SHADOWS ON THE QUEEN

SHADOWS ON THE QUEEN

A St Albans Medieval Mystery

M A LONG

Apsley Press

For Elaine

Shadows on the Queen is a work of fiction inspired by actual events. Names, characters and events other than those in the public domain are the product of the author's imagination. Any resemblance to persons living or dead is purely coincidental.

Published by Apsley Press

ISBN 978-1-3999-2371-2

Cover design by @coverbookdesigns

Glossary

A note on dates: dates in medieval England were determined by the year a monarch acceded to the throne and its proximity to Saints' days. Edward, I became king on November 20th 1270. So, November 19th 1273, would be eight days after the Feast of Martinmas (November 11th) in the first year of the reign of King Edward, son of King Henry. Likewise, just a few days later, November 22nd 1273, would be the Feast of St. Cecilia in the second year of the reign of King Edward, son of King Henry. Kings of England were not classified as Henry I, Henry II etc., but by who their father was. Edward, I was Edward, son of King Henry. His son, Edward II, was Edward, son of King Edward, but this would change with Edward III, who was also Edward, son of King Edward. Hence, a different form of the designation was needed.

Abroad – a medieval expression meaning beyond one's home

Arbalest – a small hand-held crossbow

Archdeacon – a high-ranking clergyman who serves as an assistant to a bishop

Ave Maria – Hail Mary – a common prayer to the mother of Jesus

Barons' War – the civil war in England between King John and his nobles 1216-17

Baselard – a heavy, short, tapered dagger

Benedictine – monks who followed the Rule of St. Benedict

Bothelyngstock – the butcher's area of St. Albans, located at the far end of the town

Brabant – a medieval duchy in present-day Belgium

Ca de Bou – Spanish mastiff bred originally for defending cattle against wolves

Chancery – the medieval department responsible for the production of royal documents

Chapman – a medieval seller of goods, usually itinerant

Compline – the last Church service of the day, around 9 p.m.

Coney – a rabbit

Cotehardie/cote – a long-sleeved outer garment worn by both men and women

Curia Regis – the King's Court

Curfew bell – a bell rung to signal that all were to be in their homes around 9 p.m.

Darnells – present-day Radlett in Hertfordshire

Deep in cups – drunk

Deodand – a payment to the Crown based on the value of whatever had caused a death

Dominicans – monks who were preachers and followed the teachings of St. Dominic

Dryghten – a pagan satanic deity

Eggeswer – Edgware, a village north of London on Watling Street

Elsterre – Elstree, a village north of London on Watling Street

Exacted and waived – a summons to appear in court; declared as being outside the law

Excommunicant – someone excluded from receiving the sacraments of the Church

Feast Day of St. Aurelian – May 10th

Feast of St. Bartholomew – August 24th

Feast Day of St. Chad – March 2nd

Feast Day of St. Christina the Martyr – July 24th

Feast Day of St. Mary Magdalene - July 22nd

Feast of the Nativity of John the Baptist – June 24th

French Chord – a medieval term for a garotte

Friar – an itinerant preacher who has taken a vow of poverty

Gascony – Province in south-west France that was under the control of England

Hippocras – a sweet wine infused with sugar and spices

Holy Blood – a vial containing the true blood of Jesus

Household Knights – royal bodyguard

Hue & Cry – the process where bystanders were summoned to apprehend a criminal

Huckster – a female peddler

Hutch – a wooden chest

In his cups – drunk

Jakes – toilet

Kelebourne – Kilburn, a village north of London on Watling Street

Kermes – vibrant red dye made from crushed beetles

King of the Germans – an honorific title given to the next Holy Roman Emperor

Knight's Fee – a payment by a knight to the king based on the amount of land held

Knights of St. John – The Knights Hospitalers

Liegeman – a vassal who owes allegiance and service to a lord

Le Straunde – the Strand on the banks of the Thames

Lorteburn ditch – an ancient London stream that ran from Aldgate to the Walbrook

Lord Edward - sons of a monarch, were not called 'Prince' but 'the lord —'

Magsman – a confidence trickster

Mendicant – usually a monk who relies on begging to survive

Mercartix – female merchant

Necromancy – the practice of magic through communication with the dead

Nones – the ninth hour after sunrise, about 3 p.m.

Nuncio - a messenger on horseback

Obedientiaries – the holder of a position of responsibility in a monastery

Oblate – a person, given to the Church as a nun or a monk, often a younger child

Oubliette – a single cell for holding prisoners

Outremer – the land beyond the sea; the medieval name for the Holy Land

Oymelor, Demefin, Lamair, Masair, Symofor, Rimasor – satanic deities

Palfrey – a riding horse suitable for long-distance travel

Paternoster – the Lord's prayer in Latin

Pontiff – the Pope

Porta Pomarii – orchard gate

Prie Dieu – a prayer desk

Prime – the first hour of daylight

Quarrel – the bolt of a crossbow

Queen's Gold – an arbitrary tax levied on England's Jews that went to the Queen

Quillon – a dagger with a small guard to protect the hand of its holder

Reeve –a local official responsible for oversight of a manor or village

Riffler – a common thief

Royal writ – a written order issued in the King's name

Sacrist - a senior monk responsible for the monastic Church and its contents.

Saint Edward – King Edward the Confessor, died 1066

Savoyard – from the medieval duchy of Savoy

Scriptorium – monastic writing room

Seneschal – a royal governor

Sext – the sixth hour of the day, i.e. noon

Sexton – responsible for the maintenance of a church and its graveyard

Scrip – medieval satchel

Serjeant at Law – a man of law

Shambles – an open-air slaughterhouse and meat market

Shift – an undergarment

Signum Crucis – the Christian sign of the cross

Sopwellstrete – present-day Sopwell Lane, St. Albans

Statute of Jewry – placed restrictions on England's Jews, including lending money

Stanmere – Stanmore, a village north of London close to Watling Street

Sumpter Yard – where pack animals and carts offloaded their goods

Super visum corporis – an inquest held in the presence of the dead body

Supplicant – one who asks God for something to be granted

Te Deum Laudamus – 'God, we praise you' – a Latin hymn

Terce – the third hour after the dawn

Terce bell – a monastic bell rung to summon the monks to service

Thaumaturgy – the manifestation of magical spells

Thurible – an incense holder, used in church services

Usurer – money lender

Vespers – the service of evening prayer, around 6 p.m.

Vicar General – from Latin vicarius, 'substitute' – one with delegated authority

Virii Hereditarri – the hereditary, powerful merchant families

Watlingstrete – Roman Watling Street running from London to the north-west

Wherry – a wide, flat-bottomed cargo or passenger boat

Wimple – a head covering draped over the head and around the neck and chin

Wolf's Head – an outlaw
Yester-ba-ra – a satanic deity

Prologue

Edem anno, cum anno quarto regni regis Edwardi filii regis Henrici, in festo sancte Marie Magdalene, regina et filia eius, domina Eleonora, venit ad devotionem suam ante beatam. Sancte. Cum eleemosynis egenis et manibus impositis infirmis, gratia eius in magna pietate ad septentrionem iter faciebat ad iter faciendum cum Fratribus Sancti Petri in Dunstaplia.

(In that same year, being the fourth year of the reign of King Edward, son of King Henry, on the Feast day St. Mary Magdalene, her grace, the queen and her daughter, the lady Eleonora did come to pay her devotion before the blessed Saint. Having given alms to the poor and laid hands upon the sick, her grace journeyed north in great piety to progress her pilgrimage with the Brothers of St. Peter's in Dunstable.)

St. Albani Chronica et Annales (*The Chronicle of St. Albans Abbey*) - William of Rishanger

CHAPTER 1

Fulelane, The City of London, November 1275

Across the city, late autumn rain lashed doors and window frames, seeping into cracks and crevices and pooling on windowsills. Rushlights flickering at this late hour threw tall dancing shadows onto the clean lime-washed walls of the house in Fulelane north of the Tower. Inside, three figures huddled close, facing each other in the centre of a downstairs room. The clattering of shutters against a window frame barely interrupted the hushed conversation.

The man's bearded face showed many scars on his rough, worn skin. Dark hair hung long to his shoulders, framing dark and deep-set eyes. He was a warrior, a mercenary, the sort of man you didn't cross. Only a few trusted souls knew he was here, that he was back in England, where he was both a declared traitor to the Crown and an excommunicant from the Church.

The property where the three now sat was old, but in a good state of repair. The house was well known to the wealthier merchants and officials in the city. They frequented it regularly in the evenings before returning home to their wives. Its owner, the older woman, now seated in the room downstairs, ensured that was always the case. Across from her sat her daughter, not yet thirty summers. The girl's face reminded her so much of the father, the man she had lost.

She knew the man seated across from her of old. He, too, had once pledged fealty to the man she had served and loved. A powerful lord feared and revered in equal measure when he lived, and one whose reputation and legacy lived on since his death these ten years since. Now,

loyal followers of his son, these three met up on this wild November night plotting revenge.

The warrior spoke. "I am told that who we seek may be found in Flanders, in Ghent. Our lord has gone there and put the word about that we wish the services of Benuic."

"Does that not carry a danger that the King's agents there will discover what we are about? "The woman's tone was concerned.

"Nay, the places he shall spread word have no loyalty to any king of England."

The older woman fixed the man with a penetrating gaze.

"No one must be privy to what we do here. No one must know that we have met. There must be no connection between us."

The daughter's eyes met the man, and the woman went on.

"And you and your master must be obscure in what you plot. There are spies everywhere who would betray us for a few coins."

There was an understanding between the three as to what had to be done. Each knew the risk they took and the fate that awaited them were they to be caught. Longstanding malevolence burned deep in their hearts—hatred of the man who had taken their lord's life.

They made strange bedfellows: the excommunicated warrior; a man whose sword was for sale to the highest bidder; the High Priestess of a covenstead of witches and her daughter, a common whore of the city of London. Each had a separate part to play in achieving their common goal of vengeance. The mercenary stood to make his leave, and the younger woman reached out a hand to stay him.

"Do you cross the sea now?

"Nay, I shall stay in England and await instructions from our Lord."

The younger woman smiled wanly.

"May Dryghten walk with you," she said in a low voice

He thought for a moment. "As good-a God as any, but I won't need him."

Each of the three regarded the other before the mercenary departed. No one broke the silence giving an acknowledgement of understanding. Each had a role to ensure success as they hatched their plan to exact vengeance upon King Edward of England.

CHAPTER 2

Marthe Lane, City of London, November 1275

Long afternoon shadows gradually grew to darkness as the dying winter sun slowly dipped below the city walls. A cold northerly breeze stirred and rippled the dark waters of the river. It struck the vessels moored in the packed wharves, causing them to twist and strain their ropes in protest, creaking a ghoulish chorus to accompany the stiffening wind.

The chilled air pierced the city's alleys, lanes and runnels, turning the whispered breath into a shriek as it penetrated deep into the murk of twilight London. It drove those human predators of the shadows deeper into the city streets' recesses as they waited for any unfortunate abroad on such a dark and miserable November night.

The biting cold of the winter evening caused the two figures to draw their cloaks closer, tight around their necks. Neither would have considered themselves 'unfortunates abroad' this night. Roger le Stedeman and Henry Pelliors were making for Fulelane and the house of Alice la Blunde. Beneath their cloaks, their hands rested on daggers, ready to confront rifflers, thieves or ruffians lurking in the shadowed doorways. In the stillness, a clink-clink sound came from the tools of Pelliors' trade, a circlet of lock rakes tied to his belt. These were unfamiliar streets for Henry Pelliors. Much more familiar were the lanes and alleys of Gloucester, where the dwellers of the night knew him better as 'Picklock'.

St. Paul's lay a few streets west; its precincts and churchyard were the sanctuaries for every villain, murderer and thief in London seeking to evade the law. The streets and alleys were dangerous after dark. Still, any unease Pelliors felt was tempered by the prospect of an evening of pleasure this night.' That would be a fitting reward for the dangers and hardships he had put himself through over the past weeks.

They picked their way up Marthe Lane, trying their best to avoid the patchwork of ruts and water-filled holes in the stinking mire of mud and faeces that was a London street. The bells of the Church of All-Hallows de Berkingecherch had rung for Vespers long since, and the flickering flames of its burning sconces threw just enough light to guide their way. Ahead, pinpricks of brightness indicated the lit torches of St. Olave towards the Tower, where the two men would turn onto Olafstrete. Both men knew that the darkness surrounding them was home to the creatures of the night, both animal and human. But the only company they sensed was the scurrying of predatory rodents, their bright eyes occasionally reflecting in the lit torches of the churches. But in the darkened shadows off Marthe Lane, another predatory pair of eyes followed the two men as they disappeared into the dark void of a city alley towards Fulelane.

CHAPTER 3

Fulelane, City of London, November 1275

The bustle and noise of early morning traders assaulted the ears of Henry Frowyke, the Under-Sheriff of the city, as he made his way along Cornhulle. The ale from the night before made his head throb. His mood was not helped by having his first meal interrupted to summon him to a house in Fulelane in the parish of All Hallows Colemanscherche. He had enjoyed what he had eaten of that coney pie. And the ale, freshly made by Edith, his housekeeper, was particularly good this morning. And it would be again, he thought, after he had dealt with the business at Fulelane. Yes, he was looking forward to that. As he approached Alegatestrete, the city was stirring from its night slumber. All around him were the cries of apprentices, water carriers and costers. The beggars had appeared early. A dishevelled man on a wooden sledge grabbed at his ankle, only to receive the Under-Sheriff's right boot to the side of his face.

The icy wind of the previous evening had not relented. It nipped at his nose, watered his eyes and bit hard at his exposed cheeks. Between teeth gritted from the cold, Henry Frowyke cursed the inadequacy of his fur-trimmed woollen robe. He doubly cursed the Flemish Street merchant who had sold to him with promises that it would keep him warm in the worst of winter. He quickened his step, hoping the increased movement would warm him up. His detachment of men-at-arms, even less well garbed for the chilly November weather, appreciated the increase in pace and the body heat it eventually produced.

Frowyke had been undersheriff for just under two years. He had accepted the role because of the potential for advancement in the future. He, not London's two Sheriffs, Robert Basyng and Wyllyam Meyre, did the daily grind of investigation. It was Frowyke whose days were filled investigating homicides and robbery in the seedy, murky side of the city. His nights were no better, being summoned at all hours to look into unexplained deaths. To him and his men-at-arms fell the daily duty of keeping the public peace, including presiding over executions. In time, Frowyke would assume the higher office of Sheriff and, with it, the perks and financial rewards that would make him both rich and respected within the city community.

Henry Frowyke was always conscious of his status. His leather boots from fine Cordoban leather, his elegant cloak which looked the part but failed to keep him warm and his fine-weave cote all suggested he was a man of importance. He was by no means low-born, but he was aware that as the eldest son of a city of prosperous London cordwainer, he was not high-born either. Frowyke had to earn his position, respect, and advancement. He preferred his men to see him as a hard taskmaster who demanded obedience to his commands. He liked the fact that his men both respected and feared him. Frowyke knew his was a role that he could not fulfil without the industry of his men-at-arms. Many were seasoned veterans of foreign campaigns; hard men used to trouble. And then there were the newer recruits, green and inexperienced, still with much to learn. These men did much of the groundwork for him, although he rarely acknowledged it to their face.

As he turned his stallion off Alegatestrete into Fulelane, Henry Frowyke was on familiar territory. He had been informed of two bodies discovered at a house in Fulelane. Ahead in the flickering rays of the early dawn, he could see the road bend sharply away and the shape of a man holding a candle lantern standing in a doorway. A house in Fulelane; it couldn't possibly be that house, he thought? As he rode towards the lantern light, he realised that his fear had been correct. He could make out one of his youngest men-at-arms, candle lantern in hand, standing in front of the property. Yes, Frowyke thought to himself, it was that house. It was that damned house.

Arnald atte Crosses' boredom at his guard duty at the front of the murder house was broken by the sound of horse hooves striking cobbles at the far end of the lane. He peered gloom of the dawn and recognised the Sheriff's black stallion approaching. A tall, gangly youth, Arnald was the youngest member of the Sheriff's men-at-arms and frequently the butt of their jokes. It had been after the bells had rung for Lauds in the dark of night when they had been summoned to the house. Two bodies had been discovered at the rear of the property. Arnald had arrived with five other Sheriff's men led by their wizened old Serjeant, Will Gissors. Some of the older men expressed their unease about entering the property.

"You know what this place is, Serjeant?" The ten-year veteran, Henry Ryce, said.

"Aye. It's a posh whorehouse, now get moving," said Gissors curtly, steeping towards the veteran.

"Nay, Serjeant, not that." Ryce's voice quivered with fear. "Whore house for lords it may be, but it is a place of evil where good Godly men should not go."

Arnald atte Crosse stood open-mouthed next to his fellow guards; speaking to the serjeant in this way was something he would never contemplate. Arnald watched as Gissors stood face-to-face with Ryce.

"Do your job, Ryce. Set an example." Then he pushed him roughly towards the back of the property.

The rear of the house threw little light onto the small garden, and each of the Sheriff's men carried a candle lantern to pick their way through a stinking, narrow runnel that led to the back. Some still grumbled when they arrived in the alley where the two bodies lay.

Serjeant Gissors had made Arnald guide them through to the rear. When the candle lanterns illuminated the two bodies, Arnald turned and vomited.

Gissors slapped the younger man hard on the back. "Something that's part of the job, young'un. Get used to it."

Gissors dragged Arnald back to where the two bodies lay and forced him to look upon them again. One man had his hands bound behind him. Both appeared to have had their throats cut and lay draped across a steaming dung heap. Arnald was glad when the Serjeant posted him to guard the front. He hadn't wanted to spend the cold night hours alone, close by to two dead souls who would wish vengeance upon their killer. The long hours of darkness standing at the front of a house where murder had occurred were only broken up by the serjeant checking that Arnald hadn't fallen asleep.

The Serjeant had spoken with the occupants of the house that fronted onto the midden. A witness, a serving girl, said two men had gone inside much earlier, but the owner, Alice le Blunde, was not home. It seemed that six other women, all maidens, lived there, but not one had seen or heard anything.

Arnald atte Crosse cowered, wary of his master's acid tongue as the undersheriff pulled his mount to a halt.

"You! My horse," Frowyke didn't waste words as Arnald grabbed the reins and stroked the horse's nose to calm him as Frowyke deftly dismounted.

"Well? Where is your Serjeant?" Frowyke hoped his impatience didn't show.

He didn't want his men to know his familiarity with this house in Fulelane. Frowyke wanted to spend as little time as he could here. Of all the houses in Fulelane, it had to be this one. This was a house of evil and somewhere he wanted to get far away from as soon as possible. That hadn't always been the case. He chuckled to himself. Had this crime occurred three weeks past, he would have been found here, enjoying the pleasures of one of the ladies of the house, the delightful Notekina. His mind drifted. Oh! Notekina. Sweet Notekina, who did things his wife would never do.

"My Lord?" It was Serjeant Gissors. Frowyke's impatience teetered on the edge.

"Have the jurymen been?" Frowyke snapped. "I want this mess cleaned up."

He ground his teeth, visibly shaking. His Serjeant could see the agitation.

"Has the Coroner been sent for?" His question was addressed to no one in particular, and it received no reply.

His patience snapped. "Well?" he shouted

"Aye, My Lord," stammered his Serjeant. "We expect him shortly."

Frowyke gave a harrumph. As Undersheriff, it was expected that he viewed the bodies where they lay, and he had been putting it off. He turned to Will Gissors, the impatience disappearing.

"You'd better show me then, Will." Gissors slowly led the way through the runnel that lay beside the property. In the half-light of post-dawn, Frowyke regarded the noxious, sticky glop in the passage ahead of him and gazed down at his fine, supple leather boots, wondering if they would ever recover. Passing to one side of a mostly brown, barren garden, save for a few cabbages, they came upon another alley beyond. The other men-at-arms milling around the midden heap parted as the Under-Sheriff arrived.

Frowyke peered at the two bodies lying there, one atop the other. One had a thin purple gash on its neck, looking like a second mouth. Like Arnald before him, Frowyke recoiled at the sight. He wondered how many dead bodies he saw in his two years as Undersheriff. Yet the sight still sickened him. And they turn up dead here, at this place, he said to himself. Was that significant? This house?

Frowyke turned and addressed his Serjeant.

"I am for Guildhall. Once the Coroner has been, have the bodies removed. I want a report by noonday. Is that understood?"

"Aye, My Lord."

"And men, the women of the house. Have them brought to me at the Guildhall for questioning."

His men shuffled nervously, peering at the floor and reluctant to speak.

"The women. I want them brought before me," Frowyke demanded angrily.

"My...My Lord Under-Sheriff." It was Will Gissors who broke the silence. "The women...the women in the house...the women are gone."

"Gone! What do you mean gone?"

"We posted guards on the front and the back of the house all night, ever since them bodies were found. But..." Gissors gulped nervously. "They are not there."

"They cannot just be gone." Frowke snapped. "Your guards must have been asleep. I will have them flogged, everyone."

"Nay, My Lord. Some of the men," he gulped, "did say they was uneased about this house, knowing what it is."

Frowyke wiped at his forehead, seemingly flustered by this. "What do you mean, knowing what it is?"

"That it is a house of the devil, my Lord." Gissors paused. "And a stew for the rich as well." Frowyke was certain Gissors gave him a knowing look. "Anyhows, my Lord, knowing some of the men were unsettled like, I made sure I checked on them regular. They were not asleep. Not one. I checked throughout the night. Nay, The front and back were both guarded. No one went in or out. The women. They just disappeared."

CHAPTER 4

The Royal Palace of Westminster, March 1276

The chill of the morning was lifting as Simon Lowys walked up to Leadenhall. The Queen's nuncio made sure to stay towards the middle, far away from the overhanging windows. Careless servants were already dumping the urine, faeces, and detritus of the night onto the heads of the unwary below.

The City authorities had condemned such practices and even appointed surveyors to fine offenders and catch and kill any animal found rooting in the refuse. It was a grand pronouncement, thought Simon, typical of the city authorities, but no one was paying any attention.

Beneath his cloak, one hand rested on the handle of his long baselard dagger he kept on the left of his belt. Made by an armourer to the French King's Brother, he had acquired it in Florence four years earlier. Feeling the 'T' at its hilt gave him a sense of reassurance. His twenty-nine years had made him streetwise enough to know that walking the city streets, even in daylight, was dangerous. Even at this early hour, gangs of young rifflers roamed the streets, and the Hue and Cry were regularly raised in an often-futile attempt to apprehend some youthful malefactor.

As Simon threaded his way, London was stirring, ready for a busy day ahead. Cries of "Stand there. Make way" rang out as crudely made barrows loaded with produce were pushed blindly down the street. The sound of iron-rimmed cartwheels on stone reverberated everywhere. Even at this hour, whinnies and neighs filled the air, along with all the animal noises of livestock being traded, auctioned, or prepared for slaughter. Tradesmen and early risen merchants began to tout for business. Hucksters, fish vendors and coal boys emerged to ply their flourishing trade. To a backdrop of Church bells tolling the canonical hours, young boys darted here and there with their wooden buckets and clay jugs full of drinking water to sell.

Lowys ignored them, and their competing trader calls seeking to attract his attention to buy their fresh fish or newly baked bread. A very young costermonger's boy tugged at his sleeve.

"Apple Mister? Best in all England."

Simon broke into a grin, took one, tossed the lad a coin and made his way down to the mooring steps on the Thames to hire a wherry to take him upstream through the heaving waters of the Thames to Westminster.

The journey upstream against the stiff current and choppy waters was thoroughly unpleasant. By the time he had reached the mooring steps below the royal palace, he bitterly regretted not having hired a palfrey. He left the bobbing wherry and scampered up the steps to a muddy pathway that led to the King's grand royal Palace of Westminster.

Simon felt himself at ease in Westminster, its remoteness from the city and its tranquillity, lying as it did next to the Benedictine Abbey. Some thirty years before, the old King Henry, father of King Edward, had begun rebuilding the Church in the new gothic style. Wooden scaffolding surrounded the abbey Church hiding its future magnificence.

Two guards at the gates of the royal palace of Westminster eyed Lowys suspiciously when he announced himself as a royal official.

New, Simon thought, at least new to me. One, an older man with a wizened face and a stubbled chin, stared at the Royal Serjeant-at-Law.

"Who are you then?" he demanded. The guard thought the man in front of him didn't look like a Queen's nuncio. His straggled brown hair pulled up and tied in a 'Q' knot, his weather-worn cote, battered scrip, and worn leather boots didn't give him the appearance of one engaged in royal business.

Simon reached into his scrip, pulled out his royal writ, and handed it to the guard. Simon doubted the man could read, but he could recognise the Queen's seal affixed to the bottom. The guard regarded the document warily, handed the writ back to Lowys and grudgingly waved him through into the palace complex.

The great vaulted Hall of the Royal Palace of Westminster was thronged with people. In its alcoves sat different royal courts, each cordoned off from the others. Here, red-robed judges, soberly dressed clerks and black-robed Serjeants-at-Law, Simon's everyday fellows, dispensed opinions, judgements and justice. In rooms just off the Great Hall, the King's clerks went about the government's daily business. This was Simon's usual place of work, but today it was different. He caught the eye of one guard at the Chancery Office entrance and showed him the writ he had kept in his scrip. Then, one of the King's valets led him down labyrinthine corridors to arrive at the royal apartments.

In an antechamber waiting for him was John of Berwick, Steward and Treasurer to Queen Eleanor of Castile. Simon bowed deeply in obeisance. The man before him reminded him of a carved statue he had seen beside a wall fresco in Viterbo. Yet there was nothing holy about the beak-like nose, thin slash for a mouth and tight pursed lips that never knew a smile. John's flint-hard eyes were more like those of a bird of prey. These eyes now studied Simon intently. In a surprisingly high-pitched, clipped voice, he bade him sit down on a stool a harassed clerk had swiftly brought across the room before being summarily dismissed.

Once the clerk had left them, closing the door firmly behind him, John of Berwick rose and sifted through some documents strewn across the desk in front of him. He plucked one from the pile, giving a grunt of pleasure as he unrolled it and scanned its contents. He suddenly looked up as if he had half-remembered something.

"Ah yes. Master Lowys, I offer you my sympathy on the loss of your dear wife. May her soul be sanctified in the holy company of Heaven." His words threw Simon. John of Berwick was not known for his compassion. But the words stirred a memory etched on Simon's heart of his dear sweet Amy, his wife of three years, whom he had lost in childbirth not six months since, and their stillborn son. The hurt was still there.

In his usual abrupt manner, Berwick brought Simon back to the present. He tossed a vellum document towards him. "These are your instructions," His tone was now curt and peremptory. "They come from her Grace the Queen herself. It will take you four, perhaps five weeks to fulfil your commission." John of Berwick's expression appeared dismissive. Simon was all too familiar with the man standing in front of him. The older man was methodical and liked immersing himself in detail. From personal experience, Simon knew that John would explain the document's content to him before he was ever permitted to read it.

"You are to go to Langlei. You know of it?"

Simon shook his head. "Nay, My Lord."

"That's not surprising. It is a village near to the old Roman road towards the castle at Berkhamstede. It is one of the manors her Grace, the Queen, is...." Berwick paused, clearing his throat, seeking the correct word, "....*acquiring*... as her own. The Lord of Langlei is

Stephen de Chenduit, a liege-man of the King's cousin, the Earl of Cornwall. Frankly, de Chenduit is in over his head. He has managed to get himself deep in debt to Jewish moneylenders, and her Grace is buying out this debt. *"You,"* he placed great emphasis on the word, "are facilitating this."

Simon nodded and took this in, but his expression must have given away his surprise at the nature of the task.

"You are wondering," began Berwick, "why a personal nuncio to Her Grace the Queen, a man trained at Oxford as a Serjeant-at-Law, is being asked to undertake such a routine task?" Berwick had read Simon's mind.

"This needs to be done and facilitated with all despatch, but there is another, more dangerous charge you must undertake, one that may place you in great peril. If your arrival attracts interest, you say that this is the reason for your presence," said Berwick.

"Dangerous and peril, my Lord?" Berwick's use of the words unsettled the royal nuncio. He was a man of letters, not a man of the sword, and that he may be in peril implied violence, he was not used to.

"And the real reason?" inquired Simon, trying not to show concern in his voice.

John of Berwick straightened, his face tightened as he fixed Simon with his stern gaze and in a lofty tone quoted from St Paul. "Put on the armour of God that you may be able to stand against the wiles of the Devil. Wrestle not against flesh and blood, but against the rulers of the darkness of this world, against wickedness in high places."

CHAPTER 5

The King's Highway towards the Guildhall, London, March 1276

Simon had been in the saddle since shortly after Prime as he trotted his palfrey along muddied and rutted tracks that were the King's Highway into London and the Guildhall. He shifted his weight in the saddle, trying to find some comfort, his rear unused to long periods on horseback.

What was it John of Berwick had told him yesterday? The enigmatic reply had been from the Book of Ephesians; it warned of satanic practices and links to powerful people in the realm. The very thought had made Simon uneasy as he thought back to their meeting and Berwick's use of the word dangerous. John of Berwick's expression had remained stern. He had taken a deep breath, exhaled and begun to speak.

"Are you privy to the murder of two men in Fulelane three months since?"

"Aye, I heard discussion of it in the Chancery. Two rifflers were killed in strange circumstances, and their bodies dumped in an alley. Two Frenchies are suspect if I recall, and none was apprehended."

"You have the right of half of it at least. I am told that one of the men, Henry Pelliors, was indeed a riffler, a locksmith and a thief, the best in the west country." Berwick seemed to look beyond Simon as he spoke wistfully as if recalling something personal.

"The other man, Roger le Stedeman, was my man. One of the best," Simon had given him a look of surprise. He couldn't be sure whether that was because this was information he hadn't known or because John of Berwick was showing emotion.

"Aye. Le Stedeman was on the trail of a coven of witches, the Daughters of the Shadows, and that is as much as I know. I had hoped he had sent a despatch, but none has yet been found."

Simon had watched Berwick's face as he spoke. The words seemed to come hard to the older man, and when he spoke of le Stedeman, Simon thought he observed genuine sorrow on the Royal Steward's face.

"Le Stedeman had made progress in tracking down this coven of witches; now it is for you to take over and progress this. They must be hunted down and destroyed, but we must, at all costs, discover what evil they plan."

"My Lord, may I ask...." The King's Intelligencer stopped Simon in his tracks and waved him away.

"The Guildhall. Find Frowyke." And with that, Berwick had dismissed Simon to familiarise himself with the Coroners Roll records for the city on this unsolved murder, and to pick up the trail of the Daughters of the Shadows.

The village of Charing was quiet as he passed through, picking up le Straunde and the highway to the city. As he passed the Temple Church, bells rang out for Terce, the service of the Third Hour.

Simon was still thinking about Berwick's enigmatic words when a raised voices brought him back to the reality of the city of London. He was approaching Ludgate, the western entrance beside the

Dominican Priory known as Blackfriars. A cart laden with animal fodder had shed a wheel and its load and blocked the narrow gate. There was enough room for horsemen but not other wagons. A three-way heated and animated argument between cart drivers and guards had drawn a crowd.

"I don't care how you moves it, but I need to get my goods through to market," shouted an indignant old carter waiting impatiently to get through.

"And how do you expect me to repair it?" said the beleaguered driver holding up part of the broken wheel.

"You are blocking the King's Highway," one of the guards shouted unhelpfully. Get it shifted." Already his colleague was grabbing hold of the oxen that pulled the stricken wagon, ready to drag it to one side to keep the King's route open.

Simon picked his palfrey through the melee to pass through the city gate. Such was London life. Mishaps, arguments, problems to be overcome. Was that what he now faced in this commission for John of Berwick? His life could be in peril from whence he did not know. Simon Lowys, royal nuncio and man-of-law, was ill-prepared for that.

CHAPTER 6

The Guildhall, City of London, March 1276

Henry Frowyke, the Under-Sheriff of the city, sat in a dim cubby in the Guildhall. The window high above him threw down gloomy shadows accentuated by three rushlights. The remains of a hearty meal lay on the table in front of him. It was neither his breaking of his fast, which he had done just after dawn nor his dinner, which he planned for Sext. He had received word from the Queen's Steward that a King's Man would call on him this morning, which irritated him. He was a city official, not a royal appointee. The Sheriffs and Under-Sheriffs of London had been independent of the Crown since the reign of King Stephen. Yet a King's Man was coming here to question him. Frowyke ran a finger around the rim of his goblet. He felt uneasy, not at the impending questioning but because he would be questioned about '*those*' murders and the women from Fulelane who disappeared from the house of Alice la Blunde months before.

The six women, those six beauties, whores everyone. Margery de Pyritton, Agnes de Bilda, Dulcia le Blunde, Maud Blount, Notekina de Hoggenhore and Isabella la Rus. He wasn't sure that all of them were whores. He had only known Notekina with her comely appearance, soft skin, shapely body, alluring eyes, and enchanting smile. Oh, dear sweet Notekina. He had wanted Dulcia; he had stared at her in the house but had never lain with her. She and the others, or so he had heard, brides of Satan all. All six were members of a depraved coven of witches, the Daughters of the Shadows, so said the street boys around Fulelane, who he paid to keep their eyes and ears open. Frowyke hadn't known this, of course, when he first came across them in the house of Alice la Blunde. He could not believe it, but more and more lurid stories about the Daughters of Shadows and their depravity had circulated over the past weeks and months. And now, Henry Frowyke was scared.

Frowyke had never met Simon Lowys, although he had heard of him. Acquaintances in the Chancery shared gossip over ale in the Westminster inns. Lowys had a good reputation as a man of law, and her grace, the Queen, trusted him.

Frowyke was still deep in thought when Simon Lowys arrived. He stood to welcome the nuncio. "God give you good day, Master Lowys."

Simon bowed his obeisance. "And you, My Lord Undersheriff."

Frowyke thought the man in front of him young to be a royal Serjeant-at-Law. Nor was his dress suggestive of a royal nuncio. Perhaps he did give off the appearance of a man of law, thought Frowyke. He was tall, maybe two fingers short of six feet and not muscular. Not a fighting man at all. His round face was unlined and studious, hands soft, not calloused from hard labour or swordplay; a man of book learning. He gestured to Lowys to sit.

"How may I be of assistance?" A bead of sweat appeared on the Undersheriff's brow, and he was in a hurry to get this over.

"Do you recall the slaying of two strangers in Fulelane this November past, Master Frowyke?"

The Undersheriff paused, his eyes avoiding the royal nuncios. Those murders at that house, and he had thought the case was closed once the Coroners proceedings had finished. Now, here was a royal agent asking him about it. Frowyke tensed, sensing that something was not quite right.

"Aye....um," he stammered. "I recall the night well. Twas a cold wind blowing, that I remember. What would you like to know?"

"That's helpful," said Simon. "I was afeared you might not have the recollection of it. Did you find the men responsible?"

"Nay. None was indicted. But twas a strange affair. But why is it of interest to a royal nuncio?"

"It is of interest to the Crown," Simon replied calmly. "Such an unsolved murder by foreigners on Englishmen would always be of interest."

Henry Frowyke relaxed slightly. In his mind, he had feared that it was he who was being investigated and that the crime in Fulelane was the mechanism for that inquiry.

"So, Master Frowyke, apprise me of your recollections of that night."

The Undersheriff let out a long low breath. "Well, I'll tell you, Master Lowys, there was something strange indeed. Now By our Lady, I've seen many a dead body over the past years, but this was, it made my soul go cold." Frowyke's eyes were in a wide-open stare. He could recall the stench of the blood mingled with the shit of the midden heap. The recollection of the events silenced his speech as if an evil presence had entered the room.

"Master Frowyke." Simon raised his voice to shout. "Master Frowyke."

The Undersheriff shuddered, and the vacant stare disappeared. He refocused on the nuncio.

"Pray continue, Master Frowyke."

"Do forgive me, Master Lowys. I have not thought on that night for a long time. I have tried hard to forget." Frowyke wrung his hands together and closed his eyes.

"When we got there, it was after Prime; I'd heard the bells of All Hallows ring out as I was making my way. When we got to Fulelane, I knew Alice la Blunde's house was below halfway up; the dead men were lying behind the property atop the midden used by all who live there. A maid said she opened the door for the two men at the home of Alice le Blunde, and one of the women who live there told my man that she saw an argument with two Frenchies. One with arms out wide and their legs all splayed-like. And he lay on top of one whose hands were bound. And the strange part is that the six women who lived there were gone."

Frowyke paused, staring up towards the high-beamed ceiling as if to better recall the sight he had seen. "That is the very strangeness of all of the matter. At first glance, it appeared that the two men had their throats cut both, but the Coroner says that both were strangled by a thin cord that cut into the skin. One had his hands bound behind him. There were no other wounds, eyes wide open, mouths agape, but their throats were cut. Damn Frenchies."

"I have read the Coroner's report," said Simon, "and it speaks of these two foreigners who quarrelled with the dead men."

"Aye, that is what the women said. Two foreigners, possibly Frenchies, one with a fine cote and embroidered cloak and the other shabbily dressed but of the appearance of a man of violence."

"A man of violence, you say. But you didn't find the men or any trace of these women?"

"Nay, no trace of them."

"Everyone there was questioned, and each of the women said the same. Not one said they saw le Stedeman or Pelliors save for the servant who let them in."

Frowyke regarded the royal nuncio, impassively taking in what he had said. Frowyke prided himself on his ability to understand what suspects were thinking. But from this royal agent, he got nothing.

"And the six women of the household didn't appear shocked or frightened?"

"Master Lowys, it was as if the two men weren't there. No one admitted they knew the men were dead, and no one said they knew why they were there."

"Before I returned here, I placed guards on the bodies and the front and back of the house. I gave instructions to my serjeant to take the six women under guard to the Guildhall for further questioning after Terce that morning.

"But, after I'd gone, the red-headed one, Isabella la Rus, pleaded with one of my guards, a new lad, inexperienced, to let them all get some rest, and the young fool agreed. By the time the Terce bell rang, the six of them had gone."

"Gone?" Simon's eyebrows raised in enquiry.

"Aye gone; with guards on the front and the back, they disappeared. No trace of them. What is strange is that when we searched the house, we found two wax dolls with pins driven through the heart." As he spoke, Frowyke became unsettled once more

"It is the Devil's work Master Lowys, the Devil's work."

"When the case came to the Coroner, the six women were exacted and waived according to the custom of the city. No one has heard of them since, and they are now beyond the law, and their goods and chattels are seized. The Coroner determined that there had been a quarrel and that the two strangers killed le Stedeman and Pelliors, but we shall never know the why of it."

"And what are you not telling me, Under-Sheriff Frowyke? What is it that causes you unease when you speak of this?"

Henry Frowyke took in a long breath. The air in the small cubby became oppressive, and he longed to be outside. This young royal agent had drawn from him much detail that he had hoped never to recall.

"I admit to you, Master Lowys, many a time I took my pleasure at the house of Alice la Blunde. It was not like the stews of Lambeth and good men for company if you take my meaning. The whores were captivating, clean and fragrant. Roses, saffron and lavender. The smell Master Lowys, oh it was just so...." His words trailed off into nothing. He breathed in a gulp of air, recollecting the aromatic fragrance.

"If you could have seen the six of them, you'd know what I mean. But whenever I went there, it always felt dangerous; *they* were dangerous. Frowyke paused his thoughts elsewhere.

Opposite him, Lowys sat impassively, taking in what the Under-sheriff had told him.

"Have you ever heard of the Daughters of the Shadows, Master Lowys?" As he spoke the name, Frowyke's eyes widened, looking left and right as if expecting someone else was here with them.

"That is why I am here, Master Undersheriff. I am to discover more about them and what threat they pose to the realm."

Frowke exhaled, and sharing the information took a weight from his shoulders.

"Those six women, Master Lowys, I didn't know it at first when I started to go to Fulelane." Frowyke's words came out quickly. "Had I known at first, I would never have gone there. Those women, they are but all part of a witch's coven."

"These Daughters of the Shadows?"

"Aye. I have eyes all over the city, and back around the Feast of St Chad, I began to hear stories about Margery de Pyritton and Maud Blount. The owner, Mistress la Blunde, has not been seen by the neighbours these months since. Gone north to kin, the women said, but I don't know for sure. Just disappeared."

As Simon Lowys repeated to himself Frowyke's words, it brought to mind what John of Berwick had said, that this undertaking would be dangerous and perilous. A coven of witches could not just disappear unless they invoked dark magic. If that was so, Simon thought, how prepared was he for the jeopardy that lay ahead?

CHAPTER 7

Distaflane, City of London, March 1276

As he made his way back to the Chancery, Simon turned over in his mind all that Henry Frowyke had told him and, more importantly, what his next step should be. He had not forgotten his task of overseeing the transfer of the manor of Langlei to the Queen. However, events were getting in his way. Confirmation of a coven operating within the city of London was deeply troubling. More disturbing was that, as yet, he did not know what they might be planning. And to add to his worries, he could not shake the sense that someone was following him. He kept his vigilance and frequently stopped.

Simon listened but heard only the sound of metaled wheels on cobbles and the snorting of horses. He looked around him but saw no one.

Off Distaflane, he came across a small dark square and saw the dim light from the open door of an inn. A draught of ale might help to clarify his thinking. As he entered, the rushlights flickered. The large stuffy room was half-full of an array of customers seated around rough wooden tables. Beneath his feet, strewn rushes, likely freshly laid that morning, had now turned into a mushy mess that clung to his battered leather boots.

As he made his way deeper into the inn, shadowed eyes followed him warily from under hoods and cowls.

The usual hucksters were plying their trade; a tooth-puller with a filthy wooden bucket and pincers: a seller of the finest squirrel fur with his stinking dried pelts hanging from his dirty belt: an apothecary with a large scrip full of herbs, lotions and potions.

A group of city apprentices were baiting a Chapman, a one-eyed man with a wooden tray slung across his chest selling the wonders of the world. His wares included a tooth of John the Baptist, breast milk from the Blessed Virgin Mary, a rock used in the martyrdom of St Stephen and a single white feather from the wings of an Archangel.

Simon pushed his way past the pedlars towards the far end of the inn, where a bald, white-faced man in a soiled apron stood guard over substantial oak casks. Young maids rushed back and forth with dirty pots brimming with froth-topped brown liquid. Deep in their cups, four men sat huddled close around a table, deep in shouted conversation about a woman they all knew and what delights she had performed for them.

He sat at a small table in the corner, and a young maiden brought him over a jug of tangy, frothy ale. He laid coins on the table and thanked her; she smiled coyly.

"I have not seen you in here before, sir," Simon thought about how learned her speech sounded for a serving maid. The girl loitered at his table as if awaiting a response.

"Nay, I um, I er," he was struggling to make conversation with a pretty girl, perhaps the first time he had done so since the death of his beloved Amy. " I have had business nearby and chose to slake my thirst."

She scooped up the coins, more than was necessary for the ale.

"Thank you, sir, for the coin,"

A guttural shout in French from the innkeeper caused her to turn abruptly. She responded to him in French whilst wiping nearby tables. She half-turned, smiled again, and inclined her head in thanks. He regarded her heart-shaped face with its dimple, made pretty by its slightly tilted nose, small lips, and hair like wet straw in the sun, platted to hang down halfway down her back. She looked about eighteen or nineteen summers, and, being unmarried, wore no wimple. Her hips swaying as she moved between the tables had more to do with avoiding the groping hands of lecherous customers than acting in a saucy manner.

He lingered a long time over the brew she'd brought him. Alone with his thoughts, he reproached himself. He was regarding this maid in a comely manner. Guilt flashed through him as this was not the appropriate behaviour for a widower of but a few months. Another ale might help, and when it was finished, he ordered another and then another.

Simon looked around the inn, now far noisier and thronged with customers. Thoughts were becoming less clear to him; that last brew had been a mistake. The Chapman approached his table and produced a small phial containing tears from the Virgin Mary, which he assured were genuine and purchased from a poor monastery in Outremer. Simon politely declined, but the peddler's wares stirred a memory for him about the Cistercian monks of Hailes Priory.

The lord Edmund of Almain, nephew of the late King Henry, had donated to the Abbey at Hailes a vial of the Holy Blood of Jesus. He discovered the precious relic at Trifels Castle in Franconia six years before and brought it back to England, giving it to his favoured Cistercians. Simon had read the Chancery reports of a recent attempted theft of the holy relic from its temporary shrine inside the Abbey. It had failed, and the perpetrators escaped. All very strange, he thought.

Simon looked up from his now empty tankard, gazed hard at the customers and recognised that it was time he departed. Now he felt uneasy, perhaps the way Henry Frowyke had done. It was as if an unholy presence were watching him, but it could be anyone or no one. As he peered around the gloomy room, the eyes which furtively weighed him up slid away when they met his. Fear gripped him. He was a nuncio to the Queen, a Serjeant at Law, not a common street brawler. Here was not a good place for him to be. He felt the hair on the nape of his neck rise, and he fought down the urge to rise and run from the inn. The strong ale had made him weary, and he tensed, realising it was too late to get to Westminster, so he had to make his way back to the Tower where he could get lodgings overnight.

A woman approached his table. She wore an undyed loose-fitting shift that exposed her breasts. Her dark hair, parted in the middle, hung in two long plaits halfway down her back. She smiled, leaning in appealingly towards his table. He realised she was no more than a girl with a sweet face and thousand-year-old eyes. She spoke softly and promised him delights he had never experienced in return for a drink and a few coins. Simon panicked; he got up, pushed her aside and, ignoring her stream of profanities, pushed his way through the crowd towards the door.

Three rifflers barred his way; hoods pulled low and exuding menace. The glint of a knife reflected from the flickering rushlights as the three fixed their gaze on Simon and fanned out slightly, ready to jump him. The middle of the three opened his palm to reveal a wooden cosh. Simon's sheer panic of moments earlier was exacerbated. Men who frequented this inn were unlikely to come to his aide. He had his baselard dagger, but it was inevitable that all the thugs were armed. It was three against one.

A firm hand gripped his arm. Simon turned in consternation and looked into the face of the smiling, pretty serving maid with the round face and long dark straw-coloured plait who had waited on him earlier.

"Come now, good sir; you are going the wrong way. Here, let me help you." She addressed Simon but looked directly at the three thugs as she spoke.

"These good men here are not about to give trouble. I'm sure they just want more ale and to continue drinking in this inn."

With her gaze fixed firmly on the thugs, she steered Simon briskly backwards away from his would-be assailants, her hand strong on his arm, guiding him towards one side of the inn. As they moved, the mass of men drinking and shouting filled the void behind them, obscuring them from the three rifflers.

Close to a side door, the young serving maid stopped him and addressed him sternly.

"You needs must be more careful, sir; dangerous people are drinking here, and you so stand out as being different. That could get you killed."

Her words reinforced how close this encounter could have been.

"I thank you.... Mistress." He wished he knew her name, but she supplied it for him as if reading his mind.

"Alia. I am Alia Parys."

"I thank you, Mistress Parys; you have saved me there from great injury. However, I cannot think why you would risk yourself for me. You do not know me, and yet you put yourself in danger for me."

She smiled at him once more. He thought to himself; she did indeed have a lovely smile to go with her pretty face.

"Nay, I am in no danger from them. I did so because you showed me kindness and respect, sir. I do so rarely get that. And you didn't deserve to be robbed and stabbed by those three."

Her hand still rested on his arm, and he laid his own on top. His other hand went to his purse to give her coins.

Her free hand came up in a gesture of displeasure.

"Nay, sir, I seek no coin as thanks for my actions."

"Mistress, I am sorry for the offence I have given for that action. I am greatly in your debt this night. And somehow, I must need repay you. If you ever require help, find me at the Chancery; I am Simon Lowys, Serjeant at Law." He thought there was no need to add and nuncio to her grace, the Queen.

She freed her hand. "God go with you, sir."

He looked at her, smiled and nodded his head and, as almost an afterthought, asked, "Those three men, will they give you bother for what you did?"

"Nay, by now, they will be so deep in their cups that they are likely to have forgotten and mind, one serving wench looks much like another to men like them."

"Stay safe, my maid." And with that, Simon made to leave.

He pushed open the door, took in a lungful of cold air and stepped into the silence of the night. The panic of the previous minutes had dissipated, and he stood taking in refreshing breaths. That had been too close, and he recognised how lucky he had been. Out of the darkness ahead, a cowled figure approached. Simon scrambled for the handle of his baselard dagger strapped to his belt, but the figure was upon him.

The dark figure's cowl was suddenly flicked back, and a gap-toothed boyish face smiled back at him. For the second time in the space of a few minutes, Simon Lowys was propositioned. He pushed the youth away, composed himself, let out a deep breath and began to make his way through the winding streets towards the river steps to hail a wherry to the Tower. He had taken out his long baselard dagger and held it in his right hand high against his chest.

As he passed shadowy lanes to the left and right, he was aware of being watched by thugs and rifflers. Seeing the glint of his dagger reflected in the moonlight, they let him pass unmolested. He made his way down Pasternosterstrete, which he knew led to a mooring by the river. He stopped. His senses were heightened, and the hairs on his neck stood up. He was sure he heard footsteps behind him, something quiet, sliding across the cobbles. Simon whirled around, but there was nothing.

He continued onwards, but he could not shake the sense that he was being followed, observed by some presence. He reached the riverbank at Brokenwharfe, where a burning torch flickered, illuminating the wherry steps. As he moved towards the boat, he was sure he heard a noise behind him again. It was footsteps, of that he was confident, and his sense that someone or something was following him did not dissipate.

He gathered his breath, sheathed his dagger, and ran the final few steps. The chill wind whipped his cloak behind him, and he almost fell onto the wherry. Simon gabbled his instructions to an astonished boatman as he scanned the riverbank for a pursuer. There was only the city's silent baleful darkness, which was soon lost as the wherry nosed its way downriver towards London Bridge and the Tower beyond.

As the wherry pulled away into the river mist blending with the darkness, a woman in a hooded cloak stepped out from the shadows of the riverbank. A lock of soft red hair peeped out from under the edge of her tight wimple, framing one pale cheek. Her dark, penetrating eyes followed the path of the wherry as, for the second time that night, she watched Simon Lowys disappear from sight.

CHAPTER 8

Pendley Manor, Hertfordshire, early April 1276

John of Berwick's duties as the Queen's Steward and Keeper of the Queen's Gold masked his other primary responsibility as King Edward's Chief Intelligencer. His duty was to keep the realm safe and free of peril to the Crown. Tracking down the threat posed by the Daughters of the Shadows had deftly been passed onto Simon's shoulders. John of Berwick wished to know more of this witch's coven and any danger they might pose to the King and the realm. Hence Simon's early morning ride to the manor of Pendley close to Akeman Street belonging to Maeve de Thornby, widow, spice mercartix and, according to Berwick, a woman who was exceptionally well-informed through her contacts in almost every southern and eastern port and across the continent.

The dawn had brought slate grey clouds rolling in from the west, but the rain held off, saving Simon from a soaking. The King's Highway curved gently following the line of distant hills as a large dwelling came into view that Simon immediately knew must be the manor house at Pendley.

It was evident that the Merchant Spicers of London were doing well. The dwelling lay just off the main road, and clear instructions had been given for trees on either side of the road to be pruned back. Simon urged his palfrey onwards at a gentle trot. The track up to the manor house was compacted earth and stone, and a high, flint-stone wall protected the whole manorial complex.

The stout, high oak gates were open, and Simon entered a neat, cobbled courtyard. He picked up the smell of jasmine wafting in the breeze, knowing the scent from his time in Italy with the King and Queen a few years before. It had been grown in southern Europe's Moorish gardens, and he didn't imagine it was widely grown in England. The sun shining from a mostly blue sky accentuated his senses, and for a moment, he was back in Sicily.

The courtyard was empty. He could smell the stables off to one side and heard sounds of activity as wooden shovels scrapped on cobblestones. Simon dismounted and took his palfrey by the bridle. Ahead was an imposing two-storey building with a ragstone base set onto a sturdy oak timber frame. The wattle and daub infill had been limewashed and sparked in the April sunlight. A young lad of perhaps ten or eleven years ran towards him and grabbed hold of the bridle.

"My job, Meister," He tugged the harness, and Simon loosed his grip and dismounted. The young boy walked the palfrey towards the stable block.

Simon approached the imposing wooden door protected by two sturdy iron locks, continental, he thought, having seen similar on his travels in Europe.

"May God give you good day" A tall, muscular had approached silently from behind. The lilt of his words made him not English, but it was an accent Simon had heard before. The man was Welsh. The man held up a raised palm and enquired about Simon's business.

"I am about the King's business to see Mistress de Thornby."

The man's eyes slid up and down the royal nuncio and then, without a word, turned and beckoned him to follow. They walked deep into the property; there was a smell of beeswax with fresh rushes on the floor and neat limewashed walls. Even though it was daytime, cresset torches and candles threw out their light. The wooden boards beneath Simon's feet were polished and sprinkled with sweet herbs to keep the room fragrant, lavender, marjoram, and something exotic that Simon could not identify.

He was so engrossed by the perfume that it took some time for him to notice a woman seated at the far end of the chamber. The woman lifted her head and gazed nonchalantly at the King's Clerk.

"You are Master Lowys, King Edward's man?" Her words came out like honey, spoken in a soft Welsh lilt. He had not been announced and had not sent word he was coming, yet she was aware of who he was.

Maeve de Thornby was a woman whose elegance seemed to grow with each passing year. Strands of fair hair peeked from beneath her white wimple. She wore multiple layers of garments that showed her wealth and status. Her cotehardie, dyed with expensive kermes, was tightly fitted with a wide scalloped neckline. She had it drawn in at the waist by an intricately woven Flemish cord.

Simon studied her face. She was a mercartix in her own right now; her wealth had grown in the years following her husband's death thanks to her business skill and insight. Maeve de Thornby was a woman who negotiated with experienced foreign merchants and gave little away in her expression. She was perhaps not yet fifty summers in age, although her round face did not show the lines of years as others might.

"Do you have business with me, King's man, or are you here to gaze like a moon-struck manboy?" Maeve's words broke Simon's intense focus on her face. Her rebuke hit him hard. She gestured for him to take a seat.

"Mistress, I am here on the King's business, and he has need of your good offices."

Maeve laughed derisively. "When King Edward has required my help, he has always summoned me to him. Now he sends you. Why is that, I wonder?"

"Mistress," Simon suddenly realized the hole he was digging for himself. "His Grace has told me you have generously lent him money for his foreign wars in the past, but now he needs your good offices."

Simon knew a great deal about the imposing woman opposite. John of Berwick had spent some time informing him about her background. The third daughter of a minor Welsh lord, she had been intended for the Church as an oblate. Then, her father had arranged a marriage to a Bristol pepper merchant, Henry de Thornby, when she was fourteen. More than twenty years of marriage saw de Thornby's fortunes rise considerably. When he died of pestilence years before, Maeve had taken control of the business herself. She had not just increased its profits but expanded its trade to the furthest parts of the continent. A year earlier, King Edward, on hearing of Mistress de Thornby, had approached her for a loan to help finance his campaign in Gascony. Maeve de Thornby had been only too happy to oblige her King.

"Men underestimate her," John of Berwick had told Simon. "She is a most comely woman. Her looks seduce them, and they do not see her ability. Pray, don't make that mistake."

Maeve's wealth and success, Simon knew, had been built on information and contacts. She was a highly desirable widow, yet she had not remarried. Simon was sure there must have been suitors amongst the most prominent merchants and minor nobles who would welcome her fortune. She had resisted them all and remained a wealthy, independent and powerful woman possessing the freedom of the city of London.

"There are few better placed than her, with eyes and ears in many ports and trading cities," Berwick had told him, and that was why

Simon was here. He had no intention of underestimating Maeve de Thornby.

Simon sought to focus. "His Grace, the King needs your assistance, Mistress."

"Forsooth, he has not already burned through the £1,000 I lent him a year since. Mind my manners, Master Lowys."

She turned to gesture at a man standing silently by the door. He left, almost immediately returned with a glass container containing Hippocras and two small Murano glass drinking vessels. She poured two drafts of the amber liquid and offered one to Simon.

"What the King needs from you, his loyal subject, is information. Have you a knowledge of a coven who go by the Daughters of the Shadows?"

Maeve's face lit up in an engaging smile. "Probably more than you, Master King's Man."

Once again, her soft, melodic Welsh lilt drew him in. "You suspect this coven of ill-deeds?" It was a statement rather than a question. "But I fear you are misdirected. It is but six months since that word spread of a coven of witches in the city up to no good. But these shadows you chase are merely that."

Simon showed surprise at her apparent indifference to the threat such a coven of witches posed to the King and his family.

"I fear you are wrong, Mistress. There is a rumour abroad that this coven intends harm to the life of His Grace the King."

"So, you have said it yourself, King's Man. You are dealing with but two things; a coven of witches and a threat to the life of His Grace. They may be one and the same, or they may not be."

There was no one better informed than Maeve de Thornby. She frowned, dropping her eyes and breaking into a thin smile, which only served to make her look more intriguing. It was her eyes, he thought, that drew him in, deep eyes that looked right into his soul.

"Here you are, King's Man, chasing those shadows just as they would have of you. Are you looking for what you know to be true or for what you think you know to be true?" Her reply was enigmatic. This mysterious Welsh beauty was slowly casting a spell upon him with her golden words. He wondered if she was flirting with him.

She suddenly broke the spell. "You must need ask yourself where this coven has come from. If they are so dangerous, why have they only just appeared, and what serious wrong have they done up to now?"

She leaned in closer to him, her grey-green eyes fixed upon him." My agents and people know what happens in London, York, Bristol, Dover and the southern ports, yet they tell me of no danger. But you seem to think different. I fear you are the victim of misdirection, Master Lowys. You are being encouraged to look here when needs must have you look elsewhere."

She inclined her head. "You may close your mouth, Master Lowys, or have my words taken you by surprise?"

Only then did Simon recognise that he was staring at her and, worse, at the scalloped neckline and the suggestion of her bosom beneath.

"Pray you to forgive me, Mistress," he exclaimed. He had gone red. "I was but taking in your words." He felt she probably knew what thoughts he had in his head and that he was not the first man to look at her in such a manner.

"It would be folly of me to ignore intelligence about this coven, Mistress, but that is was you are suggesting. A plot against His Grace, the King, must always be taken seriously and fully investigated. You suggest that I dismiss this plot as insignificant."

She leaned in towards him, her tone serious.

"Ask yourself, King's man, who does it serve to have you chase these shadows? How can you be sure that the genuine threat to His

Grace does not lie elsewhere? A plot there may be, but can you be sure you are hunting your true quarry?"

"Pray do have more Hippocras, Master Lowys." Having planted a seed in Simon's head, Maeve de Thornby suddenly switched the conversation. She, not he, was in control, and it made the nuncio feel frustrated. He had the sense that she was still gently teasing him to make him feel uncomfortable. In an instant, she put down her Murano glass on a side table, turned to look at him and frowned. The atmosphere abruptly became grave.

"If you are set upon chasing these shadows, Master Lowys, I would caution you to have a care for your safety. You would do well to go to St Albans, do you know it?"

"Aye, I know it well."

"And needs must you may go there soon after you have met with the Jewish Moneylender in Berkhamstede. Do you know the inn with the sign of the Wheatsheaf? I have been told that women of the coven are known to frequent the inn."

"Thank you, Mistress; I will heed your advice." Simon tried hard to shield his sense of alarm. John of Berwick had warned him of danger and peril, and now, here was Maeve de Thornby cautioning him to have a care for his own safety. Simon could not be sure that Maeve read the alarm on his face, but he imagined she had.

"I have more Master Lowys. I cannot vouch for the accuracy of this, but I am privy to news that a woman who would interest you, Mistress Maud Blount, resides in St Albans, where her husband was a merchant trader."

"Was, you say?"

"Aye, she is a widow now. But those who are happiest in the darkness do say she is one of the Daughters you seek."

Simon tried not to show any recognition of the name. Maud Blount had been one of the women Henry Frowyke spoke of who had been at Fulelane for the slaying of the two strangers. Moreover, she was one of the Daughters of the Shadows identified by the Under-Sheriff.

"There is gossip Master Lowys. Some do say that there are those who plan imminent evil against His Grace the King." Simon regarded her intently, wondering how she gathered such information.

"Do you know who?"

"Nay, just rumours abroad. But when you are in St Albans, seek out one Mistress Isabelle de Brun. Ask John of Berwick of her and follow that path."

Simon was puzzled as to how she knew things. How was she privy to his impending visit to see Abraham of Berkhamstede, the moneylender? This woman was all that John of Berwick had said she was. He had never come across one so well-informed, not least a woman so versed in current information.

When Simon came to leave Pendley Manor, he felt a tinge of sadness. He had actually enjoyed the company of Maeve de Thornby, even if she made him feel like a man-boy. His palfrey was brushed down and given a good feed of oats and was ready for the return journey to St Albans. He swung his mount towards the road just as the rain began to beat down from the dark clouds above. He now had a trail to follow to the Daughters of the Shadows. He had to take the King's Highway that would lead him to Berkehamstede, where he had the Queen's business with Abraham, the moneylender. After that, he had to travel the few miles to Langlei to meet with its Lord to facilitate the transfer of the manor to the Queen. Things were coming together for him, and for once, Simon felt pleased with himself, although he also knew that such thoughts often led to events going awry.

CHAPTER 9

Berkehamstede, Hertfordshire, April 1276

It was a short ride from Pendley Manor along Akeman Street to the royal castle at Berkhamstede. The fortress appeared on the eastern horizon long before he arrived. He descended Castle Street and crossed the moat towards the gatehouse. Alert guards appeared, all wearing the livery of Edmund of Almain, Earl of Cornwall. Simon's royal writ gained him immediate access. Around him, building works to improve the defences continued unabated. The castle had changed somewhat since he had last been here a few years before with new inner walls and a stately range of domestic accommodation.

He knew that time was of the essence, but protocol demanded that Simon apprise the Earl, the King's cousin, of what he knew. Again, his writ gained him access to the Earl's outer chambers, but he had to wait once there. Of course, Simon knew of the Earl and had seen him at court, but they had never met or spoken, for there had never been a need. But now there was.

At length, the Earl's Steward came out. "His Grace the Earl will see you now, Master Lowys." He bade Simon through a polished oak door into the Earl's presence.

Simon bowed and stood before Edmund of Berkhamstede, Earl of Cornwall. He was slightly younger than Simon, still far off his thirtieth year. He was the grandson of old King John and the half-brother to the murdered Henry of Almain, slain some five years before in Italy. Edmund's heritage marked him out as one of the premier lords of England, but the man standing in front of Simon did not cut such a figure. Edmund of Cornwall looked like a man out of his depth.

"Master Lowys, I bid you good day." The Earl's reedy voice seemed appropriate for his spindly frame. "You need to see me on urgent business?"

"I needs must inform you of pressing matters, My Lord and beg your good offices to send a despatch to the Chancery." As briefly as he could, Simon explained what more he now knew about the witches' coven and what Maeve de Thornby had said regarding a threat to the life of the King.

"I have business to conduct here in the town on behalf of Her Grace, the Queen, but I must get word to the Chancery to search documents. May I beg ink and parchment and then use one of your nuncios with the fastest of horses?"

Minutes later, Simon found himself at a desk scribing a message to Hugh Ferre in the Chancery requesting any information on the Wheatsheaf Inn on the Magna Vico in St Albans, and especially its proprietor. He thought it would be an act of folly to go blundering in without first knowing something of its owner and the people who frequented it.

He folded his message, wrote Hugh Ferre's name on the front, and sealed it with wax. A servant waited to take the despatch to one of the Earl's nuncios, but Simon dismissed him, preferring not to lose eyes on the message until it was in the scrip of the rider.

At the stables, a lean youth lounged against a gatepost. Tall with long, fair hair and boyish looks, he seemed too young to be a senior messenger. In the stall beside him was a fine, powerfully muscled black stallion. On seeing Simon approach, the youth straightened, and a beaming smile came over his face.

"Master Clerk, I am Arnulf de Bullen, your nuncio."

Simon greeted the young man and looked him up and down, his face betraying what he was thinking. The youth's face had wisps of fair facial hair as if he struggled to grow a beard. "For how long have you been a messenger to the Earl?" There was a note of concern in Simon's voice.

"You think me too youthful, Master? I have been a nuncio to the Earl these two years past. I know the roads well, and my horse can reach the royal palace for you by dusk." He toyed with the dagger in his belt. "And I know how to use this if I have to."

Satisfied, Simon passed the sealed despatch over to Arnulf, who placed it in his scrip. The mount was led out, and in one swift movement, Arnulf mounted. Then, almost as another concerning afterthought, Simon grabbed for the reins.

"You do know the layout of the Palace at Westminster? I wish this despatch to be placed only into the hands of Hugh Ferre, the Under Controller of the Royal Household. Do you know him?"

"I know of him, Master, and I know what he looks like. Afear not, I will put it into his hands only."

Arnulf grabbed back the reins, kicked his heels into the stallion's flank, turned and trotted purposefully towards the gatehouse and up Castlestrete to the main road south to London.

CHAPTER 10

The manor of Langlei, Hertfordshire, April 1276

With the spring rain still stinging in his eyes, Simon turned off the track that served as the King's Highway from London to Berkhamstede. He made his way down the gentle slope towards the river crossing that would lead him to the village of Langlei. He urged his palfrey forwards across the wooden bridge, which he noted was in desperate need of repair. Clearly, Langlei was not a prosperous village. Back in the time of the old King Henry, third of that name, in the years after the First Barons' War, prosperous villages and towns had built stone bridges to encourage trade at their market and annual fairs. Langlei had not shared in such prosperity. The bridge was perhaps thirty paces in length and the width of a cart, but it rattled and shook as his mount crossed skittishly. The planks were lashed together with hempen ropes, and alarmingly, he could make out the swirling river below, swollen by rain. Two boys stood knee-deep in the still water at the river's edge, setting wattle eel traps amongst the river reeds off to his right-hand side. Startled by his sudden appearance, both stared at him intently; strangers were an unfamiliar sight in this village, he thought. Once across the river, he passed an old horse pulling an even older cart loaded with dung. The wizened old driver eyed Simon with suspicion, holding his gaze until he had moved beyond him. Far beyond the bridge, he could hear the clank, clank and sound of rushing water suggesting the paddles of a mill wheel somewhere close by.

The track sloped gently upwards towards the village. Langlei was a small settlement, with groups of homes on either side of an ill-defined muddy street. The simple, single-storey, wattle and daub cottages were all thatched with reeds from the riverbank. Setting eyes on the village confirmed his view that this was not a thriving community.

Wood smoke emanated from the roof of each house. A few children in rags played outside. The rutted roadway curved gently uphill towards a church sitting on a small, grassed plateau off to Simon's left. Beyond, a patchwork of barren strips fanned out towards the southern horizon, broken only by the occasional smear of green growth. The silhouettes of figures could be seen here and there, low-bent weeding or tending to precious winter crops. Simon saw few other people about on their business this chill winter's morning, just a young flaxen-haired maid stacking rushes plucked from the riverbank.

The sight of the girl brought Simon's thoughts back to the inn of Distaflane and how the maid, Alia, had rescued him from the three rifflers. Like most men, Simon carried a dagger but had never used it. That night in the tavern had not been the first time he had been threatened and not the first he had been incapable of doing anything about it.

CHAPTER 11

The Royal Camp of the Lord Edward of England, Trapani, Sicily 1270

As his bay palfrey made its way up the gentle slope towards Langlei Church, memories rolled over Simon like waves. It was the summer of the fifty-fourth year of the reign of King Henry, third of that name. Simon was a retainer of Her Grace the Lady Eleanor, wife of the Lord Edward, heir to the Crown. The couple were to embark on a crusade to Outremer and Simon, as the Lady Eleanor's nuncio and Serjeant-at-Law was to accompany them.

They had embarked from Dover in August and, for three months, travelled overland through France towards Aigues-Morteson, on the southeast coast and thence onto Sicily. The Lord Edward was joining the crusade of the French King, Louis IX, to liberate Jerusalem. Upon the arrival of the English crusaders in Sicily, Edward learned that King Louis had died from dysentery in Tunis. His younger brother Charles of Anjou and his eldest son and new French King, Phillipe IV, were making ready to take the late King's body back to France.

Simon's crusade ended there; he never saw Outremer.

The merciless Sicilian afternoon sun beat down on the Lord Edward's crusader camp in Trapani, only tempered by the cooling breeze that blew in from the northwest. It succeeded in blowing in a fine dust that coated everything no matter how much Simon tried to cover his possessions. The biggest problem he faced was the dust tainting the ink he used. On several occasions, he had trimmed his quill, dipped it in his inkhorn and started to scribe the parchment, only to find the ink clogged with fine Sardinian sand blown across the water.

The time waiting in Trapani was interminable. Simon busied himself studying documents and scribing correspondence for Her Grace the Lady Eleanor. Although far from England, she kept in touch with her bailiffs and relatives, so Simon was busy scribing her letters and despatching nuncios under the royal seal.

The monotony of this Monday was broken by the arrival of a royal messenger at his tent. The knight was a member of the Lord Edward's Household Guard. At more than six feet in height, years of experience were etched onto his face, tanned olive by the sun. He stood at the entrance to Simon's tent silhouetted as the sun's rays shone past his muscled torso, framing him against the opening.

"I bid you good day, Master Lowys," said Sir Thomas of Ashberne with a smile, "How go things with you? Do you find the day warm enough for you?"

Simon had not known Sir Thomas before they embarked on crusade. He got to know him during the perilous sea crossing and the journey south to the Mediterranean coast. Simon had been surprised at how learned Sir Thomas was for a man of violence. He enjoyed the company of this knight and the discussions they had on the knowledge of the ancient world.

For his part, the veteran knight found his conversations with the young nuncio stimulating. He had taken him under his wing, ensuring that he was not the butt of pranks by others in the royal camp.

"His Grace wishes to see you before Vespers, Simon."

That brought the young nuncio up with a jolt. In theory, Simon was the nuncio and Man-of-Law for the Lord Edward's wife, the Lady Eleanor of Castile. She had accompanied her husband on crusade to Outremer, so Simon had gone too. That was why he was here in Sicily.

He had been in the service of Her Grace, the Lady Eleanor, for three years, firstly as one of her Serjeants-at-Law, drawing up legal agreements for property and wardships. Initially, he had little contact with the future queen. Still, his diligence and service were noted. More recently, he had acted as her personal nuncio, delivering correspondence and confidential communications on her behalf. Simon was in awe of her husband, the Lord Edward; his presence intimidated him, yet now he was summoned to his presence.

"His Grace wishes to see me? Me.......why? What does he want with me?"

"Strangely, he didn't confide in me why he wants to see you. Shall I go back and ask him?"

"Nay, nay..... I'll be there. I wonder...."

"Simon," Thomas' tone was calm and reassuring. "Whatever His Grace wishes of you, he knows he can rely on you. Her grace will have told him that. Be there before Vespers."And with that, Sir Thomas turned and left.

Simon made sure to be at the royal enclave in good time for Vespers. The Lord Edward's tent held the prime position within the encampment, with his household knights guarding it day and night. Nonchalant eyes watched him as he approached, ready to spring to the defence of their Lord at a moment's notice.

Although attached to the royal party while on crusade, as a nuncio and Serjeant at Law, Simon had little daily contact with the Lord Edward. Standing before his Lord, he shuffled from foot to foot with nervous apprehension.

There were only a few people inside the royal tent. The Lord Edward, the heir to the throne of England, stood gripping a trestle table deep in the study of correspondence. He appeared unaware of Simon's presence. Sir Thomas was behind him, in full mail and longsword by his side.

Edward was an imposing figure, standing a full two fingers beyond six feet with long, black wavy hair, a stern face and a left eye that drooped. Next to him stood his cousin, Henry of Almain, the grandson of King Henry. In their mid-thirties, both royals were a similar age, young, vigorous men who inspired others to follow them.

Henry's father was the Earl of Cornwall, who had been made the King of the Germans, one step removed from being elected Holy Roman Emperor. As a result, his eldest son was always called Henry of Almain.

The hawkish eyes of the Lord Edward looked up and, it seemed to Simon, glared at him.

"Master Lowys..." any sternness was not reflected in his welcoming tone. "We have need of your services."

"My... My... Lord," stammered Simon.

It was then the Lord Henry of Almain who spoke. As the Lord Edward's cousin and representative, he would accompany the dead King's funeral procession back to France and then onwards into Gascony to control rebellious local lords.

The funeral procession would travel up through Italy and stop at the small hilltop city of Viterbo. There Henry would act as the English Ambassador to the College of Cardinals, still arguing over a successor to Pope Clement, who had died two years before. As such, Henry would balance the presence of Charles of Anjou, uncle, to the new young French King, who sought to pressure the cardinals into accepting a pro-French Pope.

Henry of Almain turned his head to look at his cousin standing next to him.

"Charles of Anjou is a snake," said the Lord Edward. "He harbours resentment at not being firstborn and that the Crown of France went to his pious brother Louis. Anjou is someone who uses his ambition to further his own interests. He rules Tuscany through his enforcer, his Vicar General in the region, who is ruthless and much hated."

Simon nodded at the explanation but inwardly couldn't see how this involved him.

"Viterbo is Charles of Anjou's administrative centre," Edward continued. "When he is there, he will likely meet with his Vicar General, which is why my cousin is travelling with the French party." Still, Simon didn't grasp the relevance of this.

"Charles of Anjou's Vicar General in Tuscany is our cousin, the traitor, Guy de Montfort."

Guy was the hot-headed youngest son of Simon de Montfort, the rebel brother-in-law of King Henry, who took up arms against the King, defeating him in battle at Lewes in 1264. The following year, the Lord Edward was victorious at Evesham. He sent a hand-picked squad of knights onto the battlefield to kill de Montfort and hack his body into pieces. That, Simon recalled, was the catalyst for the familial feud. Guy de Montfort had sworn blood vengeance on the Lord Edward and his family. Simon de Montfort had been the brother-in-law of King Henry and, thus, the Lord Edward's uncle by marriage.

Guy had been wounded and captured at Evesham. Along with his older, more cautious older brother, Simon the Younger, they had escaped, fled to the continent and served as mercenary commanders for the highest bidder.

"My cousin, the Lord Henry, will arrange to meet with Guy and Simon de Montfort in Viterbo and offer them reconciliation with the Crown, effectively a royal pardon. Your role, Master Lowys, is to give legal effect to that pardon and bring the document back to me for royal assent on behalf of my father. Until you reach Viterbo, this part of the mission must remain secret." Simon had been excited to embark on a crusade, looking forward to seeing Jerusalem. And now, having heard what his Lord had said, he was resigned to never setting eyes the holy city.

CHAPTER 12

Viterbo, central Italy, March 1271

The interior of the small Church of San Silvestro gave off a distinctive musty yet perfumed scent of incense, beeswax, dampness, and decay. The odour of sanctity Simon remembered. The ancient Church lay to one side of a small, cobbled square in the centre of Viterbo, some fifty miles northeast of Rome. On its whitewashed walls were holy relics and ancient wall paintings, illuminated by small shafts of light streaming through the stained glass of the high windows. The interior chill, familiar to all churches, was accentuated by the cold marble floor. From the ornate thuribles hanging down from the ceiling, a fug of incense hung at head height throughout. As the purified incense burned, it travelled heavenward, transforming the worshipper into a state of exceptional holiness.

It was a Friday in March, the Feast Day of St Christina the Martyr, in the fifty-fifth year of the reign of King Henry, son of King John. The slow-moving funeral procession of the late French King Louis had arrived in Viterbo three days before, and with them Henry of Almain and his small party, which included Simon Lowys.

Although only a minor city, Viterbo was an obvious choice to break their journey. It, not Rome, had been home to the Popes for almost fifty years. The last Pope, Clement IV, had died there in 1268, and no successor had yet been chosen. Tradition dictated that the election should take place in the city where the previous Pope died. Many cardinals had been resident in the Papal Palace at Viterbo for more than two years, unable to break the deadlock and elect a new Pontiff.

So frustrated were the Magistrates of Viterbo at the indolence of the Cardinals that they had them locked in the Palazzo dei Papi. They allowed them only bread and water for food and removed the roof to focus the Cardinal's minds on choosing a new Pope.

Simon found Viterbo to be a fascinating and enchanting city. He had never seen so many fountains fed, he was told, by a system of underground conduits built in ancient times by the Romans. The fine houses were characterized by a profferlo, a decorated external staircase leading to the ground floor's main doors for stables and people who lived above.

It seemed that every available inn and room in Viterbo was full. Although Henry of Almain's party was small, a detachment of household knights, squires, servants, valets, scribes, chaplains, cooks and officials needed accommodating. But the funeral cortege of the late French King was enormous and took precedence for all but the Lord Henry.

Viterbo, usually a sleepy city, was heaving with people. Henry of Almain's household knights had gone ahead to take the best rooms they could find for their Lord. They found him lodgings in the small Franciscan Priory on the Piazza San Lorenzo, the city's central square and a stone's throw from the Papal Place. Simon among them, many of the party found themselves sleeping in the stables.

While the French royal party used chapels within the Papal Palace for devotions, Henry of Almain and his followers heard mass in the tiny church across the square from the priory. On this Friday morning, the church was not full. It was an intimate church some forty paces by twenty wide. Henry of Almain and a few of his senior household knights and officials were hearing mass at this eighth hour between Prime and Terce. As the nuncio to Her Grace the Lady Eleanor, protocol demanded Simon join the church party. However, he was careful to loiter towards the rear of the church, as befitted his status. The faded, peeling frescoes along the sidewalls looked ancient to Simon but added to the intimacy of the old building. The Lord Henry took his place at the front as the service commenced.

Padre Giulio, an old priest with a booming voice, had just reached the invitation to pray, the Oremus. "Oremus pro ecclesia Sancta Dei," he intoned. We pray for God's Holy Church. "Flectamus genua," responded his archdeacon. Let us kneel. As the archdeacon uttered the Latin incantation, the heavy oak doors were roughly flung open and armed knights poured into the chapel.

Swords and other weapons were banned from the church, so Henry of Almain and his household knights had left theirs inside the main door. There was noise, chaos and confusion. A tall, lean man with flowing dark hair and a short beard strode into the church, and a path opened up between the armed men storming into the chapel to allow him through to the front.

From his demeanour, it was evident that he was the leader of these men. His face was weather-beaten and a scar traced from his right eye towards his mouth. Although he was giving orders, he was the youngest among this invasion force. His suit of chainmail was dusty from long days of riding; his coif pulled down to his neck. He held no shield, and his long sword was drawn. Alongside him, but keeping slightly behind, stood another man barking instructions. Although a few years older, there was a strong facial resemblance. It was then realization struck Simon. It was Guy and Simon, the sons of the traitor, Simon de Montfort.

It was evident that Guy was in charge. Members of the congregation and mercenaries were pushed aside; his eyes fixed firmly on his cousin, who stood frozen.

"Proditor Henrice de Alamania, non evades!" he screamed. "Traitor, Henry of Almain, you shall not escape!"

The knight retainers of the de Montfort's brandished their swords, violently pushing the congregation towards the walls holding them there with the drawn blades.

A whirring blur slashed down onto the left arm of one of Henry of Almain's household knights who had stepped in to help his Lord, almost severing it at the elbow. None of the Lord Henry's party wore protective armour; there had been no need. The blade bit deep into the flesh and broke the bone. The knight fell to his knees, clutching his arm, though no sound came from his throat despite the pain. The attacker, a burly mercenary with a red face and split nose, raised his sword and drove it down hard, deep into the neck of the wounded knight, laughing as he did so.

Simon gave an involuntary movement towards the dying man. Another mercenary half-turned towards him and pushed his sword hard against Simon's neck drawing blood. He pressed the tip hard up against Simon's Adam's Apple.

"Non!" His head slowly moved left and right, indicating that Simon moved at his peril, his scarred face showing a venomous sneer.

Henry of Almain dashed towards the altar; Guy de Montfort, sword raised, strode down the aisle towards him. Padre Giulio stepped forward and put himself between the rushing Guy and the Lord Henry.

"Out of my way, priest, out of my way!" cried out Guy in French, brandishing his sword. He placed his hand on Guy's shoulder; as he did, the blade ripped into the old priest's stomach, and he collapsed to the floor. Bravely, Padre Giulio held up his hands in pacification and began to plead with the younger man. Blood seeped onto his violet vestments and began to pool on the altar floor. The few women in the congregation, wide-eyed in terror, screamed as one at this act of blasphemy.

Although his eyes occasionally flickered left and right, the mercenary holding Simon at bay had kept his focus on the sword point. His face showed the scars of experience. He wore a coat of long mail, ill-kept and rusty. His long dark hair hung lank to his shoulders; his beard peppered with a grey that matched his years.

The sword point pressed hard under Simon's chin forcing his head to the left. He had to turn his eyes far to the right to glimpse the unfolding horror. The congregation, small as it was, had been pushed to the side and held at sword point, interfering with Simon's line of sight.

Guy de Montfort stepped over the body of the dying Padre Giulio and moved towards Henry of Almain, now cowering beside the altar. Henry, his face flushed, stared at his cousin, now just a few feet from him.

"For the love of Jesus, mercy cousin, mercy."

"You had no mercy for my father and brothers," sneered Guy.

The elder Simon de Montfort had been King Henry's brother-in-law. He had led the baronial opposition, forcing reforms on the King in 1258 that limited royal power. The struggle culminated in war, with the King captured at the battle of Lewes in 1264. Simon de Montfort became the effective ruler of England. The following year, royal forces under the Lord Edward met de Montfort in battle at Evesham. De Montfort was hunted down and killed on the battlefield. Once he lay dead, the Lord Edward's hand-picked killing squad deliberately mutilated the body. Although Henry of Almain had not fought at Evesham, he had once supported Simon de Montfort before finally going over to the King's side.

For a moment, both men's eyes locked. The shrieking of the women continued. Oblivious, Guy de Montfort raised his sword; anticipating the blow, Henry raised an arm to defend himself, gripping the altar with his left hand. Guy slashed hard against Henry's head, cutting deep into the brain. The Lord Henry of Almain fell to the marble floor. Guy rained down further blows upon his cousin's defenceless body as he fell.

Henry of Almain lay on the marble floor of the altar, his head and upper body a bloody mess. His breathing was shallow, dying moans emanating from his mouth. Three of his unarmed household knights moved to aid their Lord. They were mercilessly cut down by the sword-wielding mercenaries guarding them.

The shocked congregation watched in horror as the younger de Montfort, Simon, moved towards the dying Henry. He, too, drove his sword into the body, exclaiming as he did so, "Revenge! Die traitor, die."

Satisfied, Guy de Montfort turned on his heels and stomped towards the doors of the church. "Come, Walter," he said to the mercenary holding Simon at sword point, "I have taken my vengeance!"

"Nay, My Lord," exclaimed the mercenary Walter, still with his sword tip at Simon's throat. "At Evesham, they hacked and mutilated the body of your father. Your revenge is not yet complete."

Guy de Montfort paused, thought momentarily, and exclaimed, "You have the right of it." He turned and strode back towards the altar, passing his brother as he did so. Both grabbed Henry of Almain's long hair and roughly dragged the now lifeless body along the church floor and out onto the square. A trail of blood marked their path.

When Guy de Montfort spoke to this mercenary Walter, the knight turned his gaze away from Simon for the first time since the church had been stormed. The pressure of the sword point at Simon's throat eased momentarily. Still, it resumed the moment Guy turned and went back to the altar to drag the Lord Henry's body outside.

The de Montfort mercenary knights followed their swords, pointing at the congregation as they retreated towards the door. As they left, four of them blocked the exit, their swords menacing, keeping the Lord Henry's few unarmed household knights at bay.

Outside, the de Montfort brothers dumped the lifeless Henry of Almain onto the church steps. Guy again raised his sword high and brought it down onto Henry's chest. Further blows rained down, partially dismembering the corpse before them.

"Maintenant j'ai pris ma vengeance!"screamed Guy de Montfort. Now I have taken my vengeance! He spat on the mutilated corpse of Henry of Almain as it lay draped on the steps facing away from the church. Blood no longer seeping from his wounds; his face no longer recognisable; death had taken him. Some of de Montfort's men mimicked their Lord, spitting on the corpse and disdainfully hacking at the body as they descended the steps. A light drizzle had begun to fall; in the square, de Montfort's young squires held the reins of thirty horses, nostrils flared, tails rising and skittish and jumpy now they had smelt blood in the air.

With Guy de Montfort at their head and without a glance backwards, the killing party mounted their horses, manoeuvred out of the tight square and rode off. All inside the Church of San Silvestro were terrified, shocked, and confused at the brutal sacrilege they had witnessed.

Screams and shrieks emanated from the oppressive atmosphere inside the church. Men shouted instructions amid the uproar. Once de Montfort's men had departed, knights raced to the lifeless body of the Lord Henry. An older knight with a leathery face, hollow eyes and receding hair cradled Henry's head in his arms. Tears welled in his eyes; a woman joined him, wailing and crying.

In less time than it would take to say a few Paternosters, Henry of Almain, the King's nephew, had been slain. There was anger and disbelief at what had just occurred in this holy city.

It took Simon more than two months to travel to Acre with news of the assassination. Two of Henry of Almain's Household knights accompanied him. Both feared the wrath of the Lord Edward for permitting the murder of his cousin. Simon had already despatched fast messengers to England to the King and to Henry of Almain's father, the Earl of Cornwall, with a written account of what had occurred.

The Household knights were correct to fear the reaction. The Lord Edward and the Lady Eleanor sat on a slightly raised dais in their quarters inside the compound of the Knights of St John in Acre. Simon's eyes welled with tears as he recounted the events inside the Church in Viterbo months before.

The Lord Edward's Plantagenet temper, always close to the surface, boiled over, and he lashed out in rage at all present.

His mood swung from anger and rage to tears and wailing. When his fury subsided, his rage turned towards revenge upon Guy de Montfort and his brother. He and Henry of Almain had grown up together and had been as close as brothers.

Even now, years later, Simon could recall the Lord Edward's icy stare and the silence that lingered for a long time. For many months afterwards, the Lord Edward was cold on the occasions he had to see him as if blaming the messenger for the deeds of others.

Simon never forgot the scarred face of the man who held him at sword-point in Viterbo. He had witnessed a callous act of revenge by the de Montfort brothers and reproached himself that he had not been able to help his Lord.

CHAPTER 13

The manor of Langlei, Hertfordshire, April 1276

As his willing palfrey trotted uphill towards the Church, Simon took in the building. It was modest, a nave and chancel both in need of renovation, and it didn't strike Simon as being that old, perhaps one hundred years. Like the homes in the village below, its roof was thatched with a patchwork of reeds. The lower courses of the nave were of flint set in lime-mortar, but it was mainly wooden in its upper section layered with wattle and daub. Yet further evidence that Langlei, and its Lord, Stephen de Chenduit, were not prosperous enough to have God's house entirely stone-built.

On a ridge just above the church stood the Old Manor House. Simon could see why it was called thus. He thought it had centuries of age, possibly from the time of the Confessor, before the conquest of old King William. It had been a fine building in its day with oak beams holding up a second storey. Like the church, it showed signs of requiring urgent repair, its thatched roof likely home to nesting birds and rodents. The wattle and daub walls were cracked and crumbling in places and had not seen fresh limewash in many summers.

From his conversation with John of Berwick, Simon knew that this had not been the de Chenduit's home for many decades. After the First Barons' War in the early years of the late King Henry, de

Chenduit's grandfather had built a new manor house on top of the hill that rose a few hundred feet west of the village. This older house, nearby the church, was now the likely home of the de Chenduit's Reeve.

The road to the 'new' manor house was a well-defined path that snaked up towards the top of the ridge, falling away gently to the south. It meandered along the edges of the now bare-brown field strips of the Lord's demesne, the fertile south and west-facing land that here and there held winter crops of unpicked peas and beans.

Unlike his tenant's wattle and daub cottages, the de Chenduit moated manor house was built of flint courses laid with mortar. Its size reflected his status as the local Lord and a former household knight in the service of the late King's brother, the Earl of Cornwall. Its location atop a hill suggested that it was part fortification and part home. That was understandable given the de Chenduit's chequered past serving Simon de Montfort.

The grandfather Ralph de Chenduit had fought against the Crown in the civil war in the reign of King John that followed the Magna Carta and had his lands seized by the Crown in 1217. The family fortunes had improved in the years that followed to a point where the estates were restored. Despite loyal service to the Earl of Cornwall and his son, Henry of Almain, the present Lord, Stephen de Chenduit, had fought for Simon de Montfort at Lewes against King Henry and his son, the current King, Edward. Only his past service and connection to Henry of Almain had allowed him to retain his manors.

The house was dominated by its great hall. At one end, large windows were visible, which threw light into the solar, effectively the de Chenduit's private chambers. As he crossed the moat, two guards at the gatehouse stepped out and halted his progress, enquiring about his business.

Mention of the King's Writ served to gain Simon immediate access to the inner courtyard of the manor house. It was precisely the type of home one might expect of a former household knight to the royal family. Although it dominated the local landscape, it could by no means be considered large. Moreover, just as Langlei village showed signs of tiredness, so too did Stephen de Chenduit's manor house. Tiles were broken on the chapel roof; thatch on the outbuildings went unrepaired. Langlei Manor was drab. The whole effect reinforced the impression of a village and its Lord that was not thriving. The de Chenduit's were short of money.

Simon Lowys' eyes blazed with fury at the sight of the man seated at Stephen de Chenduit's table. You do not forget the face of a man who held you at sword point in a church. That face had haunted his sleep for five years. The memories of his own inadequacy that day years before overcame him. A sword pushed hard against his throat, and Simon had done nothing to help his Lord as he was hacked to death on the altar. How he had taken the news to the Lord Edward in Acre and how the future King had broken down and sobbed uncontrollably on hearing of his cousin's death.

"You bring a traitor under your roof, Sir Stephen?" enquired Simon, controlling his anger.

"I am no traitor to the Crown," snarled the man seated.

Simon's eyes bored in on him. He spoke slowly. "Walter de Baskerville, traitor, rebel, mercenary, liegeman to the excommunicated Guy de Montfort, murderer and heretic. You are all those things and more. You are tainted with the mark of Cain, and I find him here with you, Sir Stephen."

De Chenduit's reply was almost apologetic. "William is family; his wife Lucya is my wife's cousin, Master Lowys. He intends to petition His Grace the King for royal pardon; that is why he is here."

"A pardon?" Simon exploded with rage. "Your wife's kin killed the grandson of a King. Slain in cold blood in God's house. He was party to that murder. I know; I witnessed it. He is a man whose soul is damned. An excommunicant. He can have no pardon."

"And yet, I am here," replied de Baskerville in a slow sneering tone that only served to anger Simon even more. "I am a supplicant before the Crown asking for forgiveness and His Grace's pardon, as is my right. I plan to seek absolution for my sins from Holy Mother Church and expunge the stain of excommunication."

Simon Lowys glared at the seated mercenary.

"You dare to set foot in England. His Grace the King will hunt you down before he ever grants you a pardon."

A smile cut across the gnarled face of Walter de Baskerville. A thin malevolent smile Simon had seen years before and could never forget. If blame were to be laid for what occurred at Viterbo, it partly lay with the man who sat in front of him now at Stephen de Chenduit's table, idly chewing on a chicken leg. The presence of Walter de Baskerville here, now, was no coincidence. The news of his reappearance would need to be known to the King's Intelligencers in Westminster. He had to get the information John of Berwick as quickly as possible.

As flushed with anger as he was, Simon had the Queen's purchase of the manor to execute. Still bristling, he turned towards de Chenduit. Avoiding de Baskerville's penetrating stare, Simon said, "We needs must discuss your business with Her Grace. In private, I think."

Stephen de Chenduit paused and looked to his brother-in-law. Walter de Baskerville just inclined his head as if to assent. De Chenduit considered, and then ushered Simon into a small side chamber.

The antechamber was almost bare of furniture. It had a musty smell as if it had not seen use in many months. Simon and de

Chenduit sat on the only two benches in the room. This wasn't to be a negotiation; de Chenduit was deep in debt to Abraham of Berkhamstede and Manassas, son of Aaron. The terms of the 'agreement' had already been worked out months before. Simon was here to put the charter into effect and get de Chenduit's seal of acknowledgement. Stephen de Chenduit had been living beyond his means for many years. Although he held many manors across Hertfordshire, Buckinghamshire and Oxfordshire, eleven Knights Fees in total, his income was diminishing year by year.

Once, he had been a knight in royal favour serving in the royal household. He had been appointed to accompany the late King's brother, Richard of Cornwall, to Cologne in 1258, where the Earl had been crowned King of the Germans. In that royal retinue was another promising household knight, Walter de Baskerville.

But de Chenduit's chequered past, supporting de Montfort and fighting against his King at Lewes had cost him politically and financially. Now Her Grace, Queen Eleanor, was buying out his debt. Simon had already scribed the document weeks before he arrived in Langlei. The Queen was buying out the debt.

Alone in the small room, resignation set in. All of Stephen de Chenduit's movements were slow. He had no choice but to affix his seal to the bottom of the parchment, and Simon scribed his name. He took a green wax bar from his scrip and, taking a candle from its holder, melted the wax to drip onto the document. Simon removed a gold signet ring from the middle finger of his left hand and pressed it into the wax, affixing the royal seal on behalf of the Queen.

Stephen de Chenduit regarded the royal nuncio with mixed emotions. As unhappy as he was with the situation, de Chenduit was debt-free, and Queen Eleanor now held the manor of Langlei.

CHAPTER 14

The Benedictine Abbey of St Albans, April 1276

From high on the ridge above Langlei, Simon Lowys surveyed the fields stretching out towards the eastern horizon. The morning was bright but chilly, and the earthen strips looked like fingers of brown. He had spent all of yesterday, and most of this morning, riding the tracks and roads that defined the boundaries of the Queen's new manor. Now satisfied, he had planned to head east towards St Albans. A journey to the Chancery and back would take up a day, which he could ill-afford. But the presence of Walter de Baskerville meant he had to get to the Chancery and receive new instruction. His final task in Langlei was to survey the property boundaries to ensure they were clearly defined in the charter. In his despatch to Hugh Ferre, Simon had instructed that the reply should be sent, with all speed, directly to him at St Albans Abbey.

The Benedictine Abbey containing the shrine of the first English martyr lay just ten miles east of Langlei, and it was an easy-paced journey of a few hours. Simon had some knowledge of the town, having an older widowed woman who lived there and who, on occasions, helped him with his work. If ever he was asked, Simon always called her his wife's kin, for it made explanation easier in matters of propriety. In truth, they had first met three summers before, at the behest of John of Berwick. Matilda Heacham was a point of contact for Berwick's men in St Albans. She provided safe lodging and necessary supplies for royal agents passing through the Abbey town. She accepted and forwarded messages, passed on instructions, and provided good food and a comfortable bed.

It had been her husband who was Berwick's man, and when he had passed to God, Matilda continued his work. She possessed valuable connections throughout the town as well as inside the abbey from its lay servants. John of Berwick had others in towns across the realm who performed a similar function for him. Simon had come across two of them in the past when engaged on royal business; one in York and another in Bury St Edmunds. Matilda Heacham, like those others, was discreet and fulfilled her role diligently. To all intents and purposes, she was a well-to-do widow of the town, of middle-years, one of many such women following the pestilence of a few years past.

The Spring air was fresh, and Simon saw few people on the road. When he reached the hamlet of Bedmond, he came upon a flurry of activity. It seemed as if the whole village were out early planting the strips. He stopped at the green and drank from his wineskin. Refreshed, he mounted and headed northeast for St Albans.

Simon's arrival at the northern gatehouse of the Abbey promoted a flurry of activity, with servants, ostlers and stableboys rushing to assist the King's Man. Amid the activity, Simon noticed a young man lounging against the upright of one of the stables, a huge grin on his face. As Simon approached, the smile on Arnulf de Bullen's got bigger.

"Master Bullen, what do you here? I did not expect to see you."

"I have your reply, Master Lowys. Sir Hugh gave me instruction that I was to await your arrival and hand the despatch directly to you."

"Will you not be missed by the Earl?"

"Nay, Sir Hugh sent news that I would be delayed. I have been instructed to act as your nuncio for these next days, he said."

"Then come, I must see what Sir Hugh has for me

Arnulf went to his scrip, took out the despatch from the Chancery, and handed it to Simon.

Have you eaten? Come and take some food, Master Bullen."

They headed off in the direction of the guesthouse to partake of ale and cheese. An hour later, having eaten their fill, the abbey ewe's milk cheese being particularly delicious, Simon laid the paper despatch on the bench. He took his knife and carefully slit the underside of the wax seal. He folded open the paper and read the uncoded information it contained.

Although Simon's request to the Chancery was for information about the Wheatsheaf, one of Hugh Frere's clerks had itemised each point in this despatch. The tavern was known to the Chancery, and it had been owned by a vintner, one Thomas de Brun. It appeared he had died, and the ownership had passed to his widow, Isabelle. There then followed a list of known or suspected felons known to frequent the inn. However, Simon found most interesting that witnesses had placed Margery de Pyritton and Agnes de Bilda regularly using the alehouse. The Chancery clerks also informed him that Isabelle de Brun also owned another alehouse in Berkhamstede and had links to another in Barnet. However, they were uncertain whether she was the proprietor.

That name, Isabelle de Brun. Maeve de Thornby had told him that he should seek out Mistress de Brun when he was in St Albans. Maeve had also suggested that he ask John of Berwick of her, which he had yet to do.

So, two of the coven members of the Daughters of the Shadows had a connection to the Wheatsheaf. The despatch also confirmed that the widow Blount lived in a townhouse in St Albans. He now had two leads to follow: Maeve de Thornby's about Maud Blount, here in St Albans, and a further connection to Berkhamstede. He already had business in that town with the Jewish moneylender who held the de Chenduit mortgage for Langeli; he now had an additional reason to go there. But before he could contemplate that, he had urgent business at the Chancery in Westminster.

CHAPTER 15

Watlingstrete outside the village of Park Hertfordshire, April 1276

Ivo Shaldeforde worked his way cautiously between the Alders, Field Maples and Sweet Chestnuts that thrived in the woodland beyond Watlingstrete, outside of the village of Park. His movement startled a busy squirrel digging for long-buried nuts, its red fur and tail standing up in high threat alert.

Ahead of him, the ancient highway snaked its way north towards St Albans. Here at Park, the woodland encroached close to the road, despite an ordinance to cut back by thirty yards. Not that Ivo was disappointed at such failure. It made his life much easier.

Ivo lived on the fringes of society. Years before, he honestly couldn't recall how many he had killed a man from his village. Ivo had been in the tavern, deep in his cups, when a rival for the affections of the raven-haired widow, Joanna, began to taunt him. Ivo's temper exploded, and he drew his dagger, fatally stabbing his opponent. Knowing that witnesses would identify him, his guilt was assured. Ivo ran from his village. Abandoning his feudal obligations, he chose to live his life outside the laws of England. Now those same laws of the land considered Ivo Shaldeforde akin to the creatures that roamed wild in the forest, a Caput Lupinum, a Wolf's Head.

From his cover behind the trees, Ivo could make out one of his companions, John Pyecart skulking behind some scrawny hawthorn on the far side of the Roman road.

The Wolf's Heads around the village of Park accepted Ivo as their leader. There had been challenges to his authority from disaffected rivals, but he had seen off all of them. Ivo revelled in the violence; he found that he enjoyed killing. Thus, his fellow Wolf's Heads looked to him for leadership out of their fear of him and his ability to meet their needs of shelter, food, drink and warmth. Ivo had an uncanny prowess in procuring goods through stealth and bribery, but primarily through violence and intimidation.

He and his band of outlaws were, by necessity, nomadic. Staying in one place for too long risked detection by the Sheriff. They preyed on travellers along the old Roman road, moving either north or south depending upon where their last attack had been. Here at Park, where the woodland closed close to the verge, was a favoured location for robbery. Ivo placed his men at crucial points on both sides of the road where it curved slightly, creating a blind spot for travellers coming north from London towards the abbey town.

Ivo knew that he faced a slow execution should the law catch up with him. What matter, therefore, are a few more deaths? They could only make him do the gallows dance once. Some among his fellow Wolf's Heads remained unhappy with his decision to leave no witnesses alive; their fear of Ivo outweighed their conscience. Ivo's accomplices knew the fate that awaited them if the Sheriff's men apprehended them. They would receive no mercy. The law forbade giving assistance, aid, and food to outlaws. Anyone could take them dead or alive for a guaranteed cash reward, so Ivo always thought it best to avoid towns and villages whenever possible.

The Spring had bought renewed warmth and greenery to the forest. The winter had been harsh. Growing up, the old people in his village used to call January the Wolf Month. Wolves, driven by snow or cold, would shelter in the woodlands the same way as the outlaws. Stories were told around the fires of starving wolves overcoming their natural fear of man and entering nearby villages. They carried off livestock and even small children on more than a few occasions. Though, as he thought about it, Ivo had never actually seen or even heard a wolf. Just stories, he thought, to frighten young children.

But life for him and his fellow outlaws in the forest in winter was harsh. Roads and tracks simply disappeared for weeks in the rain or under snow and ice. Even Ivo called the month of March the Mud-Month. Which was why he welcomed the Spring, not least because it would bring travellers back to the roads and provide him and his men with likely targets to rob.

Although Ivo's Wolf's Heads in the forest numbered around a dozen, he had taken just five other men with him to the ambush at Park. Three outlaws lay in wait on the far side of the road, concealed by overgrown shrubbery. Ivo placed two others fifty yards apart, covering the entrance into the curve and its exit. He hid deep in the trees, waiting to pounce.

In normal circumstances, Ivo would lay in wait for his prey. He avoided larger groups or mounted knights and men-at-arms, as the risk would be significant to him and his men. On this day, he had been forwarned about a traveller on the road and had laid his trap accordingly.

Ivo Shaldeforde did his best to avoid the local inns; there was always the danger that someone might recognise him. If he ran low on supplies, then he chanced to go somewhere remote. The inn beside the crossroads lay at the intersection of two old Roman roads off Watlingstrete. An inn had existed on the site for centuries and was always known as the inn beside the crossroads. Now it was old and run down, and its clients were a few ale-sodden villagers and the less well-to-do travellers on the road.

Ivo wasn't a frequent visitor at the crossroads, but his appearance always caused consternation to the innkeeper Thomas Fyssh. Fyssh was frightened of the Wolf's Head and the violence he brought with him. But Fyssh acted as a messenger for Ivo. A conduit from the Daughters of the Shadows to their enforcer in the woods.

Ivo knew a message from Alice le Blunde awaited him when he saw the dead sparrow nailed to the water butt. That was her signal that Fyssh had instructions for him. For his part, Ivo Shaldeforde was afraid of no man. Years of a life outside the law, living alongside tough men who would slit your throat for a penny, had hardened him. Yes, few things scared Ivo; but Alice le Blunde was different. He was afeared of her and the demonic sisters in her coven of witches.

Ivo waited in the shadows at the rear of the inn until a potboy came out to relieve himself. Silently, Ivo crept up behind the boy, placing a hand on his shoulder.

"Don't turn around."

The boy's sudden urge to relive himself disappeared.

"Go inside and send your master out here. Understood?"

The potboy quivered and nodded his acknowledgement.

Minutes later, the bulky figure of Thomas Fyssh appeared at the rear door. Peering into the gloom of the evening, Fyssh could not see anyone, so he called out.

"Who is there? Who calls for me?"

"I do, Fyssh." A shudder of apprehension ran through the innkeeper as he recognised the identity of the hushed voice.

"Greetings, my friend." Fyssh was careful not to use Ivo's name lest anyone was listening. "How can I help you?"

"For a start, there's a dead bird here that says you have a message for me."

"Aye. Our friend has passed on the details of a task for you. You are to..."

"Hush!" Ivo abruptly interrupted him. "Follow me to that copse behind the inn and give me the message there. In the meantime, I have things I need."

Ivo gave Fyssh a list of the provisions he required.

"Send them by cart two days hence. Take the road north and be before the village of Darnells at Nones."

Fyssh knew what Ivo planned, and he knew Ivo's reputation for leaving no witnesses alive.

"My carter," Fyssh's voice was pleading. "He is old, his sight is failing, and he has a family."

Ivo screwed his face pondering on the response. "His sight is failing, you say. That is good. Fear not, Fyssh, he will be left unharmed, provided he does see nothing."

It was but a few minutes later, deep in the thicket, that a nervous Fyssh passed on Alice le Blunde's message

"Mistress le Blunde wishes you to intercept a traveller on the road north from London. He travels from the royal court to St Albans on the morrow. He will leave at first light and should be in the town by mid-morn."

"And who is this person, and how will I know him?" inquired Ivo.

"Mistress says he is a royal clerk. He is perhaps thirty summers, dark-haired and slim of build. He will be riding a bay palfrey and travelling alone. His profession is the law, not the sword. And she instructs you to leave no trace of his existence on the road."

Alice le Blunde had issued a death contract on this royal clerk. Ivo neither knew nor cared why. She had given her command, and Ivo Shaldeforde would comply rather than risk the ire of the Daughters of the Shadows. Thus, Ivo and his band of Wolf's Heads were concealed on Watlingstrete, waiting for Simon Lowys to come upon them.

CHAPTER 16

St Albans, Hertfordshire April 1276

The King's Intelligencer, known as le Reynard, felt a sense of unease. Things were not as they should be. For too long, the Daughters of the Shadows had evaded detection and stayed at least one jump ahead of those pursuing them. Le Reynard suspected, though could not prove, that someone inside the Royal Chancery was passing information to Alice le Blunde.

But le Reynard had informants at Westminster inside the royal complex. This day, a message had come saying that Alice le Blunde knew that the King's Man, Lowys was en route to St Albans on the morrow. Le Reynard suspected that Alice would not want a King's Man snooping around the Daughters of the Shadows and thus, would order Lowys' death. That could not be allowed, so le Reynard began to formulate a plan to prevent his murder.

Some eight miles to the south of St Albans lay the manor of Titeberst, an ancient, once-thriving settlement. Its past prosperity had been linked to its proximity to the Roman road north, but it now had just a few houses Titeberst had a once fine manor house built during the reign of Saint Edward. Its owner, Margery de Clyderode, was the widow of a Household knight of the old King Henry, slain at Lewes defending his King.

The death of her husband left Margery de Clyderode responsible for the running of the manor, which she did with excellent efficiency for the benefit of her young son Ralph. She still had an elegance about her; not yet past her fortieth year, literate, fluent in both French and the local English and with a keen mind. And Margery de Clyderode was a close ally of le Reynard.

On this last day of April, the sun was just setting as the messenger arrived. Margery had been picking the last of the winters' sage leaves in her herb garden when he approached. He took a sealed despatch from his scrip and handed it to her. She instantly recognised the wax impression as belonging to le Reynard. The messenger bade her farewell, and Margery went inside.

Breaking the seal, she scanned its contents. It was written in English, which would make it unintelligible to most educated people. If they could read and write, it would be in French, not English.

Le Reynard had made an urgent request of Margery to save the life of a King's Man who would be on the road tomorrow at mid morn. It came with risk. Le Reynard did not know the specifics of the threat to the King's Man, only that there would likely be an attempt upon his life when on the road. Margery was to nullify that threat through ingenuity and guile.

Titeberst lay close to Watlingstrete, and the King's Man would pass close by the manor on his journey. Margery did not know precisely when this royal nuncio would be close to Titeberst, so she planned her diversion and waited.

CHAPTER 17

Watlingstrete, May 1276

It was the sort of day to make even an unaccomplished horseman like Simon Lowys feel good about being on the road. The early May sun shone brightly from an almost cloudless blue sky as Simon picked up the King's Highway to Padintun. He had left Westminster early, passing through the huge Magno Porta to exit the royal palace. His route took him north towards the village of Hyde to skirt the marshes beyond the Hospital of St James and its leper colony.

He had been right to leave for the Royal Chancery. More intelligence had come in from agents in Ghent and other royal intelligencers that John of Berwick shared with him.

After a time, he came upon the gallows at Tyburn, where the bodies of two common criminals twisted in the gentle breeze. At the junction of the two Roman Roads marked by a monument known as Oswulf's Stone, he found Watlingstrete and made north for Kelebourne. The ancient road was arrow straight as he passed through one similar village after another: Eggeswer, Stanmere and Elsterre. There were few travellers on the King's Highway, some merchants and pilgrims and the occasional royal nuncio, who he greeted enthusiastically. Simon's bay palfrey made easy time despite being tied to his packhorse carrying his legal baggage, inks, quills, parchment, and bedding.

After Elsterre Watlingstrete became more rutted and cartwheels had worn away some of the surfaces, forcing Simon to slow his palfrey and packhorse to a walking pace. He rounded a shallow bend and ahead was a stationary carriage. It had once been a fine vehicle, with bright colours long since faded. Red silk curtains hung from its windows. Two horses should have drawn it, but one appeared to be missing.

Simon stopped beside the carriage and hailed the driver.

"God give you good day. Is all well?"

"Nay. A problem with one of our horses, Meister," came back the response.

"Who is it, Hamo?" It was a woman's voice coming from inside the carriage.

"A stranger upon the road, Mistress," answered the driver.

"I am Simon Lowys, nuncio to Her Grace the Queen and engaged on the King's business."

A delicate pale hand pulled one of the curtains aside, and the beguiling face of a woman peered back at him.

"May God and his Holy Host give you good day, Master Lowys. I am Mistress Margery de Clyderode, the lady of the manor of Titeberst."

Simon gave Margery his greetings and inquired of her what had occurred?

"I am en route to the Shrine of the Martyr at St Albans, but it appears one of my carriage horses has gone lame. My man has taken it back to the manor, but it will be many hours before he is back here with another to allow me to complete my journey." Simon could hear the frustration in her tone. Unbeknown to him, Margery de Clyderode had just scattered the seed for le Reynard's plan.

"I too am for St Albans, Mistress. See, my palfrey is much the same size as your remaining horse. Your man can tie him to the harness, and the pair can pull your carriage to the Abbey. I can ride atop with your driver."

"You would do that, Master Lowys?" she asked hopefully.

"Aye. Of course."

"But I would not hear of you riding atop with my man. You shall ride in here with me."

Simon's first thought was for Margery's virtue and the scandal of a man riding alone with a woman he did not know. As if reading his mind, she added, "You may share the carriage with myself and my maid of the chamber, Joan."

Simon Lowys sat inside Margery de Clyderode's carriage, happy to be carried north in the presence of such a fine lady. He regarded Margery, her round features perfectly framed within her white wimple. In the minutes he had known her, she had never lost the gentle smile. Her face was pale, with few lines and piercing blue eyes.

Simon had anticipated a pleasant ride north to St Albans. The company of this lady, he thought to himself, would be much nicer.

It hadn't taken Margery's driver long to unsaddle Simon's bay palfrey and hitch it to the carriage harness. Simon's saddle stowed in the rear with the packhorse tied behind. As they made their way a sedate pace along Watlingstrete, Margery conversed politely in French with both Simon and Joan.

Ivo Shaldeforde squinted his eyes as he stared south down Watlingstrete. He had watched the sun progress in the sky, and it was not far off its high point of the day, and still, the man had yet to appear. He and his fellow Wolf's Heads had been waiting for this King's Man. Not many travellers had passed them. The occasional merchant, trailing packhorses, slow-moving carts and groups of pilgrims, going in both directions, to and from St Albans.

In the distance, he made out horses pulling a large carriage. This would present a tempting target for his Wolf's Heads in normal times. But, this day, with their specific target, he could not risk an attack that might alert the King's Man to their presence.

Ivo waved his arm to signal Godric, concealed in the trees on the opposite side of the road. His fellow Wolf's Head acknowledged his leader as Ivo shook his head, pointing at the oncoming carriage. They would allow it to pass.

Inside Margery de Clyderode's carriage, the small talk continued.

"Have you been in Her Graces' service long, Master Lowys?" inquired Joan. Simon felt very relaxed in the company of these two women.

"I served her grace as a nuncio before she became queen, and I went with her to Outremer these six years past."

That he had gone on crusade to the Holy Land fascinated his two companions, and they began to question him about his crusading exploits. He could see the disappointment on their faces when he told them that he had never actually set foot in Outremer.

"I was sent north from Sicily by his grace, the King, to accompany the Lord Henry of Almain."

At the mention of the slain cousin of the King, both ladies made the sign of the cross. Simon averted his gaze as they did, looking out of the open window, the silk curtains pulled well back.

He thought he caught a glimpse of brown moving behind the shrubbery. A deer, perhaps, or a Wolf's Head? Simon tensed, awaiting an attack if, indeed, it was a band of robbers. He knew this stretch of the Roman road was notorious for outlaw attacks, but he was conscious of not alarming the women.

"Do you plan to make devotion at the Holy Shrine?" he hoped they could not sense concern in his voice.

"Aye," replied Mistress de Clyderode. "It is many months since I have done so, and I needs must make an offering for the repose of my late husband's soul."

Simon listened intently but kept watch on the close-by shrubbery from the corner of his eye, hoping above hope that it genuinely was a deer.

Ivo Shaldeforde peered at the carriage as it passed slowly in front of him. It pulled a packhorse, which in itself was strange. There was a single driver and two women, and a man inside. The colourful decoration of the carriage told him it belonged to someone important. A lady of the manor or the wife of a wealthy merchant. Ivo felt a pang of regret at having to allow such a valuable target to pass through his fingers. He took solace in the knowledge that there would always be others and that he had a more important task to fulfil for Alice le Blunde.

CHAPTER 18

St Albans Market, May 1276

Simon left his lodgings in the Abbey guesthouse early. He could have stayed with Mistress Heacham and intended to call upon her later that day. He had confirmed what Maeve de Thornby had told him and was eager to follow the leads to the Daughters of the Shadows, so he skipped breaking his night fast. One of the Daughters, Maud Blount, resided in the prosperous part of town in a house in Bothelestrete, up beyond the Market Place.

He smelt the market long before he saw it. It was a layered tapestry of putrid, aching stenches: rotting offal, human excrement, stagnant water, foul-smelling fish, the burning of tallow candles, together with animal dung on the streets.

The market at St Albans was a large triangular open space to the northeast of the Benedictine complex. Over time it had evolved into separate sectors for different traders. The meat market was situated in the lower marketplace, the fish market, higher up. Along French Row, given that name after the forces of Prince Louis of France occupied the town in 1216, was the 'Women's Market,' selling butter, eggs and poultry. Further along, were the leather sellers and the wheat merchants. The butchers had their stalls at the end of the marketplace beyond Bothelestrete.

What had begun as temporary booths in the reign of the first king Henry had evolved into permanent structures with an attached stall at the front, facing onto the street. Even at this early hour, the market was thronged. A pie seller peddled his wares on a board slung from a shoulder with a cry of, "*Many-a-pie. Fine coney. Many-a-pie...*" A toothless old woman, her face aged with lines, sat cross-legged on the earth, a worn blanket laid beside her on which she displayed a motley selection of gnarled vegetables. A man deep in his cups, even at such an early hour, was throwing up over the corner of a building.

Simon had to fight his way through a flock of recalcitrant geese being driven to the far end of the marketplace, where only the sharp blade of the butcher's knife awaited them. It was noticeable how sellers used wooden carts or tables to display their wares, and some had awnings or sides made of heavy cloth hanging from poles to create a makeshift booth.

Simon waited in a doorway close to Maud's house, prompting suspicion from passers-by. When Maud left at Terce, long after the sun came up, it was relatively easy to follow her despite the market crowds at such an early hour. Her cote of deep crimson easily stood out, and he caught frequent glimpses of her among the throng of people.

Many hucksters were selling their wares from blankets laid out on the ground. Ale sellers abounded, all beckoning and calling out to anyone who might listen to sample their brew.

He noticed the young men creeping along the stall front, their eyes not on the goods but the crowds. These were the lookouts for the gangs of rifflers and cutpurses who operated in every town on market day. Always seeking a suitable victim, they worked in twos and threes. Once they had identified their mark, they moved in to bump accidentally into them, skilfully slicing the purse from the victim's belt and handing it on to the fellow gang member.

Simon identified several youthful lookouts as he trailed Maud through the square. Their eyes always gave them away, he thought. She visited several stalls before making her way to Bothelyngstock, where her late husband had traded. Despite his death a few months before, the business thrived. Maud, it seemed, also sold her wares from there, making cheap candles from tallow. The frontage of Butcher Blount's stall displayed a surfeit of cuts of meat, hams, sausages, ducks, chickens, black puddings and many rabbits dangling from the awning. It all looked very fresh, Simon thought, as would be expected of a leading member of the town.

A single mendicant Friar screeched out his warning of hell and damnation for all sinners. A single bony finger pointed heavenward, intoning the Lord to strike down the unworthy in his midst. The Dominican Friar's voice boomed out above the hub-up of the market noise, "For ye are sinners, and the wrath of God awaits you!" Two armed guards in the employ of the Abbot stood by and grinned at this early entertainment.

The surrounding crowd appeared disinterested in his invocation. Their eyes were fixed on a young woman wearing just a thin shift, sobbing and kneeling at his feet, a grubby leather halter around her neck. Her matted dark straw-coloured hair hung down well below her shoulders. She seemed to Simon no more than nineteen summers and beneath the grime on her face, might be considered quite pretty.

"She has sinned against the Lord," cried out the Friar with globules of spit. He jerked roughly on the halter, dragging her to her feet. "And she must repent. Repent, I say! For she is a sinner!"

The wide-eyed crowd in front of him waited in anticipation for what the Friar might do next. Simon had all but gone past when the Friar grabbed the neck of the girl's shift and ripped it down, exposing her naked upper body. The crowd jeered as she tried to cover herself up, drowning out the Friar's screams, "Rahab; Jezebel; Tamar; sinner; harlot! We must punish her for her sins!"

A flicker of recognition came over Simon as he hurried past, causing him to stop abruptly. He looked at the young maiden, screaming now and pathetically, trying to hide her nakedness as the Friar continued to jerk the halter around her neck. He knew this maid. Then, he looked more closely. Her heart-shaped face made pretty by its slightly tilted nose and her long dark straw-coloured hair in a plait hanging down her back; this was the young maiden Alia who had saved him in the tavern in Westchepe.

For a moment, Simon was conflicted. His task was to trace and find Maud Blount, but this maiden had saved him from serious injury at the hands of three thugs, and he owed her a life-debt. He could find Maud later, as she would most likely be at her shop. The issue with the maid, he felt, was more pressing.

The Friar produced a three-corded knotted whip, pulled down his robe to expose a hairy back and began flagellating himself, chanting as he went. Occasionally he would bring down the whip on the young girl's back, drawing blood. The cheering crowd surrounding the girl was driven into a frenzy by the mendicant Friar. They whistled, jeered and cat called. They wanted a show, and Simon was about to put a stop to it.

"You... and you," Simon shouted at the two guards still enjoying the entertainment.

The taller of the two eyed Simon warily uncertain of this man whose clothing marked him out as someone of standing.

Simon walked towards them. "I hold the King's Writ, and you and you will help me now... *Now!*"

The taller man looked nervously at his partner, clearly reluctant to obey the instructions of this stranger.

"We answer only to the Abbot," came the indolent reply.

"You answer to the Crown," bellowed Simon. "And you will follow my instructions, or I will have you both arrested." Simon knew that the law wasn't on his side and that he had no authority to have them arrested, but he relied on their ignorance.

Both guards looked uneasy, unsure about the authority invested in this stranger and wary of his wrath. The shorter guard made the decision for both men.

"How can we help King's Man?"

"Follow me!" And with that, Simon moved into the crowd surrounding the Friar. He pushed his way towards the small dais where the mendicant Friar stood. He gave a glance around to ensure that the two tardy guards were following; to his relief, they were.

As he confronted the mendicant Friar, Simon knew that he had walked into a lion's den. The Dominican worked up the crowd who wanted a show and would likely turn their anger against him.

"Yea. And on her forehead, a name was written, a mystery, Babylon the great, the mother of harlots and of the abominations of the earth." The Friar was chanting his incantations in rhythm to the cracks of the whip on his back. The crowd cheered each stroke even more loudly when he moved the whip to cut into the back of the young maid, Alia.

"King's Man! You! Monk! I command you to cease in the name of the King!"

The Friar brought his eyes from their heavenward gaze down to look at this interloper.

"Stop! I command you. You and you," Simon addressed the two abbey guards, "stand here and face out towards this crowd. Make sure no one interferes."

The sense of reluctance in the guards was clear. Simon fixed their gaze, and both Abbey guards moved into position after a few moments.

The Friar had stopped his self-flagellation, and he, too, stared at Simon.

"You cannot command me, King's Man or no. Only God commands me."

"You will desist now, or I will have you arrested."

"You cannot have me arrested. I do God's work here, and I hold the benefit of clergy. You have no authority over the Dominicans."

The young girl, Alia, stopped cowering for the first in what seemed like an eternity and looked up into the face of the King's Man who had intervened.

A spark of recognition came across her eyes; the Serjeant-at-Law from the tavern a few months before.

Simon stepped onto the dais and grabbed the Friar's whip, throwing it to the ground.

"I will have you arrested and thrown into one of His Grace's donjons. It will be years before you can claim the benefit of clergy."

The Friar was suddenly hesitant. He saw the resolve in Simon's eyes, unsure who this King's Man was and how far his authority extended. His hand holding the halter around the young girl's neck lowered, and Simon reached out and took it.

"This maid," Simon began, "is under royal authority .... my authority. Churchman or not, you have no right to be holding her in this spectacle." With his legal background, Simon knew he wasn't correct in law. Nonetheless, he was determined to stop this circus. He hoped he wouldn't be challenged if he said it forcefully enough.

"The maid comes with me."

The crowd, sensing they were to be denied their spectacle, became even more agitated. The two guards nervously waved their spears in front of the disaffected faces.

Simon drew his baselard dagger and pointed its sharp tip towards the Friar.

"The maid comes with me!"

"But she is *mine*," lamented the Friar pathetically.

"Nay, monk, on my say-so, she belongs to the Crown and comes with me," dropping the halter and reaching out to take the maiden's arm to steer her away, just as she had once done for him.

The monk stood mouth agape as Simon steered the maid through the jeering crowd. As worked up as they were, none dared go up against two armed guards and a man carrying the King's writ. The monk continued his whining protest, and the crowd, no longer getting their anticipated spectacle began to drift away.

Simon offered his thanks to the two Abbey guards, handing them a few coins for their trouble. They beamed with joy at the cash and the prospect of the story they would tell in the alehouse that evening and the ale they would be stood as a result.

Once through the crowd and onto the open street beyond the malt market, Simon stopped. Alia was trying with one hand to hold her torn shift over her semi-naked torso. Simon unbuckled his woollen cloak and threw it around her shoulders.

He hailed a young boy and gave him a penny to purchase a skin of wine, promising him two more for himself when he returned. The boy was back within minutes. Simon offered the wineskin to Alia, and she drank greedily.

"Mistress. Alia. You know me. I am Simon Lowys. You did rescue me in the tavern in Westchepe some months back."

Alia stared at the face of her rescuer. A flicker of recognition came across her face, and she acknowledged what he had said with a nod of her head while continuing to gulp down the wine. After a while, she stopped drinking and handed it back to Simon, who took a short swig.

"I thank you, Master Lowys, for saving me." The voice was scratchy and hesitant.

"How did you come to be the monk's prisoner?" Simon enquired.

"The innkeeper, Doderell, was angry when he found out what I had done in stopping those men from robbing you. He sold me to the monk." Tears filled her eyes as she spoke.

"*Sold* you? .....The monk *bought* you?" Simon was shocked. "He's a Dominican; he's meant to *save* lives."

"Nay, he is a fraud. He is no Dominican but a common huckster, a magsman pretending to be a preaching Friar and using girls like me as his prop to wile alms from the crowd. He goes from market to market and fair to fair; always the same trick."

The tears flowed down her soft cheeks as she recalled the monstrous weeks with the huckster, unable to escape his grasp. Simon moved to untie the halter about her neck gently, but she flinched her head away from him.

"It is alright, my maid; you are free of him." He hoped his soft words reassured her.

Her words spat back at him. "How can I be free? He will find me."

"Nay, he will not. With me, you are under the protection of the Crown, for as I told you once, I am a Serjeant-at-Law and..." he paused "...nuncio to Her Grace Queen Eleanor."

She looked up, her eyes wide and red. "The Queen? Why would you protect... me?" her words came out in sobs.

"To repay a debt of kindness and a debt of honour. Now we must to a place of safety."

The darkness of Alia Parys' world had disappeared in a few short minutes. This King's Man had saved her. She felt blood trickle down her back, and her first thought was that she would ruin the woollen cloak Master Lowys had lent her to cover her nakedness. Alia coughed; her throat still tight. Her hand moved to her neck, and she loosened and then removed the halter, throwing it to the ground.

She walked close beside him, this King's Man, as they picked their way through the filthy streets of the town. She wondered whether she could trust him. Men had often let her down and used her. Still, she felt she must. After all, he had rescued her from the huckster when he didn't have to.

On Sopwellstrete, below the abbey church, Simon guided Alia towards a small two-storey cottage with pristine lime-washed walls and tidy thatch. He rapped on the stout door, and shortly, a smiling, red-faced woman of middle years opened it.

"My! 'Cousin,' hale be thou. I had not expected you."

"Cousin Matilda," he replied with a smile. "God, give you good day." Matilda looked beyond her cousin to the maid standing beside him draped in his cloak.

"Cousin Matilda, I give you the maid, Alia Parys." And Simon introduced the woman to Alia as his cousin, Mistress Matilda Heacham.

Mistress Heacham welcomed Alia into her home without judgement or question. She brought hot water and towels for Alia to wash, but not before shooing Simon into another room. Matilda lightly applied cooling salve to Alia's flayed back. Her soothing words matched the gentleness of her hands. Then, without being asked, she produced a clean shift for Alia to wear. Alia couldn't help but wonder if such a situation had occurred before.

The bed Mistress Heacham provided was soft, warm, and welcoming, and darkness had fallen long before Alia awoke. A fresh shift and cote were laid across the end of the bed. She had no way of knowing how many hours she had slept.

Dressing, Alia crept her way slowly downstairs. Mistress Heacham was busy at the table darning by the light of a rush candle. She appeared unphased by Alia's presence.

"How are you, my dear? You have slept these many hours."

"I feel much-rested, Mistress," Alia enquired after Simon. She wondered if he had explained the circumstances of what had occurred to Mistress Heacham.

"He is away on the King's business, in the town, I think, but he will call in before curfew. You are to stay here for the time being if that meets with your approval."

"I thank you, Mistress Heacham, but I fear I cannot pay you; I have no coin."

"Hush now. That is all taken care of, and you are safe here for as long as you need."

Matilda Heacham, still darning as she spoke, bade Alia sit with her. Alia again thanked her and sat. Matilda Heacham had a kindly face, with it seemed a permanent smile. She looked every bit a town wife, thought Alia, somewhere in her fourth decade, a woman who had worked hard all her life but one who still had elegance. But not of low birth, she thought. No, the house was well appointed, a sure sign of modest wealth. A thought struck Alia, was Mistress Heacham, a widow? There was no sign of a husband in the house. Was she Simon Lowy's Mistress? That thought was unwarranted. But was she? He seemed very familiar with her when they had arrived hours earlier.

"My dear," Matilda Heacham broke Alia's thoughts. "Tell me about yourself. Master Lowys has told me the circumstances he came to... rescue you from that bad man."

Matilda looked hard at Alia and took her hand. "You do not strike me as a common street maid, and I suspect you are of gentle birth. Please do tell me about yourself." Her face beamed with that engaging smile again.

"My name is Alia....... Alia Parys." The words stuttered out. "You have the right of it, Mistress. I am of gentle birth. My mother was the daughter of a land-owning family near Coggeshall. She married beneath her when she married my father. He was the Reeve on a large estate nearby. My mother taught me to read and write until I was in my eleventh year. I know some Latin and can read and write in French too. But my dear mother and father were taken by the pestilence when I was eleven, and I was taken to live with one of my father's cousins." At this thought, tears emerged in the corner of Alia's eyes.

"But not two years later, he passed away, and I was made to be indentured to the innkeeper in Westchepe in the city. And I worked for him these past years, beating off his advances and those of his riffler customers."

Matilda could see the sadness in Alia's eyes as she spoke, sad remembering's of a happy life now lost to her.

Through tears, Alia explained how she had intervened and saved Simon from the attack and robbery in the inn off Westchepe. And how then that act had cost her liberty. The innkeeper, Fulberg, angry at what she had done, sold her to the huckster monk.

"And then, in the depths of my suffering, Master Lowys appeared in the market this morn to rescue me." The relief showed on Alia's face.

"He is your cousin?"

"Aye, we are kin."

Alia raised her head, surprised that she felt disappointed at this. Seated across from Alia from Alia in her parlour, Matilda Heacham didn't see the change in Alia's expression, but her thoughts were on the maid. Matilda saw strength and genuineness in the young girl opposite. Having washed and rested, she looked nothing like the poor victim who had accompanied Simon to her door earlier. She was very pretty, her hair somewhere between dark and light that she had roughly plaited, so it hung down her back below her shoulders.

Matilda Heacham believed herself to be a good judge of people. She regarded a face that had witnessed loss, pain and suffering but still portrayed understanding and experience. She looked upon this young maid, not yet in her twentieth year and saw something of herself at that age. Here was someone at ease with others and well-liked by those who knew her. Behind Alia Parys' comely appearance was a strong and determined woman. Matilda Heacham smiled; she liked this maid.

CHAPTER 19

Berkhamstede, Hertfordshire, May 1276

It was mid-morning when Simon Lowys turned his palfrey to leave Watling Street, where it joined the old Roman road to return to Berkhamstede. It was a short journey of but a few hours from St Albans before he arrived in the thriving town of streets lined with inns, shops, and merchant houses. He left Akeman Street, where it met St Peter's Church. The main road ran gently down towards the castle-built centuries earlier by the first King William. The house he sought lay somewhere in a triangle between the road from the castle – Millstrete – and what the locals called Backelane.

Abraham of Berkhamstede had been a successful moneylender with a reputation for being highly unprincipled. He had accompanied the Earl of Cornwall's commissioners in collecting taxes from other Jews, often with great cruelty. Abraham had been a banker and financier to the Earl. All that had changed a year before with the King's Statute of the Jewry. That law placed restrictions on England's Jews, forbidding usury, lending money with interest, and regulating where they could live.

Rumours circulating a decade before alleged that Abraham had murdered his wife. Abraham was granted to the King's brother so that, in effect, Richard, Earl of Cornwall, had his own personal Jew.

Debts owed to Abraham totalling £18,000 were signed over to the Earl, who ruthlessly exploited this income stream.

Abrahams was a well-kept property located at the end of a parade of timber-framed dwellings behind Castle Street. There was nothing ostentatious about the house. It was clearly kept in a good state of repair, and the thatch was recent; there was nothing to indicate that this was the home of one of the town's wealthiest inhabitants. Only when Simon approached the heavy wooden door did he notice a tiny hollow gouged out of one of the uprights and into which had been placed a small roll of parchment.

Simon was puzzled, suspicious of what it meant. His look of uncertainty was still there when the door half-opened. A short, dark-skinned man stood behind, peering out of the doorway casting anxious glances down both sides of the street. His tanned skin, pronounced cheek bones and black curly hair suggested a foreigner.

"I am Simon Lowys, a King's Man. I have business with Abraham of Berkhamstede. I am expected."

The servant bowed obsequiously and invited Simon inside. He led him through into a large wood-panelled room that smelt heavily of wax and herbs. As the progressed through the house, Simon realised that the property was far farther than he imagined from the road. They entered a large room with glass windows that allowed sunlight to flood in. At the far end of the chamber, a man of middle years sat seemingly toying with an abacus. On Simon being announced, the man rose from his chair and bowed.

"Peace be upon you, Master Lowys, I am Abraham Maybaum. I give you greeting." He had introduced himself in fluent French.

Simon was surprised at what he saw. He had come looking for Abraham the Jew, anticipating a foreigner. Aside from the beard, which was fuller grown than most men, he appeared English. His perfect, courtly French held no trace of an accent. Clearly, surprise showed on Simon's face, for Abraham broke the moment.

"Am I not what you expected, Master Lowys? Have you come across many Jews in your work for Her Grace?" Before he could answer, Abraham invited Simon to sit on a beautifully carved elm chair. It was but one of many delicate and valuable objects in the room.

"Most people, even here in Berkhamstede, treat me as an outcast. My family have lived in this town since the reign of the second King Henry. My Grandsire came to this country from Portugal and served His Grace as a usurer. Once, we Jews enjoyed royal protection. My people are hated, and we are pariahs because we lend money, yet your Christian Church encourages us to do so. Now the king's Statute of the Jewry, but a year past has forbidden even that. When we go abroad, we needs must wear a yellow badge on our clothing to identify us. I can no longer live alongside Christians and can only make my living as a farmer, merchant or craftsman." The words came out with genuine sadness.Simon looked at the man before him, who seemed to have visibly aged as he spoke.

"We enjoy protection from the Crown, but we pay heavily for the privilege and accede to royal requests for funds to pay for their wars. I am past fifty summers, Master Lowys," he lamented." I am not suited to the land or to make things with my hands, and I have nothing to sell. A year since I was wealthy; now I have no source of revenue and no prospect of any." Abraham spoke sardonically, a man whose life had been ripped from him. Simon found he struggled to make small talk with Abraham and felt an urgency to conduct his business and be gone.

"Master Abraham, we must down to business. The Queen's business." Abraham Maybaum's shoulders drooped, and he had sadness in his eyes.

"I know this, Master Lowys."

"I am to arrange the transfer of the mortgage document for Langlei to Her Grace the Queen."

CHAPTER 20

St Albans, Hertfordshire, May 1276

A sense of unease gripped Simon Lowys. The royal business with the moneylender Abraham had gone as well as he might have expected. Abraham had little choice in the matter other than to agree to the Queen's wishes. But that was not the cause of his unease. His enquiry to the Chancery had produced confirmation that the Wheatsheaf in the centre of St Albans was frequented by women believed to be members of the Daughters of the Shadows. Perhaps that was the reason behind his concern. The task of chasing down the members of this coven had fallen to him, and, he felt, they couldn't have been more aptly named. He was hunting shadows.

The bells of St Peters' were ringing for Sext when Simon again made his way along the wide Magno Vico, where the triangular marketplace of the town gave way to the expanse of the Great Street in St Albans. He was looking for the alehouse of the widow, Isabella de Brun. Trade in the town appeared brisk, and even though it was mid-afternoon, it was still bustling.

Simon found the inn sited halfway along the Magno Vico. It was an elaborate two-storied building with its upper chambers jutting out over a central entrance and walls brushed with recent limewash.

A large ale stake fixed to the first floor with a roughly painted sheaf of wheat made it the most conspicuous building in the parade of shops. He pushed open the heavy oak door and entered. Inside was dark but comfortable, much cleaner than many such establishments. That was reflected in its smell. It didn't have the aroma of stale ale and vomit common to many

alehouses. A long chamber with lime-washed walls and fresh sweet rushes on the floor lay ahead of him; its high ceiling had blackened rafters from the hearth in the centre of the room. Tables and benches were laid out in an ordered fashion, occupying the length of the room.

A tall willowy man scrutinised Simon, his beady eyes darting left and right to ensure this visitor was alone. Young serving lads moved from table to table, cursorily wiping them down and removing ale jugs. It seemed there were more of them than customers at this hour. Simon beckoned the willowy man to come over, which he did so with much reluctance.

"I am Simon Lowys, nuncio and King's Man, and I am here on royal business. I wish to see Mistress de Brun." The man gazed long and hard at Simon, assessing the integrity of his word. Then, satisfied without a word, he turned, beckoned with a gesture of his hand, and walked to the far end of the inn. Simon followed, entering a hot steamy kitchen. A hogget was slowly roasting on a spit. They moved through into a larger, longer ante-room through another stout door. This chamber, too, had fresh rushes on the floor and neat lime-washed walls.

Tiny dust particles danced in the beams of sunshine pouring through the windows. The room smelt of wax and crushed herbs, lavender, rosemary and the subtle perfume of something else, Simon thought, a fragrance from his past. He was so engrossed by the surroundings' aroma that he initially didn't notice the slim figure of a woman sitting at a table, deep in the study of a parchment. Upon seeing Simon enter, she looked up and pushed the parchment to one side. The willowy servant approached, whispered something in her ear, bowed and withdrew.

As he moved closer to her, Simon gave an involuntary gasp; he had never seen such beauty. A white-laced gorget headdress, bound under the chin, framed a small pale face. Her large, penetrating dark eyes, a perfectly chiselled nose, and thin inviting lips drew him in. A lock of soft red hair had escaped from under her headdress to lie across a perfect cheek. She was small, but her deep green gown and golden belt at her slim waist emphasised a womanly body. This was a woman who would always enchant men.

"Mistress," Simon said in a dry voice, his throat caught by this woman's beauty. "I am here to ask you questions. I am Simon Lowys, a servant of the Crown, and I hold the King's writ and..." He was aware of the mocking laughter in her eyes, and his voice trailed off into silence.

The woman beckoned to a place on a bench beside her table. He sat, staring at the patterns of the woodgrain of the table before him. He was drawn to this woman like a hunted and thirsty deer is drawn to the clear, inviting waters of a cool spring brook. He brought his eyes up and stared at her. Her eyes were not dark as he had first thought, but deep blue. He felt shy and tongue-tied, keen to keep gazing into those deep mesmerising pools.

"Mistress Isabelle de Brun?" He stammered the words out. "What do you know of the Daughters of the Shadows?" He hadn't meant to say that, not at this point. He intended to be more circumspect, but his mind was scrambled, and he had difficulty formulating his questions.

Isabelle stared at him, her thin lips pursed and her fingers steepled beneath her chin. "What should I know, King's Man?" she replied.

Simon could sense the woman's calm superiority opposite him and decided to reassert himself in a mood of official brusqueness. He was, after all, a trusted royal clerk holding the King's commission.

"Mistress, common report has it that you may be and likely still are a member of that black coven, the Daughters of the Shadows."

Isabelle de Brun stared back at him, her lips pursed with fire burning in her eyes. Then she broke into laughter, which burst out like drops of rain in a spring shower. "Master Lowys... I am a vintner's widow. What would I know of such things?"

Her words jolted Simon back to reality. Isabelle was studiously watching him. She seemed to sense his mood and the danger posed by this inquisitive King's Man breaking free of her cleverly woven spell. She placed one delicate hand on Simon's.

Simon's mind was tearing him in different directions. He knew that she was leading him away from his questioning about the Daughters of the Shadows. At the same time, he was happy that this was happening and that her hand lay upon his.

He tried to focus, despite always staring at those honeyed eyes drawing him in. He shook his head, trying to clear his mind. "Mistress, I know that you married a vintner, Thomas de Brun, a man older than yourself. I also know that he died soon after the marriage, and you, his widow, inherited his business and taverns. I know you own this inn, one in Barnet on the King's Highway north and another on Churchstrete in Berkhamstede. You are now a wealthy widow."

He looked at her face. He observed the delicate curl of soft red hair that had fallen from her wimple. A loop of red hair, he said softly to himself. A train of thought began to come together in his mind.

"Before your marriage, I suspect you were known as Isabella la Rus. I know you were at Fulelane at the home of Alice la Blunde. I know that you were there when two men died three days after the feast of All Hallows last. I know, too, that you are part of a dangerous coven that goes by the name the Daughters of the Shadows. And, for all I know, you may well be a common whore."

He had not known that Isabelle de Brun was Isabella le Rus when he entered the inn, but the lock of red hair convinced him that they were one and the same. Her reaction confirmed it.

Her eyes blazed with fury, and she abruptly withdrew her hand from his and slapped his cheek hard. Simon smarted from the blow and shook his head, as much in surprise as anything else.

"Then you know much, King's Man, and understand very little." She was angry, her face red and eyes bright and brittle with temper. "You come into my house and suggest that I am a common street whore. You forget yourself and your manners."

And yet, those eyes still drew him in. The fury, her flared nostrils as she raged at him; he was entranced by her temper, his mind whirring.

"Master Clerk, Kings Man," she spoke softly, switching from anger to mellow in an instance. "I am sorry. My words were harsh and uncalled for, but you have it wrong."

Simon sat captivated, staring at her face as Isabelle spoke of her youth as an orphan child. She described her marriage to Thomas de Brun, and her widowhood following his loss at sea bringing a cargo of wine to England. She told him of her inheritance of all his business interests, taverns, and dealings in the Gascon wine trade. As she spoke, her fingers moved rhythmically, toying with the hem of her silk gown.

Simon sat as if in a trance, hanging on every word she uttered, enthralled by the movement of her slim gloved fingers. Yet, his thoughts were conflicted. He reminded himself that he was here on royal business and that the woman opposite may pose a threat to his grace, the King. But how could a woman so elegant and comely pose a menace to the Crown? These thoughts swirled around in his head, only for them to be pushed aside by a remembrance of Sandalwood. That fragrance he could not place was the waft of Sandalwood on the skin of Isabelle de Brun. Now he recalled that rich, warm smell from his time in Sicily. The sweet, spiced fragrance on her body.

"You call me a common whore Master Lowys, but I deny that. I know Alice; I stayed with her at her house in Fulelane, but I swear I am no common doxy, and I am not a member of this coven of witches you speak of. Whoever told you else is bearing false witness."

Her denial was passionate and forceful, and Simon so wanted to believe her. His heart was beginning to overrule his mind.

"But you were at Fulelane when the two men were killed by 'strangers', and you did flee along with the other women against the undersheriff's instructions?"

Isabelle bit the side of her lip and gazed beyond Simon, seeking the right words to respond. "I did not kill those men. I didn't know them, and yes, we left, but we didn't flee as you claim."

"So, you were there when the killing occurred, but you didn't see or hear anything or hear the 'strangers' leave the house?"

"It is as you say," she said again, moving her hand to cover his. "You must believe me in this. I am not being false. What would their deaths gain me?" Her deep blue eyes pleaded with him.

Simon continued to press his questions, and Isabelle continued to push back, always maintaining her innocence. He decided that he should withdraw and take stock of what Isabella had told him and marry that with what was learned from Frowyke and that he had gleaned from the Coroners Record.

He rose quickly, pushing the bench back behind him. "Mistress," he bowed clumsily and turned to go, but she too stood, a soft hand on his arm, restraining him, her gaze fixed on him. "You must believe me. You have me very wrong, Master Lowys."

She began to move to a door on the far side of the room. She turned and looked at Simon, her eyes penetrating his very soul.

"Your visit has saddened me. I feel angry that you would think so of me." And then she was through the door and gone.

Even though she was no longer in the room, Simon gave an involuntary bow and walked away pensively. He left her inn, still deep in thought.

As he made his way towards a bustling Cheapside, he realised how measured her answers had been. *"I am not a member of this coven of witches you speak about,"* she had told him. That wasn't a denial that she was a witch, just that she wasn't a member of the coven of the Daughters of the Shadows. *"I didn't kill those men"* did not mean that she didn't know who had.

As he walked, his mind began to clear from the fog of her beauty. Just as he imagined, she had truly enchanted him, much as any skilled practitioner of the dark arts might. She had avoided successfully answering his questions. She had succeeded in turning his questioning to make herself appear the victim, but had she, he wondered, also spun him a web of lies and deceit?

From an upstairs window, she watched him leave, this King's Man. He both intrigued and worried her in equal measure. He had done well to trace her to the Wheatsheaf Inn and make the link that Isabelle de Brun was, in fact, Isabella la Rus. Her hand touched her cheek and fixed the soft curl of red hair that was forever escaping from her wimple. King's Man or not, this Simon Lowys was blundering around in things he did not understand. That made him dangerous, and she resolved then and there that she needed to do something about it.

CHAPTER 21

Sopwellstrete, St Albans, May 1276

Mistress Matilda Heacham baked her own bread each day from dough she always prepared the evening before. This bright morning, she placed the additionally baked loaf on the table along with butter from the market and honey from her neighbour Mistress Gordine. Simon had been up early, having returned from Berkhamstede the previous afternoon. He sat down to break his fast, and Alia joined them. Immediately Simon had said grace Alia began with her questions.

The questions came one after another. Alia was keen to know about his work for the Queen; had he seen the King, and why had he gone to Langlei? As the purchase of Langlei was not a private matter, he was happy to tell her and not a little proud of his involvement, and he glowed at telling her about the king.

"It is no secret that Her Grace, the Queen seeks a location for a royal palace, to be both a stop-off for northern and eastern journeys and one that can serve as a safe residence for the royal children. Both she and His Grace, the king, passed this way two years since, on royal progress towards Aylesbury and beyond."

"Did you go with them?" Alia seemed excited at the prospect.

"I did. We passed along the old Roman road from St Albans to Risborough. Locations were inspected, including Langlei, which seemed to serve Her Grace's purpose. Do you know the village?"

"Nay. I have never heard the name."Alia replied, helping herself to some of Mistress Heacham's excellent bread.

"It is a pitiful place, but its manor sits high on a hill and has the benefit of being a calm day's ride from Westminster. Her Grace's agent, Richard de Hoo, discovered that its holder, de Chenduit was deep in debt to the Jews and that the title could be bought."

"I don't understand why the Queen had to buy the manor from the Jew in Berkhamstede and not Sir Stephen de Chenduit."

Through a mouthful of sweet bread, Simon tried to reply. "Now that becomes a complicated matter of law..."

As simply as he could, Simon explained how all the Jews of England were chattels of the Crown in legal terms. All debts owed to them legally belong to His Grace the King, in his capacity as 'Protector of the Jews'. One 'benefit' held by a Queen of England was 'Queen-Gold'. If the King levied an arbitrary land tax on the Jews, called tallage, a percentage was added to go to the Queen. That was called Queens-Gold. Stephen de Chenduit had borrowed 400 marks from the money-lender Abraham of Berkhamstede. As security, Abraham held the mortgage for the manor of Langlei. But, under the Statute of Jewry passed by the king the year before, a Jew could hold a mortgage but would no longer receive interest payments.

Moreover, he went on, Abraham was not allowed to evict de Chenduit as a debtor for non-payment. So, Abraham held a valuable mortgage that earned him no income. Queen Eleanor offered Abraham 100 marks for the mortgage on Langlei, in effect buying out de Chenduit's debt. Abraham owed 'Queen Gold' to the tune of 600 marks to Queen Eleanor, making her offer more tempting. Abraham surrendered the mortgage for Langlei to Her Grace the Queen instead of the Queens Gold payment he owed her. Once he had done this, Stephen de Chenduit was consequentially in debt to Queen Eleanor. She now held his mortgage for 400 marks. Her Grace the Queen remitted de Chenduit's debt in lieu of the manor of Langlei forever.

Alia looked open-mouthed at him as if she was ready to speak, but Simon continued.

"It is complicated... Not easy for most people to comprehend."

"You are a Serjeant-at-Law, so it must be legal, though it doesn't sound very fair to my way of thinking."

"Her Grace is buying out de Chenduit's debt. He and his family will move to one of his other manors, most likely to the adjacent hill hamlet near Hempstede or Islehamstede a few miles further west."

Alia held onto every word of Simon viewing him differently now. She had not really noticed what he looked like back in the inn when she had saved him from his attackers. Now she saw a confident young man, someone who was trusted by the Crown and who she could trust. She had stayed in the house of Mistress Heacham for more than a week now and felt she could not impose on her hospitality much longer. The weal's on her back, and her cuts and bruises were healing well thanks to Mistress Heacham's cooling salves, but when she closed her eyes, the demons still lurked inside her head.

Her future, she knew, was uncertain. What would she do when she left the safety of Sopwellstrete? She feared the monk would hunt her down and that there would be no saviour this time.

She became aware that Simon had stopped speaking, and she was staring at him.

"What troubles you, Mistress Parys?"

"I fear for the future Master Lowys. What shall happen to me when I leave here?" She hadn't meant to be as blunt as that. Simon and Mistress Heacham had been very kind to her.

"What shall I do? I cannot return to my past life, and I am sure the monk seeks vengeance for what happened."

"Fear not, my maid, Mistress Heacham and I have talked about this, and there is an obvious solution. Mistress Heacham is in need of a household maid and companion, and we think it would suit you well." Alia's face beamed, her eyes bright and lighting up her face at the news.

Matilda Heacham, who had slipped back into the room, added, "I would welcome your company Alia if you will accept, and you can be of help to me when I assist Master Lowys in the future."

No more words were said, but the sense of relief Alia felt was written in her still-smiling face.

CHAPTER 22

Bothelyngstock, St Albans, May 1276

The area around Bothelyngstock in St Albans contained three or four rival butchers' stalls with produce not quite as fresh as Butcher Blount's. Blood and animal dung pooled on the ground. At this end of the market, the noise was a tapestry of shrieks, whines, grunts, screams, and roars as butchers slaughtered animals. Drains running down the middle of the street flowed with blood and offal, and Simon had to be very careful where he placed his feet.

Yet as Simon kept watch on Maud's shop from a distance, he remained puzzled. Maud was the widow of a well-to-do town butcher, Rauffe Blount. Until his recent death, Blount had been a prominent figure in the Blessed Brotherhood of St Bartholomew, the loose trade association of St Albans butchers. The Abbot would not permit guilds.

None of this made any sense to Simon. Henry Frowyke had identified Maud Blount as a common whore; he had described her to him. Small in stature, prim with penetrating eyes, a small mouth and a mouse-like face. There was no doubt in Simon's mind that the woman he was watching was Maud Blount. Yet this was the respectable widow of an influential merchant, not some low-born woman who sold her body to men.

He was missing something. He knew it and couldn't put his finger on what it was, which troubled him. Simon felt hungry, having loitered by Master Butcher Blount's stall for a long time. He paid a young lad a penny to buy him a rabbit pie from one of the nearby bakers, which he devoured with relish.

Simon reflected on the situation. As a widow, Maud inherited part of her husband's business. The Brotherhood were very protective of their widows. She would now be wealthy and a target for ambitious younger men seeking advancement. For all intents and purposes, there could be no-more respectable citizens of the town than Maud Blount.

Long hours passed, and Simon struggled to keep his focus. Maud left her husband's stall at the ringing of the middle-day bell for Sext. Once more, she moved busily through the market, visiting fellow stallholders, greeting, laughing and jesting. There seemed nothing suspicious in her actions.

From a distance, Simon followed and observed. If she were going to leave the town and meet with the coven sisters, it appeared it would not be during daylight hours. When the bell rang for Nones in the late afternoon, the market ceased trading with the sun going low. Quickly, stalls closed, the crowds thinned, animals were penned, and the market square reverted to a more normal existence.

The inns filled up, and too much ale was drunk. Women made their way home with their purchases to produce an evening pottage. As the sun slipped below the western horizon, the town of St Albans quietened and remained so until the inns closed before the curfew bell.

CHAPTER 23

Sopwellstrete St Albans May 1276

The hooded figure moved silently through the shadows of a dark St Albans night. Maud Blount crossed a lane and turned down an alley as the moonless night enveloped the tightly packed houses. The gables of the upper stories jutted out so far that they almost touched and, in the daytime, blocked out the weak winter sun. She turned onto Sopwellstrete, which lay at the south-eastern edge of the town, with its heavy gates controlling access to and from the London Road. As it had gone beyond the hour of curfew, she had to avoid the guards and the town Watch. Maud moved forwards and then stopped to listen rather than look and then moved again. She slipped into a passage of a house well-known to her, whose rear vegetable garden and alley beyond would give her unseen access out of the town. Once there, a cleverly concealed gap in the town ditch gave her access to the flood meadows of the River Ver.

She moved silently, at home in the night hours. Every now and then, she stopped, turned, listened, and looked behind her towards the town she had just left. Was she being followed? She thought she heard a trace of footsteps behind her. But if so, where were they? Perhaps, she thought to herself, it was her imagination. Maybe she wasn't being followed.

Maud made her way quickly west, away from St Albans, across the meadow towards the haunting ruins of the old Roman town. This was a place townspeople avoided, for the ghosts of the dead walked at night among these fallen walls. But Maud felt at peace here in this world of shadows. She breathed in the blackness of the new moon as she skirted the monastery wall. She had been a coven member for almost all her life, not yet at her thirtieth year, this spirit world, where they often met, was familiar and welcoming to her.

The smell of the recent shower in the air brought childhood memories flooding back. As a young child, she recalled how her aunt, who had brought her up as her own, took her to night-time meetings of the Daughters of the Shadows. There, standing in drizzle, eyes wide with fascination, she witnessed the rituals of the thirteen hooded witches of the coven. As the years passed, she became more involved, finally becoming one with the pentangle.

Maud Blount crept silently, her senses alert to any sudden sounds or movement. The close-by hoot of an owl caused her to stop and look back. Satisfied, she kept heading west towards the ancient ruins.

To the east, Simon Lowys watched as Maud Blount stopped and looked around again. He froze, keeping as silent and as still as possible to not alert her to his presence. Following Maud had been straightforward. He gambled on her leaving that night, having discovered the secret way through the town ditch. How did the coven avoid being seen by the Watch at night? At first, he suspected that the Daughters left the town during the day and simply did not return until the gates were open the following day. But following Maud at a distance as she went about her daily business made him realise that this wasn't the case.

Simon suspected that Maud must have a way of leaving the town unseen. The next day, despite the cold and drizzle, he spent

many hours exploring the town's boundary ditch. After many fruit-
less, frustrating, hard hours, he discovered a cleverly concealed gap
hidden at the back of a garden in Sopwellstrete, close to the southern gate. It had been skilfully constructed where the ditch turned
away from the river. A small, uprooted bush draped itself across the
sloped bank. Behind it, cut into the earthen rampart, was a narrow
passage, just wide enough for a person to get through, leading out
onto the meadow. Once Simon had discovered its existence, it was
a case of watching each night to see if Maud or anyone else left the
town via this secret way.

It was just the second occasion he had sat, cold and miserable,
hidden behind some hawthorn bushes. After the monastery bell
rang for Compline, he saw a solitary figure emerge furtively through
the concealed gap in the ditch. He couldn't be sure it was Maud
Blount, but he thought it most likely. He watched her ferret-like
movements, her wimple-covered head moving, checking left and
right that she wasn't being followed. While she moved stealthily
across the meadow heading north, Simon kept low and close to the
ditch to ensure Maud wouldn't see him.

Again, she turned her head and peered into the night, one way
and then the other. She stopped and listened. She could hear the
rustle of the wind in the trees and the occasional call of an owl.
Was there someone there? Was that a shape she saw? Was she being
followed? She certainly hoped so!

Ignoring the unseasonal cold, Maud picked her way across the
dew-covered meadow. A late-spring mist hung low above the sparse
pasture. She couldn't see the King's Man, but she knew he must be
there, well hidden, somewhere behind her. Days before she had been
alerted by one of the coven's friends in the King's Chancery, a royal
official was on his way to the town to investigate her sisters. They
hadn't given her a name. One of the lay workers in the monastery

had identified him when he arrived and passed on the news. After that, it wasn't that hard to have him followed by one of her fellow coven members while he sought to keep out of sight following her around the town market. She kept moving, using the ancient stones to guide her, occasionally stopping to check to make it seem that she wasn't being followed. Soon she would be beyond the skeletons of the Roman city and reach her destination, the village of Kingsbury.

Ahead, framed against the night, Maud could make out a dimly lighted torch burning by the door of the Church, throwing shadows onto its semi-circular arches. With sudden speed, she darted behind a tall section of a ruined Roman wall. Maud pressed her back up against it and listened, trying to hear any sound of the King's Man following her. He was there; she knew it. She had gone about her business in the town quite openly, hoping that he would see her and choose to follow her. So arrogant, so typical of a man, she thought, not noticing that he himself was being spied up by a woman who was hiding in plain sight. How easy it had been. And now, she would lure in her prey.

Maud became aware of someone else there with her behind the wall. All she could make out was an indistinct shape, but that of a giant man. Maud could not see him, but she could undoubtedly smell him. Alone at this time of the night, she should have been afraid. The hairs on her neck should be standing up. Turning her head slowly, she looked towards the shape.

"You smell worse than pig shit, Roger."

Had the man been able to see her face in the dark, he would have seen the huge grin that came over her.

"Ready?" she asked.

"Aye." Roger l'etranger responded in a deep guttural voice and a broad London accent. He was indeed a big man, flat-nosed, swarthy and a killer. The bastard son of a Gascon sailor, he had been brought up in London's runnels, back streets, and alleys. As he grew, he had progressed from the thieving and fighting of his youth to become a Wolf's Head, a man outside of the law. Now he was a hired assassin, skilled at his job. He lovingly unsheathed a long quillon dagger and pulled a short wooden cudgel from his belt, which he rolled lovingly in his left hand.

Abruptly, Maud moved from the wall and stepped back onto her route towards St Michael's Church. She now hoped that the King's Man could see her clearly against the light that was thrown out from its burning torch. Slowly but assuredly, she walked towards the graveyard. There were no walls, no stones marking graves, just a few newly dug internments and some yew trees, one of which loomed large in the gloom suggesting great age. He was out there, the King's Man. All she needed now was for him to catch a glimpse of her in the murk of the predawn.

CHAPTER 24

St **Michael's village, St Albans May 1276**

For a short time, Simon had lost sight of Maud Blount. He guessed she was making for St Michael's because of her route towards the ancient Roman ruins across the meadow. He was pleased to have followed her this far without her realising it. He momentarily lost sight of her. A chill mist hovered just above the ground as he moved cautiously alongside the ancient wall, his eyes scanning left and right, his head turning to try to pick up sound. That was when a ball of pain exploded inside his head.

Awareness returned only slowly. Opening his eyes had never been so difficult. His face grimaced; his head throbbed, and he felt a trickle of liquid seeping down behind his ear onto the nape of his neck. Simon struggled to make sense of where he was, trying to recall what had happened.

He tried to focus on what he had been doing and realised he was seated but could not move. His hands were bound behind his back and his feet tied together. He struggled against his bonds as they cut into his wrists but was held fast, and the movement seemed to deepen the pain.

His heart was pounding. He blinked and screwed up his face peering left and right, but the deep blackness of the night made it hard to distinguish much beyond the shape of the odd tree or bush. *I'm somewhere open,* he thought, *but where?*

Straightening his back, he met something hard, which he took to be a tree trunk. He sensed movement ahead of him, and two figures emerged from the black gloom. A man, a hulk of a man and – he squinted, trying to make sense of the shapes in the murk ahead – a woman. Maud Blount. Even in his befuddled state, he recognised the Daughter of the Shadows. He now remembered that it was she he had been following. He recalled trailing her towards St Michael's Church and then... Nothing.

"King's man." His thoughts were interrupted by the reedy tones of Maud's voice. She slapped him hard across the side of his face.

"Can you hear me, King's man?"

Her words echoed in his throbbing head, and Simon groaned and nodded. Eyes now closed, he tried to assess his situation. It didn't take long to arrive at the conclusion that it was desperate. He felt a sharp pain in his chest, opened his eyes and could make out the shape of a dagger pressed hard against him. Then his jaw exploded with pain as the hulk punched him with a swinging fist. Simon shuddered.

"I want to know what you know about my sisters. Why are you here following me? Who sent you? Who have you told?" Maud's questions coming one after the other.

"You will tell me now, or Roger here will amuse himself with you... and he would enjoy that greatly."

Simon's blood chilled as the point of Roger's sharp quillon dagger moved to his neck, nicking the skin and drawing blood. Despite the imminent danger of death, Simon could only think about the overwhelming, foul smell emanating from the man in front of him.

"Who have you told about us?" came Maud's shrill voice, from behind Roger's bulk. The dagger pressed a little harder, and she repeated the question. Silence.

Fear pricked the back of his neck, and he fought to calm his breathing. Simon knew that he would be dead before dawn lit the eastern sky. He chose to say nothing, not out of stoic bravery but simply from the realisation that whatever response he gave wouldn't save him. He silently repeated the Ave Maria to himself, over and over.

"Take out his eye," Maud ordered Roger, who smiled at the instruction.

As the quillon dagger moved to hover over Simon's right eye, he thought he heard a dull noise in the distance, but he focused on the imminent danger in front of him. He sensed the point of the quillon and blinked involuntarily before closing his eyes tight shut as if that would be any help. His breathing quickened, and he was sure he could hear his heart pounding. Roger dropped the tip of his dagger below the eye. With a flick of his wrist, he opened a cut on Simon's cheek. Simon was breathing even more heavily, feeling blood running down the side of his face and its iron taste in his mouth.

Awaiting the impending savagery of the dagger stabbing at his right eye, it was almost as if his senses were heightened. Simon was aware of a metallic click. He heard a familiar whirring as a quarrel from an arbalest rush close to his head to thud into something in front of him.

A grunt and a strangled cry told him that the quarrel had struck Roger. The big man fell backwards. The quillon was no longer at his eye, and Simon opened both to see Maud Blount charging towards him, a club in her hand ready to smash it into his head. She let out a scream of anger, and Simon turned his head away, grimacing, unable to do anything to defend himself against the blow that must come.

But it did not come. He heard a piercing scream. Slowly Simon opened his eyes again and could make out the figure of Maud lying at his feet with a quarrel embedded in her chest and around it a dark wet patch.

Emotions of relief followed by confusion and then alarm raced through Simon's head. He was aware of light footsteps approaching behind him. In his bound state, he was vulnerable, powerless to defend himself. His alarm turned to panic. His mouth went dry, and he tensed against his bindings as he heard the scraping sound of a knife being unsheathed.

Simon's breathing, which had only just slowed, now quickened once more as a gloved hand pushed his head forwards and down with considerable force. The hooded figure reached down and pressed harder on Simon's neck. Eyes now again shut, he tensed, fully expecting the assassin would draw the blade across his throat to finish him. Despite his miserable situation, he gave a momentary chuckle to himself at what a fickle mistress fate was.

But the misericordia, the killing blow, didn't come. Simon could sense the knife being brought down behind his back, and then the bonds holding his hands were slit with one deft stroke.

Simon's relief was palpable. He exhaled and then gulped in the cold night air. As he did so, he saw the faint smudge of the dawn light in the eastern sky, heard the chorus of birdsong, and the unfamiliar smell of an aroma of lavender. So many questions swirled around in Simon's head.

"What? Why? Who are you?" Simon swung around in an ungainly manner, his feet still bound. The figure was silhouetted against the pre-dawn, their face in shadow. He could make out the small hand-held arbalest slung over one shoulder that had saved his life.

"Cut my bonds," Simon pleaded. The hooded figure paused, sheathed the knife, turned, and slowly walked away into the gloom, leaving his feet still tied.

Inelegantly he shuffled over to the now-dead Roger and grabbed his quillon dagger; it took Simon no time to slit the hempen cord that bound his feet. He threw down the quillon, and his own baselard and arbalest were nowhere to be seen. He stood and, with difficulty, took a few constrained steps; his unknown 'saviour' had disappeared into the dawn murk.

Looking around him, Simon took in that he was in the middle of a churchyard, probably St Michael's. The first weak winter sun fell onto the wet earth as the darkness retreated. Simon shivered; he could not be sure whether from the cold or the fear. The full magnitude of what had passed in the last hour swept over him. He knew he should be dead, but he had been saved. Why was that? He didn't know. No one was aware he was here, yet as he followed Maud, he too was being stalked as a lone deer in the forest.

Someone knew, and that person could only be inside the Royal Chancery. They must have alerted Maud, and she was prepared for him following her. The relief he genuinely felt at cheating death was tempered by the insecurity that swept over him as if he were a pawn in a chess game. But he returned to the questions that were at the forefront of his mind. Who had saved him, and how had they known he was there?

Simon wiped his hand across his face and looked down. Even in the half-light of dawn, he could see smearing of blood. His head still throbbed, and he was not yet thinking clearly. There were two dead bodies on the ground beside him; he could not just walk away even had he wanted to. St Albans was a monastic town; more than a century ago, the English Pope, Adrian IV, had granted the Abbot diocesan rights over the townspeople. As a royal official, he had to report the deaths to the Abbey authorities and the Sheriff's men. So, a royal coroner wouldn't investigate these deaths as happened elsewhere.

Once again, Simon tried to piece the parts of the story together. Had Rauffe Blount known about Maud's association with the

Daughters of the Shadows? He thought that given Rauffe's position within the St Albans Brotherhood, that was highly unlikely. But for how long and exactly how had Maud lived this double life?

His gaze fell onto the corpse of the big man. He bent down, and in the dawn's light, he examined the quarrel embedded deep in the dead man's chest. It was fletched with two wooden fins, and just about two inches protruded from his chest. There was nothing particularly unusual about it. Finding more about the big man would likely lead him closer to the Daughters of the Shadows. Given his size, he would probably be well known in the inns of the town. Who was he, and how did Maud know him, he wondered?

Simon's own baselard and arbalest lay just a few yards away on a grave mound, tossed to one side by the big man. Simon picked up and examined Roger's quillon. It was over twelve inches in length, tapering to a sharp point with a short metal crossguard. Its ivory handle was finished with a round polished pommel. It was an exceptionally well-balanced dagger and must have been expensive, not the sort of weapon a town thug could afford to carry. So, mused Simon, the big man was not some local riffler. That would make it more challenging to discover his identity, but Simon already knew where he would begin.

CHAPTER 25

Sopwellstrete, St Albans, May 1276

The hours that followed the deaths in the churchyard were a blur for Simon. Once he had freed his remaining bonds, he summoned the local priest from St Michaels and sent for the Constable. The news of the killings spread quickly, for, before Terce, when the sun had long since risen, a small crowd gathered in the churchyard, eager for information.

When Simon arrived back at Matilda Heacham's house in Sopwellstrete, it was well past the hour of Terce, and the town bustled with activity. The lack of sleep and the effects of being struck with a club, gagged, and bound gave Simon a haggard, weary appearance. His long brown hair was matted, dried blood caked his face, and the wound on the back of his head still oozed red.

Alia was busy in the kitchen when Simon entered by the door from the garden. She looked at him and shrieked.

"Master Lowys," her voice expressed genuine alarm. Then she took in his appearance. "By Jesu, you are hurt." Alia rushed over to him, grabbed his arm, and guided him to the bench. She called out for Matilda Heacham, the tone of her voice alerting the older woman who appeared at the door. Mistress Heacham took in the situation, reached into a small cupboard, and took out some small pots containing salves.

"Alia, my dear, there is a lidded hutch at the end of my bed. In it, you will find some linen strips we can use as bandages for Master Lowys. Could you fetch them for me, please?"

Alia did as was asked, as Matilda calmly applied salves to Simon's cuts and the back of his head, Alia boiled some water. She washed the open wounds, all the time following Matilda's instructions.

"Keeping the wound clean before you apply salve is essential, my dear. It promotes better healing."

When they had finally finished cleaning and dressing Simon's wounds, Alia asked how Matilda had come by the knowledge to treat injuries?

Matilda Heacham shrugged as if it were nothing. "A long time ago, when my husband was here and trading out of Marseilles, we had an acquaintance. No, more of a friend, really, a Moor, he was a physician, and he taught me much about the art of healing. Though, I fear our Holy Mother Church would frown upon such knowledge."

Once she was satisfied that his wounds had been treated, Alia turned to Simon to inquire how he managed to get himself into such a state?

"I seem to have a familiarity with trouble these days." It was a feeble attempt at humour and brought neither laughter nor smile from Alia.

Simon's eyes rolled and closed, his head tilting forward, the after-effects of the blow to his skull. Alia reached out towards him and lay her hand against his chest to stop him from falling.

Matilda looked impassively at the two but could sense the mutual attraction played out in front of her. She saw Simon slowly open his eyes, and the tender gaze he gave the young woman in front of him, as if for the very first time.

As his eyes opened, Simon saw Alia's face. Unfamiliar sensations stirred inside him. Her lovely face, beautifully formed with her deep sparkling eyes and sunny disposition. How had he not seen that before? She was no longer the beaten, bloody, and bruised maid he had rescued in the market. There was an aura of innocence about her. He took in her round face with a high forehead, the soft dimpled cheeks, and milk-smooth skin. With the look that gazed back at him now no words were exchanged, but their expressions said much.

Matilda Heacham broke the moment. "You must rest now, Master Lowys. That blow to your skull has left a nasty wrent which must be given time to heal."

"Nay, I cannot rest. I have work to do that cannot wait. There will be an inquest at the Abbey, maybes even as early as tomorrow. I must be prepared."

"I will not hear of it. You must rest, Master Lowys. Your tasks can wait, or someone else can undertake them for you."

"I can do whatever you require," Alia volunteered.

"Alia and me both," agreed Matilda.

Simon shook his head and immediately regretted it. "Nay, you are women. What I do this day is work for a King's Man, not for a widow or a maid." He spent the next few minutes, outlining between deep gulps of air and long pauses to catch his breath, that, even though Maud was dead, he had to keep watch on her shop on Bothelyngstock to observe who came and went

"King's man you may be, but you too see only as far as other men. Do we not have eyes to see as well as you?" inquired Matilda Heacham? "It is us women who go unseen and unnoticed. Women can be places and be invisible to men. Who bothers to notice another widow or a young servant in the town? But a man marked out as a King's Man, then all in the know will see him and see what his business is about."

Simon was unused to a woman expressing such forthright opinions though he recognised that what she said was correct.

As the abbey bells pealed out their ring for Nones, Simon Lowys attempted a fitful sleep in Matilda Heacham's house. A few hundred yards away, Mistress Heacham and Alia carefully made their way along Peter's Street. They did their best to avoid the animal dung, effluent and other rubbish scattered beneath their feet. To any who noticed them, they appeared as Mistress and servant, out for the morning. But, as Matilda had promised Simon, no one saw them save the rifflers eyeing up opportunities. There were many men in the market; most traders were male, but the majority of the customers at this hour were women. Matilda knew that if she peered into any of the many inns in the town, she would find them full of men this time of the day. Up until his death, five years since, her husband Effric would have been one of them.

Simon Lowys did not know, but Matilda Heacham had done such a task before for other royal intelligencers. Discretion had always been one of her qualities, which was why John of Berwick valued her. As the two women perused the stalls, Matilda instructed Alia on how to go about their assignment.

"Always place yourself in the direction you wish to observe. Pick up an item and look upon it while at the same time gazing on the target of your observe." She showed Alia what she meant and invited the younger woman to try.

Alia picked up a small square of cloth, held it up to the light as if to inspect it, but keeping her gaze upon Maud Blount's butchers stall where Bothelyngstock met Peter's Street. The young maid smiled at her success. Maud was dead, but nonetheless, Matilda was watching the stall to see if the wealthy woman Simon spoke of, who met with Maud the day before, would return.

Mistress Heacham and Alia spent many hours meandering through the market stalls, occasionally conversing with other wives, stopping frequently but buying little. At length, Matilda took Alia's arm, leant in close and whispered that they were going to make their way to Maud's shop to buy a leg of hogget. A look of surprise came over Alia until Matilda said, in a low voice, "To see who has just gone into the rear of Mistress Blount's stall."

Matilda Heacham made a great fuss about her purchase of the hogget. This one was too big; that one too small; too little flesh, too big for her hearth. All the time, she hoped to get another glimpse of the woman Simon had observed previously meeting with Maud. Matilda had observed such a woman entering the rear of the shop. Matilda hadn't recognised the woman, and Alia hadn't seen her. There had been many other women going into Maud Blount's stall. Still, there had been something about this one, Matilda thought, something striking, something that was not quite right.

Simon had said that the look on Maud Blount's face had first alerted his interest. It had been more than a look of surprise; certainly not one of joy, a look of recognition, a look of fear. That had been yesterday. And now, with Maud dead, and now it seemed that the woman had returned.

There was an elegance about the woman Matilda observed that fitted with Simon's description. She was older, well into her fifth decade. Her face was strong, and even from afar, Matilda noticed her eyes, her piercing eyes like those of a hawk, aware of her surroundings. She was dressed as a lady, a cote of deep blue trimmed with pale fur, not the type to frequent such a stall, one who would despatch her servants instead. Simon had spoken of the look of recognition on Maud's face yesterday. Maud Blount appeared a strong, confident woman, but Simon said she had visibly deferred to the woman when she appeared at her shop. Maud was dead. So why had this woman returned?

There was only so long Matilda could string out her purchase of a leg of hogget. Settling on a well-aged mid-sized one, she left the stall and met up with Alia, who had been watching the rear of the shop. Matilda had hoped to see or hear something in the rear. But it was to no avail. Alia assured her that the woman had not left through the back. She had to be in there still, but for what reason?

CHAPTER 26

Chirchestrete, St Albans, May 1276

It was four days before the inquest opened. The Seneschal, Brother Gilbert, who would conduct the coroner's inquest, looked a man in a hurry. His small eyes, sunk deep into his fleshy face, gave him the appearance of a squirrel. The constant movement of his head, one way and then the other, as if on alert for danger, reinforced this.

Brother Gilbert sat at a long oak refectory table at the end of the ground-floor room of an inn opposite the Abbey Guesthouse on Chirche Strate. The inquest would be held in the large tap room as the two deceased were laypeople. Gilbert sought to display an air of lofty detachment, but his agitated eyes continually scanned the room. Documents were strewn across the table in front of him. The deep carved wooden chair he sat on lifted him slightly higher than the two clerks that sat on either side of him to emphasise his authority over the proceedings.

The Benedictine Abbey enjoyed historic, privileged legal rights, including the liberty to conduct its own coroner's court. The Abbey Seneschal, Brother Gilbert, who combined his office with that of Coroner and Sheriff, would preside over a coroner's court. Another much younger Brother, who seemed to be serving as the coroner's clerk, called the inquest to order. Thirteen freemen from three local villages, St Michaels, Kingsbury and Childwick and four burgesses from the town made up the jury. The clerk, in a dreary tone, swiftly swore them in. Because it took so long to arrange the inquest, Brother Gilbert had decided to waive the traditional 'super visum corporis' whereby the inquest proceedings were to occur within sight of the bodies.

The Jury, the Coroner, Simon, Father Peter and his housekeeper, her son, and a few witnesses, were conducted by the clerk to the mortuary chapel to view the bodies.

Beneath the drab Mortuary Chapel altar, both corpses lay on trestle tables draped with a plain white linen shroud. The gloom of the chapel was broken only by narrow shafts of light streaming down from the high windows. The warmth of the May sun accentuated the stench of death that already permeated the air. How ironic, Simon thought, that Maud, a coven member, should have her corpse lying for days before a holy altar. He thought again of the paradox of the priest shriving her in death in the lonely churchyard.

A young monk pulled back the linen shroud exposing the naked bodies of Maud and the big man. Everyone present made the *signum crucis* – the sign of the cross. The jury inspected each corpse for marks of violence and recorded the nature of the wounds. Some of them grimaced, turning their heads away at the gruesome task. Simon, Father Peter and his housekeeper Miriel Tulle all testified that these were the bodies found in St Michael's Churchyard four nights before and were among the first finders. Two witnesses from the town testified that these were the bodies of Maud Blount and Roger l'etranger. It seems Roger was an itinerant thief and ruffian for hire known to frequent the inns and whorehouses of St Albans. The inquest then adjourned back to the Abbey guesthouse to the relief of all. There, the jury members quickly established that the cause of death was a quarrel bolt in each case.

Brother Gilbert began a monologue about how a tragedy had come to pass that the wife of a respected townsman was so brutally slain in the churchyard of St Michaels. He opined that it seemed clear to him that she must have been abducted by Roger l'etranger, taken to the churchyard, and killed there. There could be, he said, no other explanation.

Simon listened to the monk's speech with incredulity. There was not a shred of evidence to support Brother Gilbert's interpretation. Not that he had yet given evidence about what had occurred.

When Brother Gilbert resumed, he seemed agitated, tapping the ends of his fingers together as he steepled his hands. "Master... Lowys," he spoke Simon's name slowly, half-turning towards him and with not a little menace.

"You have sworn on oath before me to being the first finder to these dead bodies, yet..." he paused and smiled falsely, "as far as I can establish, you failed to rally the hue and cry, is that not so?"

"To do so was impossible," Simon retorted. "I saw both Maud and the big man killed."

"So, you witnessed this murder, *primum manus scientiam*?" He used the Latin phrase for 'first-hand' to assert his superiority, Simon thought. "Yet despite being a man of law, you did not rally the hue and cry as was your obligation under the law?"

"I heard the sound of quarrel bolts from behind me, but I did not see who loosed the bolt. By the time I had cut my bonds, the killer had disappeared. It was but late night and in God's acre, and the hue and cry would not have found anything."

"How very convenient... So, having witnessed this crime, you permitted the murderer to flee?" Brother Gilbert was deliberately taunting Simon, gleeful in the power he was asserting.

"I could have done no more." Simon was irritated, and Brother Gilbert's haughty manner was annoying him.

"Once I had cut my bonds and established that both were dead, I made my way to the nearest house – the priest's house – and summoned Father Peter. He and his housekeeper, Mistress Tulle, and her young son accompanied me to the churchyard where Father Peter did shrive both bodies. Because of the early hour, Mistress Tulle sent her boy to inform the Bailiff and the Abbey as you hold the liberty of Coroner. We discharged our duties as first-finders. There was no sign of the killer and no one else around. There would have been little point in raising the hue at that hour."

Brother Gilbert gave a snort of derision. "And now the nub of the question. Why, pray, were you there at that hour, Master Lowys, beyond the curfew bell?"

"I was following Mistress Blount, engaged on the King's business." Simon's response was techy. "Despite her position within the town, she was implicated in a Crown investigation. I can offer no more in this public court."

Gilbert, his lips pursed and his face red, bubbled with rage.

"This is a lawful inquest, and you will respond fully to being questioned, King's Man or not."

"Brother," Simon sought to be conciliatory, "I did say, I can offer no more in this public court. But I am fully prepared to tell you as the Court Official, in private, the circumstances relating to my enquiry."

Recognizing that Simon's royal writ held greater authority than his own, Brother Gilbert adjourned the hearing for a few minutes to meet the royal nuncio in an antechamber of the inn.

"Holy Brother," Simon began. "I have been tasked by the Crown with investigating and hunting down a coven of witches that have been operating within the city these past months. As surprising as it may seem to you, Mistress Blount was a member of this coven."

Brother Gilbert shook his head. "Nay, I cannot believe..." Simon cut him short.

"Believe it or nay, it is true. This coven poses a threat to the Crown and the life of the King. That was why I was following Maud Blount. But it appears that she knew I was here in the town and following her, for she led me into a trap. That was the circumstance of my being in the churchyard. But I do not know who killed her or her man, for I did not see them."

"So, the killer followed you to St Michael's or was already there?" added brother Gilbert.

"You have the right of it, Brother," said Simon. "But the killer remains unknown to us."

The monk reluctantly accepted what Simon had told him, and the pair returned to the inquest.

Brother Gilbert resumed his place and began addressing the jury. "Master Lowys, as a King's Man, has satisfied me that the circumstances of his presence in St Michael's Churchyard were related to his royal duties."

He cleared his throat, and in an attempt to reassert his authority, he asked, "And who gave the instruction to move the bodies?" Most present knew that the jury was required to view the body where it was found, and a fine would be levied if the body was moved. The clerk answered Brother Gilbert's question.

"It was our...the Abbey Bailiff who gave the instruction. The bodies had to be removed from where they were desecrating the holy churchyard."

The monk cleared his throat. "Irregular, very irregular."

At length, Brother Gilbert asked the seventeen jurymen to deliberate. It took them but a few minutes of hushed discussion before the foreman announced that they had reached a decision of unlawful killing by a person or persons unknown. Brother Gilbert declared that he concurred with the decision and then began the process of announcing fines.

He declared that the value of the murder weapon be set at one penny and that the deodand, therefore, be the same. Then he turned his attention to the failure of the first finder to raise the hue and cry.

"Master Lowys, being a man of the law," he was almost gleeful as he spoke, "is fully aware that it is incumbent upon the first finder to raise the hue and cry. By his own admission, this he failed to do. A most serious breach of the law at any time but made worse by his situation as an officer of the law. I have no choice, therefore but to levy a fine on the said Master Lowys of one shilling, to be paid forthwith."

A wry smile passed over Simon's face. It was a petty act by the monk and, he thought, very typical of someone like Gilbert. Simon approached the younger monk who had served as clerk, took twelve silver pennies from his purse, and laid them upon the table. At least the clerk looked embarrassed as he picked up the coins and offered Simon a perfunctory thank-you.

CHAPTER 27

St Peter's Church St Albans, May 1276

The funeral of Roger l'etranger was a pitiful affair. There were no mourners, and his body was wrapped in a dirty, ill-sewn shroud and laid to rest in a pauper's grave in a remote corner of St Peter's. Simon Lowys was there, but he did not grieve over someone who had tortured him and would have slit his throat without compunction. In contrast, Maud Blount's funeral was lavish. The Blessed Brotherhood of St Bartholomew insisted on meeting the cost for the widow of one of their esteemed members. A stout wooden cart pulled by two horses carried her coffin in procession from the wool market along the wide triangular street, past the shambles to **Bothelyngstock**. Heads bowed, and caps were solemnly doffed as it slowly passed by. All the members of the Brotherhood gathered to pay their respects at the Butchers' stall and shop owned by her late husband. Afterwards, all walked bare-headed in a silent procession to St Peter's Church a few hundred yards to the north.

Maud Blount was laid to rest in the churchyard alongside her husband. Her body had been ceremonially washed, and devotions were made as it lay in front of the altar. The priest conducted a funeral mass with incense from a thurible wafting through the church, and elaborate prayers were said, befitting her widowed status within the

Brotherhood. Simon Lowys watched the burial from a corner of the churchyard. He was intrigued to know if Maud's fellow coven members would attend. From the descriptions, he knew two for sure: Notekina de Hoggenhore, and Alice le Blunde. But much to his surprise, Isabella la Rus was also there. Other women were present, older, perhaps other coven members, but he didn't have a description of all of them. Something to put right, he noted to himself.

A light drizzle began to fall as the funeral party broke up and went about their business. The women Simon knew to be members of the Daughters of the Shadows left with three other women; Margery de Pyritton, Agnes de Bilda, and someone he could not identify. A thought nagged him. Who was the third woman? Was she another member of their coven, and how would he identify her?

Simon himself had pressing business in Langlei to finish his work surveying the northern boundary of the Queen's new manor. He needed to get the completed documents to her as soon as possible. He wasn't looking forward to being soaked through from the sort of rain that got in everywhere. At the stables opposite the Abbey gates, he found his bay palfrey and set out on the short ride to Langlei to arrive there before darkness fell. Leaving the churchyard, he watched the burly sexton begin the task of filling in Maud Blount's grave and silently cursed as the light drizzle turned to rain.

The rain had stopped by the time the curfew bell rang and the dark of a moonless night descended on the town. Puddles of mud pooled in Maud's grave, with the recently filled-in earth now once more piled up beside it. At the bottom of the deep dark hole, Maud's open coffin lay empty.

CHAPTER 28

Nottingham Cloth Fair March 1276

More people were at this year's Cloth Fair than he remembered from years past. The noise of activity and selling was all around him—the fusion of animal noises mixed with human shouts and screams of enjoyment and pain. Merchants called out to no one in particular, extolling the virtues of their products. Women gathered, gossiping, making their slow path along with the many stalls lined the High Street. Although Nottingham Cloth Fair was an annual event attracting cloth merchants from beyond England, there were also many other traders dealing in a wide range of goods: fleeces, spices, timber, oils.

Adam de Brazbourn hauled another heavy ell of finished cloth from his master's wagon onto the stall. Trade had been brisk that morning. The journeyman to the cloth merchant Peter of Berkham-stede had worked up a thirst, which he intended to slake at one of the local inns once his Master returned from lunch.

Adam hailed from a small West Flandrian village. He had been with his Master since his tenth year and thought of himself now as English. The long years of apprenticeship had been burdensome. He frequently received the lash on his back for some mistake or accident. Despite the pain and humiliation he had endured, he was no longer an apprentice but a journeyman to his Master. He had learned his trade, and now Adam had plans – plans that would take him beyond England's shores to become an international merchant. Adam had always been a dreamer; he often spent his days imagining how it would be in the future when he returned to Berkhamstede, a wealthy and successful merchant trader. His apprenticeship had ended two years before when he had reached his eighteenth year. Adam knew that the Master's wife Agnes had intended for him to marry their only surviving daughter Matilde. The Master and Agnes once had had a son called Peter, but the boy had died in the pestilence a few years after Adam's apprenticeship had begun.

Matilde was a year younger than he, and he enjoyed their fumbling in the outside barn and the hayfields. But he did not find Matilde attractive, although she was captivated by him. He had fumbled with other girls in the town and even swived with a few. They seemed drawn to his lean, muscular body. He knew the town girls liked him. He had not yet reached his twentieth year, but he had already begun to grow a beard, albeit more of a fair-haired fuzz than full-grown. Soon, he hoped, it would frame his square, chiselled face and long fair hair, making him look older than his years. He wasn't ashamed to say that he had a way with the maidens; he could always charm them by talking and laughing. He would draw them in with his friendly banter, and it would often lead to a fumble or better.

Mistress Agnes frequently scolded him for being a daydreamer, and she was probably right. Adam did dream and always hoped for a better future for himself. He stacked another ell of cloth onto the stall; the first rush of trading had waned, but he kept busy organising the scantillions.

Later, Adam could not be sure why he stopped and looked. He just remembered that he had. Watching as she moved slowly, sensuously picking up a trinket, caressing and admiring it.

She wore multiple layers of garments that indicated her wealth. Her green cotehardie fitted tightly with a wide scalloped neckline and suggested what lay beneath. She wore an overgown with enormously large armholes to complement the cotehardie, making the garment effectively side-less. The Church, of course, disapproved, calling such slits 'windows to hell'. But Adam was both captivated and intrigued, drawn in by her.

Her long dark hair was parted in the centre and styled in two long braids, coiled and brought back towards the crown of her head and topped with a mesh crespine. As he gazed at her, Adam's throat went dry. She meandered from stall to stall but didn't cast a glance in his direction. He was invisible to her. Who was she, he wondered?

She walked right past the cloth stall of Peter of Berkhamstede. As much as Adam had willed her to stop and examine the rage of damask silks, linen and tiretiraine laid out in front on the stall and converse with him, she didn't. Disappointed, he carried on with his work, putting the vision of the lady to the back of his mind.

He looked up, aware that a customer was handling the rolls of cloth – and then she was there in front of him. He took an involuntary gasp of breath. It was difficult to identify her nationality; she did not appear English; her flawless skin was an olive hue. She had piercing brown eyes set in a strong, pleasing face. Her cheeks were slightly dimpled, her mouth wide, with full lips; he noticed her slim wrists framed by the open ends of her sleeves and her delicate hands. Though small in stature, she seemed tall for a woman, not beautiful but captivating in her looks. Adam stared at the scalloped neckline of her cote and the curve of her torso beneath. Just the cut of her clothing and bearing told Adam that this was a rich woman, not noble but from the affluent merchant class.

She spoke. Adam stood motionless, not taking in the question as she posed it in French. Again, his mouth opened, but no words came out. She spoke again, this time asking the question in hesitant English. "Your Master has agreed to supply me with three ells of finest damask. Do you know if he has it?" Happy to be speaking to this woman, Adam enquired of her name.

"I am Jasliena van Leuven." How she pronounced her Christian name, with a strong emphasis on the 'Yas,' reinforced his view that she wasn't English.

Her voice was soft and melodious. Anxious to be of assistance, Adam scrabbled beneath the counter to locate her order. He had always struggled with letters. The Master's wife had tried to teach him, but he had made little progress over the years. He knew the sounds the letters made so quickly found her order pinned by a small offcut of linen onto which had been scrawled her name with a large letter 'J.'

"I have your order here, Mistress; will your servants take it?"

"I wish you to bring it to me at my residence. You can do that?" It was an instruction more than a question. She tilted her head, smiled at him, fixing her penetrating eyes on Adam. It seemed to him that they bored directly into his soul.

"What name do you go by?" she inquired. Her gentle tone was honied, her face wreathed in a melting smile.

His usual way with the maids suddenly left him as he stammered out a reply, "A...A... Adam, I am Adam, Adam de Brazbourn."

She broke into a thin smile, and the tip of her tongue ran seductively across her top lip. "God give you good day, Master Adam." She looked at him and then cast her gaze to the ground.

"Thank you, Mistress. Are you new to these parts? I have not seen you before." He blustered out his questions, only then realising how forward his behaviour was.

"I am sorry, Mistress, I did not mean...."

She held up a hand, stilling his flow. "Fear not, Master Adam of Brazbourn, I have no offence with your words." She used the term 'Master' as though she were teasing him, and he enjoyed it.

CHAPTER 29

House of Jasliena von Leuven Nottingham, March 1276

Adam had gone to Jasliena's lodgings nearby the Vintry with the three ells of damask she had purchased. His Master, Peter of Berkhamstede, was ready to send the youngest apprentice, Ralf. But, Adam had volunteered, implying he might be able to sell the lady even more fine cloth. At the prospect of more sales, his Master had relented. Now he stood outside her house. The south-westerly aspect ensured that the sun bathed its rear rooms with warmth and light. This was an expensive part of the town, close to the monastery walls and set above the market, so the smells didn't pervade. He took in a lungful of air and rapped hard on the imposing oak front door. A few moments later, a young olive-skinned servant girl opened the door and enquired about his business. She looked him up and down, and from the look of disdain on her face, she wasn't much impressed.

With a curt, "Wait there," the door was closed on him, and, he supposed, the maid went off to inform Mistress van Leuven. She has a foreign maid, a Saracen perhaps, he thought; further confirmation, he thought, that Jasliena was not English.

Moments later, the door reopened. "The Mistress is free and will see you in the solar." Her tone was more conciliatory now.

The young maid bade him enter and escorted him through a hall and up a flight of stairs into the solar. On one side, framed against the leaded glass window, was Mistress Jasliena van Leuven. She wore a different dress from when he had seen her earlier, and she had changed into a blue sleeveless surcoat with an embroidered mantle trimmed with fur. On her head she now wore a white coif under which was a crespinette to hold in her hair.

She turned towards him and beckoned him to sit. Still holding the ells of cloth, Adam awkwardly took a seat. Jasliena made her way over to him, positioning herself opposite a small chair. He gazed at her, his throat once again dry. He still could not place her nationality; she spoke French, that much he knew; and English as well, and she had dismissed her maidservant in something that sounded like Spanish. Her olive hue and her dark hair, almost black, made him believe that she was from the Mediterranean, possibly Iberia. Her skin seemed flawless, and her eyes... those piercing brown eyes. Adam was drawn to her like a moth to a flame.

She was older than him, perhaps by ten or more years. Yet, she seemed vulnerable and in need of protection. Jasliena brought her hands together and steepled her fingers. She inclined her head but didn't speak. Her silence was bewitching him.

Her words broke the spell, "So pray do tell me about yourself, Master Adam." She spoke so smoothly, and her accent was exotic, but he still couldn't place it.

Jasliena indicated that he place the ells of cloth on the table next to him, and he clumsily complied. He felt awkward around her, fumbling and lost for words. He was never that way around the girls he knew, but this Jasliena von Leuven was different.

"You, Master Adam. Tell me of yourself."

The dry throat had reappeared, and he gave a low cough and began telling her about himself. A man of few words, within a few sentences, he was finished. Jasliena had to tease out of him further details about his ambitions, plans, and life as a journeyman. It occurred to Adam that this was the first woman ever to be interested enough in him to ever ask.

Silence followed, and Adam realised that he was once more staring at Jasliena's swan-like neck. He plucked up the courage and blurted out, "And tell me about you, Mistress."

He hadn't intended to be so direct. He had thought of the different ways he might subtly find out more about her, and in the end, it had just come out of his mouth.

Across from him, Jasliena van Leuven lifted her head and nodded. She ran her tongue lightly across her lips. "I will if you wish."

She closed her eyes, looked down, and spoke in a soft, sultry voice.

"I was born in Flaviobriga, an ancient hamlet in what is now Aragon. My father was a fisherman, and when I was twelve summers, he sold me to a spice merchant whose vessel had been driven onto shore by a storm." Adam thought he could see the trace of a tear in the corner of her eye.

"My husband, Jan van Leuven, was a good man and treated me well. He was a spice merchant from Brabant who traded across the Mediterranean and was very successful. We were married for more than twenty years, and they were good years. I was widowed four years since, and Jan left me well-provided for, and the business passed to me. There were immediately suitors pressuring for marriage, other widower merchants all old and anxious to get control of my business."

Her story touched Adam. She appeared so demure though he wondered why she told him all this. Conversation with anyone, not just women, was not his strong point. Usually, there were just a few words, and then the fumbling began. Jasliena continued, telling him of her struggles to survive widowhood and how she had taken the business her husband left her and improved its fortunes. His attention had wandered, and his gaze moved from her body to her face. Her words passed over him. All Adam saw was meekness and vulnerability in this woman.

Her use of the words 'abducted,'' seized', and 'rapere' brought his attention back to her.

"What?" His exclamation came out with a spittle that flew onto her seat. "Rape?" At her mention of those words, anger had overcome him.

"Why would these men make to seize you?"

"Ah! Adam of Brazbourne, your innocence is sweet. I am still of marriageable age. My husband left me a thriving business and a great deal of money and property. Since his death, the business has flourished. Many in the guild are old and widowed and who covet my business for their own. Such men are hard-nosed and would think nothing of seizing me, taking my virtue and forcing me to marry, and the holy church would turn a blind eye to it all."

Adam allowed his outrage to show.

"That is monstrous, and I shall never allow such a thing to happen." He stood up, adopting a defensive pose, arms splayed.

"You may always rely on me, Mistress, should you need someone to defend your honour."

Jasliena's face broke into a smile, and she took in the young man's brave words. She reached out a hand towards him.

"If you truly mean what you say, Master Adam, then I would gladly have you as my protector."

She placed her hand on his arm and gave him a gentle squeeze. "I thank you, sir."

And with that, a hope flickered in Adam of Brazbourne that his future was assured. And he was correct; at that moment, his future was assured – but not in a way he could ever have imagined.

CHAPTER 30

Westminster June 1276

Although the business of the transfer of Langlei was not yet completed, there was a necessity to get back to Westminster. Simon was required to inform John of Berwick about progress and what was to be done regarding the arrival of Walter de Baskerville. The royal palace was half a day's journey from St Albans, and Simon planned to depart after the breaking of his fast. He wished he could spend more time reassuring Alia, but his duty was his priority. But even that would have to wait some hours, for he also had a pressing need to get to his lodgings at the Tower to collect both coin and documents.

He had stabled his palfrey at the inn opposite the monastery gates into the town. On arrival, he tossed a silver penny to the young groom who had cared for the horse, who accepted it gleefully. He mounted smoothly and began the journey through towards Sopwell Gate, above which the severed heads of three miscreants stared hollow-eyed at the horizon. Simon crossed where the gate straddled the town ditch and, in a gentle canter, headed south along the King's Highway towards London.

The route south down the old Roman road took Simon through some ancient villages and hamlets. At Park, the road passed through a large wood, a known haunt for Wolf's Heads and thieves who lived outside the law, so Simon moved at pace. He anxiously scanned the trees to the left and right, but his luck was in for this day; it appeared that the outlaws were elsewhere. Beyond Darnells, he felt more at ease and slowed his speed. With luck, he would be at The Tower by mid-morning.

If there was a day to cross London, then this was it. The sun shone down at this late morning hour from a cloudless sky.

The building works on the Tower commissioned by the late King Henry were ongoing. Masons and labourers scurried busily. The royal apartments on the first floor of Blundeville Tower looked magnificent. He exited the Tower through the western gate built into the new curtain wall. He crossed the Watergate over the moat heading west up Tourstrete towards Eastcheap. There he picked up the old Roman road and headed west towards the Lud Gate. He passed the ruins of Baynard's Castle and Mountfitchet Tower, both destroyed in the past on the orders of old King John.

The shadow of Great St Pauls loomed to his east. Workmen were busy there, too, replacing the old roof timbers with new oak. Simon left the city at the Lud Gate and made his way along le Straunde, crossing the River Fleet and passing the properties of the Knights Templar and their Temple Church.

Aside from a few important palaces, such as the Savoy, built by relatives of the old queen, Eleanor of Provence, all around him were green fields and pasture. After a mile, Simon passed through the sleepy, isolated hamlet of Charing and, beyond it, the royal palace of the King of Scotland.

The early June skies were still blue when he finally arrived at the Palace of Westminster. He bade an ostler take his mount and instructed that the palfrey would be well rubbed down and well-fed. Simon left the stables and made his way up through the warren of passages to the royal apartments on the riverside and the ante-chamber of John of Berwick.

Simon found John of Berwick intensely studying a parchment stretched out on a table before him. It was a few moments before the King's Intelligencer looked up. There were no wasted welcoming words.

"I was not expecting you. I am hopeful you have good news for me, Master Lowys." The emphasis was placed on the 'good'.

Simon began giving an account of his meeting with Maeve de Thornby and what he had gleaned thus far about the Daughters of the Shadows. This he followed up by relaying the details of the property transfer of Langlei.

"Have you seen the Jew yet?" John of Berwick's distaste for Abraham of Berkhamstede seemed obvious.

"Aye, I went there after I had seen de Chenduit." He paused, taking in a deep breath. "But... when I was at Langlei with Sir Stephen... it was who was staying with him that I had to report to you urgently... Walter de Baskerville."

John of Berwick's eyes widened, and his face reddened. "De Baskerville!" He spat the name out. "What is that treacherous dog doing back in England?"

"He claims he seeks a pardon from His Grace, but I fear he is false in his words."

Berwick looked thoughtful, appreciating what he had just learned.

"If de Baskerville is here, he intends trouble, which will be linked to his master, the younger de Montfort. Are you aware that the younger de Montfort brother, Simon, died of pestilence in Sienna these three years past? But Guy, the elder, is still making trouble, protected as he is by powerful Italian lords."

John of Berwick paused and remembered. He looked up at Simon. "But of course, of all people, you know about their crimes. You were there in Viterbo when His Grace the Lord Henry was slain."

Simon nodded and made the sign of the cross in remembrance of the slain lord.

"I was, and it is fixed in my head. I can never forget, for de Baskerville held me at sword point in the church as My Lord was mercilessly hacked down."

Berwick sat down. He steepled his fingers and began to ponder. Simon knew not to interrupt him in such situations and let the silence run. After a while, Berwick jumped up.

"You are to go back to Langlei and finish your duties transferring the manor, and when you are there, seek to establish what de Baskerville is up to. You said Mistress de Thornby had steered you towards an alehouse in St Albans?"

Simon told him of the talk about the Daughters of the Shadows and their connection to the inn.

"Ah, yes." It was not really a question. "And you are heading there next?"

"Aye. I have needs to go there to meet once more with the Jewish moneylender, and I can go on to St Albans, and the Wheatsheaf inn Mistress de Thornby spoke of."

"What?" Berwick appeared startled. He had told Berwick about the inn, although, he realised, he hadn't actually named it.

"The Wheatsheaf? What did Mistress de Thornby say of that inn?" Berwick snapped.

Simon was surprised at Berwick's interest. "She told me that it was her belief that some members of the Daughters of the Shadows frequented that place. I sent word to Sir Guy at the Chancery for information about its owner, a Mistress de Brun. I saw her when I went there...."

"You've been there? You went to the Wheatsheaf inn?" Berwick shouted his response as if Simon had done something wrong.

"Aye. I went there after I had seen the Jew." Simon was rather pleased with himself for his initiative. "I saw Mistress de Brun, and I believe that she and Isabella la Rus are, in fact, one and the same."

John of Berwick was staring at him, eyes wide.

"Oh, by Christ's eyes. You have no idea what harm you have done...." Berwick was flustered and agitated, his face reddening by the minute.

All Simon could do was stare back, mouth agape, perplexed. "Master Berwick, I do not understand...."

"No, by God, you do not understand. Why did you not tell me you intended to go to the Wheatsheaf and see Mistress de Brun?"

"I did not know you wished to be privy to that. I received the information from Sir Guy in the Chancery. You entrusted me to seek out these Daughters of the Shadows, so I followed the trail to St Albans and thought... I do not know how I have failed you."

Berwick leaned forward and fixed Simon with his gaze. "You are to continue with your duties for Her Grace the Queen. You are to continue with your investigations into this wretched coven of witches. Still, you do not go to the Wheatsheaf inn again or do make contact with Mistress de Brun. Is that understood?"

"Aye, that is clear to me, but I do not know why. I am certain that Mistress de Brun is a member of the Daughters of the Shadows...."

Berwick cut him off. "I have my reasons, Lowys. I cannot tell you... yet. The Wheatsheaf Inn and its people are part of another investigation I am conducting in the name of the King. I do not wish that to be undermined by you."

The reproach stunned Simon. "Now what else?" demanded the senior man, his face no longer so red. "Go on."

"Mistress Maud Blount is believed to be one of the coven members. I followed her to St Albans."

"And?" Berwick's agitation seemed to be returning.

"And I followed her one night to the old Roman ruins outside the city, only for her accomplice to jump me. They had a knife and would have killed me too, but... um...." Simon was thinking quickly about how best to put this to John of Berwick.

Berwick drummed his fingers on the desk. "They would have killed you. So how is it that you stand here now?"

"I was tied, and the thug employed by Mistress Blount would have taken my eye and then my life were it not for a good Samaritan intervening. I know not who it was, but they slew both before freeing me from my bonds."

A thin smile broke across Berwick's lips. "And who was this good Samaritan?"

"I know not, for he fled after cutting my ties. All he left were the two quarrels used to kill Maud Blount and her man."

"And you did not see this man?"

"Nay, nothing at all. The Abbot's man was not happy that I did not raise the hue and cry, but there was no one else abroad, alive at least, so there seemed little point."

Simon relayed the findings of the inquest and Brother Gilbert's fine imposed upon him.

Berwick gave a harrumph. "You may claim that coin in expenses once all this is finished. For now, you must make haste and make your way back to Langlei and Berkhamstede to complete the Queen's business."

Berwick put down the parchment he was holding in his right hand and pointed a finger at the nuncio.

"You have done well to locate de Baskerville, but we must find out why he is here. I am of the view that you need greater knowledge about the Daughters of the Shadows. Once your business in St Albans and Berkhamstede is done, you must proceed to Hailes Abbey with all speed."

CHAPTER 31

Hailes Abbey Gloucestershire June 1276

Simon Lowys had the sense that he was being watched ever since his meeting with John of Berwick. He could not shake the feeling. Was there a spy in the Chancery, a follower or sympathiser of the Daughters of the Shadows? Did John of Berwick know? Simon sensed he could not rely on the information on the coven from the Chancery and, going there, risked his subsequent movements being betrayed. However, he knew what his next move must be.

Simon understood John of Berwick's thinking. To combat the Daughters of the Shadows, he needed greater knowledge and understanding of them and their practices. There was one man in England who held vast expertise about the practitioners of the dark arts, one person he knew he could trust and could rely upon to help him. That was why Berwick was allowing him to travel the west country.

The King's writ gained Simon immediate access to the Cistercian Abbey of Hailes. The days had been fine, and he had made good time covering the one hundred miles from Westminster west along old Roman roads to Gloucestershire in just over two days. Passing the abbey mill, he entered the abbey precinct through its eastern gate. The sprawling abbey complex, less than thirty years old, was bounded by a grey ragstone wall that ran downhill be meet the gateway to the London road. Simon rode up a gentle slope, past God's

Acre, where the monks lay awaiting the Day of Judgement, towards the Long Stables, where a young lay brother took charge of his palfrey. Simon tossed the Brother a penny and requested that the horse be given an extra bag of oats and a good rub down.

He had sent word ahead, so another Abbey servant awaited and escorted him through the Cloisters and Chapter House to the Abbot's lodgings next to the abbey church. Clouds of acrid stone dust billowed around the Abbey, caused by extensive building works, a sure sign of a thriving community.

Even behind the veil of dust and the ching-ching of metal tools on stone, Simon could not help but admire the abbey church. Frantic building work took place behind a mass of wooden scaffolding and winches at the eastern end, and the activity enthralled him. A workman was approaching him, holding a short semi-circular wooden board that looked like a deformed horseshoe. A cloth tied behind his head covered his mouth and nose, and his hair was almost white with dust. What remained visible on his face showed fine lines ingrained with years of powdered stone, and he seemed busy in conversation with one of the monks.

"It so reminds me of the Benedictine Chapter House at Westminster." Simon expressed his thoughts aloud as he made his way past the stonework.

"Well, it will be when it is finished, Meister." The workman had stopped to respond. "It's familiar because it is designed in the same style. I worked on the Chapter House at Westminster, and now I'm supervising the extension of the Abbey to house the shrine of the sacred Holy Blood."

It turned out that the man was not what Simon first thought. "I am Brother John, John of Waverley, Master Mason and a lay brother here at Hailes."

"God give you good day, Brother John," Simon replied. In between lungfuls of stone dust, Simon asked the monk about the frenetic activity all around. Noise, shouts, the creaking of winches, the clanking of metal on stone and workmen rushing around with carts full of rocks and young boys hauling wooden buckets full of lime mortar showed the urgency with which the new shrine was being constructed.

"We are extending the eastern end of the Abbey, beyond the high altar, to make a polygonal apse, called a chevet, from local yellow Cotswold stone," explained Brother John. "Each of the five circular bays will contain a separate chapel. At its centre will be the new shrine to the Holy Blood presented to us by the Lord Edmund, Earl of Cornwall. The swelling beauty of each of these deep chapels will eclipse anything previously built by my Cistercians or the Benedictines in England. But I am thinking it will be two or three more building seasons before it is complete. Father Abbot would like it sooner, of course!"

The Master Mason explained how once Cistercian churches were simple, austere buildings. Over time, coloured glass, wall hangings and paintings that once were considered wasteful and incompatible with the purity of Christ were now accepted practice.

Brother John then gave an interested Simon a very brief tour of the progress.

"And pray tell me, brother, your revered treasure, the Holy Blood of the Lord; where do you house it?"

The Brother stopped and pushed a hand across his hair, releasing a snowstorm of fine white dust.

"'Tis a holy icon indeed. We have built a temporary shrine for it before the High Altar. But I fear it may be temporary for many years yet, until the Holy Chapel to house it is complete."

The fine stone dust covered every surface and made Simon and the monk appear prematurely aged. Simon covered his face and mouth with a cloth, making breathing and speaking easier.

"And how secure is it?" inquired Simon. "A holy treasure such as that must surely be a temptation for Wolf's Heads, thieves and rogues. Is it well guarded?"

"That it is! A holy brother kneels in prayer before the shrine in between services. So, it is attended for all daylight hours and only left in the dark hours between Matins and Lauds. Then the abbey church is locked, and the only entrance is from the monk's dortoir."

"And at night?"

"The external site is guarded at night by a pair of watchmen. We've had no problems with theft these past years. None at all."

Not what I have heard, Simon thought. The Master Mason seemed confident that the site and the Holy Blood had always been safe and secure. Perhaps he was unaware of the reports of an attempted theft that Simon had read of in the Chancery. Or maybe he was not prepared to reveal details of the robbery. At some point, Simon resolved he would ask the Abbot.

Time was pressing, and Simon bade his farewell to Brother John and was shown to the imposing Abbot's house, built from the same mellow Cotswold stone.

Jordan of Beaulieu had been Abbot of the Cistercian community of monks at Hailes for nearly thirty years. He and twenty other monks from Beaulieu had founded the community in 1246 at the behest of the old King's Brother, Richard, Earl of Cornwall. It was hard to determine the Abbot's age as life had left a deep imprint on the old monk's face. He seemed to be looking into the distance, and his eyes reflected either deep sadness or relaxed tranquillity. Those eyes, once deep blue, now bore the colour of a pale winter morning. Abbot Jordan's demeanour gave out an air of serenity. He sat behind his large oak desk, his long fingers weaving together. Having paid his respects with the Cistercian salutation – "Pax et Bonum" – Simon explained the reason for his visit.

Abbot Jordan sat and listened. His eyes widened, and he seemed astonished that a royal official asked to meet with one of the Hailes community's lay brothers.

"I know brother Thomas of old," Simon explained. "I am in need of his expertise."

Abbot Jordan's eyebrows raised in interest. "His expertise, you say?"

"Aye, you do know of brother Thomas before he joined your community?" Simon was pleased that he had succeeded in capturing the older man's attention.

"Of course, I am aware he had served His Grace and had taken the cross to Outremer."

"That is where I first met him. But as well as being a capable knight, Brother Thomas was also a learned one was skilled and knowledgeable in necromancy and thaumaturgy knowledge of which he learned from the books of the Saracens."

Abbot Jordan made the sign of the cross as if to protect himself from an unseen evil.

"Sir Thomas was unusual for a knight in being somewhat of a scholar. He fuelled his interest in books and the learning of the east while in Outremer. He became an authority in the practice of the dark arts of magic, learning from the works of Arabic scholars. And as you know, upon his return to England in the autumn of 1273, Sir Thomas gave up being a warrior and embraced the monastic life of the Cistercians here at Hailes Abbey."

A wide-eyed Abbot Jordan had not been aware that the mild-mannered Brother Thomas, who had only been at Hailes for a few years, was so skilled and knowledgeable.

"Ummm. I think I understand you," replied the Abbot enunciating his words slowly. "You do tell me Brother Thomas' knowledge is in such matters you need in the fight against satanic evil." He gave a long, thoughtful pause. "We must, of course, give whatever assistance we can to a King's Man engaged in royal business. You may, of course, meet with Brother Thomas. My Prior, Brother Anselm, will take you, and I believe you will find him in the Cloisters at this time of day."

Simon thanked the Abbot and became aware that a bird-like, pale-faced cleric had slipped silently into the room behind him, ready to act as escort. This Simon guessed was the Prior.

On the way to the Cloisters, Simon sought to engage Brother Anselm in conversation. But Prior, Anselm was not one for small talk. When they arrived, a solitary figure in a greyish-white habit sat engrossed, deep in thought, on a stone aisle bench. Brother Thomas' face beamed, eyes wide showing pleasant surprise at looking at a man he had last seen in Sicily more than five years before.

Brother Thomas was now well beyond his fortieth year. His narrow, tanned face under greying tonsured hair looked calm and kind. His eyes twinkled with mischief just as Simon remembered them, creating sharp lines above his brows. Thomas's ill-fitting black habit covered the length of his body, exposing just his bony, sandalled feet. Yet Simon knew that beneath the habit and cowl was the muscular torso of an experienced knight.

Seeing the man again after all this time, Simon recalled his excited, young self who until then had never set foot out of England and who had never reached Outremer. It was later, when he arrived back in England, that he heard the stories. It had been Sir Thomas who was first on the scene in June of 1272. A Syrian Nizari assassin, posing as a friend and armed with a poisoned dagger, attacked the Lord Edward in his bedchamber. The soon-to-be King succeeded in killing the assassin but not before he was wounded in his arm. It had been Queen Eleanor herself who had sucked out the poison.

After this, Sir Thomas acted as the personal bodyguard to the Lord Edward and screened everyone who came before the heir to the throne until the new King sent him back to England as a personal envoy to the Royal Council.

Brother Thomas listened as Simon gave a brief account of what he knew of the Daughters of the Shadows.

"And that, my friend, is why I am here at Hailes, to seek your help and advice to better understand the nature of what it is that I face."

Brother Thomas bit his lower lip as he reflected upon what he had just been told.

"The coven will be meeting somewhere remote, a woodland glade, a disused church, churchyard, or some ancient site," he began. "They will be conducting a purification ceremony."

"Purification?" Simon expressed surprise.

"I mean purification from God and the Holy Church."

"Ahh. At night?" asked Simon.

"Always at night. And on some important date associated with the transit of the moon." Simon nodded his understanding.

"They will stand in a circle surrounding a pentangle drawn on the earth," continued Brother Thomas. "That they call the coven-stead. Each present will make a sign on the ground in front of them, but outside the circle. It would be a triangle with a hole in its centre. Every coven has a different middle, but the principle of the pentangle remains the same."

"The coven will be dressed in black robes," he paused. "Probably black, hooded, and naked beneath. There will be thirteen in the coven, but I believe they may perform with less than that number."

Simon nodded. "The woman murdered in the churchyard at St Michael's days past was one of the coven."

Brother Thomas paused, thinking, inhaling. "You have the right of it. The Daughters of the Shadows will seek to recruit one further sister, and very soon. The coven is stronger when it numbers thirteen."

Thomas looked at Simon intently, his gaze stern and hard. "Do not underestimate these sisters of Satan, my young friend. For a coven like this to operate must mean that there are some highly influential people supporting them or who, may the Good Lord forbid, are actual members of the coven themselves. You must beware. Their influence may extend to the very royal court itself. You have to ask yourself, Simon, what is it these Daughters of the Shadows are seeking to achieve? When you know that, you will know how to stop them. But be careful, my friend. Whatever you discover will place you in great danger."

Thomas then began to muse, his eyes in fixed, far-reaching contemplation, his head tilted. "Did I ever tell you that King Alfonso of Castile, the brother of our dear queen, employed Jewish, Christian, and Muslim scholars to translate magical texts from Arabic and Hebrew into Latin and Castilian?"

"Nay, I did not know that. Why did he so?"

Thomas continued. "There were five treatises, the Lapidario, the Picatrix, the Libro de las Formas et las Ymagenes, the Libro de Astromagia and the Liber Razielis. Together they explain how mortals can manipulate the natural forces of this world."

"And you have read them?" enquired Simon. "Is that not heresy in the eyes of Holy Mother Church?"

"Let us say I have seen them, and I did scribe thoughts on parchment. Although if that were ever revealed to my superiors, I would have seven years of subsisting only on bread and water, spending all my days on my knees reciting the Paternoster."

Simon chuckled as the image of a penitent brother, Thomas surviving on such a meagre diet, flitted through his mind.

Simon began to think out loud. "We may assume that the six women from the house in Fulelane were members of the coven. We know one member is dead, Maud Blount, killed in the churchyard at St Michael's. So that leaves five. Is Alice la Blunde alive, and is she also a Daughter of the Shadows? If she is, then there are six witches unaccounted for."

Simon shook his head. Where to begin? He had to track down the women he knew to be witches, and he felt that was an impossible task. Then a thought started to form in his mind.

When it came to the dark arts, he was floundering because of his lack of expertise. Here in front of him, was someone who possessed such knowledge. Although Brother Thomas had taken the holy oath of a Cistercian, his prowess as a former knight may be particularly useful if danger indeed lurked in the days ahead.

"Would you leave here to come with me?" Simon blurted out. "I am going to ask Father Abbot if he might spare you for a few weeks to lend me assistance in this fight against sorcery and necromancy. You are skilled in these ways, whereas I am not." Thomas sat wide-eyed, although Simon couldn't make out whether from surprise or alarm. Thomas began to shake his head.

"My friend. I cannot leave this place. As well as the vows of poverty, chastity and obedience, I have also taken a vow of stability. That means I must remain here. Only an instruction about a most serious matter from my superiors or a dispensation from Rome would permit me to leave these walls."

"But I could persuade Abbot Jordan,"exclaimed Simon.

"Nay, my friend. If you think to take me with you for protection, then I needs must disabuse you. I cannot take up arms. That man no longer exists, and it would be contrary to my vows."

Despite brother Thomas' protestations, Simon still tried to persuade the Abbot. He began by flattering him and his monastic community, emphasising that the Crown requested Abbot Jordan's help. It would be to the Cistercians' renown to allow one of his brethren to assist the Crown in pursuing the malefici.

The elderly monk was polite in his refusal to comply with the request. "Brother Thomas has become used to the routines and strictures of the monastic way of life these past years. He has taken vows and would find returning to his 'old world' a difficulty."

Having rejected his request, to Simon's surprise, the Abbot insisted that Simon borrow one of the Abbey's prized holy relics. A holy sackcloth belonging to the famous Cistercian Saint, Guillaume de Donjeon. The Abbot explained that the mystical power of the sacred saint's relic would protect Simon and ward off the threat from the evil demons when he confronted the Daughters of the Shadows.

Before he left Jordan of Beaulieu's presence, Simon raised the tricky question of the attempted theft of their own precious relic some months before. But Abbot Jordan was adamant that the Holy Blood was safe and secure even in its temporary shrine. Thanking the Abbot, Simon took his leave. Brother Thomas asked permission to walk with his young friend to the guesthouse.

Brother Thomas grasped Simon's arm when they had left the Abbot's lodgings and took him aside.

"You should know something, my young friend. You are pursuing these witches, the Daughters of the Shadows. You said Alice le Blunde was one of the names of those in the house in Fulelane."

"Aye, you have the right of it. Why so?"

"Because if Mistress le Blunde is one of the Daughters of the Shadows, then we have a connection to Walter de Baskerville."

"We do?"

"Aye, we do. Alice le Blunde served Simon de Montfort as the wet nurse. She raised the infant, Guy de Montfort. Walter de Baskerville serves Guy as his liegeman."

Simon thought about this. "It is not a straightforward link, but it can be no coincidence."

"Aye, tis not." Brother Thomas showed deep concern etched across his face.

"You must track down de Baskerville with all speed and see where this link takes you, but my young friend, know that ahead of you lies darkness and danger." Brother Thomas gripped the arm of the young nuncio. "You needs must be ready to face it without hesitation."

Before he retired for the night in his chamber in the Abbey Guest-house, Simon went to the gloomy Church. He knelt before the unfinished tomb of Henry of Almain, spending some time in prayer before the shrine to the dead Lord. Some of his prayers asked for forgiveness for not being able to save the King's cousin in Viterbo. Simon left feeling sombre and retired to a comfortable bed.

So the following day, having broken his fast, Simon left Hailes Abbey and headed east on his two-day journey to St Albans. His palfrey pulled a pack-mule with the holy cloth of St Guillaume, stored safely in a small chest. As Simon rode the King's Highway towards Akeman Street, the words of Brother Thomas resounded in his head.

"Be careful, my friend. Whatever you discover will place you in great danger." That word again; first John of Berwick, then Henry Frowyke and now Brother Thomas. The next few weeks would prove the monk correct.

CHAPTER 32

St Peter's Church St Albans, June 1276

It took a few moments for Walter de Baskerville's eyes to become accustomed to the darkness of the interior of St Peter's Church. It appeared empty at this hour save for a solitary old woman kneeling in her devotions before the altar in a side aisle. It held the cloying aroma of godliness; de Baskerville thought, incense and beeswax. Walter had never liked churches and, if truth be told, had no time for the Church. It had been many years since he had been inside a church; Viterbo had probably been the last time, and that certainly wasn't for devotion. He chuckled to himself at the paradox of the situation; here he was, a man excommunicated by the Church and whose soul was condemned to eternal damnation by the Pope, entering the house of God.

The praying woman rose from her devotions and made to leave, disturbing the bats roosting in one of the side aisles. Ever the soldier, de Baskerville surveyed the church to ensure he was alone. He was always a cautious man; he had thought it a strange location to arrange to meet, a pilgrim church on the fringe of St Albans, but Benuic had chosen the time and place. Walter had come to St Peter's without his sword and armour; wearing it would arouse suspicion. Carrying his dagger hidden beneath his cloak made him feel less vulnerable.

This meeting had been arranged many weeks since. When de Baskerville arrived at Langlei, a sealed message on parchment awaited him. Cryptically all it said was: 'The Pilgrim Church of St Peter's, St Albans, Nones, on the feast day of St. Aurelian.'

Thus, it was that he found himself five days before midsummer, in the fourth year of the reign of King Edward, in a church awaiting an assassin he only knew as Benuic. He understood why Benuic had chosen this day; it was the first day of St Albans' annual fair, and the town was thronged with merchants, sellers and visitors.

"Do not turn around, Walter de Baskerville." A hushed female voice came from somewhere close behind him. He had not heard anyone enter the church and had heard no footsteps approach.

"Benuic has words for you." Walter tensed as he heard the heavy church door creak open. He went to turn. "No! Do not do that." The woman was nearby, he thought, but he had no sense of her presence earlier when he entered. How was that? He had surveyed the interior and had caught no sight of anyone apart from the single woman at prayer, but she had left.

"Go through the fair and make slowly past the stalls as if inspecting the goods and produce. You will be contacted."

Walter anticipated further instruction, but none came. He turned and peered into the gloomy, chill interior of the church but saw just three pilgrims who had entered and whom, he presumed, had made the door sound he heard earlier.

Of the woman, there was no sight.

St Albans fair was by no means the biggest. The greatest of all medieval English fairs was held at Stourbridge, near Cambridge. There, flocked merchants and traders from all over Europe. Flemish merchants brought their fine linen and cloths from the great commercial cities of Belgium. But the annual St Albans mid-summer fair attracted a fair share of prominent merchants. It was, de Baskerville thought, an excellent place to hide in plain sight. The three-day fair was held annually, towards the start of the third week of June, always eight days before the Feast of the Nativity of John the Baptist.

The stalls ranged from the practical to the exotic. A fascinating array of cloth, clothing accessories, dress-making equipment, jewellery and trinkets, toiletry articles, groceries, and assorted containers and pots were offered for sale. Jongleurs, jugglers, acrobats and musicians performed, each seeming to have their own pitch.

In vain, a jovial merchant sought to persuade Walter to examine his fishhooks, awls for leather, lancets for bleeding and crimping irons. Walter was offered combs, mirrors, razors, tweezers, ear-picks, toothpicks, and soap as he passed down the various stalls. Then there were the well-covered stalls of the more prosperous merchants selling dried fruit, nuts, ginger, saffron, spices, cumin and pepper, all for sale at exorbitant prices.

De Baskerville listened to the babble of many tongues, the odd word of which he grasped. Flemish merchants brought their fine linen and cloths from the great commercial cities of Flanders and Brabant. Genoese and Venetian traders called out promoting their stores of Eastern goods. Spaniards and Frenchmen brought their wines. The merchants from the Hanseatic towns of Germany sold furs and flax, ornaments and spices.

Walter de Baskerville moved along the stalls set up in the market triangle, constantly aware that Benuic could be anyone and approach him at any moment. Beyond French Row, at Chepping, he stopped at a stall belonging to a Genoese merchant selling the finest eastern spices. The booth appeared to be making a brisk trade. He was distracted by two women haggling with the owner over the price of pepper and cloves.

Amongst the throng of heaving people moving in all directions, it was difficult to identify individuals, but few would have trouble identifying the Frenchman at the butcher's stall on Bothelyngstock.

As Walter de Baskerville was Guy de Montfort's man, so Bertrand du Guesclin was Walter's man. He was short but so obviously a man of violence; his long black greasy hair fell lankly down to the nape of his neck. His torso was squat but well-muscled. The man was flat-nosed, swarthy and a killer. Men said of him there was none so ugly from Rennes to Dinan. Bertrand du Guesclin had no eyes for the merchandise in front of him. His gaze was fixed on his master idly examining the market's goods, awaiting word from Benuic.

Walter de Baskerville had been lazily inspecting the stall goods for a long time, and he still awaited contact. The choice of name, Benuic, was perhaps informative. Benuic had been the resistance leader of the Lusitanian against the Romans in western Hispania in ancient times. Did that have relevance? He stood in front of a spice stall. The seller, a foreigner by his appearance, sought to make a sale.

"Only the finest peppercorns and cloves, to be appreciated by all with good taste." His heavily accented tone was obsequious.

"You will find no better quality here today," came another voice behind him, a woman's voice. Frustrated, Walter turned to his left. He had not been aware of anyone approaching, but that was not surprising in the throng of the crowded market.

"Begone, Mistress. I have business here and have no time for small talk."

"I too have business here... Master de Baskerville."

To Bertrand du Guesclin, some thirty yards behind, it looked as if his master was flirting with one of the townswomen. *Lucky Devil*, he thought.

"Excuse me, sir, could you assist me. I cannot reach that roll of cloth there." It was a young servant girl addressing Bertrand. She spoke in excellent French, not English, and gave him a warm smile.

"That one there..." Bertrand gazed where she pointed and then back at the maid. He took in her comely body. Evil thoughts entered his head. Perhaps she's a fighter? He reached up and brought down the roll of cloth she had requested, passing it to her. He received in return a smile and a thank you from her. He tried to make small talk, something he was not very good at, but she did not respond and having inspected the cloth, she walked away.

"Bitch!" *Typical of my luck*, Bertrand thought to himself, wondering why he bothered being nice.

He refocused on his task of watching his master. He looked at the spice stall, but, to his horror, Walter de Baskerville was nowhere to be seen.

CHAPTER 33

The lanes behind St Albans Fair June 1276

In one of the cramped back alleys of the Marketplace, hidden by a doorway, Walter de Baskerville conversed in French with the woman from the market stall. To a casual observer, they made a strange couple standing in one of St Albans less desirable lanes. From his appearance, he was a man whose trade was violence; from her demeanour and clothes, she could not be a common whore of the town. Walter was exasperated, and the conversation hushed.

"When do I meet Benuic? I am tired of these games."

"Benuic has sent me. We shall finalise the arrangements, and my master will carry out your wishes once his bankers confirm the payment."

"How do I know you can trust you? I wish to meet Benuic."

"I am here, now. My master has received your message. Now you deal with me, and I pass on your message to him." The tone was firm.

Walter wasn't used to a woman giving him instructions, and he felt uncomfortable. He warily studied this strong woman and could tell much from the cut of her clothes. It was an elegant gown. Walter did not know about cloth, but it suggested that she was well-off. Perhaps a widow, he thought. She wasn't English, of that he was sure; her accent and the dark hue of her skin suggested she was Mediterranean, southern French or maybe a Savoyard.

He was distracted and not taking in her words. She repeated herself.

"You are aware of the terms of our agreement?" He knew, of course; these were his terms agreed with an intermediary in Ghent earlier in the year.

"A Letter of credit for one thousand florins, payable in advance deposited, with the Peruzzi bankers in Florence. That has been done these weeks since."

"The deed will be done before the feast day of St Mary Magdalene."

"My master would wish to know the details."

The woman pursed her lips. "Let us say that the deed will not be as clumsy as your master's fiasco in Viterbo."

Walter blanched at the rebuke. "And when will I know? When will it happen?"

"Master de Baskerville, the world will know when this deed is done. Remember, it was you who sought out Benuic. You know his reputation. It really becomes a question of how much Benuic can trust you." With that, the woman walked away, merging into the packed St Albans streets.

Walter de Baskerville turned to watch her leave. He bit his lower lip with a sense of unease. Something told him to follow her, but the crowds in the town made that impractical. Slowly he made his way back towards the bustling fair to locate his liegeman, Bertrand du Guesclin. Around him, people continued going about their business, shouting, smiling, laughing, all unaware that he had just sealed a deal with the assassin to kill the Queen of England.

CHAPTER 34

The Bull Ring St Albans Fair June 1276

Wild-eyed children pushed their way to the front of the temporary wooden arena opposite the Leather Shambles on the Magno Vico. Over the past days, Simon had watched half-a-dozen carpenters construct a wooden semi-circle with tiered stands to accommodate bullbaiting. It was always one of the most popular attractions at St Albans fair. Twice each day, a scrawny old bull was chained to a post at the front of the arena and a pack of well-muscled mastiffs set upon it. It was a rather one-sided affair as a sport, with the mastiffs almost always prevailing. That was why the bull ring was constructed so close to the main butchery area at Bothelingstock – to facilitate the speedy removal of the carcass.

Crowds thronged the arena and betting on which mastiff would produce the kill was equally popular. Given the mass of people in such close proximity, the bull ring was also a haven for rifflers and cutpurses. Every so often, a cry of 'thief!' or 'robbery!' would arise from the crowd as some unfortunate had their coin stolen.

Simon kept one hand on his baselard as he moved towards the bull ring through the crowds. Usually, such sport had no attraction for him, but Alia and Mistress Heacham had expressed an interest in watching. They found a spot on the third tier of the stand with a good view of the wooden post where the beast would be tethered. A rope tied tight around the root of his horns tethered the bull securely to the post situated in the centre of the ring. The dogs were already being paraded in front of the crowd. Each animal was held on thick chains and pulled along by a youth who struggled to control them.

Matilda Heacham seemed almost giddy with excitement.

"Tis said that baited flesh is tastier and more digestible. Prolonged exertion does render tough meat tender and palatable. That is why there is a town ordinance that it is illegal to slaughter a bull unless it had first been baited with dogs."

Simon was unsure how true that was but didn't say anything contrary.

"See. They have loosed the hounds," exclaimed Alia.

The dogs darted at the bull, seeking out its weaknesses. The wary bull attempted to strike the dogs with his head and horns and toss it into the air, but the hounds proved too cagey.

"Aye. See that one there, the light brown one." Matilda pointed to a lean, well-muscled hound, larger than the other mastiffs.

"I am told that is a Ca de Bou from Iberia and bred to control cattle and fight off wolves."

Simon looked at Matilda, a playful expression across his face.

"We seem to have found ourselves in the company of an expert, Alia. Do you think she will be laying some coin on the outcome?" That earned him a dig in the ribs.

"Look!" Alia needed to shout over the din of the crowd. "Do you see that dog crawling towards the beast?"

One mastiff had circled to one side of the bull and flattened itself on the ground, creeping close as the dogs on the other side distracted the bull's attention. Suddenly, the flattened dog leapt at the bull's face and attempted to bite its nose. As one, the crowd gasped and then cheered. But the bull's jaw caught the dog as it tried to bite, tossing it into the air. Again the crowd let out a collective gasp.

From the other side, the Ca de Bou took the opportunity to launch its own attack at the bull's head, clamping its fierce jaws onto the bull's snout. The animal bellowed in pain. The Ca de Bou held on, refusing to release its grip as the other dogs attacked its head and belly. The bull stamped, lashed, bucked and rolled in an attempt to shake them off.

The crowd cheered as the Ca de Bou refused to release its grip. That was the signal for the dog handlers to move in. Accompanied by a tumult of noise from the crowd, the youths attempted, amid much snarling, to prise the dog's jaw apart to release their hold on the bull. With its strength ebbing away, the unfortunate bull gradually gave up the fight.

Although Simon could see no sport in what he had just witnessed, the crowd cheered their acknowledgement.

"How impressive was that Iberian hound?" asked Matilda.

"I suppose you have the right of it," Alia replied. "But I found myself out of steps with the crowd, and I did not enjoy that spectacle."

The snarling, still-growling mastiffs were being dragged by chains away from the prone bull. At length, the beleaguered animal staggered to its feet and let out a bellow of defiance, which was answered by a chorus of barking from the frustrated dogs.

CHAPTER 35

Ghent May 1276

From his vantage point on the corner of the Markt on the pave outside the tavern of the widow Stebenhethe, Benoit Marguet watched the busy townspeople of Ghent go about their business. He took in the merchants with their wives and those with their mistresses. He observed the poor, the artisans, the newly arrived, staring wide-eyed at sights they could never have imagined. Benoit Marguet took in his world at his corner by the Markt in the centre of Ghent. This was his spot, where he had begun his days for years. Once, he had been a man-at-arms in the pay of the Duke of Flanders. All that had ended when he was trampled by a destrier. It was a minor skirmish suppressing a nothing-revolt in a place he didn't even know. After that, his legs didn't work. For these past years, he had been reduced to begging on the streets of the city he now called home.

A kindly carpenter in the docks had crafted a wooden sledge for him years before. With the help of his two paddles, he scraped his way along the cobbles, back and forth to the Markt and back to his ground-floor room half a mile away. Many were kind to him. Mistress Stebenhethe of the tavern he now sat outside always welcomed him in the evening. The heat from the fire was always much appreciated in the colder months.

Benoit appreciated this. Although only a very few kind people bothered to speak to him, Benoit no longer minded. He was good at listening and frequently picked up snippets of interesting information, overheard when the conversation grew louder as the ale made men drunker. And always, some would pay Benoit for such information.

The merchant was one of those kind men who always had time for words with Benoit. He didn't know for sure that the man was a merchant, of course, but his fine clothes and educated accent showed he was both wealthy and influential. The merchant would affectionately pat Benoit on the shoulder, placing a few coins into his hand and always buying him an ale. Begging, especially in the winter months, brought little money. Benoit liked the merchant, and when the man asked if he would pass on snippets of news in return for coin, he was happy to do so.

On this night, Benoit was in a corner near the roaring fire. There were few men in the tavern when the merchant came in. As usual, he came over to Benoit, greeted him heartily and purchased him an ale. The two spent a few minutes in banal conversation before the merchant reached down to pat Benoit's shoulders.

Benoit gripped the merchant's arm and whispered a message into his ear. The merchant's eyes widened, and he nodded understanding.

"God, go with you, my friend." The merchant placed coin into Benoit's palm before sitting alone at a table where a frothy ale awaited him.

The merchant spent long minutes staring at the jug of ale, deep in thought. He had no way of verifying what Benoit the Beggar had just told him, but that was for others to concern themselves with. Now he would do what he always did with important news.

Having supped his ale, he hailed a serving maid and ordered another, which he quickly downed as he took in the tavern's patrons. There were more customers now than before. At an adjacent table, three burly sailors sat drinking and hardly conversing. Two whores had come in, their faces painted and their bodices open, giving a clear indication of their profession. They, too, eyed the clientele seeking potential customers. Their eyes met the merchants, and he glanced down at his empty jug.

The merchant pushed the table away and headed towards the door, nodding goodbye to Benoit as he departed. Once outside, the merchant looked down the street to check that there was no one there. His route home would only take but a few minutes, and as always, men alone on the streets had to be wary of robbers and cutpurses.

The merchant's journey home turned out to be uneventful. His large house lay in the wealthiest part of Ghent, an impressive three-story property located close to Saint Bravo's Cathedral.

Benoit believed the man to be a merchant, but he was wrong. Jaque Routaert was a trusted senior clerk to a leading member of the Virii Hereditarri, the elite ruling class of the city. He had served in that capacity for over ten years. He was well-respected in the city, known for his fairness and attention to detail. What would have been a surprise, had it been known, that he was an agent in the employ of John of Berwick.

Jaque's mother was from Bishops Lynn, and his father was a Ghent merchant. He didn't consider what he did was spying for the English, for Flanders and England were frequently allies. Jaque passed on the news that was of interest to the English. He had first met John of Berwick fifteen years before in Bruges, and over time, the two became friends. Jacque passed on news to John of Berwick, how it got to him, once it left Ghent, he was unsure. He only knew his part in passing on the information to the man who would carry it to England.

Upon his arrival home, he made straight for his downstairs chamber. His maid had left rushlights in the passage to illuminate his way. He lit a beeswax candle and, moving around the room, collected the various items he would need. He placed a small inkhorn and a quill onto the table in front of him. From a drawer, he withdrew a sheet of paper. It had come via Venice from the East, and more and more clerks like him were using it to record information.

He placed a copy of Psalm 27 on the table and smoothed it out with his palm.

The Lord is my light and my salvation- whom shall I fear?

The Lord is the stronghold of my life- of whom shall I be afraid?

When the wicked advance against me to devour me, it is my enemies and my foes who will stumble and fall.

Though an army besieges me, my heart will not fear; though war break out against me, even then, I will be confident.

He began transcribing Benoit the Beggar's message to him in the tavern using a cypher and Psalm 27.

When the message reached John of Berwick, one of his scriveners would use their identical copy of Psalm 27 to decode the message. Jaque completed his task, placed his quill on the table, sprinkled fine sand over the coded message to dry the ink and shook the paper over a small receptacle on the floor.

He reread his work then folded the paper five times before sealing it with red wax. As the liquid flowed across the folded paper, Jaque pushed his ring into it, leaving an impression that John of Berwick's men would recognize as authentic.

Two nights later, the first Thursday of the month, Jaque went to an inn near the docks on the River Scheldt at the hour before Nones. The dingy interior had the smell of the sea, fish and wood smoke.

Jaque ordered an ale from a disinterested serving girl and sat alone at a table in the corner far from the entrance. He took in the customers, sailors, fishermen and dock labourers. At a far table, an older man sat alone. From the finer cut of his clothing, he was a sea captain. His face was burned from the sun, and it emphasised his deep lines. His hair and beard were greying. He sat toying his ale jug, turning it as if in contemplation.

After two strong ales, Jaque decided that it was time he left. He stood, swaying uneasily, perhaps from the strength of the ale. He lurched towards the door, passing the table of the sea captain. If any of the other customers were interested, they would have seen a man in his cups struggling to make it to the way out.

Trying to stay upright, Jaque grabbed at the corner of the table where the sea captain was seated. Alarmed, the captain reached out a hand to push him away, but Jaque managed to straighten himself and, without a glance backwards, lurched towards the door.

None in the tavern were sharp-eyed enough to have seen the small, sealed paper fall from Jaque's right hand. It landed on the table only the be swept up by the Sea Captain as he raised his hand to push the drunken Jaque away. The paper was deftly slipped into his pocket, and the Sea Captain continued the contemplation of his jug of ale.

Alban Savage had been at one with the sea all his life. He hailed from Dunwich and first went to sea as a ship's boy on a merchant's vessel. That had been in the reign of the old King. Now he commanded his own merchantman crossing the North Sea with ells of cloth and other goods into the port of London every other week. He had been a messenger for the Crown for more than five years, passing on messages from the Crown Intelligencers as well as reporting what he observed in the ports where his vessel docked.

He ordered himself another ale and spent a long time over it before returning to Le Bon Vente, his sea-going cog. Once in his tiny cabin, he opened a wooden crate containing a dozen earthenware pots the length of his hand. He opened one with a slightly raised lid, pushed the message deep down into a jar of dried peppercorns, and carefully reaffixed the cover. The cargo of pepper was too valuable to place in the main hold, so it resided in his cabin, which made it a perfect medium for passing on the messages.

Le Bon Vente sailed on the morning tide, the calmness of the Scheldt estuary giving way to the rough Northern sea, which hampered their crossing. Three days later, Le Bon Vente entered the calm of the Thames estuary. It took half a day to progress on the tide upstream to dock at Herberds Wharf below London Bridge.

The arrival was anticipated. The Under Controller of the Royal Household, Hugh Ferre, waited on the docks with four men-at-arms and three officious-looking clerks. Two large black carthorses attached to a royal wagon strained at their bonds, anxious to be moving. Ferre already had to assert his authority over two keen port officials who were eager to board and inspect the vessel and its cargo. He and his Kingsmen would board first and conduct their official business.

Alban Savage stood pensively in his small cabin in the upper stern of Le Bon Vente, awaiting the arrival of Master Ferre. The wooden crate of earthenware pots of peppercorns was stowed innocuously to one side of the entrance. The drape that served as the door was pushed aside, and the Under Controller of the Royal Household entered. A nod of recognition passed between the two men, and Hugh Ferre stepped aside as his two clerks followed him in, lifted the wooden crate, and left.

They picked their way through the bustle and activity on deck down to the dockside. There they loaded the crate onto the guarded wagon, and in just a few minutes, they were gone, headed for the royal palace at Westminster.

CHAPTER 36

The Royal Palace of Westminster May 1276

Deep inside the royal palace, two men sat huddled over desks illuminated by expensive beeswax candles. In this small dingy chamber with just two small windows, Raynold Dodderell turned the sealed paper message this way and that, bringing it close to his eyes intently studying the wax to ensure that the seal had not been tampered with.

When he was satisfied with his examination, he took a thin blade and sliced open the seal, unfolding the paper and flattening it out on the desk in front of him. Dodderell was one of three specialist scriveners tasked with deciphering coded messages that came into John of Berwick. Now he placed his copy of Psalm 27 alongside the paper from Ghent and began to translate the message. Allowing for double-checking his work, the whole translation took him the time it would take a priest to say a mass.

He took his translation and went next door, where Hugh Ferre was waiting. Ferre, as well as being Under Controller of the Royal Household, was one of the King's senior intelligencers. A man of very few words and little emotion, Ferre grunted a noise that served as thanks and snatched the paper and rushed to the chamber of the senior Royal Intelligencer.

"This is not good, Ferre. Not good at all." The contents of Jaque Routaert's message agitated John of Berwick.

"Guy de Montfort, the son of the traitor to the Crown, has been seen these weeks in Ghent, and our agent reports that de Montfort puts the word out in the taverns that he seeks Benuic." Berwick finished the sentence with a deep sigh.

"Benuic?" Ferre had never come across the word and was unsure if that was a person or an object.

"Benuic is a ghost. An assassin for hire. The name is well-known beyond England. But none knows who he is. Benuic has killed more than a dozen men these past years. Always important people but has never been caught nor does he leave any trace of his being there."

Berwick stared at the wall in reflective thought, trying to put the pieces together. "If de Montfort has hired the services of Benuic, then the appearance of his man de Baskerville in England can be no coincidence. There is a link here, but as yet, I cannot see it."

"Master Berwick, you have mentioned this de Baskerville fellow before to me, but how does he link to Guy de Montfort and how does all this connect to this Benuic?"

"Walter de Baskerville is.... was, a mercenary captain. He was once loyal to the Crown, serving the late king's brother as a household knight. But de Baskerville fell under the influence of Simon de Montfort these fifteen years past. He fought for de Montfort at Lewes when they captured the king and was with him again at Evesham the following year when we slew de Montfort."

Berwick paused, recalling events from ten years before as if they were yesterday.

"De Baskerville fled, but Guy de Montfort was wounded and held prisoner. It was, we believe, de Baskerville who engineered his escape from England and his passage to the continent. De Baskerville served both de Montfort brothers as a mercenary commander and was with them at Viterbo five years ago when they murdered the

King's cousin in the church. Like de Montfort, he was excommunicated by the Church and declared a traitor to the Crown. If now the traitor Guy de Montfort seeks the services of an assassin, and de Baskerville is here, then the two must be linked. What we must do is find out how and who is de Montfort's target?"

Ferre spoke to help clarify what Berwick had said. "De Montfort would have only hired Benuic to kill a person of importance. We must ask ourselves, who would de Montfort wish to kill? Can we be sure that it is not an enemy he has on the continent? But if it is one of his rivals in Tuscany, then why go to Ghent to seek his assassin?"

Hugh Ferre stood in front of the small fire burning in the hearth. He took the liberty of thinking aloud, formulating the questions as they came into his head.

"Do we assume that de Montfort seeks harm to someone here in England? What other reason would he have for hiring an assassin in Ghent? If he could kill someone himself, he would do so. So... we might assume that his target is someone he cannot get close to, but someone he wishes dead."

"By Jesu, you have the right of it, Ferre." Berwick turned towards his underling.

"De Montfort is already condemned as a traitor. He plots revenge for what happened to his father. He has hired Benuic to kill His Grace the King."

It was a leap of thinking, but Berwick was sure he was correct. The reason behind de Baskerville's return to England had puzzled him. The traitor's explanation to Lowys at Langlei didn't hold together. Church and Crown condemned him; he may want a pardon, but that lay at the King's whim. He risked ending his days disembowelled on the scaffold by returning to England secretly and without royal permission.

A procession of thoughts entered Berwick's head. He had to get news of his suspicions about Benuic to Lowys and his royal intelligencers. The ports had to be alerted, but Benuic was this ghost; he had no description. Indeed, although he strongly suspected the assassin was a foreigner, he could not be sure he wasn't an Englishman in exile in Flanders.

The King! He had to alert His Grace to the threat. He knew from experience that King Edward paid scant attention to his safety. The attack on his person, in his personal tent, by an assassin in Sicily five years before had demonstrated that. Nonetheless, John of Berwick feared an assassin getting close to His Grace whilst on royal progress or pilgrimage.

Walter de Baskerville's movements had to be followed; he would summon Lowys immediately to put that in place. Berwick paused in thought and then left Ferre to see his scrivener Dodderell.

"Master Dodderell. I wish you to encode a message to le Reynard and send it by the quickest nuncio within the hour."

Berwick gave a brief outline of the threat to the King and of de Baskerville's arrival in England. Dodderell quickly wrote down the words and, without prompting, took a fresh sheet of thick paper and a copy of Psalm 61 and laid both in front of him.

'Hear my cry, O God; listen to my prayer. From the ends of the earth, I call to you.'

He used the psalm as his cypher code and, within a few minutes, poured sand onto the paper to dry the ink, blowing off the excess. Folding the document to envelop it, he took a red wax stick and melted some onto the centre. He proffered the envelope to Berwick, who placed his ring onto the liquid wax to leave his seal.

"Within the hour... Send me confirmation." Berwick's command echoed in the corridor as he left to return to his chambers.

For John Pedderton, this was the third occasion he had journeyed with such messages over the past months. He didn't know the identity of the King's agent who would receive the despatch he carried. Indeed, he wasn't entirely sure that the message was for an intelligencer. His job was to deliver it to an inn on the road west urgently. From there, he guessed, the message would be passed on to one of the King's agents. His fast horse glided over the miles, and in under three hours, he arrived at a country tavern. Typically, a customer would enter through the front door. Still, the arrangement had always been that he came in via the kitchen.

He gave a cursory greeting to the cook who was busy basting a roasting hoggett and went through into the inn and approached the innkeeper, a stocky man wearing a leather apron. He had done a similar thing three times, handing over messages to the innkeeper, but no words had ever passed between them.

As before, the innkeeper took the sealed message without any acknowledgement. He slipped it into a pocket in his greasy apron and continued with his business. Although he had worked up a thirst on his journey, Pedderton chose not to have an ale here. Quite why, he didn't know, but he preferred to find another tavern where a pretty maid might serve him if he were lucky.

The flickering from a fine wax candle illuminated the solar as the evening shadows of moonlight danced on the window shutters. Le Reynard handled the page on which John of Berwick's message was written and began to think through its implications. The translation, using Psalm 61, had been straightforward; it was the message itself that presented the problem. Le Reynard had been told Walter de Baskerville's presence in England by Berwick weeks before. Now, Guy de Montfort, seeking an assassin's services, had to be linked to de Baskerville's presence. It was how they connected that le Reynard didn't yet know.

And then there was another factor to consider. Le Reynard knew that de Baskerville had been at Langlei meeting Sir Stephen de Chenduit. The manor of Langlei was in the process of being transferred to Her Grace the Queen. Was there a connection there?

Berwick had said in an earlier communique that the royal nuncio, Lowys, was facilitating the transfer.

Lowys, le Reynard thought. The inexperienced royal nuncio. Lowys had been at the Wheatsheaf inn at St Albans and had been to Pendley to meet with Maeve de Thornby. Bit by bit, the King's Man was getting closer to the heart of the conspiracy. Le Reynard wondered whether or not Lowys knew how close he actually was.

CHAPTER 37

Berkhamstede Hertfordshire June 1276

The sun threw its morning warmth onto the damp landscape, gradually burning off the early mist. Alice le Blunde sat staring out of a narrow window, grey-eyed, deep in memory. The window in the merchant house looked out onto Berkhamstede's main street, which led down to the castle. It was flanked by other impressive merchant homes and businesses. But Alice's eyes saw the imposing stonework of a Midlands fortress she had called home.

Today was St Mark's Eve, the day the child had been born three decades since. Alice was dewy-eyed as she recalled. It had been a difficult birth. In the confinement chamber, deep inside Kenilworth castle, coal braziers threw out oppressive heat. There were no men in the room; there was no place for them in the birthing of a child. The mother's screams in her labour had been constant since the bells for Lauds had rung as the day broke. The sun had passed its mid-point when the child finally arrived. Alice was there as one of the mid-wives, just as she had been for two of the woman's previous births. How strange, she thought, that all women were equal in childbirth. Lady Eleanor de Montfort, daughter of a King of England, lay on the bed sweating and exhausted, having delivered of a fourth son.

But the son was sickly. She gazed out, oblivious to the hubbub of activity outside on the Berkhamstede street, fondly recalling how it was she who had been his wet nurse. It was she who had cared for the child in those fraught early days as he lingered on the cusp of life and death. That had formed a special bond with the infant, watching over him, nursing him through those early years, the milk from her breasts slowly building up his strength. As the years passed, the bond between them remained. The bond between Alice le Blunde and Guy de Montfort.

Guy was the son Alice never had. He may have been borne from the loins of the lady Eleanor de Montfort, but Alice saw herself as his true mother. And then there was his father, the Lord Simon de Montfort. A fondness came into her eyes as she thought of the great man. Tall, strong, imposing, he was the grandest Lord in all England. He showed great interest in the sickly child, visiting the nursery chamber when he was at Kenilworth, holding the swaddled infant while he made small talk with Alice. Those conversations had developed into a friendship, as much as any great Lord could be friends with a servant. From this fellowship, they became lovers.

They remained lovers for more than two decades. As her youth bloomed into womanhood, Simon de Montfort always returned to Alice's bed; her beauty didn't fade with the years. It was she, not the Lady Eleanor, who was his true love. Alice was set up with private chambers within Kenilworth. If the Lady Eleanor was aware, Alice neither knew nor cared. Just two years after Guy was born, Alice gave birth to a de Montfort's illegitimate son, a boy. He was given the name Alix de Montmorency, after his ancestor, but he lived just a few days. Less than ten months later, a tiny daughter was born that Simon insisted be called Dulcia, the Latin word for 'sweet'.

Alice played her role in the de Montfort household as the dutiful children's nurse. She had always attended the church services, although her relationship with the priest, Pere de Taney, was always strained. De Taney, for his part, was cold and distant towards her and viewed Alice with tremendous suspicion. She could not be sure whether he was aware that she shared a bed with the lord Simon and had done so for many years or whether he knew of her other life as a Daughter of the Shadows.

For as long as she could remember, Alice le Blunde had been at one with the night. It had never frightened her. One of her earliest memories was being woken by her mother and taken in the darkness of a midsummer night to an open clearing deep in the forest. There she watched as her mother and other women danced naked around a log fire, speaking words she didn't understand.

But she would come to understand them as the years passed by her. As a young girl, she had acted as a handmaiden to her aunt, the High Priestess of the Daughters of the Shadows. She had taught her the ways of a cunning woman; how to make up potions to cure, heal, and harm. Alice learned how to set bones and heal wounds. She had always found great joy in her walks in the woods with her aunt. There she learned about the plants and the fauna and the medicines and tonics made from them.

Alice also learned the ways of the coven, the spells and incantations and its rituals. By her thirteenth year, she had been enrolled as a member, and when her aunt died of the pestilence four years later, she took her place as the High Priestess of the Daughters.

That had been so long ago and yet, yesterday in her mind. It had been Alice who held the Daughters of the Shadows together when pestilence took four others of the coven. Their number was never the thirteen they should have been. Still, Alice had identified local women, wives or widows who demonstrated an independent spirit and would fit well within the Daughters of the Shadows.

Alice had married; it provided the respectability a woman needed. But her husband Roger le Blunde had been a pathetic man, sickly, incapable in bed and hopeless with money. He, too, had been taken by the plague, which was when Alice found employment at

Kenilworth Castle. All he had left her was the title to the house in Fulelane in the city of London.

Even as she worked as the wet nurse to the infant Guy de Montfort and shared a bed with his father, she carried on the traditions of the Daughters of the Shadows. Fewer in number, they would meet under the dark of the new moon marking their festivals such as Imbolc, Ostra, Litha, Mabon and Samhain, the crossing of the Hallows. When the garrison slept, Alice would slip silently out of the coffin door in the chapel and meet with her fellow daughters in a clearing as the hour of midnight turned.

Just as her relationship with Simon de Montfort had been an essential part of her life, producing the daughter she loved, so too were her other daughters, the coven of the Daughters of the Shadows. Alice had nurtured the coven, weaving their magic spells as a collective and holding it together.

The murder of her lover at Evesham ten years past had hit Alice hard. The man she loved, her protector, the father of her child, had been slain mercilessly on the battlefield on the orders of the King's son, the Lord Edward. Her beloved Guy, bloodied and wounded, was taken prisoner and awaiting trial for treason.

The mighty fortress of Kenilworth did not surrender to the forces of King Henry. If the King wished to reclaim Kenilworth from the followers of Simon de Montfort, then he would have to do so by force. Still, there was no escape for the civilians. The King, emboldened after his victory, attempted to persuade the garrison to surrender. For months they refused all his overtures. His patience finally snapped after his herald, sent to parley with the defenders, returned with his hand severed before the Easter of 1266.

The year following the death of her lord were desperate times for Alice and her young daughter. Alice could not count how many wives, children, servants, and defenders were inside the fortress, but she thought it would fill a church ten times more.

At midsummer in the year following the death of Simon de Montfort, the King's forces began an all-out siege on Kenilworth. As she closed her eyes, Alice could still remember the noise of the continuous stream of stone missiles bombarding the castle walls – the noise that never stopped and the screams that pierced the hours as another projectile struck human flesh, maimed and snuffed out life.

And her recollection of that gnawing hunger seemed so vivid; Dulcia crying from the pain in her belly. All around them, there was death, not always from the siege engines. Disease stalked the de Montfort fortress. The summer and autumn had come and gone before the castle defenders surrendered to the King. The men were allowed to leave with their arms, horses and harness. Only two days' supply of food remained in the castle.

Alice and her daughter were turned out with only the possessions they could carry. Kenilworth and its Lord had been her world. Her future now was uncertain.

Behind her vacant expression, Alice flitted between her past and her present. The years had once been kind to Alice's looks, but her face, now lined, showed her years. Beneath her white whimple and veil, her hair was thinning. Her mother had once told her that she had been born in the fourth year of the reign of the old King Henry, the year the first Dominicans came to England. Alice was now past her fiftieth year, she had outlived the old King, but the aches and rhumes plagued her ageing body.

The tears fell down Alice le Blunde's face. Her memories of her life at Kenilworth with her Lord and lover were still vivid. He was still so real to her, despite his death at Evesham. She had promised herself that she would avenge his death one day. She had made that promise the hour she had learned that Simon had been slain in battle and how his enemies had desecrated his body.

Alice focused on retribution as she brought her mind back to the present and the busy Berkhamstede street. She shared a common purpose with her beloved Guy. They would have their revenge on the man responsible for Simon de Montfort's death, and she would use her Daughters of the Shadows to achieve it. The man and his family would know their wrath; they would have their revenge on King Edward of England.

CHAPTER 38

The ancient Roman ruins outside St Albans, June 1276

The city curfew bell had long since struck. The gloom of the moonless night made tracing the trackway through the wood harder than it should be. The weather was incredibly chilly for early summer. He knew it would be the dark of the moon when they met. This night that belonged to those who more comfortably dwell in darkness, alone, with nought but starlight and candle flame to light their way. Gnarled, twisted branches laid bare by the chill winds closed in around him. Simon picked his way forward, ignoring the cold seeping through his boots and stabbing his feet. The arbalest slung across his back clattered his shoulder, and he held onto his baselard dagger for reassurance. An owl, deep within the trees, hooted dolefully. Simon paused and shivered; wasn't that an omen of ill tidings? Ahead, the woodland began to thin; keeping to a line of trees, he approached the edge of the old Roman ruins. This place, he had been told, had once been an important town when the Romans ruled, but now it was a collection of scattered walls and fallen stones.

He stared across the misty clearing, flanked by the ancient walls. A fire crackled in the centre at a point where the ground rose slightly to a plateau. At first, all Simon could make out were just black silhouetted shapes, moving around in a circle of silence. Then pitch torches were lit, illuminating the ground, and he could make out the rough shape of a pentangle marked by stones on the earth. The women, he thought they must be women, all wore dark garments, black, Simon presumed. All of their heads were hooded, hiding their faces. Simon counted. Eleven now around the pentangle.

Then as one, the eleven began to chant. Simon strained to hear the words, some of which were indistinct, but he could make out one which kept recurring, 'Caper', the Latin word for male goat, an incarnation of the Devil. He shivered again, from the cold or something else; he could not be sure. The chanting grew louder, now their incantation implored, "Oymelor, Demefin, Lamair, Masair, Symofor, and Rimasor, your sisters summon you..." Simon felt the hairs rise on his neck. Suddenly the chanting stopped, and, as one, the eleven of the circle fell to their knees. Then out of the silence, one stood. She held her arms aloft and intoned in a high-pitched voice.

"Dwellers of the Yester-ba-ra. Your sisters of the shadows summon you."

A large black raven swooped down and circled the centre of the pentangle, cawing loudly before flying off. The standing witch, who Simon thought must be the High Priestess, summoned the demons to appear before her sisters. Then the circle parted to reveal a single figure.

A woman, again, Simon was sure it was a woman, robed in an all-white hooded gown and led by another dark cowled figure, entered the circle. The woman in white slipped off her gown and, naked, lay down in the middle of the pentangle, her red hair billowing in the breeze. Simon let out an involuntary gasp. In the light from the pitch torches, he could see Isabelle de Brun.

As she lay within the pentangle, a dark liquid was daubed over Isabelle's naked body, probably blood, Simon thought, but what kind – human or animal? The High Priestess mumbled an incantation that, this time, Simon couldn't make out. She brandished a flaming torch rhythmically over Isabelle's body, muttering all the time.

Isabelle stood, her white garment now replaced by a dark-hooded gown draped over her shoulders; she moved quickly to take her place within the knelt circle. Simon lost sight of her, garbed as she now was like the others, as they all rose and began circling the pentangle, once more chanting their calls to the demons. He counted. They now numbered twelve. In the distance, an owl hooted.

From his vantage point behind the trees, Simon continued to observe the ritual. Make a mental record of all they do, Brother Thomas had said. The coven stood as one and began to circle the pentangle. A low-hanging summer mist rolled in off the river Ver and hung eerily above the pentangle. The now twelve hooded figures of the Daughters of the Shadows stood. On an imperceptible nod from the Priestess, they began to circle the magical pentangle marked out on the earth, always moving left. The Priestess of the Coven began her incantation, and Simon's chill intensified.

"One of our sisters has been destroyed! "She spoke in French, her voice high pitched and almost a shriek. "We have the King's Man to thank for that! Oymelor, Demefin, Lamair, Masair, Symofor, and Rimasor, your sisters in darkness summon you!"

"We must seek vengeance; we must kill him!" intoned another, hatred spewing in her voice. "We will have vengeance; will destroy the King's spy!"

The coven stopped. All hands rose to the sky. The High Priestess spoke once again.

"We must prepare for the Gathering. We must bring down misery and suffering on he who has offended us by striking down his path of parturition!" There was excitement in her voice. "And the King's Man will see his death, and we shall celebrate the shedding of his blood!"

The words of the Priestess frightened him. Alone, in the dead of night, Simon suddenly felt very exposed and vulnerable. A twig cracked behind him. He half-turned his head just in time for his world to go black.

CHAPTER 39

The Bull Ring, St Albans Fair, June 1276

He became aware that he was no longer cold. Simon Lowys screwed his eyes, trying to remember. His head throbbed, and for the second time in a matter of weeks, he found himself lying on the ground, his hands bound. Recollection came slowly. He remembered the meeting of the coven, the sinister incantations and seeing the naked body of Isabelle de Brun, seemingly involved in some kind of initiation. He remembered the chanting and the threat to his life by the priestess. Then he recalled the coldness of the night and being struck over the head.

And now he found himself here. But where was here? He was lying on the cold earth. It smelt of damp and animals. His head throbbed. He opened his eyes and gazed at his surroundings. It was no longer night but that time when the sun rose above the horizon and darkness blended with the light. He could make out some sort of wooden structure around him, with gaps that allowed the semi-light inside. Above him, a rough canvas awning covered most of the structure and served as its roof.

Having taken all of that in, he had no idea where he was. He focused. There was a noise, animal noise, a low rumbling sound, close-by but not within view. Snarling and yelping followed. Dogs, it was the growling of dogs he could hear.

As he sought to sit up, a wave of nausea rushed over him. In the distance, the dogs were becoming more agitated, their barking more aggressive. He looked left and right to see if he could make out where they were. They were close by, he sensed that, but he couldn't see them.

"You have come back to join us, King's Man", A woman hailed him, speaking in French. Her voice came from somewhere above him. Simon arched his head to try to locate where she was.

"Who are you? What do you want"?

"Now, King's Man, you know who I am. And as for what I want, I thought that would be very obvious to you. You were there watching my sisters and me in the woods, and I called vengeance on you, and now," she paused, "Here you are."

Simon lay on his side, his head craned to locate the woman. He groaned. He did indeed know who this was. It had to be the High Priestess. He struggled at his bonds but was bound hard, hand and foot. He rolled on the earth, trying to get a better view to find the woman.

"Struggle all you will, Master Lowys. It will do you no good."

The voice now came from behind him. He shuffled around. A woman stood in front of him, garbed in dark robes and holding a flickering cresset lamp. She was beyond her fiftieth year. The flames illuminated her face and its lines of age, but she had once been a beauty. Then he saw the glint of a knife she held in her hand, and he shuddered.

She approached him slowly. The blade was raised high and brought down with force, slashing at his shoulder. Pain surged through his arm, and Simon sensed the blood flowing from the wound. She had wounded him, not killed him. That she hadn't done so only served to exacerbate his unease.

"And now Master King's Man, my friends are hungry. I am sure you have heard them, and most certainly, they know you are here.

How fares your shoulder wound? Now they can smell blood... and very soon they will feast on your flesh."

A shiver of revulsion swept over Simon. At that moment he realised where he was. He was in the bull ring set in the middle of the fair. The damp earth and the smell were from the savaged bull, its blood and innards. That would now be his fate.

The dogs he could hear must be the bulldogs and mastiffs, trained to kill a chained animal with their teeth. Now, as he lay on the wet earth, he was to be their prey.

"I bid you goodbye, King's Man. When your body is discovered in a few hours, no one will recognise you. They are hungry, you see; they've not been fed for a day since. I would like to watch it, but you must realise I cannot be seen here. Die painfully King's Man. Your death will avenge my sister Maud. Pray to your God now, for you will die unshriven, and your soul will spend eternity in hell."

Alice le Blunde laughed as she left the bull ring, her chortling ringing in Simon's ears. The yelping and excitement from the dogs increased. Alice closed and bolted the wooden door behind her. Outside she paused, then lifted a latch by the door, which released the catch on the pen holding the baying hounds.

Three burly, muscular mastiffs raced into the enclosed arena. Even in the dim moonlight, Simon immediately recognised one, more prominent than the others. The Ca de Bou; the Iberian wolf killer. Struggling in vain with his bonds, he kept his eyes firmly on the dogs. But they, in a display of cunning and intelligence, split up so that he could not keep all three in vision at the same time.

The mastiffs bared their fangs, and the growling and snarling grew deeper. They seemed to lie down, but, Simon realised, they were keeping low to the ground to stalk their prey. And that prey was him.

Simon kept moving his head, one way and then the other, to keep the dogs in his sight. From seemingly nowhere, he was hit on his side by a huge force as one of the mastiffs charged him. He sensed rather than felt a weight on his leg as the teeth punctured flesh. Then the pain came, followed by the sensation of liquid pulsing down his leg. The dog, enjoying the sport, released its bite as the others continued to circle him.

He had briefly watched the dogs fight the bull at the fair a few days before. Fight wasn't the right word. For the chained bull had little chance of victory. The dogs didn't go for a quick kill as if they were aware that they had to prolong the 'sport.' Desperate thoughts came to him. This was how he would die; alone, unshriven, and savaged by the teeth of these killer dogs. From the corner of his eye, he caught sight of another mastiff leaping towards him. It was the Ca de Bou, the wolf killer. He tensed, screwed his face, and waited for the pain that would follow as it sank its massive teeth into his flesh.

Simon had turned his face away from the charging dog. When the force of the hound striking him at speed and the subsequent pain didn't come, he was at a loss to understand why.

Slowly, he rolled over, peeking towards where the mastiff had been. The Ca de Bou was still there, but instead of sinking its teeth into his leg, it was sitting down on the earth, panting. Puzzled, he rolled the other way and saw, to his amazement, the two other dogs also seated and standing next to them was the figure of a woman dressed in white holding out a candle lantern in front of her.

His first instinct was to flinch; the priestess had returned after all to witness the dogs finishing him off. It took but a few seconds before he recognised the face silhouetted in the light; it was Isabelle de Brun.

Her face was impassive, but Simon's wasn't.

"So, you have come to watch me die? Are you to be the witness for the Daughters of the Shadows? I always thought I couldn't trust you!" The anger in his words was apparent.

"You may well be a good King's sergent-at-law, Master Lowys, but you make a right poor Royal Intelligencer."

Confusing thoughts were flying around Simon's head. Then he turned his thoughts to the killer mastiffs sitting quietly beside her.

"The dogs?... What magic is this? How have you... what has happened to...?"

Ignoring his words, Isabelle de Brun approached the bound and helpless royal nuncio. She swiftly drew a small but deadly dagger from inside her white cloak.

Simon flinched, sure that she meant to slit his throat to allow the dogs to feast on his dying corpse as the life ebbed from him. She stood before him, dagger pointing at his face. She slowly bent. Involuntarily, Simon closed his eyes; his heart raced. He felt the tug as the sharp blade sliced through the hempen rope binding his hands, then the bonds that bound his feet were slit, and he was free.

Free he might have been, but he felt the danger still.

"What game is this? Am I to be chased down like sport by these dogs?"

"Fie, Master Lowys. Do you not recognise a saviour when you meet one?"

"A saviour? You? You are an accursed witch, a member of that damnable coven, the Daughters of the Shadows! I watched you... In the pentangle. In the ceremony in the woods."

One of the mastiffs, the large Ca de Bou, stood, tensed and growled fiercely. Isabelle gave a sharp hiss, raised her arm and gently lowered it in a curving motion. The Ca de Bou stopped its growl and lay down as if mesmerised. The effect was to make Simon even more terrified and wary.

"What kind of sorcery is this? By what magic do you control those beasts?"

"Ah, Master Lowys. It is not sorcery; it is but a particular skill I possess with hounds." With that, she raised her arm once more, gave a low whistle, and the two remaining bulldogs lay down, their heads on paws.

"And to answer your question as to whether I am witch or saviour? What you see with your eyes and what you know are not always the same."

Just as in their meeting at the Wheatsheaf Inn, Simon found her reply enigmatic.

"I will explain all, but first, we needs must get you out of here and to the safety of Mistress Heacham's house."

At her mention of Matilda Heacham's name, alarm and confusion swept over Simon, and it must have shown in his face. How did she know? And then he groaned; the Daughters of the Shadows knew about Mistress Heacham's house in Sopwellstrete. They knew! Then, in a moment of clarity, he returned to his original, never framed questions.

"How did you know I was here? You came with the Priestess. What game are you playing?"

"No game, Master Lowys. And we must be away now. I will explain all, but we needs must get away from here."

Uncertain and unsatisfied, Simon remained where he was as he fell silent, tension building up inside him. She began to get frustrated by his inaction.

"Look, you can come now with me to safety or perhaps you'd prefer the company of these killing dogs and end your days here?" Still, he didn't move.

"Jesu knows, you've blundered around enough these past months, but even so, I doubt John of Berwick wishes to lose your services."

Simon blinked, his eyes now wide, his mouth agape. How did this woman know this? It was worse than he could have imagined. These Daughters of the Shadows had penetrated the King's intelligence operation.

CHAPTER 40

The Bull Ring, St Albans, June 1276

"Master Lowys, we must be gone. I did not save you in St Michael's graveyard these weeks past for you to end up dead here. Now let us be away."

"You? You were the one who killed Maud Blount and the big man? Why...? How...?" Now his thinking was more muddled than ever. He got to his feet and moved tentatively towards Isabelle. The dogs, as one, began low growl. Once again, she hissed, gestured with her hand, and the dogs stopped and lay back down.

But Simon's train of thought was stuck in St Michael's Churchyard. "You killed them; Maud and her riffler, and you saved me. How did you know I would be there?"

She ignored his question. "Come quickly; we must move down the back lanes and alleys to get to Sopwellstrete without the watch seeing us."

He followed her out of the bull ring and down a maze of small lanes and alleyways. They heard the Abbey church bells ring for Lauds as they arrived at the back gate of Matilda Heacham's house in the southeast part of St Albans. Mistress Heacham had already risen and was in her kitchen baking bread. If she was surprised at their arrival, she did not show it.

"Master Lowys, it is good to see you, sir, even at this hour. And you Mistress...?" There was a long awkward pause.

Isabelle looked upon the older woman. "De Brun. Mistress Isabelle de Brun, of this town, Berkhamstede and Barnet."

A faint, knowing look came to Matilda Heacham's face. She stared at the other woman, garbed in a white cloak, standing in her small kitchen.

"Isabelle de Brun." Matilda Heacham spoke the name slowly. "Le Reynard, it is a pleasure to meet with you finally."

Simon looked from Matilda Heacham to Isabelle and back again, puzzlement etched across his face.

"Le Reynard? Le Reynard is one of John of Berwick's intelligencers!" he said. Confusion scrambled his thoughts. "You cannot be le Reynard! No, you cannot be! You are a woman."

Simon turned to Mistress Heacham. "What do you mean? How do you know of le Reynard?"

Then he remembered the previous night and the witches' ceremony in the woods. Accusingly, he turned to Isabelle.

"You are not le Reynard! You are a member of that vile coven, the Daughters of the Shadows!"

Isabelle pushed back a stray lock of red hair. "Do sit, master Lowys, before you fall from your wounds and between us, Mistress Heacham, and I will explain all to you."

Simon did as he was bid and sat on a wooden bench by the fire. Matilda Heacham finished putting her loaves into her bread oven. Then, she disappeared into a cupboard and emerged with some linen and small pots containing wound salve. She laid them down on the bench next to Simon, and then both women positioned themselves opposite him.

It was Isabelle de Brun who spoke. "Master Lowys, do you recall I told you what you see and what you know is not always the same? Well..." she gave a long pause as if to collect her thoughts. "Aye, you have the right of it. I am a member of the Daughters of the Shadows; you saw me initiated this night past. But I am firstly an agent of the Crown, a secret intelligencer for John of Berwick. He calls me le Reynard; I think it is his humour for my red hair. I was to get near to the coven of witches and discover what they planned. I used the inns at St Albans and Berkhamstede as a base, and I got close to the women we believed were members of the Daughters. After a time, they introduced me to the High Priestess, Alice le Blunde. It was she who locked you in the bullring earlier tonight."

Simon went to hold up a hand as if to interrupt her. He grimaced from the discomfort of Matilda treating his bite wound and spoke as if to take his mind off the pain

"If what you say is true, then why did John of Berwick not tell me of you? And when I sent a despatch to the Chancery to Sir Guy Ferre, his reply said nought of an intelligencer linked to this coven."

Matilda Heacham worked skilfully cleaning the bite wound, salving it with a soothing potion and laying strips of linen dressing across it. When she had finished, she looked up at Simon, gave a slight nod and turned to listen to Isabelle.

Isabelle smiled. "Mayhaps Ferre did not know of me. Mayhaps John of Berwick had not told him. Remember that not all in the Chancery can be trusted. I believe that the Daughters of the Shadows have someone inside the Chancery who passes knowledge to them, and I relayed this to John of Berwick."

Alarm crossed Simon's face. "At the bull ring, there will be no body ravaged by dogs. Alice le Blunde will soon find out and know that I live."

"Nay, she will not. Already, word of a man's corpse badly mauled by vicious hounds is spreading in the town. The constable has been well-paid to spread the rumour, and the corpse will be so badly mutilated to make identification possible. The authorities are most compliant in providing a body of a pauper these days past."

Simon gave a long sigh of relief. He looked across at Matilda Heacham, busy arranging her salves and potions in a basket. "And you, Mistress Heacham, how is it that you are aware of Isabelle de Brun and le Reynard? You are but a simple housekeeper who gives me help and assistance when required."

"Ah, my dear Master Lowys," Matilda Heacham patted Simon's arm. "My simple cote hides many duties that you are unaware of, and so it needs to be. I serve you when you are here, but I have long served John of Berwick and his intelligencers. Many times, I have passed on messages to le Reynard these years past. But you have the right of it. I, too, always assumed that le Reynard was a man.... I am glad she is not."

Simon sat puzzled and flanked by these two women. Isabelle broke the silence.

"I was pursuing the intentions of the Daughters of the Shadows in secret when you came to my inn. You did well to trace me, but I could not have you blundering through my investigations."

"Blundering." Simon was indignant. "I was not at all blundering! I was following instructions."

Isabelle's face showed regret at her choice of words. "Aye, perhaps not blundering. I am sorry for that word. But now, John of Berwick has sent me a despatch instructing me to bring you into my investigation."

Simon eyed her quizzically. Events were moving fast, and he was struggling to keep up.

Mistress Heacham took that moment to go for ale and check on her loaves in the oven. Simon looked at the woman now sitting opposite him.

"And what should I call you? Are you Isabella la Rus or Isabelle de Brun?"

"Aye." She laughed. "I am those and many others too. But these many months past, I have used the married name, Isabelle de Brun."

He once again found her laugh captivating, reminding him of their meeting in the Wheatsheaf. He stared at her, once more taking in her beauty. Her dark eyes drew him in, boring deep into his soul. The soft pale skin and delicate features suggested vulnerability. But the woman before him was far from vulnerable; she possessed hidden strength and abilities that belied her sex.

"How did you know I was in St Michael's churchyard?" The question had again leapt into Simon's head, and he had uttered the words without thinking.

"Master Lowys," again the smile came to her face. "You were trailing Maud Blount throughout the day and again after curfew. You even used Mistress Heacham here and that young maid previously. But, unbeknownst to you, Maud knew you had arrived in the town. While you followed her, she had her people track you."

"Nay, that cannot be. I was always careful to ensure none followed me."

Isabelle's expression made it clear he was wrong. She continued with her explanation.

"That night, when she slipped out of the town to go to the old ruins, and you followed her. I tracked both of you. It is no fault of yours that you fell into her trap. I had always planned to have Maud taken into custody and have her interrogated by John of Berwick's people at the Tower. But once she took you, I had little choice, for she would have you dead. Just as Alice le Blunde wished you dead earlier this night."

Simon's mind was reliving the events of that early morning.

"I feared you were there in the churchyard to kill me. When you came towards me with your knife, I thought I was about to die. Why did you not tell all to me then?"

"You did not need to know then, and I choose to operate alone. But my instructions have changed. We now needs must work together."

Matilda Heacham returned with freshly baked loaves, butter from the market, honey from the hive in her garden and recently brewed ale, and they broke their fast. As they ate, Isabelle explained the despatch she had received from John of Berwick.

"One of the King's Intelligencers on the continent has sent news that Guy de Montfort in person has sought the services of an assassin they call Benuic. You, Master Lowys, discovered that the traitor, de Baskerville, was in England."

Simon put down his jug of ale. "Aye. He was with the knight, de Chenduit, when I went to Langlei on the Queen's business."

"De Baskerville is Guy de Montfort's liegeman. Now, this is where I think things start to connect." Isabelle took a delicate sip of the ale.

"This is a fine brew Mistress Heacham. The full fare is excellent."

Matilda Heacham nodded a thanks at the compliment as Isabelle continued to outline her thinking.

"I was tasked with pursuing the Daughters of the Shadows. Their High Priestess, Alice le Blunde, you had her acquaintance earlier this night, Master Lowys has the link to de Montfort. She was his nurse and tutrice for all his childhood." She paused for a moment, reflecting on a thought that had occurred to her.

"Aye," said Simon. "Thomas of Ashberne at Hailes Abbey did say the same to me."

"But there is more to this. Alice was the mistress of the elder de Montfort, the traitor slain at Evesham. There is a connection there. I know from what Alice has said that her hatred for His Grace the King burns deep. She seeks vengeance for what happened to Simon de Montfort. We know that the son, Guy de Montfort harbours the same thought."

"Aye," Simon interjected. "So, we have Alice le Blunde and Guy de Montfort, both of whom harbour vengeance against King Edward."

Isabelle picked up her train of thought again. "And, de Montfort's man, Walter de Baskerville, is here in England, and we have knowledge that Guy de Montfort himself seeks the services of an assassin. If I put that together, I would suspect that de Montfort has hired the assassin to do harm to His Grace the King."

"But we do not know that for sure."Simon remained sceptical. "Is this one plot, or is it separate plots against His Grace, one by de Montfort and another by Alice le Blunde and the Daughters of the Shadows?"

"I suspect that de Baskerville is the intermediary between de Montfort and Alice le Blunde, but both are working towards the same outcome... to hurt His Grace, the King."

CHAPTER 41

The Townhouse of Matilda Heacham, Sopwellstrete, St Albans, June 1276

Isabelle de Brun was a woman with commanding detail. "These past months, I have discovered much about the Daughters of the Shadows." She spoke without emotion and in a tone of authority. "I understand that part of your remit from John of Berwick was to investigate the murders that occurred at Fulelane, months since?"

Again, Simon was taken aback by her knowledge of things secret.

"Aye. Mistress, how do you know this?" Then he remembered. "Of course, You were there, in that house when it happened? Master Berwick led me to believe that few knew of the reasons behind these murders."

"Aye, you have the right of it, Master Lowys. I was there. Yet, I only discovered what had truly occurred much later. I had been working on getting close by the Daughters of the Shadows. And, by then, they had admitted me into their coven as a novice. I was in the house of Alice le Blunde that night when the men were slain. I was to meet with another of John of Berwick's agents, le Stedeman."

A look of puzzlement resonated on Simon's face. She was to meet with le Stedeman, the agent of the Crown. For what reason? Isabelle gave him his answer.

"Roger le Stedeman was with a known riffler that night, a man by the name of Pelliors. Pelliors was a thief, a very good one apparently, who hailed from Gloucester. He had a reputation for picking the most devilish of locks. To draw out the Daughters of the Shadows, le Stedeman had devised a plan to break into the new shrine at Hailes Abbey and steal the vial of the Holy Blood of Jesus."

"I heard about an attempted theft when I was there", Simon interjected, "but Abbot Jordan assured me nothing had been stolen."

The inscrutable expression returned to Isabelle's face. "Well, It all depends on how you interpret, 'nothing had been stolen.' Father Abbot was correct and," she gave a long pause, "and not correct in his assessment." Isabelle straightened in her seat, pursed her lips and began her explanation of this riddle.

"John of Berwick came up with the idea, but the execution of the plan was always le Stedeman's, and it was a good one. The is no more wondrous a relic in the whole of Christendom than the Holy Blood. He planned to steal it from Hailes Abbey and then put out the word in the London taverns that it was available to the highest bidder. He planned that it would draw out the Daughters of the Shadows and reveal to us their leader."

"But it wasn't stolen! I know that." Simon grasp of the situation was no clearer. "The Abbot was sure that the attempted break-in had failed."

"Ah, therein lies the complexity of le Stedeman's plan. He hired Pelliors, who they called Picklock, on the streets of Gloucester. Pelliors broke into the temporary shrine one night and stole the vial of the Holy Blood, substituting it with one le Stedeman had given him."

"So, the Abbot was wrong. It was stolen."

"Nay, he was correct. The real vial was never stolen; it never left Hailes Abbey. Le Stedeman had substituted it beforehand with a second, false one, which was what Pelliors stole. Le Stedeman then had the Sacrist replace that one with the original."

Isabelle reached forward and picked up her beaker of ale, taking a sip before continuing.

"The word was put out across the less reputable taverns in the city of London that a vial of the blood of Jesus was for sale to the highest bidder. Such a relic would always interest a coven such as the Daughters of the Shadows because of what it represented. There could be no more powerful relic for sacrilegious rituals. So, John of Berwick was confident that the High Priestess of the Daughters would wish to possess it."

Simon suddenly grasped why Pelliors had been at Fulelane that night.

"Pelliors was with le Stedeman at Fulelane that night to add legitimacy to the story. He genuinely believed that he had stolen the original."

Isabelle bit her lip and focused her gaze on Simon. "Aye. You have the right of it. It was Pelliors who put out the word in many of the taverns, and it took some days before contact was made."

"Mistress le Brun." It was Matilda Heacham who interjected. "How did Master le Stedeman know that he could trust Pelliors?"

"He didn't trust him. Would you? A notorious street picklock. So, le Stedeman had Pellior's mother, wife, and two children held in a house in Gloucester. When his work was complete, they would be released, and he was to receive £20 and a royal pardon."

While Isabelle continued with her explanation, Simon stood and flexed his wounded leg, which still throbbed and was starting to stiffen up.

"There was a number interested in acquiring the vial of the Holy Blood, including a senior Lord and cousin of the King. But such enquiries were ignored. Le Stedeman had to be sure that it was the Daughters of the Shadows who were making contact. That was when my master, John of Berwick, first instructed me to become involved."

As she spoke, Isabelle's thoughts returned to that early winter's night in London when she stayed at Fulelane with her sisters in the coven of witches.

As she spoke, Isabelle's thoughts returned to that early winter's night in London when le Stedeman and Pelliors were slain. She knew le Stedman was a highly effective intelligencer and one who would not normally put himself in danger. How had he got himself into that situation? Why the house in Fulelane and why were they slain in such a public manner?

CHAPTER 42

Lamb Inn, City of London, November 1275

The chilled stillness of the early evening broke the moment Roger le Stedeman entered the rowdiness of the Lamb Inn. The atmosphere inside the taproom was heady. Acrid wood smoke hung high towards the ceiling, with most of the clientele oblivious to the fumes. The rank smell of sweat and excrement-ingrained clothing merged with the ever-present odour of stale ale and rancid floor rushes. Indistinct shouting emanated from every corner, broken by the occasional shriek from one of the local whores, as a potential customer tried to sample the wares without first laying down his coin.

Pelliors was already here, seated at a corner bench, gripping a jug of ale as if it were about to be snatched from his grasp. Beside him sat an older man, dressed in clothes that had once been fine but now appeared shabby and threadbare. His ferret-like face scanned the room, eyes nervously darting left and right as if he expected trouble.

Le Stedeman moved through the taproom and slipped onto the bench beside Pelliors. He held up an arm, gesturing to one of the serving maids to bring more ale.

"God give you good day, sirs," le Stedeman addressed both men, laying down two silver pennies on the table, as the maid appeared with three fresh jugs of ale.

"Let us to business," le Stedeman began. "Master Pelliors here, and I would meet with your buyer this night. And then we can get this business completed."

The ferrety-looking man continued to fidget in his seat. His head began to nod as he spoke.

"I have been instructed to give you the details of the meeting. You have the goods with you, I presume?"

"Fear not! I will have," le Stedeman snapped.

"In the hour after Vespers, you must away to a house of Alice le Blunde, in Fulelane. It lies close by St Olave towards the Tower. Where Fulelane bends away from the Tower, seek out the large house with glass in its windows. It lies alone on the west side opposite the Lorteburn ditch."

Roger le Stedeman lifted the jug of ale to his lips and drained the contents. He thought it was surprisingly good for such a rough part of the city. He stood and looked at the ferrety-man.

"Are you to accompany us?"

"Nay, my task is done now. I am but the messenger. You will conclude your business with Mistress le Blunde. I must away."

"As will we be." Le Stedman beckoned Pelliors, and both moved towards the door, avoiding those too deep in their cups and the ale-laden serving maids weaving their way through the now crowded taproom.

As they stepped out onto the street, both men pulled their cotes tight in against a chill November wind that had blown up. A thought nagged at le Stedeman, but he struggled to formulate his thinking. The ferrety-man, the intermediary, had confirmed the name of Alice le Blunde to him. Why had he done that? Had the ferrety-man made an error? He hadn't known that le Stedeman already knew of Alice le Blunde. Was it a concern? Probably not; after all, he needed to know where to go this night. The ferrety-man had confirmed what le Stedeman's own man, Drago Bettincourt, had already found out about Alice and the house in Fulelane. No, he thought, there was probably was no need for him to worry. He congratulated himself. All was coming together nicely.

Wriggling his toes as he walked had made little difference against the bitter chill of the evening; Roger le Stedeman's feet felt like ice despite his leather boots. Alongside him, Henry Pelliors was blowing into his hands against the cold. Both men had drawn their cotes in as tight as they could and pulled their cloaks close across them.

Both men were wary. These streets were dangerous after dark; only the dim light from burning sconces from local churches illuminated their way. As they walked, their breath was illuminated by the chill. The silence of the late evening highlighted their senses, hearing every footstep, scurry and clatter of shutters as a potential threat. Fingers toyed with the handles of their daggers for reassurance against what might be.

Fulelane was a narrow path that snaked its way up towards Aldegatestrete. At its entrance on Olafstrete, it was flanked by prominent, two-storied merchants houses, a choice site, just a few hundred yards from the river wharves. Further up, the lane opened up with just a few dwellings that backed onto the churchyard of All Hallows de Staningcherche and the open sewer of the Lorteburn ditch.

As the ferrety-man in the Lamb Inn had indicated, after one hundred yards, it turned sharply to the right, and on the corner were three houses separated by narrow runnels. A sconce burned in the glassed window of the middle one, throwing dancing shadows out onto the street. It appeared a large property, extending back towards the boundary wall of All Hallows. Inside, all seemed quiet, with some of the windows heavily draped to keep out the cold air.

Pelliors, despite the cold, appeared buoyant. Le Stedeman was more cautious, always his natural instinct. He had been uneasy since they had left the Lamb Inn, although he could not put his finger on why that should be. He glanced behind him to ensure they were alone; he saw no one, but experience had taught him that seeing nothing didn't mean that there was no one there. He turned to Pelliors.

"Let's get this finished." He raised his gloved fist and rapped hard on the solid oak door of the house of Alice le Blunde.

CHAPTER 43

Fulelane, City of London, November 1275

The dim light from the tallow candles dwindled as night drew in. Five women sat in a circle in the back room of Alice le Blunde's house in Fulelane. Their time embroidering this day would soon be finished. Most, though not all, of the women were widows of a certain age, approaching their fortieth year. Margery de Pyritton, petite, with weather-worn hands from years of labour, was the oldest. Beside her sat Agnes and Maud, women similar in looks and stature. Both were recent widows after more than two decades of marriage. In truth, Agnes de Bilda was not legally a widow, for she had never actually made marriage vows with her husband. However, they had lived together as man and wife all that time. Their union ended when Agnes poisoned him. The local reeve and her husband's family never suspected he had been murdered.

Isabella la Rus was the youngest and newest member of the group seated in Alice le Blunde's downstairs room. She had passed her thirtieth and third year. She was introduced to Alice and the other women by Notekina de Hoggenhore, who frequented the inn Isabella had inherited from her late husband. Notekina did not consider herself to be what the law defined her, 'a common whore.' She was quite an uncommon whore, practised in the ways of pleasure for payment. She only went with the wealthier sort, the older merchants who were tired of their wives, or more likely whose wives had tired of them, and prosperous knights of the shires. Notekina de Hoggenhore was no Friday-night tup. A man had to lay down good coin for her services. Notekina had progressed from earning a living from the Wheatsheaf in St Albans to Alice le Blunde's house nearby the Tower. Here she met more discerning and more prosperous customers. She had found Isabella friendly, engaging and helpful, not that Isabella was a whore. Perhaps she had been once, but not now. Isabella was precisely the sort of woman Alice le Blunde sought, and so Notekina had made the introduction.

Somewhere upstairs, Dulcia, Alice's daughter, was working. Notekina had seen her client enter. He appeared well-dressed in bright hose and a cote that strained against his belly. Likely, a merchant, probably foreign, Notekina, had thought, and one not to last too long. She had not seen him leave but had glimpsed another man with her. Older, grey flecks in both hair and beard with weather-worn features and the look of fighting man, not the usual type for the house of Alice le Blunde. But Dulcia had pushed the door closed, and that was the last she saw of him.

As their needles moved dextrously across their embroidery, the women conversed with each other and, as a collective. Their common purpose extended to more than the threads and bone needles in front of them; all five of them, six if Dulcia was included, were members of the coven of witches known as the Daughters of the Shadows.

It took some time for Isabella la Rus to gain acceptance as a coven member. She had yet to be initiated but was, nonetheless treated as if she had been. These women were now her sisters; Alice le Blunde was their leader and high priestess.

John of Berwick had passed news to Isabella of the liaison with his man planned for later. Isabella did not know who she would meet and precisely how they would contact, but Berwick's men were resourceful.

The women were to sleep here overnight. A carriage would take them to another of Alice's properties close to St Albans in the morning.

The bells of All Hallows had already rung the peals for the hour before curfew when Isabella and the others heard a loud rap on the front door.

"Customers come late and in their cups most like," Agnes offered. Muffled words came from the door area, first the voice of a woman, Alice's maid, and then men's voices. Two, perhaps three, Isabella thought. Raised voices, threatening voices and the sound of a scuffle followed by silence.

All of the women, bar Isabella, reacted as if this was nothing to do with them. They left through the rear door and made their way up to the Solar where cots had lay ready with bedding and pillows. Isabella, her interest piqued, listened intently whilst making her way to the solar with the others. She had planned to make contact with Berwick's man when she went for her jakes; that would be a plausible reason for having to go outside on such a night.

But Isabella heard nothing, no more raised voices or arguments. She settled into her bed, keenly listening for further clues as to what was happening, but all she heard was the funnelling of the wind.

CHAPTER 44

Fulelane, London, November 1275

The front door of Alice le Blunde's house opened. The light inside thrown from tallow candles contrasted with the darkness of the street. A young servant girl greeted Roger le Stedeman and Henry Pelliors and enquired about their business.

"I seek Mistress le Blunde." Le Stedeman gave his name as Roger de Vescy. He was direct, but he looked beyond the maid into the front chamber to seek a sense that might calm his feeling of unease.

"I will tell the Mistress that you are here, Master de Vescy." She left the door ajar and went into a side room. She reappeared in moments and invited le Stedeman and Pelliors inside and into a large chamber before withdrawing. From the corner of his eye, as he waited, le Stedeman caught a rustle from a long drape covering a door to his left. Immediately his senses were on alert.

But despite his swift reaction, events overtook him. Before he could draw his dagger from behind the drape, a longsword emerged, point aimed at his chest. Its owner appeared, his face sneering as he began a tirade of expletives in French.

"By Gods eyes, we've been duped, Mistress. This piece of shit is a King's intelligencer. His name isn't de Vescy; it is le Stedeman."

The sword still pointed at le Stedeman's throat; the man turned to Pelliors.

"Did you know? Did you know he was a King's Man? And you brought him here?"

A frightened Pelliors shook his head. He hadn't expected this; his trade was picking locks and theft, not violence.

"I had no idea." Pelliors was babbling his mind whirring. The man holding the sword exuded menace. Pelliors was scared. His plan with Alice le Blunde had been to bring le Stedeman here, take the holy relic from him and then....? Probably le Stedeman would be killed but not by me, Pelliors thought. He would be long gone by then.

Pelliors watched warily as the sword at le Stedman's throat twitched and the man holding it gave a short nod towards Alice le Blunde. She moved forward, running her hands under le Stedeman's cloak, withdrawing his dagger. She deftly slit the chord on his belt, which held his silk purse containing the holy relic.

Pelliors was agitated, wondering how he would extricate himself from this situation. He looked across at le Stedeman and saw no fear in the man's eyes just what seemed an expression of hatred.

Roger le Stedeman's eyes burned in on the weather-worn face from his past, the face of Walter de Baskerville. His sense of unease had been palpable, but he wondered how he would extricate himself from this?

"So, a traitor makes common purpose with witches now de Baskerville?" Le Stedeman's eyes darted around the room, his brain moving fast, seeking a way out.

"Well, le Stedeman, why not? We're both excommunicant's."

"Who is he?" There was urgency in Alice le Blunde's voice. "You know him of old?"

"Aye, we have crossed paths before. He is King's Man, who works as an intelligencer. He chased me for months after Viterbo. That he is here means they are onto us. They know something."

"Nay they cannot!" Alarm sounded in Alice's tone. "Does it mean that this relic is false?"

Walter de Baskerville pushed the tip of his sword hard against le Stedeman's throat.

"Well? Is this a game? Are you playing us false?"

De Baskerville's gaze turned to Pelliors, though the tip of his sword remained hard against Roger's throat.

"Is he playing us false? Is this the relic?"

Henry Pelliors gabbled. "I think so. It looks the same. I made a mark on its base when I took it." He pointed at the small silk purse Alice now held in her hand.

Alice took the vial from the silk purse and carefully examined the base. She showed it to Pelliors.

"Is this it? This mark here?"

"Aye, that is the mark I scratched onto it at Hailes Abbey."

Alice sighed. "So, all is good, we can..."

"Nay!" De Baskerville interrupted loudly. "This is not right. Why would a King's agent come here to trade the true vial of the Holy Blood? It makes no sense." He pushed the tip of his sword into le Stedeman's neck, drawing blood.

"It makes no sense, does it, le Stedeman? You would not be here with the true relic. You play a game here, but you will lose." Walter's free hand went down to a pocket in his cote, and he pulled out some hempen chord, which he tossed to Pelliors.

"Bind his hands... Tightly." He looked towards the other person in the room, Dulcia, Alice's daughter, who, up to now, had been an observer. "Fetch Bertrand; he will be in the alley at the rear."

Roger stared at the face at the end of the sword. It was well known to him. After the assassination of Henry of Almain, His Grace the Lord Edward had despatched le Stedeman to Lombardy to track the whereabouts of Guy de Montfort. Where de Montfort went, so too did de Baskerville. He had come face-to-face with the mercenary captain on several occasions and avoided attempts on his own life by de Baskerville. And now he was here. Le Stedeman had not expected it.

With shaking hands, Pelliors did as Walter instructed, binding le Stedeman's hands tight behind his back.

Across from Pelliors he saw Alice le Blunde look hard at de Baskerville. She seemed agitated as if things were not happening as she had planned. It seemed as if it was the ageing mercenary who had taken control.

"What now?" Alice demanded.

Alice le Blunde looked hard at de Baskerville. Alice had got what she had sought, the vial of the Holy Blood. Or perhaps not. She watched intently as De Baskerville's henchman Bertrand, entered the room from the rear, closely followed by Dulcia.

"Now," de Baskerville's tone was measured, "le Stedeman here and me are leaving." His eyes met Bertrand's. No words were exchanged, but the swarthy Frenchman moved swiftly behind the bound le Stedeman, holding tight to his arms. Walter sheathed his sword.

Bertrand du Guesclin, stiletto firmly pricked at the space between Roger's shoulder blades, pushed him towards the rear door.

"You come too," de Baskerville instructed a frightened Pelliors, who seemed wide-eyed and shocked. Moving with purpose, de Baskerville led the others to the rear door and out into the chill of the night.

CHAPTER 45

Shitebrook Alley, Fulelane, London, November 1275.

The cold November wind had abated a little allowing the first showings of a frost to lie on the ground. As Bertrand steered le Stedeman out of the rear of Alice's house and into the small vegetable garden, Roger's mind raced as to how he would extricate himself. Beyond the garden lay an alley, filthy with dung and everyday detritus that locals called Shitebrook Alley. A communal midden heap lay to one side, heat rising even in the coldness of an early winter's night.

"Stop!" de Baskerville's guttural command in French broke the stillness. The mercenary now had his own dagger drawn as Roger realised that the sharp pain of Bertrand's stiletto was no longer between his shoulders.

In the darkness, le Stedeman found it hard to make out the features of the traitor de Baskerville, now standing just feet from him.

"Tell me why you are here, le Stedeman, and what game it is you play?"

"I am here on the business of the Crown, and I walk into a nest of traitors." Even as he said the words, Roger realised that he was just provoking the mercenary. Still, he also recognised the futility of his situation.

"What do you know?"

Le Stedeman ignored the question. Better to say nothing, for he was resigned to death. He knew that a man such as de Baskerville would not let him live.

"What do you know?" This time the dagger ripped at his cheek, drawing rivulets of blood.

Roger listened to the stillness around him. No birds sang at this hour. The beginning frost created cracking noises on the ground.

He heard movement behind him, where Bertrand, the henchman, had been. In one quick action, a thin chord was thrown over his head. Without noise, it was pulled tight around his throat.

Le Stedeman struggled to take a breath; the tightness around his throat increased. He wrestled in vain against the pressure, a knee in his back holding him firm. He sensed and heard gargling noises, his mind became distant as his own as his life seeped away and then darkness.

Bertrand du Guesclin unloosed his French Chord from around the neck of the lifeless le Stedeman and pushed the body onto the steaming midden. Not that anyone could see in this darkness, but a broad grin broke across his face. The garotte was always his preferred method of taking a life; swift and silent and easily concealed. He had enjoyed that.

"You did well, friend," de Baskerville said, addressing Henry Pelliors in the darkness. "Here, this is what you were promised," tossing a purse of coin in his direction. The heavy purse fell to the rapidly freezing earth, the coins clinking together as it landed.

In the gloom of the cold night, Henry Pelliors had watched le Stedeman die. He had stood open-mouthed as he made out what was happening in front of him. Le Stedeman had already paid him for his work, and he stood to gain from this night's labour. Still, the temptation of seeking payment from the other side as well by swindling and crossing le Stedeman had been too tempting. But he had not expected this. Picking locks was his trade, not murder. He had to get out of here and back home to Gloucester as quickly as he could.

Pelliors reached down, his fingers grabbing the purse that had been tossed onto the frozen ground. "I thank you, sir..." His words were cut short by something slipped around his neck, being drawn tight to suck his breath from his body. Pelliors struggled, gasping for air, his mouth open, trying to draw in the breath that would save his life. He dropped the purse as he brought his hands to his neck to fight the garotte. His eyes bulged and then closed. On the cusp of life and death, his mind grasped what was happening to him. He had been a fool; he betrayed le Stedeman, and now these people too had betrayed him. Then came the thought of how easy it would be not to struggle any more. His mouth gave out no more sound, and blackness swept over him.

Bertrand unslipped his garotte and thrust the limp corpse of Henry Pelliors onto the midden where it half-fell on top of le Stedeman. Unable to make him out clearly, Walter de Baskerville spoke at the dark shadow of his henchman. Knowing that Bertrand took great pleasure in killing, which was why he was so valuable. "Take the purse from him, my friend. It's yours."

Bertrand picked up the purse, heavy with coin and stowed it in a pocket. His master was right, he did enjoy taking a life, and he was pretty skilled at it. He knew it would condemn his soul to eternal damnation, but it was far too late now to seek repentance. Perhaps after the first time, all those years past, in Rennes. She had been a comely maid of fifteen years, and the violence he used on her gave him great pleasure. Maybe he could have sought absolution then, but now, well, it was far too late, and he enjoyed the killing far too much.

CHAPTER 46

House of Alice le Blunde, Fulelane, London November 1275

The night was getting colder, and the frost was beginning to penetrate as the two mercenaries left the alley to return to the warmth of Alice's house. Upstairs, Isabella la Rus peered out of a window, trying to discover what was occurring. But in the gloom of the night, she could see little.

"I am out to make my jakes," she said to Margery, lying half-asleep on the bed next to her. Isabella took a small rush light from a table and slipped out of the room; on the small landing, she heard the approach of two men laughing and conversing in French as they came through the rear door. She pushed herself against the limewashed wall, shrouding the rush light with her cupped hand, holding her breath, hoping not to be seen.

As the conversation faded, she judged the men had gone into the front room of the house. Isabella made her way down the rear stairs before she stepped out into the night; behind her, the front door slammed shut.

Isabella threaded her way through the narrow vegetable garden towards the alley behind. The simple rush light threw little illumination onto the cold November earth. Taking time to accustom her eyes to the dark, she looked around to see if John of Berwick's man was here for the planned liaison. She neither sensed nor saw movement.

In the alley, Isabella could hear the scurry of rodents, their eyes occasionally reflecting from the thin rushlight. Then she picked up a strong metallic smell, like iron in a forge and very strong. In moments the reason became apparent. The rushlight silhouetted two corpses draped roughly across a heap she took to be a midden. By the flickering glow, she felt both necks for any sign of life. Both men were still warm; they had been killed recently. Her probing fingers discovered no pulse; instead, a sticky trickle on both, which she took to be blood. Her hands scanned down both bodies, and she found that the body that lay beneath had his hands bound. Strange!

Isabella's senses told her that one or both of these corpses were the men who she was to meet this night. Thoughts raced through her head. Why were they killed? Who knew these men were here?

Isabella's logical mind went into action. She had heard, but not observed, the two men coming into Alice's house via the rear door. They had been speaking French, but she knew that did not necessarily mean they were Frenchmen. All among the noble and knightly class spoke French, not English. The men she had heard coming inside were calm and jovial, in no sense agitated as if they had just committed two murders. Unless, of course, they were used to killing, men of violence. Then her thoughts went to the man with his hands bound behind him. He lay beneath the other corpse, which told her that he had been slain first and, judging by the blood around the throat, killed by a French Chord. The work of an assassin. The second man had been slain shortly afterwards. Why were his hands not bound, she wondered?

The rushlight was dimming, and Isabella had to act quickly. She judged that there was no purpose to be served in raising the hue and cry, leaving that to someone else. To do so would invite many awkward questions into the house of Alice le Blunde and may compromise her own situation. Isabella felt a pang of guilt at leaving the two men here on the dung heap, unshriven before God but hoped that within a few hours, they might be discovered.

Isabella retraced her steps towards the house with the intent to raise the other women to make them ready to leave at the first light. Hopefully, she thought, before the bodies were discovered and the questioning began. She was met at the rear door by Alice's maid, shaking and incoherent, in a highly agitated state.

"The mistress has left. She said that she had to leave urgently for her sisters in the north."

"Beatrice," Isabella's tone was measured and calm. "You needs must raise the others in the house and have them ready to leave in the morning. Do you understand?"

"Aye, Mistress, but why?"

"There has been an accident outside. Tell me, who was here earlier?"

"Do you mean, who visited mistress Dulcia this night?"

Beatrice, the maid, bit her lip and screwed her face as she thought. "Well, there was a well-dressed merchant; I let him in to see mistress Dulcia. He may have been a foreigner from his cote. I never did see him leave. And then..." She gave a long pause. "There was another. He came into the house from the rear. I never announced him to the mistress, but she knew him. He spoke to her in French, I think, and took him into the room at the front."

"Had you seen him before?"

"Nay, mistress. Never before."

"What did he look like?"

"He was not the sort we usually get here. He looked the rough sort, a hard man, with a battle scar on his cheek. I was afraid of the look of him. And then two others, they looked like merchants but not right-prosperous ones; they came later, but I never did see them leave neither."

No, you wouldn't have thought, Isabella. As she took in what Beatrice had said, a commotion occurred in the alley beyond the rear of the house. Voices shouted commands; raised tones told Isabella that the two bodies had been found.

"I thank you, Beatrice, now make ready the others. I fear we shall be getting a visit from the constable before long."

Outside, a cup-shotten apprentice had chosen the alley midden to relieve himself of the copious jugs of ale he had consumed in the tavern on Olafstrete. The sense of relief that showed on his face gave way to horror as halfway through his flow, his eyes fell upon the two corpses he was urinating upon.

His shout brought others to him, even at this late hour. The hue and cry were raised, and someone went to fetch the constable and the sheriff's men. Inside the house of Alice le Blunde, Isabella recognised that she needed to act both swiftly and deftly if she was not to be compromised in this situation.

CHAPTER 47

St Albans, Hertfordshire, June 1276

Alia Parys worked at Isabelle de Brun's ale house in St Albans, the Wheatsheaf, for many weeks. She had escaped the clutches of the bogus monk thanks to the intervention of the Kings nuncio, Master Lowys, for which she owed him an outstanding debt.

Originally, Matilda Heacham had asked Alia to be her companion and help her with her work. But Matilda had received a message from the Chancery. John of Berwick wanted Alia to go to work at the Wheatsheaf. There was no explanation as to why. but Matilda knew that the royal official had his reasons. So, on her first day, Matilda went with Alia to the inn and her new role. Alia was apprehensive, but Matilda sought to reassure her. If John of Berwick needed her to be here in this inn run by Isabelle de Brun, he had his reasons.

Alia found that her work at the Wheatsheaf was very similar to her job at the inn off Distaflane. It was work she was used to, and the customer's behaviour towards her, as an unmarried serving maid, did not differ from before. She had to endure insults, lewd comments and molesting behaviour from the drinkers. Isabelle had spoken with Alia that her comely looks were a curse in this trade. Alia spent her time serving, cleaning tables, exchanging banter and avoiding the wandering hands of customers too deep in their cups.

Her injuries at the hands of the bogus monk had cleared, and her soft heart-shaped face no longer bore scars. She still wore her dark flaxen hair plaited, falling down her back, and the younger men still sought to woo her.

Through Isabelle, Alia learned how to be strong and assertive towards the lecherous drunks who thought that the purchase of ale entitled them to grope her body. Alia grew from a girl to a woman in her short time at the Wheatsheaf.

She was keen to impress her new mistress and show that she was a good worker. Not that Isabelle de Brun was always at the inn. Alia noticed how she was frequently missing, coming and going without saying where she had been or what she had been doing. That piqued the young maid's curiosity. Her mistress was busy, yes, but it was irregular and often overnight or away for a few days. What sort of business would need her to keep such hours?

Isabelle apparently recognised that her new serving maid was taking an interest in her comings and goings. So, she invested time and trust in her. She entrusted Alia to perform private tasks on her behalf and Alia came to regard Isabelle with awe. She noticed daily the confidence of her mistress. Here was a woman who was not cowed by men, however important they were, or thought they were. Her words, her poise, her manner all impressed the younger woman.

At first, Isabelle asked simple tasks of Alia; deliver a message; leave a package in a designated place. Alia's ability to read and write and her knowledge of French allowed her to take on many administrative tasks that Isabelle clearly found mundane and too time-consuming. Over weeks, Isabelle entrusted her young protégé with more responsibility.

When they were out at Berkhamstede's market, Alia decided to ask Isabelle why.

"I am not kin to you, Mistress, and you owe me no debt as I owe to Master Lowys."

The older woman stopped her examination of a length of fine samonite and regarded the young maiden.

"I trust you with important tasks, Alia, because I see myself in you. You have been born a gentlewoman, but circumstance has dealt you a grievous blow. I can help correct that." Alia saw the seriousness in her mistress' face.

"Mine is a singular life. I do not mean I am lonely, but that what I do, needs must I do alone."

Alia could tell that her mistress did not expect her to grasp her meaning and Isabelle seemed taken aback at her reply.

"Your work is so much more than an inn owner Mistress that I have come to recognise."

Alia could see the surprise and alarm flashing in Isabelle's eyes.

"Fear not, Mistress." The younger woman reached out a reassuring hand. "I mean you no harm. It is just I have deduced that this work that you do is far removed from a widow running an inn."

Alia watched as Isabelle was stilled, apparently considering how best to craft a denial.

"This work that you do is similar to what Master Lowys does, am I right?"

That produced a derisory laugh. Isabelle once again regarded Alia. She placed a hand on her arm and studied her face.

"Can I truly trust you, Alia? I have known you but a short time, really, but I must place my trust in you. Swear to me that it is not ill-placed."

"On my life, you may trust me, Mistress. I will do for you whatsoever you ask of me."

"Alia, if the bond of trust I place in you now ever breaks, both our lives will be the price we pay."

CHAPTER 48

The Royal Chancery at Westminster, June 1276

The high windows of a work chamber on the upper floors of the Chancery filtered the golden rays of warm, early summer sunshine to fall onto a large oak desk. Seated at the desk, a man studied a written vellum despatch. His eyes scanned left and right, his head occasionally nodding and his lips pursing when he came across something that caused him displeasure.

After a long while, the vellum was rerolled and placed carefully to one side of the desk. Flint-hard eyes now stared at a second man standing before the desk.

"Now, Master Lowys," John of Berwick's familiar high-pitched, clipped voice broke the silence. "You appear to have been highly active." It didn't come across as a compliment. "And you succeeded in your task?"

"Aye, Master John, in most unusual circumstances. But I have to report that Walter de Baskerville is in the wind, and we have no sight of him."

"Ah yes, pity." Berwick leaned across his desk and retrieved and unfurled the vellum roll. His eyes scanned down the report. "And you managed to get yourself taken." He gave a long pause. "And attacked... by mastiffs?"

Berwick pronounced each syllable. His tone was both a touch reproachful and enquiring.

"I concede I have much to learn as an intelligencer. I was on the trail of the coven of witches, but they discovered me. Their priestess, Alice le Blunde, was the one who set the dogs upon me in the bull ring in St Albans."

"Ah, the Bull Ring," Simon could almost feel the censure in Berwick's words. "The hounds.... Pray tell me, were you badly savaged?"

"Nay, I suffered a bite to my leg and a blade wound to my shoulder. It throbs still and I limp, but rescue came before they could inflict further damage."

Berwick consulted the vellum despatch once more. "Rescued, you say?"

Simon was beginning to get vexed at the game John of Berwick was unfurling. "Aye, my rescuer is known to you, I believe?"

"Indeed." Berwick wouldn't be drawn further.

"Pray do tell me why you did not let me know when you despatched me on this task that you had another intelligencer working to a similar end?"

John of Berwick fixed Simon with a stare of his flint-hard eyes. "You did not need to be aware of that at the time."

"Had you trusted me enough to say so, then it would have saved much time and wasted effort." Simon was struggling to hide his anger.

John of Berwick stood standing to the full height that made him taller than most men. Looking down on Simon, his manner softened. "Have you seen the Palace gardens in Spring, Master Lowys? They are wonderful." The question threw the young nuncio. "Come, take a walk with me..."

Fresh lavender shoots draped onto the winding path of the Palace gardens as the two men strode, deep in conversation.

"So, You met le Reynard."

"Aye. It was she who called off the dogs by some magic trick. I had not expected your intelligencer to be a woman."

"The lady is a most remarkable intelligencer. Highly resourceful, and her sex hides her identity."

"I agree she is remarkable, but I cannot say that I truly know her."

"Indeed, not Master Lowys; few people do."

They strolled on, past rows of low bushes full of lush growth. Simon plucked up the courage to ask Berwick once again why the Royal Intelligencer had not taken him into his confidence.

"You traced Isabella la Rus from the coven to the ale house in St Albans. You went there and questioned her. By having a King's Man come to her inn and interrogate her, you added to the integrity of her story within the coven. It made the Daughters of the Shadows more welcoming of Isabella."

"But my lord, would it not also have the contrary effect, making them draw back from her lest she gave them away?"

"I think not. It showed her closer to them."

"I believed her to be a witch, a member of that damnable coven."

"And so, her disguise was effective. If a King's Man believes her to be a witch and a coven member, then she had done well to infiltrate so deeply."

Simon stopped and placed one hand on Berwick's arm. "Who is she really, Master John? Surely such work is not suited to a woman?"

Berwick, usually so stern and unbending in character, spoke softly. "What do you mean, Master Lowys; such a woman?"

"I mean exactly that. She is a woman of breeding. A learned woman. A widow, a rich one. Her words and manner are of the court. She is but still comely and well-suited to marriage."

"You have entirely the right of it, which is why she is such an effective intelligencer for me. Do not make the mistake of under-estimating Mistress la Rus."

"Does she not go by her widowed name now, Isabelle le Brun?"

Berwick made a thoughtful pause. "Ah yes... Mistress le Brun." He pronounced her name slowly. They continued their leisurely pace through the garden, Berwick probing Simon on the details of what he had seen, questioning him on the interviews he had conducted.

Satisfied, Berwick stooped their walk. "Now, needs must you make your way back to St Albans and meet up with..." he paused un-expectedly, "...Mistress le Brun. We may suspect that this coven may try to harm the king or his family, but we do not know when and where. I am despatching more men-at-arms to each of the locations her grace is visiting on pilgrimage. You must now away and get on the road north with all speed."

CHAPTER 49

Hawkswycke Manor, Hertfordshire, July 1276

The old Roman route south out of St Albans towards Winchester was pot-holed and muddied from overuse by carts. Simon rode his palfrey at a gentle pace for about an hour before entering a sunlit clearing. The trees here had been deliberately pruned back, giving access on one side to a well-defined track. Simon took this to be the road to Hawkswycke that Matilda Heacham had spoken of. The route arced gently through a woodland glade, with its leaves flushed in the spring sun, and he emerged at the lip of a shallow river valley. The open fields to both sides appeared meticulously cultivated, with peasants tilling the crops appearing as specks on this landscape. Ahead of him, situated on a slight rise, was Hawkswycke Manor, the home of Sir Geoffry de Bolleville, a former household knight to the late King Henry. John of Berwick had impressed upon Simon that Sir Geoffry was a man to be trusted and taken into his confidence and his manor a place of refuge in an emergency. Is that how Isabella la Rus knew of it, he wondered?

Although Hawkswycke Manor seemed steeped in rural tranquillity, its people kept a keen eye for strangers. Simon passed a young boy of perhaps nine years, busy weeding the strips' verges. As he rode slowly up towards the Manor complex, the boy's gaze followed Simon until he leapt up and ran ahead to the house to give warning.

Hawkswycke Manor was defined by its high flint wall, split by the now cobbled road, leading to a pair of impressive open oak gates. A serious-looking Steward left the house to approach him as Simon rode through.

"I am Simon Lowys, nuncio to her grace the Queen and serjent-at-law. I am here on the King's business."

"God give you a good day," replied the Steward in courtly language, some twenty years out of date. "Sir Geoffry is expecting you, Master Lowys."

"And to you, good sir," Simon replied, choosing to use a similar intonation and language towards the Steward.

Simon had not sent word ahead that he was coming to Hawkswycke and guessed that either John of Berwick had communicated with Sir Geoffrey or – more likely – Isabelle had informed him.

"Come you up," instructed the Steward, bowing and turning to make his way towards the stone-built house. Crossing the impressive rectangular cobbled courtyard, the Steward ascended an outside flight of stairs to the timber-framed upper chambers. He opened a large oak door with a flourish worthy of the King's court, and together they walked through into the Main Hall of Hawkswycke Manor.

Sir Geoffry de Bolleville was seated beside the fire at the far end of the Hall. It was set against the far outside wall with a hood projecting into the room to collect and control smoke, throwing off a great deal of heat, for the room was very warm. The wooden wall panelling was highly polished and smelt of beeswax. Under the windows along one side, trestle tables were overlaid with crisp white cloths beneath damascene bowls, which suggested to Simon that Sir Geoffry had once been a crusader in the east with a fine eye for quality.

Even though it was mid-morning, cresset torches and beeswax candles threw out their golden light. The rushes beneath Simon's feet were new and sprinkled with sweet herbs keeping the room fragrant. Hawkswycke was a well-run household.

Sir Geoffry de Bolleville stood to greet his guest. "God give you good day, Master Lowys," he spoke in French, which Simon thought was to be expected of a former crusader. The man in front of him was of an older age, part of England's Anglo-Norman heritage of the empire of the previous century. Sir Geoffry had to be in his sixth decade, but he appeared to be fit and healthy. He stood Simon's height, with long, lank hair to his shoulders, showing the silver of age. His beard, too, neatly trimmed, was fully flecked with grey.

Simon tilted his head in a questioning manner. "You knew of my arrival?"

"Of course, my niece told me you would be here this day."

"Your niece, Sir Geoffry?"

"I bid you good day, Master Lowys. I was sure you would come." It was a woman's voice that came from behind Sir Geoffry. It was Isabelle de Brun.

"Mistress..." Simon's eyes widened as he spoke. It was as much a question as an acknowledgement.

"You did not know? Mistress de Brun is my niece. My wife's sister's child."

"My uncle's house provides a safe refuge, well away from prying eyes."

Isabelle went to sit on a bench next to her uncle. Sir Geoffry invited Simon to join them and, with an imperceptible gesture, indicated to his Steward to bring refreshments.

Sir Geoffrey made small talk about life at court today and reminisced about his time in the household of the old King. A young maid brought spiced ale and oatcakes laced with fruit and laid them down on a table.

"I needs must be excused for a few minutes as I have some business that demands my attention." Sir Geoffrey rose, bowed and made his way out of the room, leaving Isabelle alone with Simon.

"He would leave you unchaperoned?" Simon's surprise showed in his tone.

"My uncle is discreet enough to know that my business must be discussed in confidence. Does being alone concern you? Why is it your plan to ravish me, Master Lowys?"

Simon's face went red. He blustered, "Fear not mistress, I...."

She touched his arm reassuringly. "Nay, I jest. I trust you with my honour. Now..." Her tone changed in an instant. "What I must say is most urgent."

"Mistress..." For once, Simon's tone was assertive. "Who are you, really? Are you Isabelle or Isabella? And are you working for John of Berwick or Alice le Blunde and the Daughters of the Shadows?"

She reached out to take his hand. "Hold your fears. Call me Isabelle, for that, is my widowed name. Like you, my allegiance is to His Grace, the King."

Simon took this in. He was sure he believed her. The circumstances all pointed to what she had said was true, and she had saved his life twice.

"Master Lowys, we must proceed. We know that the vial of the Holy Blood was in the possession of the coven after they murdered le Stedeman and Pelliors. Also, that Alice would have been suspicious that it was not the true relic once she realised that le Stedeman was a King's man."

"And we know that Alice le Blunde and presumably the daughters of the Shadows have made common purpose with Walter de Baskerville," Simon interjected.

"If she sought the authentic relic for some nefarious purpose, connected to the coven, then when she realised it was false, what would she do? Simon watched Isabelle, her gaze focused beyond him as if she sought a connection that, for the moment, eluded her.

"And then there is the intelligence from Ghent that Guy de Montfort seeks the services of an assassin," he added.

"And the connection between de Montfort and Alice le Blunde. De Montfort seeks vengeance against His Grace the King; he has struck once already, at Viterbo years past...."

"Mayhaps that is what lurks behind all of this," the thought suddenly entered Simon's head.

"I think perhaps you have the right of it. De Montfort seeks vengeance, and so too does Alice. Both seek harm against His Grace, King Edward, but his household knights and archers too well protect him for them to get close."

"What puzzles me," Simon interrupted the flow, "is why Alice seeks a holy relic presumably to make evil magic with the coven while de Montfort hires an assassin. Are these two things connected?"

"Aye." Simon's comments had triggered the train of thought that had eluded her. "We are not looking at one plot against His Grace, but a second, or even more than two."

For a few moments, there was silence, each with their gaze focused far away, deep in thought.

"By Christ's eyes." Isabelle's exclamation startled Simon back to the present. "Alice and de Montfort cannot harm His Grace, he is too well protected, but they can hurt him."

Simon was bemused by her words.

"They can hurt His Grace by harming the Queen or the royal children."

"But that would be an outrage!"

Isabelle picked up a pewter jug and took a sip of the spiced ale. "De Baskerville is already an excommunicant and a traitor to the Crown. What matter is it to him if his soul is condemned twice? He is the link."

"But we have no proof that they plan to kill Her Grace or her children," lamented Simon.

"No, but we must think as they would."

"And what of the Daughters of the Shadows?" Simon asked. "Why did Alice seek the Holy Blood? What use was she to make of it?"

"She planned to harness its holy power," Isabelle mused. "A powerful evil spell, the sort that might hurt His Grace the King. And when she realises she doesn't have the Holy Blood, she will need an alternative."

Simon looked intently at Isabelle. "Where would she get an alternative? Go back to Hailes Abbey to steal the original?"

"Nay! If she proposes a spell of great evil, she would need holy blood anointed by God."

Simon gave a sharp intake of breath. "The Queen's blood or the blood of her children."

Isabelle turned her face slowly towards him; her face had paled.

"'Tis alright, Mistress de Brun, Her Grace the Queen and her children are safely at court."

"Nay! Queen Eleanor is on pilgrimage as we speak, with a few ladies of her chamber and a small detachment of household knights." Her eyes widened as she shared a further thought. "And the Lady Eleanora, her youngest daughter, is with her."

Simon had no reason not to doubt her, but he asked, nonetheless. "How is it you know of this?"

"It is my business always to know the itinerary of His Grace and his family. We must get word to John of Berwick as a matter of urgency. This day, she resides with the Augustinians in Stanmere. On the morrow, she stays with the nuns at Sopwell, and the day following, the Feast of St Mary Magdalene, she will give her devotions at the shrine of St Albans.

"I have my palfrey stabled here, and I can leave immediately."

"Nay, you will be more useful to me here. My uncle has messengers and fast horses, and they can be at the Chancery before dusk."

Isabelle made for the door and summoned a servant waiting outside to bring her ink and parchment. When it arrived, she sat at Sir Geoffrey's table and began writing a report for John of Berwick. When it was complete, she invited Simon to read it. Once he nodded his assent, Isabelle sprinkled fine sand over the ink to dry it. She folded the four corners to overlap before melting some green wax and dripping it to make a small pool on the document. Finally, she pushed her ring into the melted wax to form her personal seal.

Sir Geoffry returned, and Isabelle gave him a summary of what they had learned and planned. He asked few questions and summoned his Steward to fetch one of his trusted messengers and send word to the stables to make ready a fast horse.

Sir Geoffry's messenger appeared at the door, a tall man with an alert visage. He bowed, doffed his cap at Isabelle and stood bolt upright as he received his directions. A soldier, she thought. If he appeared surprised that Isabelle gave him the instructions, he didn't show it. He bowed once more, took the sealed despatch and placed it in his scrip.

Isabelle impressed upon him the need to place it only in the hands of John of Berwick.

"Aye, mistress, you may rely on me," he said before hurriedly making his way towards the stables. Although unnecessary, Isabelle and Simon watched from a window as the messenger's horse crossed the courtyard and out through the gate on the road heading south to London.

CHAPTER 50

Newlane, St Albans, on the Feast day St Mary Magdalene, July 1276

Sir Geoffry de Bolleville's fine townhouse lay in the well-to-do part of St Albans alongside homes of wealthy town merchants. It was east of the market, away from the smells and the prevailing wind. It was a tall two-storied house built from green oak, its wattle and daub walls covered by neat lime wash, and a deep thatched roof kept out the rain and snows of winter. The onion shoots were bolting to seed in the warm earth of the well-laid vegetable garden to the rear. Isabelle and Simon sauntered along the cinder path between the thinned-out carrots and cabbages. The garden scents were at their height, rosemary, lavender and sage, but the main fragrance Simon Lowys smelled was Sandalwood.

So many questions about this woman raced through Simon's head. How should he start to discover who she was? Did he believe what she had already told him? And, above all, she was a woman. How did a woman operate as she did? He wiped his tongue across his lips, wondering if this was the best moment to ask?

"Mistress de Brun," he used her formal designation. "Pray, let me know something?"

She stopped and scrutinised him. "If I can answer you, Master Lowys, I will."

"For how long have you acted as an intelligencer for John of Berwick?"

The fragrance of newly grown lavender wafted as her skirts brushed against it. She stopped. "I am not free to say how I came to work for John of Berwick, but I have been an intelligencer for him some years."

"But what you do. It is dangerous for a mere woman. Is this not work better suited for a man?"

Just as in their first meeting at the Wheatsheaf Inn, Isabelle's eyes blazed, her face a combination of scorn and anger.

"A mere woman saved you in the churchyard at St Michael's. A mere woman who rescued you from being savaged in the bull ring. And a mere woman who prevented your death on Watlingstrete when you first came north to St Albans some months back."

"I am grateful for the first," he looked puzzled. "But I know not of what you speak about Watlingstrete."

"No. You wouldn't. Alice le Blunde planned that Wolf's Heads of the forest that adjoin Watlingstrete kill you en route. Did you not stop to give help to a lady in distress?

"Aye? How know you of that?" inquired Simon.

"Because I arranged that Lady Margery de Clyderode be on Watlingstrete with a ruse to take you off the road and travel with her to the town. A single horseman on Watlingstrete is easy prey for the Wolf's Heads. They would not be seeking a man travelling with ladies."

"I did not know that. So tis you I have to thank? She nodded.

"Aye."

"Yet Mistress, I do believe...."

"Nay, Master Lowys," she snapped back her response. "Say no more about the weaknesses of women or how the work I do is better suited to the likes of you."

Simon wisely chose to say nothing.

Isabelle stopped on the cinder path, turned and gave Simon an intense look.

"You have known death Master Lowys, the loss of your wife and child a year since. In this work we do for the King, one wrong move, one false word may betray us, and that will be when death meets with us. Are you prepared for that?"

"I had not given it thought," he replied.

"Then it is time you did. An Intelligencer mixes in a world of Wolf's Head and rifflers, who would gut you without a thought. You cannot combat such men with subtle legal arguments, Master Lowys." She reached to touch his arm. "You are a kind man, not a killer. You are inclined to reflect on things before acting. Well, what are you to do when your life is at risk, or someone else's life is threatened, and you needs must act? Do you possess the courage to take a life? Are you prepared to kill Master Lowys? Are you prepared to kill? For if not, then someone may die because you dithered?"

She could see her words struck him like one of her arbalest quarrels.

"So, you do not hold a high opinion of me, Mistress."

"My opinion does not matter. I perceive your qualities Master Lowys but also your weaknesses. It is your weaknesses that will get you killed when you work for John of Berwick."

Isabelle recognised the hurt on his face, and for a moment, she wondered if she had gone too far but then thought this was not a time to salve his pride.

"You are like all men; you believe that woman is not the match of a man. I am not your equal, Master Lowys. It is you who is the apprentice here."

With the hot summer sun beating down, Simon Lowys' self-regard withered. The cheerfulness he had felt at walking in the garden with Isabelle evaporated. Yet, his gaze never left the strong woman standing next to him despite this deflation. He understood now that there were many layers to Isabelle de Brun, not least her identity. He really didn't know her, but he so wished that he did. She gave out the appearance of a well-to-do, comely widow, but she was so much more than that. And so much more dangerous.

Simon made to say something, but she shook her head and cut him short.

"We waste time, Master Lowys. Tarry no longer." Her tone was abrupt. "Her Grace, the Queen was at Sopwell with the nuns this past night and did travel the short distance along the London Road to the shrine of St Alban this very morn."

CHAPTER 51

The town of St Albans, Hertfordshire, on the Feast Day of St Mary Magdalene, July 1276

Walter de Baskerville found that as he aged, not only did his joints ache more, but he spent more time reflecting upon his past. Being labelled a traitor to the crown and an excommunicant did not bother him much. He had spent these past ten years on the continent as the trusted captain of Guy de Montfort, and, if truth be told, he had enjoyed it. A pang of guilt overcame him; should he enjoy having killed people? Well, yes, he did! He was good at what he did; why should he regret that? He had been taught to kill, a warrior of the crown. At the age of twenty, he had been a household knight at Berkhamstede in the service of Richard, Earl of Cornwall, brother to the old King Henry. He and Stephen de Chenduit had been brothers-in-arms, knighted by the King on the same day. Both had loyally served the king's brother and gone with him as part of his bodyguard when he went to Cologne in 1258 to be crowned King of the Germans.

It had been upon their return to England the following year that both Walter and de Chenduit, his future brother-in-law, had fallen under the spell of Simon de Montfort. The elder de Montfort was a natural leader; bold, charismatic, and loyal to his followers. Walter and de Chenduit had followed de Montfort and fought alongside him against the King at Lewes in 1264. Walter had stayed loyal to the de Montfort cause and fought at Evesham when Simon was slain. Stephen de Chenduit had not, which was why he was allowed to retain his manors after the battle. Walter and many other de Montfordians were held prisoner after Evesham alongside Simon's son Guy.

A year after Evesham, Walter and Guy de Montfort were on the continent. Walter spent almost a year imprisoned at Windsor, tending to the wounded Guy, now his lord, following Simon's death. Both were then unexpectedly transferred to Dover Castle, still under arrest, but escape was too tempting. Walter looked back on those times with pride. He had demonstrated his loyalty to the de Montfort cause, and Guy rewarded him.

Five years after, Evesham Guy was the Vicar General of Tuscany, the military enforcer for the powerful Charles of Anjou, brother of the French King and King of Sicily in his own right. Walter's position had risen as Guy's power and authority increased. And then his world fell apart one bright March morning when they arrived in the small city of Viterbo.

Walter had a feeling of unease when they rode into the small piazza in front of the Church of San Silvestro. He knew his lord well, and Guy de Montfort had fury in his eyes this day. When the demons came over Guy, Walter knew that no one, not even his brother Simon could change his mind. Usually, Guy shared his plans with Walter, relying on his experience and tactical brain. But not this day. Walter hadn't known what Guy planned. No, he thought, Guy hadn't planned his actions that morning; he acted on an impulse driven by a lust for revenge.

He had followed both de Montfort brothers into the church in Viterbo. Guy had told him that his cousin, Henry of Almain, was in the holy city with the party of the French king. Walter had thought that Guy only intended to confront his cousin inside the church.

Walter hadn't remembered the King's Man who confronted him at Stephen de Chenduit's manor. Over the years, there had been so many faces, so many bodies. As the man who called himself Lowys narrated the story, it came back to Walter. He had held the young man at sword point, pressing the tip hard under the chin to deter movement.

Walter recalled hearing rather than witnessing the assassination of Henry of Almain. He had caught only glimpses from the corner of his eye, keeping his focus firmly on the man in front of him. Blood lust had overtaken Guy de Montfort that morning. On reflection, the killing of Henry, the King's nephew, had been a mistake; actually, a catastrophic error. It brought the wrath of the Crown of England and the Papacy down upon the de Montfort's. Excommunication from the Church and a sentence of treason followed. Being the liegeman of Guy de Montfort and one of his senior commanders, the punishments fell on Walter's head too.

The past years had been difficult. Guy had the protection of his influential father-in-law, the red Earl of Lombardy, but nonetheless was a fugitive. His brother, Simon, had died of plague less than a year later. Walter continued to serve Guy as they moved across Lombardy, Tuscany, and France.

And still, the fury for vengeance burned deep inside Guy de Montfort. It had been the previous year when Guy formulated his plan for revenge against his nemesis, Edward I. He would avenge his father's death at Evesham. Walter, Guy and the few followers that remained had imposed themselves of the hospitality of the Benedictine monastery at Montescudaio. Guy was determined to hurt the

King. Had it been possible, he would have challenged King Edward to single combat to the death but return to England was impossible. As a traitor to the Crown, he could be killed on sight, and most English nobles and senior knights knew him, at least by sight. But not so, Walter. As one of de Montfort's mercenary commanders, Walter was known by very few. Guy would send Walter to England to be his surrogate, his avenging angel against King Edward of England.

CHAPTER 52

Sumpter Yard, St Albans Abbey, on the Feast Day of St Mary Magdalene, July 1276

The ponderous wooden cart trundled slowly up into the Sumpter Yard, axles groaning under their weight and the heavy solid-wood wheels bouncing across the rough cobbles. It ground to a stuttering halt beside the abbey Frater, the single oxen pulling it snorting angrily at the interruption to its gait. The heavy oak barrels in the back rattled and creaked, threatening to unbalance the cart. The driver cursed and tugged hard on the reins causing the recalcitrant beast to snort again and flick its head in annoyance. The driver, hooded and muffled, took in the surroundings. The cart had entered the abbey complex by the Sumpter gate. To the right, the monk's cemetery was God's Acre, a green space with the occasional hummock marking a recent grave. The abbey lay off to one side, scarred and crumbling where one of the transepts met the nave. The effects of the earthquake thought the driver and still unrepaired after all these years. Heavy oak timbers braced the walls, and planks laid side by side the covered gaps in the flint stonework.

The barrels contained Gascon wine for the Abbot, a gift from the King to mark his wife's pilgrimage this day; at least, that was the story the driver had used to gain entry. Neither of the lay brothers on the gate had questioned the story. Knowing the Queen was visiting the martyr's shrine this day, a delivery of fine wine made sense. It had been that easy gaining access to the monastic complex.

Six hogshead barrels nestled side by side in the well of the cart, their weight pushing down onto a strained axle. Bertrand de Guescin twisted in his seat, dropped the reins and surveyed his cargo. The story that they contained fine Gascon wine, well, that was not entirely untrue, he thought. Some of them did indeed contain wine. He had stolen the cart from a vintner arriving at the fair the previous afternoon. Bertrand had dumped the vintner's corpse in a dung heap where, no doubt, it would be discovered later in the year come autumn planting time when the muck was required for spreading on the fields. Having ensured that no one was around, Bertrand tapped twice on the barrel nearest him. The lid slowly lifted upwards, and a slightly built, hooded monk appeared, gazing around to ensure that there were no eyes upon them.

The dark Benedictine habit was too large; folds of cloth hung loose, making movement more complicated than it ought to be. Alice le Blunde asked herself how these monks lived in these garments every day. Her slight figure in the habit gave her the appearance of a youth, which was why she was keeping her cowl well-draped over her head. A woman inside the abbey and, worse, a cursed witch inside their precious monastery. She chuckled at that.

Alice dropped down from the cart and landed ungainly on the rough cobbles causing her knees to ache. Now, the task was to get inside the abbey church and meet up with de Baskerville without being observed. With her face bowed as if in reverence and shielded by the cowl, Alice looked like a Benedictine despite her oversized habit. De Baskerville had identified the short-cut entrance into the Abbey frequented by the builders, which she would use. Because of the royal visit, no building work or repairs were going on this day. Alice quickly found the entrance and slipped inside the Abbey

Church; the chill of the interior hit her immediately. When was the last time she had been inside a church? At Kenilworth, she thought, many years since. It took a few moments for her eyes to adjust to the fug and gloom, but, given their task this day, that would be of great help to them.

The interior of the church was still, and the deep pall caused by the tall pillars gave ample cover to anyone seeking to shield themselves from view. Alice le Blunde hid in the shadows of a side aisle, waiting to glimpse Walter de Baskerville. Together they would abduct Queen Eleanor of Castile and gain vengeance upon King Edward of England.

CHAPTER 53

The Townhouse of Jasliena van Leuven, St Albans, July 1276

Gentle dawn rays filtered through the wooden shutters and fell onto the bed and the sleeping figure of Jasliena van Leuven. The warmth of the early day sun on her face caused her to stir. She allowed an arm to flop onto the other side of the bed, falling onto crisp, clean sheets. Her eyes only slowly opened; there was no one there. Adam had left her bed long before curfew, and she had remained in bed fitfully dozing until she fell asleep.

Jasliena liked the young man very much; true, there was an age difference, he was not yet twenty summers, but it didn't seem to matter to him. He was uncultured, rough, vigorous and not wise in the ways of the world, but he had ambition. They had lain in bed, bodies close together. Jasliena had reached out, stroking his long fair hair when he excitedly told her he planned to set himself up once his term as a journeyman was over. He would marry her as soon as he could, he had promised. If only he could have caught a glimpse of her face when she heard him use the word marriage. His boyish enthusiasm was all-consuming, so similar to his lovemaking. Despite these thoughts, her demeanour showed no emotion, her eyes staring as if far, far away.

Adam was everything Jasliena had sought. He was tall, lean, and muscular, so very different from Jan, her dead husband. He was such a happy, talkative youth and so very impressionable. As they lay in her bed in a lover's embrace with Adam sharing his plans and ambitions for the next few years, Jasliena also thought of their future, but she was not thinking beyond tomorrow.

His striking presence was just what she desired. His height and good looks, together with his like for bright clothes and fine things, made him perfect for her. As a journeyman, he was limited in what he could wear, but she could fix that.

From their first meeting, Jasliena could sense Adam wanted to be her protector. His alarm when she had told him of other, older merchants who desired her; men who prepared to abduct and rape her to force her into marriage, was genuine. Jasliena noticed how her nervousness at this thought transferred to Adam. That was why she had given him the gift of a small, hand-held arbalest that he could conceal about his person and use, if necessary, to protect her. She had made him promise that he would carry it at all times when they were together and begged him to be her saviour was she to be set upon and abducted. Adam, like some chivalric knight defending his lady's honour, had sworn that he would. He had also sworn his undying love, which, she thought, was reflected when they were together.

Last night Adam had left an hour before the town curfew bell rang. Jasliena lay in her bed watching him by the light of half-a-dozen beeswax candles as he tried to dress with one hand. His other gently stroked her, moving alternately between her face, hair, and breasts. His attempt at dressing brought a mirthful laugh from her as he once again failed to get one leg into his hose.

"Did you not learn to dress yourself as a child?"

"Aye, Mistress, but as a child, I never did have such a beautiful distraction in front of me when I attempted to garb myself."

He leant forward and kissed her passionately, wishing that he could spend the rest of the night in her arms.

"You will be there, at the Abbey on the morrow when her grace the Queen comes?" There was a pleading in her tone.

Adam's reply came as he delivered another deep, loving kiss to her lips. "Aye, my love. I will, of course, be there. And I will stay close lest one of those damnable men seek you abduction in the crowd."

Jasliena reached her arms up from where she lay on the bed, folded them around his neck and kissed him. He broke the clinch only with great reluctance. Their eyes met. The lovers needed no words to say their goodbyes this night. Adam's gaze lingered on her naked body until he finally left her solar and made his way down to her front door.

Laying back on her bed, the sheets rumpled around her, Jasliena heard the front door latch close. The hour was late, her eyes were heavy, and she had dozed before falling into a deep slumber.

CHAPTER 54

The Abbey Church of St Albans on the Feast Day of St Mary Magdalene, July 1276

At seven years old, the lady Eleanora did not have her mother, the Queen's piety or enthusiasm for religious shrines. She found the inside of the church chilly with a strange smell of things old. And she thought, thinking of old, Abbot Roger seemed to be showing her mother every statue and wall painting inside the Abbey Church and Eleanora was bored. At first, she had been impressed with the colourful wall paintings on the squared-off piers in the nave. Images of the crucifixion of Jesus and the Blessed Virgin in terracotta, blue and gold, seemed to leap out from the walls. The Virgin Mary, her head surrounded with a holy halo, looked down on the awed Eleanora. But the fascination soon wore off, and the boredom set in.

Standing behind her mother, the Queen, Eleanora made faces at Roger de Clare, Queen Eleanor of Castile's stern and austere Dominican chaplain. She didn't think she had ever seen his face break into a smile or laugh. There were others there, all men; the senior obedientiaries of the monastery, Eleanora didn't remember their names nor cared much. And then there were three members of her mother's household guard, who felt uneasy at being denied their swords inside the Abbey Church. They were kind, but they spent their time around her mother, which Eleanora thought, was their role, but it meant they were no fun to be with.

This tour seemed to go on for an interminable time, and Eleanora was no longer listening to the Abbot's explanations. She would have much rather been playing with her toys back at Langlei. In time, Eleanora found herself loitering at the back of the group, as the Abbot pointed out yet another chapel dedicated to yet another saint. Eleanora knew she really should be interested, but no, she was not.

No one noticed her indifference and weariness, and as the party moved on towards some wall murals. Eleanora stopped and looked up. By the time she looked back down, her mother and the Abbot and the entourage were many yards ahead, so Eleanora turned and walked the other way. It wasn't devilment. Eleanora planned to wait outside, out of the chill of the church and in the warmth of the sunshine. She heard a scraping sound behind her, and when she turned to look, she saw Robert, one of her mother's men-at-arms. The burly guard smiled.

"You must not wander off on your own, my maid. His Grace, your father would flay me alive if anything happened."

"You may return to my mother's party, Robert. I am but going outside. I am bored."

"Nay, my maid. I must keep eyes on you at all times for your own safety."

Eleanora wasn't best pleased with his reply.

"I am grown in years, Robert, and well capable of passing through a church without incident."

"Be that as it may, Your Grace, I must keep you under watch for your own safety."

Robert watched as the lady Eleanora spun and raced down the nave, keeping his eyes on her, walking purposefully behind at a respectable distance. He never saw the predatory shadow to one side lurking behind a pillar. A hand smothered his mouth, and he felt the pain as a dagger slid between his ribs into his heart, ending his life. The slaying was silent, the work of one who had done this many times before. Walter de Baskerville took the weight of the dead man-at-arms and lay him silently on the floor before following the young maid down the church.

No sound had interrupted Eleanora's wandering eyes, raised towards the high ceiling, looking at nothing in particular.

"Can I help you, my child? Are you lost?" Alone with her thoughts, she had not noticed a monk approach behind her.

Even though she was young, her mother had taught her well. "Thank you, Brother," she replied in her best courtly French, "But I am going outside to wait." She looked beyond the monk for Robert, but when she couldn't see him, she deduced he had returned to her mother's group as she had wanted.

Eleanora regarded the monk. His hood was pulled up over his head, but even shrouded, she could make out his features. He had a well-worn face and stubble, which she thought unusual for a Brother; she could make out a scar on one side of his face running down towards his mouth; perhaps he had been a soldier, she thought. Maybe the Abbot used such Brothers as guards. She really didn't know.

The Brother smiled at her. "Come, my lady, I can show you a quick way out into the gardens if you wish," Eleanora liked being addressed as 'my lady.' The monk's manner was gentle and kindly. She already liked this cleric.

"Yes, I'd like that. I find I don't like the smell inside a Church."

The monk chuckled and placed a calm hand on Eleanora's shoulder, and guided her towards a side aisle off the nave. At just seven years old, Eleanora was trusting of adults, for her days were spent in the company of grown people. The sound of the Abbot's voice, droning on about another mural, waned into the distance. Another monk, hooded and head bowed, stood reverently beside a pillar just ahead of Eleanora. Was he deep in prayer, she thought?

Eleanora and the kindly monk passed the praying brother, the sound of her shoes and his sandals hardly making a noise. A sweaty hand shot across her face and jerked her backwards. She tried to scream, but no sound emerged; a rag had been stuffed into her mouth. The no-longer praying brother swept Eleanora up and threw her across his shoulder. The once 'kind' brother forced a sack over her head, and a sense of terror and revulsion swept over the young maiden.

The plan had begun well. During its mid-summer fair, St Albans was a town full of strangers. People expected to see a monk; they wore the dark monk's garb of a Benedictine. No one gave Walter de Baskerville and Bertrand a second glance. Walter had found it surprisingly easy to play the part of a Benedictine Brother. There was no problem stealing the habits. Once inside the monastic complex, no one questioned Walter and his henchman, Bertrand.

Walter had been here a few weeks earlier. Then he had brought with him the tools of a surveyor and spent some time posing as a mason. Their story was that the Crown sent them to survey the unrepaired damage from the earthquake in the thirty-third year of the reign of old King Henry. Walter had forged letters of introduction and hinted that His Grace, the King wished to know what the repair cost would be so he could make a commensurate donation.

His 'journeyman', Bertrand, accompanied him, busily taking a sham measurement with a rod stick and making marks onto a slate. His experienced military mind took in what he saw. The significant unrepaired damage of the Abbey lay to the south-eastern side close to the crossing. The force of the quake had brought down a large section of the wall and destroyed small chapels and the vestry. In the years following the earthquake, the standing walls had been shored up with timber and oak planks to cover the large holes in the nave wall. Most of these timbers, now weathered and aged, still remained. Simple doors into the nave had been constructed, allowing workmen access to both sides of the walls without disrupting the daily services. Those entrances would provide an excellent escape route toward the monk's cemetery and the western gate.

The Queen and her young daughter had arrived at the Abbey later than expected. Their journey was short, having spent the night at Sopwell Nunnery just a few miles to the southeast. Walter and Alice had secreted themselves in the upper clerestory. All the monks were in the choir stall singing a '*Te Deum Laudamus*' and dressed as they were; all brothers would be expected to be there.

Walter heard rather than saw the royal party arrive. From the clerestory, they became aware of the Abbot's tour beginning. Muffled noises, the shuffling of feet combined with the sound of a male voice. A monk's nasal voice droning on and on. Beside Walter, Alice began to scratch.

"How do they wear these things?" she whispered. "This must be riddled with fleas."

De Baskerville raised a hand to silence her and, pointing his finger downwards, indicated they should move down into the heart of the Abbey. Once in the nave, they kept to the shadows, Walter trying to keep the Queen in his sights. She was accompanied by three guards – household knights probably, Walter thought, but unarmed; he hadn't expected that. But of course, the Benedictines didn't permit weapons inside their churches; they had to be left in the porch prior to entry. That evened things up because both he and Bertrand still possessed theirs underneath their monk's habits.

Lurking in the semi-darkness, Walter perceived that the Queen was unlikely to be alone at any time. Her three guards flanked her, always at a distance of a few yards, eyes scanning left and right, indifferent to, or unimpressed by, the Abbot's running commentary. Unarmed they may be, but they still provided a formidable obstacle to killing his Queen.

To the rhythmic chanting of the monks, the royal party continued their progress through the Abbey Church.

"And if Your Grace will follow this way, I would like to show you the beautiful lectern that the old King Henry, your beloved father-in-law, commissioned Jean of St Omer to copy for his abbey at Westminster."

Walter observed as the Queen's group moved towards the altar. In such a confined space, the task became even more complex – and then, Walter spied an opportunity.

A young girl, the King's young daughter Eleanora, Walter thought, hung back and then moved in the other direction from the group. For Walter, it was a golden chance. If he could not fulfil the plan of abducting the Queen, the alternative was to assassinate her. But now, Walter saw a third choice, the opportunity to seize the King's daughter and gain vengeance that way. The tall man-at-arms following the young girl would potentially be a problem, but when, after speaking with her, the man-at-arms hung back, Walter saw his chance. He pushed himself tight behind a pillar, the gloomy shadows allowing his black habit to blend with the darkness. The unsuspecting and unarmed man-at-arms had walked right past him; his death was swift, silent and simply done.

The young girl was very trusting. She had genuinely believed that Walter was a monk; well, he did look like a monk, dressed as he was in one of their shabby habits, albeit with his sword hidden beneath it. She had followed him willingly, and it had been simple for them to grab her and force a cloth into her mouth and a sack over her head.

Keeping her silent and stopping her struggle had also proved straightforward. Walter's time in Italy as Guy de Montfort's captain had once taken him to another Benedictine house, the Abbey of St Martin in Montecassino. There he had learned of a sleeping draught perfected by the monks, a mixture of opium, henbane, mulberry juice, lettuce, hemlock, mandragora, and ivy. The monks called it '*Il sonno del Lazio*', the Sleep of Lazio. Very quickly, Alice removed the sack and forced the potent liquid down the girl's throat. After a few minutes of futile resistance, she fell into a deep slumber. All he had to do now was improvise their escape. He planned to use the same route through the ruined south-eastern wall he had devised on his last visit where Bertrand should be waiting.

Thinking quickly, Alice ripped down a beautiful wall tapestry; together, they rolled the limp Eleanora inside and began to carry her towards the workman's door in the building works. They gave the appearance of two lay brothers about their daily work, not rushing but proceeding cautiously towards the southwest wall where Bertrand waited with the ox cart.

CHAPTER 55

The streets of St Albans, on the Feast Day of St Mary Magdalene, July 1276

Cockerels in backyards across St Albans still crowed despite the arrival of the dawn being many hours before. A woman picked her way through the narrow lanes of the town; she attracted little attention. She was one of many beginning their day in the chill hours of the morning. She was dressed in drab brown clothes and acting demurely, just one of many wives or servants, out early to buy bread for the table and blending in with her surroundings. She received the occasional salutation of *"Mistress"* from merchants and traders, also early to business. The basket she carried drew no attention, for it was like many others on the street carried by women no different from herself. No eyes looked at her in recognition as Jasliena van Leuven, the wealthy widow.

The news that Her Grace Queen Eleanor was to visit the shrine of the martyr St Alban had spread quickly through the town in the past days. There was little love for the Abbey and its Abbot among the townspeople, but the Queen was highly regarded. A rumour spread that His Grace King Edward would accompany her, but Jasliena disregarded that. Queen Eleanor was frequently alone on pilgrimage to various holy shrines across the land, Bury St Edmunds,

Walsingham, Canterbury. However, the shrine of St Alban appeared to be one of her personal favourites.

Whenever the Queen went on pilgrimage, her royal retainers would hand out generous alms to the poor, ensuring a crowd would gather. Jasliena was relying on that crowd being present today. She had convinced Adam that they must not stand out in the crowd for fear of attracting attention. Adam had wondered what she had meant by this, but he had become so besotted that he trusted her and complied with her request. He dressed in his everyday work clothes, whereas Jasliena appeared transformed, no longer the elegant merchant widow but a working wife of the town.

"In these clothes, none of the merchants who seek to abduct me will recognise me," she had told him while gently caressing his wispy beard. Such was the effectiveness of her appearance that he had not recognised her at first. Adam had been struck by how many women appeared similarly dressed to Jasliena, many carrying the ubiquitous baskets. Almost as if she had copied them, he had thought.

They had walked together towards the Abbey, but Jasliena was somewhat distant as they went. She brushed away his arm when he tried to link it with his and rebuffed his clumsy attempts to kiss her. There was a fair gathering of the townspeople outside the main west door of the Abbey.

The wicker baskets of the townswomen held contained cheeses, vegetables and other products from the market stalls. Some women were regrators, buying produce cheaply and hoping to sell it at a profit. Jasliena's basket, although outwardly similar in appearance, was quite different. It had a plain cloth covering to keep the produce cool, with some root vegetable leaves protruding from its side. However, Jasliena's had a narrow rectangular slit at its front to facilitate the tiny, deadly arbalest hidden inside. The weapon with which she would kill the Queen.

The arbalest was identical to the one she had given to Adam. Jasliena had made sure of that. While Jasliena's arbalest was concealed, Adam's hung at his side, ready to defend her honour.

In the sunshine, she took in the good-natured crowd beside her outside the Abbey doors. Some men-at-arms stood by the closed wooden doors, eyes fixed firmly ahead of them. Other well-dressed men, royal officials, she surmised, mingled to one side, deep in conversation

Beside Jasliena, Adam stood alert, his height allowing him to survey the crowd to the left and right. Jasliena was aware of some of the townswomen around them engaged in risqué banter, but her focus was mainly on the abbey doors and anything that might interfere with her plan. In front of her, she noticed a small, crippled boy clutching a crutch with stuffed rags for his padded shoulder rest. The boy was seated, massaging his calf, but his gaze too never shifted from the closed Abbey door. Jasliena had positioned herself in front of Adam to get a better view, she told him. Adam had commented that she was looking around her as if expecting danger.

"Are you afeared for your safety?" he inquired.

"Aye. A crowd such as this would afford someone seeking ill against me perfect cover."

"I will protect you, my lady. "As he too began to look around him at the faces gathered beside him. In addition to the town's wives and children, many men of all ages gathered to view the queen. Adam was regarding their faces. She was sure he was asking himself, could he be here to seize Jasliena? Or him? Or him? From the corner of her eye, Jasliena caught the movement of Adam's hand going to arbalest hanging at his side. A wry smile came across Jasliena's lips. Adam had become so infatuated with her that he would do anything she asked of him. Jasliena was relying on this for her plan to succeed.

CHAPTER 56

The west door of the Abbey of St Albans, on the Feast of St Mary Magdalene, July 1276

It was Queen Eleanor herself who first realised that her young daughter, Eleanora, was not by her side. Her ladies and bodyguards all agreed that she had gone outside with the experienced Household guard Robert accompanying her.

Queen Eleanor was unhappy at what she had heard. She pursed her lips and summoned John de Bohun, her Senior Household Clerk.

"Find the Lady Eleanora," she issued her command in brisk French, "and ensure all is well, and then bring her to me at the Martyr's shrine."

The Queen turned to Abbot de Norton. "Pray do show me the Blessed Saint's shrine, My Lord Abbot, and then we shall meet beyond the Abbey doors to give alms to the paupers and the infirm."

The Queen knelt alone at a Prie Dieu, before the ornate tomb of St Alban, deep in prayer. Her fingers nimbly moved down her devotion beads, marking each Ave Maria she recited to herself. At length, she stood, bowed her head in reverence and left the enclosed altar. According to seniority, the rest of the royal party and the accompanying monks knelt in the side aisles.

As always, Abbot de Norton was slow to get to his feet, his rheumy knees aching. He escorted Her Grace towards the western door beside the chapel of St Andrew, followed by the rest of her royal entourage, keeping a respectful distance behind. Approaching the door, the Queen turned to summon de Bohun.

"Where is my daughter?" Her words were almost scolding of the clerk.

"I sent guards to the main doors to seek her out, Your Grace. I expect she will be there with Robert keeping watch over her as she runs rings around him."

Eleanor regarded the clerk but said nothing more, moving ahead towards the great doorway at the north end of the aisle.

Outside, a crowd had gathered. News that the Queen was to visit the abbey to pay her devotion to the saint had spread quickly throughout the town. The few guards there to control the crowd allowed the sick to move towards the front so that the Queen might lay her royal hands upon them to aid their healing.

A young, crippled orphan boy dressed in rags, with a crutch made from an ash staff, sat on the ground at the very front. His clothing was much torn and dirty. He did not live in the town but had hobbled his way from Redbourn, where he begged daily. The boy, who the villagers mocked as Lame Tom, had heard from a travelling Chapman that the sick would be cured were the King or Queen to lay their hands upon the infirm. It took Thomas almost two days to limp the few miles between Redbourn and St Albans, and his twisted leg hurt as a consequence. He had thought carefully about his plan. He would duck under any guards and plead with the Queen to lay her healing hands upon him.

The crowd beside Tom was good-natured, and there was much banter, especially among the town's wives, and some of their comments made young Tom blush.

A well-built woman with a rosy face taunted a man next to her.

"Get Her Grace to lay hands on your spindle, Alric. Your wife told me it needs raising like the dead."

"I don't think she'll be able to see it, from what I've heard," commented an equally buxom wife.

"She hasn't seen it in years," added another, causing a peal of laughter among the crowd.

Tom had sat down to rest his leg but was pushed forward by the wicker basket of the person standing behind him. He turned to look and saw a pretty woman with skin like dark honey standing with a fair-haired man, much younger than she. She was dressed like many of the other women, marking her out as one of the women of the town, a trader or shopkeeper's wife but she appeared nervous, constantly looking around at the crowd.

All around him, the banter continued. Thomas wasn't entirely sure what they were talking about, but he knew enough to know it was making fun of Alric.

It was the honey-skinned woman's eyes that drew Tom's attention; he was fascinated by her deep, penetrating eyes that seemed to take in everything around her. The fair-haired man was fawning over her. He's not her husband, Tom thought to himself. No, not her husband! His time begging on the streets had given him a keen sense of people and their behaviour.

The crowd behind him surged as guards emerged from the western door, and Tom got up from the cold earth. "The Queen!" people said in unison. The cry passed through the crowd like a ripple on a pond. "The Queen! The Queen!" Then Tom saw the figure of Queen Eleanor. He hadn't known what to expect, never having seen a Queen in his short life. She wore a brightly coloured long gown covered with a robe trimmed with fur. Tom had never seen such bright colours as on the Queen's gown. He had never seen silk, damask or embroidery trimming nor knew what ermine was.

Tom knew that now was his moment. He ducked under the out-stretched arm of one of the guards, and, leaning on his crutch, he hobbled forwards towards Queen Eleanor. The cheers of the crowd drowned out the tap-tap of his wooden crutch on the ground as he moved towards the royal party. There were just a few yards between him and the Queen when the tip of the crutch dropped into a small pothole, and Tom stumbled to fall flat the cobbles directly in front of Queen Eleanor.

Eleanor of Castile had walked through the western door from the gloom of the Abbey interior into the bright sunshine outside. It had taken a few moments for her eyes to become accustomed to the light, but she heard the cheers and acclamation of a crowd of the townspeople.

"The people of the town are pleased you are here again, Your Grace," said Abbot de Norton obsequiously. The Queen had been about to respond where she noticed a young, crippled boy, dressed in rags, come towards her from the crowd of townspeople. She had watched, intrigued by what was happening, only for the boy to tumble to the ground just yards in front of her.

Queen Eleanor's motherly instinct was concerned for the boy, lest he was hurt. Instinctively she bent forward and knelt to help the lad. She reached out her hand down to grasp him. In that instant, Eleanor sensed a rush of air passing across her shoulder and heard the sharp hiss of something close beside her head. A shrill scream of pain came from behind her as a quarrel hit flesh.

In the crowd, the cries of acclamation gave way to shouts of 'Murder! Murder!' as people realised that there had been an attempt on the Queen's life. People looked at each other in horror as it appeared that the Queen was struck down. The rosy-faced buxom woman making ribald comments earlier looked towards the Queen, shrieked and then shifted her gaze to the crowd around her. She spied a tall youth with an arbalest in his hand.

"Murderer!" She screamed at the top of her voice. "Murderer! See, he still holds the weapon.

"Murderer!" Others in the crowd took up the cry. "Murderer! Assassin!" Two men beside Adam grabbed at him and seized his arms, holding him fast. Others shouted out to the royal guards.

"Quick! Over here. We have him. We have the assassin."

Alerted by their cries, royal men-at-arms rushed into the crowd to apprehend the fair-haired youth with the arbalest. Before they got there, others in the angry mob administered their own justice on the would-be assassin. Blows from women and men rained down upon the defenceless journeyman from all directions.

Cheers erupted when Queen Eleanor stood, helping Lame Tom to his feet, and passing him his crutch. Guards surrounded her, and she was swiftly guided back into the Abbey through St Andrew's chapel. Events were moving too swiftly for the Queen to grasp what was occurring.

As the Queen re-entered the gloom of the Abbey, a loud cry came from deep in the interior.

"Help me! It is Robert... He has been slain!"

On hearing the plea for help, a look of realization overcame the Queen, knowing that that something terrible had happened to Eleanora. Her scream of anguish turned into an uncontrollable wail of pain.

CHAPTER 57

The Royal Palace of Westminster, on the Feast Day of St Mary Magdalene, July 1276

Simon Lowys was relieved that it had not been him that had to tell His Grace, the King, that his young daughter had been abducted. The royal Plantagenet temper was legendary, inherited, so rumour said from Henry II, the first of the line a century before. And so, it had been. Edward still seethed with rage when a royal messenger came before the King at Westminster and broke the news. A fine Murano jug was knocked to the floor. The goblet of fine Malmsey wine King Edward held was thrown against the wall, the sweet, sticky liquid running languidly down the stonework. Then the King turned his ire on the bringer of the bad news, lashing out at the messenger, with fist and foot, as if it were he that had committed the act.

It hadn't helped that the messenger hadn't succeeded in delivering the whole message before the King's temper exploded. King Edward took many minutes for his anger to reduce, only for the unfortunate, quivering messenger to outline the Queen's attempted assassination. With this, the royal fury knew no bounds. Raising himself to his full height of four fingers above six feet, King Edward veered between screaming hysteria and inconsolable wailing. An attack on his beloved wife. The King wanted the town constable, and the leading citizens of St Albans arrested and hung immediately. His drooping left eye in a constant twitch, the King ordered the Abbot seized and the guards accompanying the Queen arraigned for treason. Fresh royal men-at-arms were to be despatched to the town immediately. King Edward himself would go there to take personal command of the rescue party for his daughter. He swore vengeance upon the town of St Albans for their treason against him.

It was hard to determine what generated more anger in His Grace, the abduction of his young daughter or the attempt on the life of his beloved wife. Edward's angry rantings veered between the two, with no one at court able to assuage his fury.

It was several hours later before Her Grace, Queen Eleanor, arrived back at Westminster, distraught and weeping for the loss of their daughter. The King's anger subsided with her arrival, and he enveloped her in his large arms and held her close, whispering soft words to seek to soothe her angst.

He listened to a distraught Eleanor's anguished account of what had occurred and her belief that she was to blame for the disappearance of the young Eleanora. For her, the attempt on her own life paled against the threat to their daughter.

"I imagined she had gone outside, bored by the church interior." The Queen sobbed out the words. The sight of his dear wife, so inconsolable, tempered the King's anger somewhat.

"We shall find her. I will go to St Albans now and take personal charge of the search. No stone will be left unturned. You are to rip the town apart, and I will find and kill those responsible. All will pay both for the abduction of our dear Eleanora and the attempt on your life."

The King insisted the Queen rest. He summoned her Ladies to accompany her to her chamber and stay with her. Once she had retired, he began preparations to head north to St Albans. Instructions were given for a company of Cheshire archers to prepare, and two hundred men-at-arms and a detachment of household knights were ready within the hour.

Worry and fury in equal measure lined King Edward's face as the detachment left the royal place at Westminster in the late afternoon. The King and his household knights rode on ahead at a brisk pace, picking up the old Roman road north to arrive at the monastic precinct of St Albans after sunset.

King Edward's temper resurfaced when he came face-to-face with the Abbot. Roger de Norton visibly shook as he stood before his monarch. His face red, eyes darting and breathing heavily, he began to offer his profuse apologies for what had occurred.

"Your g... g...grace, I... I... am so..."

"By God's eyes, no words of yours.... Priest can assuage my anger. Tell me why I should not hang you this instant from the mighty oak outside?"

Roger de Norton visibly paled, his mouth agape.

"But, Your Grace, I am a man of God. This that has happened was no fault of mine."

"No fault of yours?" The spittle of anger flew from King Edward's mouth. He took a step towards the Abbot and grasped the neck of his black habit, pulling the cleric towards him. At six foot two inches, Edward towered over the quivering Abbot.

"Christ's nails, you are snivelling little runt. Who is to blame? My wife, the Queen and our daughter were here. They were in your charge. It is you who allowed this to happen." King Edward's voice boomed out.

"You allowed an assassin to get close to her in the monastery precinct. You Benedictines allowed felons to seize my daughter! I should kill you here, now."

Abbot de Norton cowered in fear. The King squeezed the monk's habit with greater force as he spoke. The Abbot tried to respond, but all that came from his lips were whimpering sobs.

Frustrated, the King pushed the wide-eyed de Norton to the ground.

"My men will speak with every single monk and lay brother. I don't care if that interferes with your services. I want to know who was responsible as soon as possible."

Roger de Norton struggled to his feet, fearful that the King's boot might send him sprawling to the floor again.

"We have held someone in custody for the attempt on Her Grace, the Queen." The Abbot's words were almost apologetic.

King Edward's beady stare fixed upon the monk. "Where is he? He shall pay dearly. He will wish he had never been born and will die slowly for this!"

"We are holding the prisoner in the oubliette we reserve for recalcitrant brothers. I shall have him brought before you straight away, your Grace."

King Edward shook his head. "Nay. You shall take me to him now. I wish to look upon his face awhile afore I send him to draw his last breath."

Relieved that the King's wrath appeared to have diminished, Abbot de Norton led His Grace and four household knights across the monastic yard towards the Gatehouse. To one side lay a compact stone-built building that housed a small oubliette used to discipline young errant novices.

The Novice Master, Brother Hubert, produced a large key from his girdle. The sturdy iron lock creaked as he turned the key, opening the heavy oak door. King Edward roughly pushed the monk aside and entered the cramped cell, followed by a well-built knight in full mail.

The only light came from a barred window high on the wall. A whimpering figure lay slumped on the cold stone floor.

"Stand before your King!" The imposing mail-clad figure of Bogo de Knoxville barked out the command, aiming a kick at the prone Adam's midriff.

Adam groaned from the blow and attempted to scrabble onto all-fours. De Knoxville gave him another kick sending Adam back to the floor.

"Up, you dog! Stand!" The knight's mailed glove grabbed Adam's hair and pulled him as upright as his wounds would allow. The beatings Adam had received at the hands of the royal body-guards and then the King's household knights had left him unable to hold his weight. They had broken his jaw; his ribs were broken, and he had lost teeth. Deep cuts above his eyes wept with one closed completely. Blood caked his fair, wispy beard and seeped out from open wounds. His words came out as guttural garble thanks to his damaged jaw and swollen tongue.

De Knoxville held Adam up as the King inspected him, his eyes fixed on the mangled, bloodied face. Edward regarded the pathetic youth in front of him. There was not an ounce of compassion in the King's body. Anger coursed through the royal veins. Edward's urge was to draw his sword and drive it deep into the youth's chest. But he resisted and instead raised his fist and smashed it into Adam's already damaged face. A piteous, deep-throated groan emerged from his bloodied mouth.

"A thousand deaths would be too good for you. You bastard cur, you attack my Queen and seize my daughter... I should kill myself, but mark my words, traitor," King Edward spat out the word. "your head will sit on a spike before another day turns."

The King gave de Knoxville a look, and the Household knight let go of the apprentice, who dropped to the floor with a cry of pain.

"He will go on trial this day, Bogo. Ensure Abbot and his Seneschal make the arrangements. I will preside over a Curia Regis. See too that the Abbot has the gallows made ready outside the gates. We shall need them soon enough."

CHAPTER 58

Magpie Lane, St Albans, on the Feast Day St Mary Magdalene, July 1276

The Widow Abury's house lay in Magpie Lane on the eastern fringes of St Albans, at the end of a row of five homes, all of which had seen better days. Once, in the reign of the second King Henry, Magpie Lane had been the affluent part of the town; not so now. The cracked wattle and daub finish was grey in appearance, a sure sign of damp rising from the ground. Two tallow candles lit the gloomy interior, whose burning contributed to the fug and the unhealthy smell.

What few possessions Widow Abury had were strewn across the hard mud floor as royal soldiers searched for clues to the missing lady Eleanora.

A stern, thick-set guard held up two glass discs bound by wire. He called out to Edith Abury, who stood frightened in one corner.

"Woz this?"

"They are illumination glass for seeing objects close up." Edith paused, composing herself. "They belonged to my husband. He bought them on his travels in Pisa some years ago. They are made on an island, Murano."

The gruff guard eyed the old woman with suspicion.

"Some sort of foreign magic. I'm taking these." He stuffed the reading glass into his pocket. He continued his search, which in reality meant overturning objects and sweeping others to the floor with his arm.

Edith pleaded with him to return the glasses to her.

"Tis one of the few things I have of his. Please do not take it." The guard was unmoved. He picked up a small wooden box. He found a small blanket, a crucifix, and some infant's teeth inside. Edith wailed. The guard recognised what it was and what it meant to the old woman. A malevolent grin came over his face.

"Nay, I beg you. Nay... Nay!"

Impervious to her pleas, he tipped out the box and tossed the blanket onto the small fire. The guard pushed the tiny teeth into the earth with his foot. Edith fell to her knees, tears of grief falling down her face.

"Wilkin. Wilkin, my precious boy..." she cried out the name of her long-dead infant son as she scrabbled to locate her last links to him on the cold earth floor.

Across the town, the same scene played out. The King had ordered that every house, warehouse, outhouse, cellar, barn, and brothel be searched. Royal Men-at-arms were systematically going through every building and alienating many within the community.

Two streets to the south of Widow Abury's house, more guards, searched the henhouse of John Baker in Ivelane. The raucous noise of the birds gave way to stillness. Once their search was complete, not a single bird remained, all destined for the guard's cook pot that night. King Edward's royal guards were most diligent in their endeavours. Rifflers and crooks were discovered in their hiding places, seized and arrested by the Constable.

Four men-at-arms and their Serjeant, William atte Garstang, a bull of a man with battle scars to prove it, arrived at the door of the last house in Melkstrete. The property was one of the more desirable houses in this part of the town, with glass, not thin horn in its windows, and recently fresh limewash on its walls. None of the soldiers had ever been here before, nor had ever visited St Albans. Still, all recognised a house of pleasure when they saw one.

The four men-at-arms were excited, nudging and pushing to be first through the door. William atte Garstang soon put a stop to that.

"We're here to search for the missing maid, not for you four to dip your naggle and get the pox."

He prodded the oldest of the men, Will Bassie, and fixed him with a look that could kill. "You understand me?"

"Aye, Serjeant," the four replied as one. With that, Garstang rapped on the door with his mailed glove.

"King's men. Open up now." He rapped again and heard the shuffle of footsteps beyond, and the door opened slowly.

A young maid stood before him, from her clothing, clearly a servant rather than one of the house ladies. She made to speak, but Garstang pushed her aside, and the five entered the House of Pleasure.

The men-at-arms fanned out, each taking a separate room to search. Garstang heard screams and shrieks and the sound of a male voice protesting.

"Who the fuck are...." The noise of a mailed glove on flesh stopped the man in full flow.

Another voice, a woman's, laced with anger and hostility, challenged the Royal Serjeant.

"By what right do you come into my house and disturb the privacy of my guests?"

Garstang eyed the woman. She was the proprietor by her tone and manner, although she seemed too young, certainly no servant and not yet beyond thirty years. She was pretty, with long dark hair framing her pale face. So, he thought, unmarried for now married woman would wear her hair in such a manner.

She took a step towards him, repeating her question. Garstang responded to this by drawing his war sword.

"By this right." He waved his sword in her direction. "And by the royal command from His Grace, King Edward himself, to search all buildings in this town."

He heard more shrieks from one of the chambers to his side, followed by giggles. The woman brought him back to the moment.

"Search away; you shall not find anything." An alarm sounded in the back of Garstang's mind at that answer. A strange response.

"And who are you, Mistress?"

Her tone seemed to change with her answer. "Why, I am Dulcia le Blunde. You are in my house."

Three of his men-at-arms reappeared. One brought with him a middle-aged man, his lip bleeding and his fine shift covered in blood. He wore no garment below the waist, his hands cupped together to hide his embarrassment.

"I am an Alderman of the city," he began to protest, but a stern look from Garstang stopped him from protesting further. The remaining soldiers pushed forward young girls, naked except for sheets draped over their shoulders. Fear showed in the girl's faces, and they babbled anxiously in French.

"How many more here?" Garstang gruffly spat out the question to Dulcia. She turned and scanned the babbling girls.

"Only one more, Notekina. She is…" Dulcia's words trailed off, and she pointed towards the chamber from where the shrieks and giggles had come. Garstang fired questions at his other man-at-arms about what they had found.

"Nothing, Serjeant. No sign."

"All clear in that chamber, Serjeant." Garstang nodded.

Pointing to two of his men. "You and you, search the out-buildings... And do it thoroughly, or I will have your bollocks." He turned to the third man. "Hugh, keep an eye on this lot."

"Aye, Serjeant."

Garstang then turned his attention to the shrieks and giggles. He lifted the latch of the chamber. Will Bassie stood before him, oblivious to his Serjeant's presence, grunting with pleasure. His back was turned to Garstang, his hose around his ankles. Notekina knelt in front of him, enthusiastically giving French love.

Garstang called out Bassie's name, and when the man-at-arms turned to look, the Serjeant's mailed glove smashed into his face.

"You, out," Garstang barked at Notekina.

Will Bassie rubbed his injured face and pulled up his hose. Before he could, Garstang brought his thick leather boot up to kick the man-at-arms heavily in the groin, and Bassie slumped to the floor.

"You, pox-ridden bastard. I gave you an order. What part of that did you not understand?"

Will Bassie, still clutching his groin, blustered a reply. "When I went in there, Serjeant, she was up to something. Then when she saw I'd seen, she distracted me."

"Oh, that's what you call it."

Bassie gulped in some air to ease the pain. "It was hard to stop her."

"I'm sure it was, by the time she'd finished. What was it she was doing then?"

"She was talking to someone outside the window. The one that looks out onto the alley."

"And?" Garstang was getting impatient.

"All I caught was a few words. She said something about a gathering, ruins. And there was a name, I think. Something like 'Morany'."

"Who was she talking to?"

"Dunno, Serjeant." Garstang gave him a withering look. "She got my attention away, like."

"So, a message?"

"Maybe, Serjeant." The Serjeant glared at Bassie and aimed another kick at his groin.

"Had you been doing what you're paid to do and not thinking with your naggle, we might have known. Get outside and search the alley. And don't think I haven't finished with you, you worthless piece of shit."

Fumbling to tie his hose with one hand, Bassie returned to the corridor. Garstang followed. Hugh held Dulcia, her girls and the Alderman at sword point. The Serjeant waved his weapon in Dulcia's direction. The Alderman continued his complaint about being detained until a well-aimed punch to his stomach silenced his protest.

Garstang regarded Notekina.

"In there." He gestured towards the chamber he had just left. Notekina gave him a beguiling smile and did as he demanded.

Once inside, Garstang closed the door. Notekina smiled and gave him her finest seductive look.

"So, Serjeant, you could not resist? I can show you ways of pleasure you have never imagined."

Garstang's reply was not what she imagined. His mailed fist smashed into her face, drawing both blood and tears.

"Bastard," she snarled at him. "So, you want it rough?" His fist struck her again, her knees buckled, and she fell to the floor, pain coursing across her bloodied face.

Serjeant Garstang loomed over her. "Bitch, who were you passing a message to?"

Notekina remained on the floor, her angry eyes not meeting the Serjeants. He lashed out at her with his boot.

"The message. Who were you talking to? What was the message?"

On the hard wooden floor, Notekina lay motionless. Her hopes that her skills in the bedroom might deflect this Serjeant had come to nought. He knew she had been communicating with someone in the alley. But she knew she must not tell for the sake of her sisters in the Daughters of the Shadows.

Garstang barked out an order to his other men-at-arms, instructing them to bind Notekina's hands behind her back.

"Her too," gesturing towards Dulcia, who immediately began howls of protest. "Take them immediately to John of Berwick at the Abbey. And don't allow them to distract you."

Once the prisoners and their escort had left, Garstang and Bassie interrogated the French girls, the maid, and the Alderman. Once satisfied that they knew nothing of importance, Garstang dismissed them and instructed the men to continue with the search of the surrounding buildings.

"So what exactly did your man overhear, William?" John of Berwick regarded the burly Serjeant. They stood in one of the Abbey guesthouse chambers that Berwick was using to direct the search of St Albans. The room was deep in the gloom, its candled sconces barely throwing out enough light to see the faces of the three men present.

Berwick knew William atte Garstang of old. Both men had fought on the Welsh borders for the old King Henry and had accompanied the Lord Edward to Outremer nearly six years before. Garstang was a man the King's Intelligencer could rely upon.

The Royal Serjeant's expression was intense. "I'm certain she was passing on a message to someone outside in the alley."

Berwick turned to the third man in the room. He sat in the shadows, thinking through the implications of what the burly Serjeant had said.

"One is the daughter of Alice le Blunde, the woman we seek," continued Garstang.

"Aye, she is. Have we questioned the two..." – Simon Lowys sought the correct word – "...*women*?"

"As we speak." It was John of Berwick who spoke. "My man, Ralph of Whitchurch, is starting with the whore. You can question the daughter."

"Dulcia le Blunde?"

"Aye. But speed is of the essence. What now must—" A knock at the door cut his words short.

"Enter!" Berwick barked, annoyed at the interruption.

A guard entered meekly. "Master, you have a visitor."

"I gave instruction that I was not to be disturbed." Berwick's face blazed with fury.

"They said it was important and gave me this." The guard placed a small ring in Berwick's outstretched palm.

The Intelligencer looked at it and nodded to the guard to admit the visitor and for Garstang to leave. Simon made to go, but Berwick raised his hand to stop him.

"I think perhaps it is best if you stay to hear this, Master Lowys."

As Berwick was receiving the mysterious visitor, a bruised and beaten Notekina de Hogenhore lay sprawled on the cold earth in the Abbey cell, which, until recently had held Adam of Brazbourn. The sound of the door creaking open registered in her head, but she didn't turn to see who had entered. A hand grabbed her hair, and she was hauled to her feet by two young men-at-arms and dragged outside towards another Abbey building.

Ralph of Whitchurch gazed at the pitiful figure bound to the chair in front of him. He had expected a beautiful young maid, comely and alluring from the reports. But the hair was matted with earth, her face bloodied and bruised, courtesy of the soldiers who brought her here. The shift she wore was dirty and bloodied. Her head slumped downwards, refusing to look up at him.

"Mistress. Can I get you some ale?" His tone was gentle and measured but elicited no reply. He went to a small barrel standing on a side table and scooped a jug of watery ale, which he put to her cracked lips. She drank eagerly.

"What message did you pass on, Mistress?" Notekina's head slumped down once again, refusal in her silence.

"You must answer me, Notekina, or you know what will happen to you." His tone was now more assertive.

This time she looked at him, but only to purse her lips and spit in his face. He raised a hand and wiped the gobbet from his cheek. His right palm lashed across her already cut face.

"You will tell me. It will come after much pain to you, but you will tell me."

"Never." For the first time, she spoke.

"Oh, you will." Whitchurch grabbed her raven black hair and twisted it violently, jerking her head backwards. As he did, he drew a thin-bladed dagger from his belt and lay its icy blade against her cheek.

"My men told me how comely you were; your soft, delicate skin; your pretty face and deep dark sultry eyes." The thin dagger pressed hard against her cheek, drawing a nick of blood that trickled down like a red tear. "If you don't tell me what I need to know, I will use my blade, and no man will ever look on your face with lust and desire ever again."

Across a cloistered corridor of fine stone, Dulcia le Blunde also sat bound hand and foot, strapped with belts to a chair in an abbey storeroom. Caskets and pots surrounded her. The smell of salt, ale, and spice permeated her nostrils. The guards had not beaten Dulcia, not a punch or slap. That had surprised her. She fully expected to be tortured when they interrogated her, but no. The fact that they had not done so filled her with dread for what was about to come.

CHAPTER 59

The Benedictine monastery, St Albans, July 1276

That it had been the King's Man, Lowys, who had interrogated her had been a surprise to Dulcia le Blunde. True, he had raised his voice, but the expected punches, pain and torture had not come. He had asked the obvious questions about the seizure of the King's daughter, and Dulcia had maintained she knew nothing about any abduction. Lowys had wanted to know where her mother was, and for that, she could truthfully say, she did not know.

"Where are the Daughters of the Shadows meeting?" He had asked her, again and again. And, truthfully, she could answer that she did not know, for only her mother knew that, although she didn't reveal that to the King's Man.

Only when he questioned her about the whereabouts of Walter de Baskerville did a flicker of emotion come across her face. Had he seen that? No! She was sure he hadn't. Dulcia liked the mercenary captain, indeed had lain with him at Fulelane. However, if her mother knew that, she would be angry. But, in truth, Dulcia didn't expect to hear from him again. Walter de Baskerville was a ghost – a most dangerous man – and she knew that was why she was drawn to him.

Screams of pain emanated from somewhere close by, followed by longs, sobs and wails. Loud cries of *"No... no... no..."* preceded more shrieks of pain. Dulcia recognised the voice of Notekina. They were torturing her for information, and Dulcia hoped her coven-sister had the strength to hold out.

Dulcia had pretended to the King's Man that she hardly knew de Baskerville, and he seemed to believe her. And with that, his interrogation ended, although she fully expected that once the torture of Notekina had finished, they would turn their attention to her next. That thought sent her blood coursing, her breath running faster and faster. The door bolt shifted, and the latch clicked upwards. Dulcia, palpitating, steeled herself for the pain that she knew was sure to come.

A monk with a protruding belly entered the chamber. What game was this, she thought?

"Fuck off, monk." Her words were spat out with contempt.

The monk threw back his cowl. "Such a kind way to welcome your rescuer."

Dulcia looked wide-eyed in amazement at the black-garbed figure of Isabella la Rus. She let out a long breath of relief and thanks. Had she believed in the Christian deity, she might have uttered a silent prayer of thanks.

"The guard. How did you get rid of the guards? Did you slit their throats?"

"Nay," said Isabella, slitting the straps binding Dulcia to the chair. "I brought him a draught of strong ale and said the Cellarer sent it. But I had laced it with aloe, myrrh and saffron so he would soon be running to the jakes."

Dulcia laughed, as much with relief as anything else. Isabella pulled out another monk's habit from beneath her own and tossed it towards her coven sister.

"Quickly, put this on over your clothes; we must be away before the guard returns."

Dulcia threw the black robes over her own dirty shift, and with Isabella slipped out of the cell, bolting the door behind them to show that the prisoner was still inside. In the cloistered corridor, their cowls pulled over their heads, they gave the impression of two novices about their business, moving deliberately slowly so as not to attract attention.

"We must be away from here as quickly as you can." Isabella stressed the urgency of the situation. "We must separate. There is a gate that the lay workers do use to come and go from the Abbey. The Porta Pomarii, beside the orchard at the foot of the hill. Make your escape that way, then meet me in the rear of the Wheatsheaf at dusk."

Isabella handed Dulcia a small wicker basket. "Clothing and some food. Go now."

Dulcia embraced her coven sister.

"Thank you! You have saved me from the pain of their torture, and I am in your debt." Dulcia headed away from the Abbey and down the path to the Porta Pomarii. She paused and turned towards Isabella, puzzled. She had a nagging feeling that she had missed something important but couldn't quite put her finger on what it was.

"Do you not leave by this gate also?"

Isabella la Rus shook her head. "Nay. I shall leave by the Porta Sumpter, as it is closer to the town, and one alone will attract less suspicion."

Dulcia gave a wave. "Until the dusk, sister," and continued her path down the hill to the Porta Pomarii and safety.

CHAPTER 60

The back lanes of the town of St Albans, Hertfordshire, July 1276

The back lanes, runnels and alleys of the town were comforting, familiar routes for Dulcia le Blunde. She had grown up on them and knew the fastest ways to avoid the Manga Vico and its crowds. That knowledge now was invaluable, as she slipped in and out of the darkness, hiding from squads of the King's soldiers still busy searching the homes and outbuildings, before making progress towards the town gates.

Dulcia thanked the Dark One that Notekina had the presence of mind to alert one of their watchers to send word to Isabella la Rus at the Wheatsheaf. That Isabella was now compromised, she was sure. That King's Man, Lowys, would realise it was Isabella who had secured Dulcia's freedom. She just hoped that somehow Isabella would make her way out of the town this night.

The two coven sisters had met in the Wheatsheaf's garden at dusk, as they had arranged. Isabella was not being hunted, and therefore, it would be easier for her to leave through the gates. Dulcia had agreed to meet Isabella behind St Michael's Church in Kingsbury village at the hour of the curfew bell, and together they would make their way to the Gathering. Her mother had not told Dulcia of all her plans for the Gathering, just the outline of the celebration. The vial of Holy Blood had been false, but her mother sent word that she now had something far more powerful. Dulcia assumed it was her mother who had seized the King's daughter. The whole town was aflame with rumour.

She heard the shuffle of boots on the earth and slipped into a dark recess between two buildings. A party of King's troops came up the lane, cursorily glancing from side to side, fatigued at the search. One looked directly into the recess where she now squatted, but the darkness saved her as many times before. Lane by lane; alley by alley, Dulcia made her way southeast towards Sopwellstrete, where the main London gate was located. Not that she intended to use the entrance. She would use the hidden gap in the ditch, the one that months before she had revealed to Maud Blount.Dulcia made slow progress, not helped by her pausing every few minutes to peer into the gloom and listen to ensure that no one was following her. That was highly unlikely. Perhaps they knew of her escape by now, but the King's men had no way of knowing where she was. Dulcia was sure she was alone in these lanes and that no one had observed her other than the occasional night riffler who also inhabited the shadows. To exit the Porta Pomarii, she had donned the simple cote and shift most townsfolk wore. She had kept the dark Benedictine habit Isabella had brought her to escape the monastic precinct, and now it served her well in the darkness of night.

By the time she reached Sopwellstrete she had evaded countless parties of royal troops. She silently slipped through a rear garden of one of the houses, crossed a stinking alley at its rear and eased through the hidden gap out into the openness of the Ver valley.

CHAPTER 61

Prae Wood, above the ancient Roman town, St Albans, Hertfordshire, July 1276

In the shadows of Prae Wood and its ancient settlements that existed long before the Romans, and some two miles west of St Albans, lay Westbrook Hall. Close by was the gentle stream that gave the manor its name. As manor houses went, it was unimposing and decidedly run down. Ivy crept unkempt up its outer walls, biting deep into the lime mortar. The house had been built sometime during the reign of the first King Henry. It had been home to the de Canefeld family, minor knights descended from the son of a mercenary captain to King William during his invasion.

The lord of Westbrook, Robert de Canefeld, had been a loyal follower of old King Henry and had fought and died for him at Lewes ten years before. In the aftermath of the battle, with Simon de Montfort in control of the King, the manor was one of many that passed into the de Montfort hands. Simon had bequeathed the estate to Alix de Montmorency, the name of his still-born son with Alice. The legal transfer of the estate bore both his seal and that of the old King.

A traveller would not come upon Westbrook by chance. It could not have been more secluded, nestled in the shallow river valley. It could only be reached by an ill-defined track off the route towards the Icknield Way.

The manor house lay on the edge of a forest of gnarled ancient oaks. The trees appeared timeless, reaching high towards the darkening sky. No rays of moonlight filtered down through the canopy this night, and scuffles from nocturnal animals broke the eerie stillness. Deep in the woodland, among the oldest of the oak, beech and wild service trees, lay a clearing, hewn from the forest by ancient tribes long ago.

Three small braziers threw out dancing light across the clearing. In its centre, large flat stones, each the size of a hand, lay tight to the grass, spread out across an area roughly thirteen paces by thirteen to form a pentangle. At each of its points stood a figure; at each of its intersections stood another; ten in all. Each draped in a dark cloak with its hood drawn. At the centre of the pentangle was a raised platform, crudely made from wood with its top draped with a white cloth with something on the top; something that looked the shape of a body.

Deep shadows from the braziers danced menacingly in the spaces beyond the platform.

This was a special night in the lunar calendar, the night the moon died. The contrast between the flickering flames in their red, blue, and yellow hues against the darkness of the sky invited the spirits to join the gathering of the coven.

From his vantage point beneath a hoary oak, whose girth three men holding hands could not span, Simon Lowys peered into the clearing. His eyes never moved from the silhouettes of dark-clad figures. He was huddled in a moss-laden gully surrounded by a tangle of large tree roots. It provided ample cover for him to observe. He just hoped he had made the correct choice of location. The creatures of the night occasionally broke the eerie silence with their calls and noises. An owl hooted far away; a vixen screamed.

The light from the braziers threw off precious little illumination beyond the platform. Despite Simon's eyes becoming accustomed to the intense darkness, it was difficult to make out anything more than shapes. He peered intently. He was sure he could make out the shape of a body lying shrouded on the dais. Could that be the young Lady Eleanora? But no! The form was too big for a seven-year-old girl. The it struck him, it had to be the corpse of Maud Blount, stolen from the grave in God's Acre in St Peter's by the Daughters of the Shadows. A shiver ran through him. What fiendish plan did these sisters of Satan have to use Maud Blount's decaying corpse?

Simon fought the fear that ran through him. He was alone, hidden in the undergrowth as a coven of witches were about to enact some devilish worship. Over the past months, he had succeeded in getting himself into some difficult scrapes and only survived thanks to good fortune. If he were being honest with himself, that good fortune had been the arrival of Isabelle de Brun each time to save him. He thought of the widow, and he recollected her beauty and poise, which helped quell his fear somewhat.

The scene inside the pentangle was suddenly illuminated as cresset oil lamps on the dais were lit. Simon could see more clearly now. It was a body on the platform, wrapped tightly in a shroud. Simon could make out a small cage on the platform with what appeared to be a cockerel inside.

Isabelle was here, one of those hooded figures draped in the dark garments surrounding the pentangle. She wouldn't know that Simon was watching the coven, watching her. He tried to determine which of the figures she was, but it proved difficult. Nor could he make out the presence of the Lady Eleanora. Had he blundered? Was the King's daughter elsewhere and the abduction not connected to this gathering of the coven?

The day's events were a blur, happening so fast as he now recalled them. Simon had been there with John of Berwick and had listened to the Royal Serjeant, Garstang's report. Notekina, the whore and the witch had passed on a message. Still, Garstang's man had only heard fragments, and they were no closer to locating the Lady Eleanora. He fully expected John of Berwick's legendary temper to surface when the guard interrupted the meeting. Simon wondered about the significance of the small wax seal the guard placed in Berwick's palm that brought about an immediate change in his behaviour. When Isabelle de Brun appeared at the door, all became clear.

"My Lord..." She addressed the Royal Intelligencer, ignoring Simon's presence. "I had to take the risk of coming here. I received a garbled message from one of the coven members, Notekina de Hoggenhore."

Berwick interrupted her. "Aye. We were in discussion about that very same communication."

"Her message came from one of Alice le Blunde's lackeys. It brought no news about His Grace's daughter, but she sent word that King's men were in Dulcia's house and likely to seize her. The Gathering is this night of the new moon. It is to be at the old ruins, but where that is, I know not."

Berwick was impatient. "Explain?" But it was Simon who answered.

"We are here in St Albans. It is sited by the old Roman town. The ruins could mean the old town or any of the other Roman remains locally, and there are many."

"Or ruins that are even older," Isabelle interjected. "There were people here before the Romans, and their ruins still remain."

Berwick stood and stretched himself out to his full height. "The solution is simple. We flood the whole area with royal troops to flush out the coven and find the maid."

"Nay, My Lord," Isabelle shook her head. "That will not work. The troops will be seen miles off, and Alice will go to ground with the Lady Eleanora. We needs must find where the Gathering is and take Alice and question her."

"But we do not know where Alice le Blunde is," added Simon. As if acknowledging his presence for the first time, Isabelle turned to regard the young King's Man.

"No, Master Lowys, we do not know where Alice is. But her daughter likely knows."

John of Berwick leapt on this idea. "My man, Ralph of Whitchurch, is a most skilled interrogator. He will get the mother's location out of her."

"But not in time, My Lord." Isabelle's eyes sparkled as she outlined a bold plan.

"We allow Dulcia to escape and follow her at a distance. That will surely lead us to Alice and to the Lady Eleanora."

"That is too much of a risk," Berwick interjected.

But Isabelle was determined. "Nay, My Lord. It is a risk, I agree, but a risk we can control. Dulcia will trust me; after all, Notekina sent the message to me at the inn. It would only seem right for one of Dulcia's sisters in the coven to rescue her."

Berwick remained sceptical. "It carries too much of a risk. Our priority is to locate and rescue lady Eleanora."

Isabelle was insistent. "This is our best chance to find the maid alive. We must ask ourselves why the maid was taken? If, as we suspect, Alice le Blunde was behind it, then what is her purpose with the girl?"

"To kill her," Simon said what all were thinking.

Isabelle shook her head. "They could have killed her when they seized her. And then there is the time when she was taken. Her abduction coincides with the new moon and the Gathering."

Simon picked up on Isabelle's thinking. "You suspect that Alice plans some nefarious plan with the lady Eleanora, linked to this Gathering?"

"Aye, I do. And we needs must ask ourselves if the mysterious disappearance of Maud Blount's body has aught to do with this?"

Until now, Isabelle hadn't made this connection. Now her thinking became more precise.

"We had the theft of the Holy Blood from Hailes Abbey, even though it was all staged by le Stedeman. Why did Alice le Blunde want the vial of the holy relic?"

Simon picked up on this. "To perform some evil magic aimed to hurt His Grace the king."

John of Berwick had yet to grasp the implications of Isabelle's thinking. "What do you mean? What do you suspect is planned?"

Isabelle paused, looked at Lowys, and spoke in an earnest tone. "My Lord Berwick, what I suspect is that, at the Gathering this night, Alice le Blunde seeks to raise the corpse of Maud Blount using the blood of Her Grace, the Lady Eleanora."

"God's teeth!" Berwick was shocked. "You think she plans to kill the maid?"

"She plans to sacrifice the child. This night is an auspicious date for the coven; that is why they call it the Gathering. All in the coven who can be there will attend. But we do not know…"

"What we do not know," Simon cut in, "is the location of this Gathering."

Isabelle admired the King's Nuncio for his speed of thought. "Aye, I do not yet know the location."

Berwick regarded Isabelle, and then the full implication of what she was proposing began to strike him.

"You surely don't just propose to allow her to escape?" He paused, his mind racing.

"You plan to escape with her, to find the location of the Gathering and the location of the lady."

"Is he correct?" Berwick asked.

"Aye, I will go with Dulcia, find the location and where the maid is being held, and then I will give a signal for the soldiers to come."

"And what if this Gathering happens elsewhere?" Berwick appeared sceptical.

"That is always a possibility, which is why Master Lowys must keep watch upon the ruins of the old Roman town, which is a likely location. It may be that the Gathering is held there, in which case we both can give a signal... but it may be at other ruins."

"Le Reynard..." it was John of Berwick who spoke now. "The stakes could not be higher, and the risk you take is great. Between locating the maid and giving a sign and the arrival of His Grace's men, your life will be in great danger."

"I know that, My Lord. But I have faced danger before. I shall trust in God to protect me." Simon reached out a hand and placed it on Isabelle's arm, his instinct to protect her surfacing once again. "Stay safe, Mistress, and take as few risks as possible."

She gazed at him, placed her hand on his. His heart raced. "You also face risk this night. I have a plan, Master Lowys. You needs must have one too before this night is out. I will be in contact with you."

With that, she swept out of the chamber. Simon called after her, "Isabelle! Isabelle!" but it was as if she didn't recognise her own name.

"Mistress!" This time she turned, fixing her deep penetrating eyes on his.

"God protect you this night." She inclined her head as her face broke into a thin smile. "And you, Master Lowys. And you."

CHAPTER 62

Prae Wood, Hertfordshire July 1276

Lying in the mossy gully beneath the ancient oak, he thought again of those last words Isabelle had said to him. It was she, not he, who was in control of the situation. She directed him earlier to watch out for the coven's Gathering in the ruins of the old Roman town. There he had been, the King's guard hidden a few hundred yards away in the trees. Was he in the wrong location? There was no certainty that the Gathering would be in the old Roman city.

The spot he had selected to view the ancient ruins was well chosen. A wide flint wall protected him from view on one side, with a copse of beech trees growing on the other. As he lay there, he imagined the ghosts of a past age, people like him, like Isabelle who lived their lives here, who loved and died here. That triggered thoughts of his dead wife Amy and brought with it a tinge of sadness.

Simon wasn't sure how long he lay beneath the beeches on this moonless night, but it probably hadn't been too long when he heard a shuffling sound behind him. Twisting around, Simon saw one of the King's men-at-arms, crouched low and moving crab-like towards him.

"Master Lowys," he whispered. "There is an urgent message arrived for you. You go back to the trees; I shall watch here."

Keeping low, Simon scrambled toward the treeline, one hundred yards away from where the detachment of royal troops hid. A Serjeant hailed him in hushed tones.

"Over here, Master Lowys," indicating for Simon to follow his voice. When he got there, the Serjeant was crouched with a young maid beside him. It was Alia.

Even in such desperate circumstances, Simon felt a glow of pleasure at seeing her again. Still, he couldn't understand why she could possibly be here.

"Alia, how come you here?" He blurted it out, his voice too loud for the situation.

"Hushed tones, Master Lowys," the Serjeant reminded him. Simon nodded his apology.

Moving close to Alia, he asked again what brought her here?

"Mistress de Brun has sent me with a message."

"Mistress de Brun?" He was taken aback. "How did she find you to get a message to come here?"

It was too dark for Simon to make out her eying him closely, deciding what she should tell him.

"She had arranged with me to meet with her in Prae Wood. Do you know it?"

"Aye." Simon's response was laced with anxiety.

Alia composed her thoughts. "I must make sure I give the message as Mistress gave it to me. I am to tell you; she came by the wood with Alice's daughter."

Although Simon couldn't see her clearly, it was evident in her speech that Alia had memorised the message from Isabelle.

"Mistress de Brun said to tell you that the Gathering is to be held this night in the ancient ruins in Prae Wood. But she believes the young *Lady* is not yet there. She says the soldiers are to keep a good furlong away to the north, deep in the woods. And... oh yes, she will give a clear signal once she sees the maid is there."

"What sort of signal?" inquired Simon.

"I know not. She did not say, other than to tell you that it will be a clear signal that will easily be recognised."

Simon began to stand, stretching his frame to its full height. "I must be away to Prae Wood now." But Alia held out her hand to restrain him.

"Mistress did say you would say that. She instructed me to tell you if you come, then you and the King's troops must approach by the southeast so as not to be seen."

It had taken Simon more than an hour to work his way stealthily towards the northern edge of Prae Wood. As he did, Isabelle's warning ran through his head. He was ill-prepared for this. A man of words, not weapons; yet this night he would face that danger others had so often warned him of.

The royal guards followed some minutes behind in a single file. All had divested themselves of any armour and held just swords or bows. They positioned themselves deep inside the wood, away from any prying eyes. Simon worked his way through the mass of trees and to the clearing where Isabelle had said the Gathering would occur.

He now lay in the mossy gully, eyes fixed on the stone pentangle and the dark, hooded figures at its edge. The rhythmic chanting that broke the stillness took him by surprise. The figures began to move purposefully around the pentangle. Simon watched as another figure appeared, walking into the centre of the pentangle towards the dais. It was too dark to see features, but Simon suspected that this was Alice le Blunde, the High Priestess of the Daughters of the Shadows. The figure seemed to be carrying a small animal in front of them. Then it struck him that this 'animal' had to be the lady, Eleanora. He had to act, but Isabelle had to be here, and she would surely take action.

Her coven sisters chanted incantations to Moloch, Chemosh, Dagon, Belial, Beelzebub and Satan, as Alice le Blunde lay the drugged body of King's daughter onto the dais alongside the corpse of Maud Blount. Alice allowed herself a wry smile as wispy clouds danced across the dark sky above her. She had waited ten long years to take vengeance on behalf of the one man she loved.

The chanting stopped. Alice took one of the cresset lights, bent low, and lit a circle of oil placed to surround the dais. The flames leapt up, creating a fiery ring that encircled the platform, with the maid, the corpse and Alice all inside.

The lady Eleanora lay drugged and inert on the dais, side-by-side with the mouldering corpse of Maud Blount. With a show of great theatre, Alice, mumbling incantations to herself, pulled aside the maid's cloak exposing her white linen shift.

Alice threw back her hood and cried out her appeal to the deities of the dark to witness her work this night. She drew a large bone-handled sacrificial knife from inside her own cloak, its blade twinkling in the firelight. She pulled the cockerel from its cage; grasping its legs together, she held it upside down before swiftly running her blade across its throat. The blood spurted like a fountain across the maid and Maud's corpse.

Simon tensed, realising that this had to be the moment to act. As he pushed himself up from his prone position in the gully, a loud cry of *"Loose!"* rang out from within the pentangle. A woman's voice. He saw a hooded figure dash towards the circle of fire and the platform within.

Hunched low inside a knoll between a copse of beech trees, Alia was filled with trepidation. She sought to control her fear. Her mind raced between asking herself what she was doing here and resolving to match Isabelle's expectations of her. Alia hadn't told Simon she was returning to Prae Wood. He would likely have prevented her had he known. So, she followed him and the detachment of troops at a distance. When they were positioned, she skirted to the east to approach the dense copse of beech where she now lay.

She knew what she had to do. Isabelle had made her repeat the instructions over and over. Beside her, Alia had a small, waxed leather pouch containing a tinder of fine, fibrous hemp. In her hands, she held the flint and the steel. Before giving the message to Simon Lowys, Alia had to drape the lower branches of the trees surrounding the clearing with straw bundles. She linked each tree with oil-soaked twine, the end of which ran down to where Alia now waited.

Alia heard Isabelle's signal, *"Loose..."* Without a thought for her own safety and fully trusting Isabelle, Alia struck the flint hard against the steel. Nothing! She tried again and a spark flew immediately, catching the hemp, which in turn shot blue-green flames along the oil-soaked cord.

As he pushed himself up from his prone position, the trees to one side of Simon Lowys erupted in terrible anger of hot, bright flame. The lower boughs of at least half-a-dozen trees were ablaze in a crescent of fire that would be visible for miles. The signal, Simon was certain, would be seen by every royal guard in Prae Wood.

At the points of the pentangle, the coven sisters of the Daughters of the Shadows stood frozen with fright and uncertainty. But not Isabelle, who had raced from her position towards the dais, pushed Alice le Blunde to the floor and grabbed the drugged body of the Lady Eleanora. She threw her light frame over her shoulder and ran as fast as possible towards where Alia lay hidden.

Lying on the ground, confused, and bewildered by what had occurred, Alice screamed a frightening high-pitched roar. Standing at the far end of the pentangle, Dulcia turned away from the dais and charged at Isabelle, cursing her.

"You traitorous bitch!" Her words blended into a frightening wail.

Dulcia produced a long, thin-bladed knife inside her dark cloak, which she brandished as her curses and wailing continued. She closed on Isabelle at a pace. The Royal Intelligencer turned towards the danger. She dropped the maid to the ground behind her and faced the raging Dulcia.

Isabelle swayed back as the witch's long blade swept close to her face. As she rocked backwards to avoid the knife, she reached into the pocket of her cloak for her throwing knife. With a flick of her wrist, she loosed the perfectly balanced knife at close range in one continuous movement. Even as she threw, Isabelle recognised the folly of her action. True, would probably kill Dulcia but now she was weaponless.

Dulcia le Blunde stopped in her tracks, eyes, and mouth wide open with surprise. All her body's energy had suddenly disappeared, her limbs not responding. Her mind did not register what had just happened. Isabelle's throwing knife protruded from her throat. Dulcia dropped her own blade, her hands trying to go to her neck as she struggled for breath. Rivulets of blood began to trickle from the corners of her mouth as she slumped forwards onto her knees, her life slowly ebbing away.

From inside the circle of fire, Alice le Blunde emitted a loud half-wail, half-scream, as she watched her daughter die in front of her. Brandishing the sacrificial knife, she charged towards Isabelle, hate and fury in her eyes.

Isabelle didn't linger to watch the death throes of Dulcia. The fire she had set now blazed in the trees above her, the dry beech leaves providing the perfect kindling. She spun around, scooped up the child and ran towards the gully where Alia was waiting. Reaching the gully, Isabelle roughly threw the Lady Eleanora to the ground.

"Run, get her out of here and keep her safe." She barked, pointing towards the north. "Find the soldiers. They should be here soon."

Leaving her scrip and her hand-held arbalest on the ledge of the gully, Alia lifted up the comatose Eleanora. As she did, she cried out a warning to Isabelle as she saw the figure of the anger-filled Alice racing towards them.

"Mistress! Behind you!" Isabelle spun around.

"Go! Go now!" she screamed at Alia, who rushed away, glancing backwards at Isabelle.

On hearing Alia's warning, Isabelle turned, but Alice was upon her, hate etched across her face. She screamed at Isabelle as her knife swung in a wide arc towards the intelligencer's head. Isabelle ducked to avoid the sharp, honed blade.

"I will gut you like a fowl!" spat Alice. "I knew I was wrong to trust you!" She thrust again, aiming the blade towards the heart, the speed of her movements belying her age.

With her eyes firmly fixed on the blade and not the vengeful Alice, Isabelle swept out her arm, hoping to make contact with Alice's, to push the knife away. She felt the blade bite into her forearm and the searing pain that followed. Alice reached her blade high in an arc with a cry of triumph to come down on Isabelle's neck.

Despite the throbbing pain, Isabelle succeeded in pushing herself away to avoid the killing blow. With all her weight on one side, her leather boot struggled for grip and slipped on a mossy rock. Seeking to regain her balance, Isabelle tumbled backwards, arms askew, striking her head on a stone that jutted out in front of the gully.

Alice le Blunde looked down at the motionless body of Isabella la Rus lying on the ground in front of her. *Dead,* she thought to herself, *probably...* This woman, one she thought was her loyal sister in Satan, had thwarted her plan for vengeance, and she had paid for that with her life. But Alice would not leave it at that. She would slit Isabella's throat, just to make certain.

CHAPTER 63

Prae Wood, Hertfordshire, July 1276

From his position on the north side of the copse, Simon Lowys saw the commotion that followed the flaming fire in the trees. He stood rooted to the spot as Dulcia charged at Isabelle and then as the witch fell to her knees, a knife protruding from her throat. Now he watched Alice le Blunde race manically towards Isabelle, shrieking and screaming oaths of death.

Alice swung again in a curving arc towards Isabelle's head. Simon caught the glint of the blade sweep down to bite into Isabelle's arm. He admired how deftly Isabelle swayed to avoid the killing stroke. He let out an audible gasp as she fell backwards and disappeared from his sight.

Alice moved towards the spot where Isabelle had fallen, and thoughts of her lying there injured coursed through his mind. Perhaps she had been caught with the blade? He stepped into the clearing and called out.

"It is over, witch. The King's archers are just beyond these trees." Simon spoke with a confidence he did not possess. Indeed, he did not know how long it would be before the royal guards arrived.

Hearing the shout behind her, Alice le Blunde turned to face a ghost. There was puzzlement in her voice.

"You? You are dead. The town authorities said as much." Her surprise at seeing Simon soon disappeared.

"So now I needs must kill a spirit." she sneered, approaching him with her sacrificial knife held high. Simon moved away from the Priestess towards where Isabelle had fallen. Simon's right hand went to his baselard dagger in his belt. Drawing it gave him more confidence, but, he was a man of law, not a fighter, and unskilled in its use.

The fire still burning around the platform illuminated the clearing, and the dancing flames reflected in blades. With a piercing scream, Alice lunged at Simon's stomach, a killing blow he just managed to evade. Despite being in a death struggle, his mind sent him conflicting thoughts; whether he should seek to take her alive or kill her.

His inattention almost cost him his life as Alice slashed her blade wide to cut into his only-recently healed left shoulder. The burning, searing pain made him wince. His arm felt weak and unresponsive to his will. Blood seeped through his shift spotting the ground beneath him.

Seeing the dark trickle of blood, Alice sensed her triumph. "You are wounded King's Man, and soon you will be too weak to strike back as the blood drains from you."

Simon knew she was correct. Already he was beginning to feel lightheaded, his eyes trying to fix Alice, whose voice became distant. Sweat appeared on his brow, and his skin began to lose colour.

"You are going to die here, King's Man, killed at the hands of the Daughters of the Shadows, and I will have revenge on the accursed Edward of England. This is not over. My sisters live on."

Although her voice appeared far away, Simon, swaying from side to side, could see the look of triumph on Alice's face and hear it in the words she spoke. He gritted his teeth as the burning pain in his shoulder overwhelmed him and slumped to his knees. His dagger fell to the earth, and Alice scooped it up. Simon slumped over onto one side falling into the shallow gully only recently vacated by Alia.

Alice le Blunde took a few paces forward, peering over to where he lay motionless. Satisfied he was dead or unconscious she swivelled and looked towards where Isabelle lay. The King's Intelligencer had come around and was trying to push herself up.

Isabelle was on her knees, her head throbbing. She looked up into a face contorted by hate as she sought to focus. Isabelle was powerless, even if she had a weapon. The High Priestess raised her knife above her head as she let out a demoniac howl. Isabelle screwed her face, only half-looking at Alice, waiting for the pain of the slashing strike that would end her life.

A click and the familiar loud hiss of a rushing bolt through the air broke the silence of the moment. Through half-opened eyes, Isabelle watched Alice le Blunde's malevolent expression change. Her lips opened as if surprised, but blood, not words, trickled from the corners of her mouth, running down onto her cloak. The knife slipped from her fingers, falling to the grass beside Isabelle. She reached out both arms as if to seize her neck and toppled to the ground, pinning Isabelle beneath, as Alice's life breath extinguished.

It took Isabelle some moments to extricate herself from beneath Alice's weight, made more difficult by the throbbing pain from her wound. Alice's blood seeped onto her face and clothing, making Isabelle appear more injured than she actually was. By the time she had struggled to her feet and looked about, the remaining Daughters of the Shadows had fled.

But then alarm remerged as the still-burning fires silhouetted a figure approaching her. Garbed in dark clothes and moving purposefully, Isabelle waited for the next assault. Then as the figure came closer, she recognised Simon Lowys. His shoulder was soaked with blood from the wound Alice inflicted, and in his hand, he held a small arbalest. Simon looked from Isabelle to the body on the grass beside her. Alice lay face down on the earth, a quarrel protruding from her back as if a small bird had impaled itself in her flesh.

Mouth open and gulping in air, Simon's eyes moved from Alice to the other dead woman lying on the earth close by. Involuntarily he made the Signum Crucis even though both were heretical daughters of Satan.

He exhaled deeply and then winced at the pain from his shoulder. Intelligencer and nuncio stood a few yards apart, breathing heavily.

"It is you who has saved me this night, Master Lowys, and I am in your debt. *But you are hurt.*"

Isabelle saw a thin grimace break across Simon's pale face. "She slashed me with her blade, and I toppled into the gully. I thought to die, but she didn't come to finish me."

Simon took a long deep breath. "I recalled your words to me, 'can you kill, Master Lowys?' And I saw the small arbalest on the lip of the gully. I could not let her finish you."

Isabelle reached out her good arm to touch his. "I do thank you, Simon." They stood close to one another, each regarding the other.

"The Lady Eleanora?" inquired Simon abruptly.

"Safe. Taken to the royal soldiers in the woods, yonder." He raised his eyebrows at this, the pain from his shoulder not allowing him to fully register what that meant.

"And the rest of the coven?"

"Scattered to the four winds by now, I suspect." Isabelle pointed to Alice's body. "They are without a leader now, and we can have them hunted down in the morning hours."

As she spoke these, Isabelle noticed Simon's eyes become distant, and his body began to sway. Suddenly, Simon's knees buckled beneath him, and she rushed forward to seize him.

"Your wound, Master Lowys, let me see it." Simon ignored her request, trying to push her away.

"My Lord Berwick would not forgive me if I succeeded in losing one of his Intelligencers. My cut is not deep but has bled much. Yours need to be seen by the physician as soon as we can."

Simon was helped to his feet, and by the light of the burning flames, Isabelle guided him towards the eastern copse of beech. They had managed just a few paces when the first of the royal guards filtered through the trees. One of the soldiers shouted out a challenge, but his Serjeant, who apparently knew Lowys, bade him stand down.

"The King's daughter?" Urgency laced Isabelle's inquiry to the Serjeant. The Serjeant was taken aback at the question coming from the woman and not the nuncio. "The lady Eleanora?" Isabelle asked again.

"The child is safe. A maid brought her out a while back."

Simon looked puzzled, turning from the Serjeant-at-arms to Isabelle.

"Alia," she said, enlightening him.

"Nay, I left her in the ancient ruins when she brought your message."

"Aye," A smile broke across Isabelle's face. "You did. But she came back.

"It was Alia that fired the trees?"

"Aye."

Isabelle's gaze fell onto the arbalest still in Simon's grip. He turned to regard the ugly quarrel protruding from the corpse of Alice le Blunde.

She saw his hand begin to shake. She took it in hers, steadying him.

"I had not taken a life before," he admitted.

"Fie. What you did was necessary." Isabelle wasn't about to give him sympathy. "You acted correctly to save the King's daughter. Now we needs must get back to the Abbey to have your wound seen and give a report on what has happened here."

In the first glimmer of the dawn, Isabelle and Simon picked their way carefully down a track through the wood that led to the old Roman road. Simon was very quiet, turning over the events of the last hour in his head. Try as he might, he could not stop his good hand from shaking. Was this what soldiers in their first battle felt like in its aftermath? He had killed someone and, at the same time, had saved Isabelle. Simon felt an urgent need for the *paenitentia secunda,* the second repentance that was the confessional. He had taken a life; he had broken the Fifth Commandment. He needed to profess his sin to a priest and seek God's absolution.

The King's soldiers milled around in the clearing. A rickety cart, driven by two of the King's Men-at-Arms, passed them. One of the guards hailed them.

"We've to collect the corpses and bring them back to the Abbey. Is this the right path?"

Simon was still despondent but pointed uphill. "Aye, carry on without deviation. Just follow the smouldering trees."

"Thank you, Meister." The guard deftly flicked the reins, and the two horses pulling the death cart responded, moving gently ahead.

The King's Intelligencer and the royal Nuncio made slow progress as they shuffled down the track. Simon leaned on heavily Isabelle's slight frame, his wound still throbbing. Her forearm still dripped blood, leaving an intermittent trail on the earth as they moved. At length, they came upon a party of royal troops guarding a carriage.

"Master Lowys. Good to see you." William atte Garstang hailed Simon. The Royal Serjeant was busy directing his men to search different sections of Prae Wood but broke off when he saw Simon was wounded.

He regarded Simon's blood-soaked shoulder. "Maybe's it's a clean-cut, so they will not have to cut your arm off." His attempt at humour was not appreciated.

"Her Grace, the Lady Eleanora?" Isabelle inquired.

"She is warm and resting inside that carriage there and will go down into the Abbey as soon as the light is good enough. She is with that young maid who brought down." the Serjeant replied.

"Alia, she is safe too?" It was Simon who spoke.

"Aye. I know not her name, but she is good, tending to her grace as we speak."

Isabelle pulled back the crimson curtains on the royal carriage and greeted a surprised Alia.

"I thank the Holy Virgin you are safe." Simon's warm words brought a modest smile of acknowledgement to Alia's lips. Leaving Simon leaning against a wheel, Isabelle climbed deftly into the carriage and examined the still sleeping Eleanora.

"There are no wounds," she thankfully exclaimed. "They must have kept her drugged, and we now must hope it wears off soon."

Simon gave a sharp cry of pain as he moved his arm too quickly. He felt cold and suddenly very fatigued. William atte Garstang grabbed him, supporting his weight and with the help of a few guards, sat him in the front of the wagon wrapped in a woollen cloak.

The crisp, clear dawn light allowed the carriage to move down the track towards the Roman road and the Abbey grounds. A groggy Simon sat quietly in the front with Serjeant Garstang while Isabelle joined Alia and the sleeping maid inside.

The Abbey bell rang for Lauds when the carriage pulled up inside the Abbey gate. The lady, Eleanora slept, oblivious to the events of the past day and the furore and crisis that had unfolded.

CHAPTER 64

The Tower of London, July 1276

The Caen stone of the Tower, built centuries before by King William, gleamed in the early morning sun as John of Berwick's stallion crossed the bridge over the western moat to enter the fortress. A young ostler took his horse while Berwick crossed the Inner Ward to make his way to the Wakefield Tower to question Adam of Brazbourn. He descended the steps and greeted the Deputy Custodian of the Tower, a large, muscular man with black hair dressed in a leather apron. Behind him, Berwick could see the glow from lit braziers and hanging from hooks, the implements of persuasion, the tools of the man's trade.

The oubliette lay beneath their feet, the dark, dank, godless, forgotten place that housed the prisoners.

"God give you good day, Master Custodian. I seek the young fellow sent here on my orders late yesterday from the monastery at St Albans."

The Deputy Custodian gave Berwick a hard stare followed by a perplexed frown.

"Nay, My Lord, no prisoner came last night. We was to expect one, and yes, on your orders." He paused to clear his throat, "but word came that countermanded that instruction."

Berwick was incredulous. "Countermanded? On whose authority?"

The Deputy Custodian of the Tower cowed, his reply a mere whimper. "His... His... His Grace, the King, Master Berwick. The King."

Berwick could not understand why but had to accept the royal command. "Do you know where the prisoner is now?" he snapped.

"Nay, Master. I do not, just that he never got here."

As John of Berwick was questioning the Deputy Custodian, twenty-five miles to the north, Adam of Brazbourn stood before the King, sitting as a judge in the Curia Regis in the Abbey Refectory at St Albans, passing sentence.

The King's judgement in French came out in a harsh, almost bitter tone. "Adam of Brazbourn, we have found you guilty of treason against your King. You shall be taken from this court to a place of execution and hanged. Your head will be removed from your body and displayed as a warning to all. Your body shall hang on the gallows, in chains, until there is nothing left. May God have mercy on your soul."

John of Berwick encouraged his palfrey uphill, along the old Roman Road towards the Sopwell Gates of St Albans. Upon reaching sight of the entrance, he realised he was too late to question the prisoner. High above the gate, freshly impaled on one of its spikes, was the badly beaten, contorted head of Adam of Brazbourn. Already hungry crows had pecked out the eyeballs leaving hollows that seemed to stare sightlessly towards the southern horizon. When, minutes later, a frustrated Berwick swung his horse into the main entrance of the Abbey, he came upon the headless corpse of Adam hanging in chains from the gallows, swaying gently as the breeze took it.

The trial had been swift, taking place as John of Berwick was on the road north. It had lasted no longer than the time it would take to say a dozen Paternosters. As was usual, Adam of Brazbourn was not permitted to speak in his own defence at this hastily arranged court in the Abbey Refectory. Not that he could have done so, given his broken jaw, swollen, bruised face and the broken teeth from the beatings administered to him by the royal guards.

As Adam stood, bound hand and foot before the King, confused thoughts had scrambled in his head. All of this was a misunderstanding. Jasliena could explain that to them if they would just bring her here. He had attempted to call out her name, get her here, have her tell-all, and say how they had got this so very wrong. His words came out as a mangled noise before a guard placed a gag in his mouth to prevent any further interruptions.

Few witnesses were called. Men from the crowd outside the Abbey were ushered forwards to give their oath-sworn testimony. All agreed they had seen the quarrel miss Her Grace, the Queen and had seen Adam with the weapon in his hand. Adam's guilt was a foregone conclusion, not least because he had the arbalest in his possession. The oath-swearers testified that they had seen him attempting to run away.

Adam had listened with incredulity. No! No! You have this so wrong? He was innocent! He so wanted to explain all but was not permitted.

Once the King had pronounced sentence, Adam was dragged from the court, held sturdily by two royal men-at-arms. His hands were bound behind his back and his feet scraped along the ground as they pulled him to the gallows outside the Abbey gate. Everything happened so fast. Adam looked up and saw a scaffold had been made ready. A cart stood beneath a stout noose slung across the bough of gnarled ancient oak.

Death came slowly to the young apprentice. His life ebbed away as he danced at the end of the rope, gasping for air, his leggings soiled by his urine. As he struggled, his face contorted, turning blue, his mind still racing, wondering how this had come to pass and what had happened to Jasliena.

CHAPTER 65

House of the Widow Heacham, Sopwellstrete, St Albans, July 1276

The aroma of freshly baked bread permeated the downstairs of Matilda Heacham's townhouse as it did every morning. The bread on her table was accompanied by newly churned butter, a large pot of honey, and two jugs of ale brewed the previous evening. Whitsuntide had been six weeks before, and this was not a Rogation Day, so the fare was allowed. It was two days since the King's daughter had been rescued in Prae Wood. The Abbey guest house was full, and royal men-at-arms had billeted themselves in every available ale house in St Albans. Simon and Alia had gone to Matilda Heacham's house on Sopwellstrete to seek accommodation, as had Isabelle. She had not wished to return to the Wheatsheaf just yet. All had rested well after their exertions the previous day, and Matilda had re-dressed their wounds. They had gathered in the morning to break their fast.

There was little conversation at the table, a reflection perhaps, of the quality of the food or a realization of how close to death they had been. Simon had not told them that he had found a confessor, the white-haired Sire Gerold of the pilgrim Church of St Peter's, at the far end of the Magno Vico. The cold, gloomy church had been empty when he knelt before the old priest and confessed his sins.

Sire Gerold listened and then granted Simon God's absolution but counselled him that although he had indeed broken the fifth Commandment, it was not a sin that imperilled his mortal soul because he had killed a witch, not a Christian believer.

Nonetheless, Sire Gerold gave Simon a penance to make a holy pilgrimage to the shrine of the Blessed St Thomas at Canterbury. The additional twelve Paternosters and an instruction to fast every Monday from Lamas Day until Advent had been for confessing to lustful thoughts about a woman who wasn't his wife.

"Will you have more ale, Master Lowys?" Matilda enquired.

"I will. Tis a fine brew Mistress."

Matilda poured Simon another and then offered the jug to Isabelle and Alia.

Isabelle held up her hand. "Nay. No more for me, but I will have some more of this wonderful honey." She scooped some onto her bread.

"What plans do you now have, Master Lowys?"

Simon laid down his buttered bread. "I must return to Westminster and wait on the Queen. Although the arrangement over the manor of Langlei is complete, I needs must oversee the safe transfer into Her Grace's hands."

"And you, Mistress?" Alia looked to Mistress de Brun.

"Oh!" Isabelle sighed. "There is much I have to finish and places I need to visit."

The three others seated around the kitchen table regarded her intently.

"That is an enigmatic reply, Mistress," Simon said. "Do you plan a pilgrimage?" His words could have been said in jest, but in truth, he wished to know her plans, and he wanted to see this woman again.

"Aye. A pilgrimage may suit well. And you, Alia, you are happy to stay here as a companion to Mistress Heacham?"

Alia's reply was quick and excited. "Aye. That does suit me well if Mistress Heacham does agree."

Matilda smiled. "Of course, I do, dear. I would welcome the company, and you will be of great help to me." She gave a knowing pause. "And to the King's cause."

Simon couldn't help but notice how, once again, Isabelle de Brun had deftly avoided answering the question. He tried again.

"So, where do you go from here? I go south to Westminster if you would have the company."

Isabelle's honeyed eyes locked in on his, again drawing him in.

"That is a most kind invitation Master Lowys. I truly wish I could accept your company, but I am not heading to London. I have work here in the town to complete, and then I needs must focus on my business."

That had not been the response Simon had hoped for. When all four had broken their fast, both Simon and Isabelle made their farewells to Matilda Heacham and Alia.

"Will I see you again soon?" Alia inquired of both. It was Isabelle who answered.

"Aye. For my part, you undoubtedly shall. And I am sure Master Lowys will return here in the fulness of time."

"I will," he added. "Look after Mistress Heacham, my maid." And having made their goodbyes, the royal nuncio and the King's intelligencer walked out onto a sunny Sopwellstrete.

The events of the previous days already felt distant. Simon was reluctant to leave the company of Isabelle de Brun.

"And will I see you again, Mistress?" he blundered clumsily.

Isabelle tilted her head and scrutinized him for a time. "I am sure that Simon Lowys and Isabelle de Brun shall meet soon, Master Lowys."

"When my business at Westminster with Her Grace is complete, I could call upon you if you would so permit."

She thought for a moment and then spoke in her most courtly tone. "Master Lowys. Mistress de Brun would welcome a visit from you once your royal duties are done."

She took his hand and lifted it gently to her face, placing a delicate, lingering kiss upon his fingers. Without a word, she turned and walked away from him towards the town.

CHAPTER 66

The port of Harwich, Essex, England, July 1276

The merchant cog, the Veel Geluk, laid close to the wooden jetty at Harwich. Its master Luka Zeeman eyed the two strangers suspiciously. The taller of the two claimed to be a merchant seeking passage to the continent to complete a business deal. He offered the Master two marks for the crossing when, in truth, Luka would have accepted half-a-mark or even less as fare for both.

The man's hood was pulled close to his face, understandable given the wind blowing in from the German Sea. But Luka knew merchants. Years of crossing the German Sea told him that this man was no trader in goods. His manner, bearing, and the scar on his cheek said that this was a man of war, one whose trade was violence. Luka only had to look at the man's companion to confirm this. This shorter man exuded menace with every look and movement. Yes, the ship's master thought, these were killing men seeking a hasty exit out of England. Dangerous thoughts raced through Luka Zeeman's head. If these men were in such a hurry to flee England, there was probably a price on their heads, much more than the two marks he was about to earn. But then, a more sensible line of thinking overcame him. They may be desperate to escape England and worth much coin, but he would be dead in a heartbeat if he tried to take them.

"One mark each, and I can throw in your meals if that suits?"

The taller man gazed at the Flemish captain, gave a gruff acknowledgement and handed over a small purse of coin containing three hundred and twenty pennies. The Master instructed both to follow him up the gangplank onto his vessel and took them below deck to a dark corner, where he indicated they could sleep. Walter de Baskerville sniffed the foul air beneath the deck. The odour of herring, salt and piss.

"Just for a couple of nights, eh, Bertrand?" He addressed his companion in French.

"How many days is the crossing to Dordrecht?" This time he spoke to Luka in crude accented Dutch.

"A day and a half if the winds in the German Sea are favourable to us." The taller man's ability to speak men some Dutch convinced Luka that his initial judgement about the men was correct. They were likely mercenaries.

Some hours after the church bells rang out for Prime, as the tide was at its height and on the turn, the Veel Geluk slipped its mooring and, straining against the breeze, left the jetty at Harwich bound for the port of Dordrecht.

As the turning tide took Walter de Baskerville and Bertrand du Guesclin away from England, eighty miles to the southwest, another merchant ship prepared to sail from the jetty at Baudries Wharf below London Bridge.

The Senyora dels Mars was a Castilian vessel carrying wool and spices between Donostia and Antwerp. She also provided a comfortable passage for those of gentle birth needing to travel to the continent. Its Master, Fadrique de Gijon, converted space below deck into accommodation for more prosperous merchants, lords, and ladies who paid good coin for the privilege.

For this crossing to Ponthieu, the accommodation had been taken by an Abbess, Constanza of San Andreas de Anroyo, returning from a pilgrimage to the major shrines of England. Fadrique de Gijon thought Constanza very young to be an Abbess. He judged that she had just passed her thirtieth year and assumed she must have had family links to the nobility to attain such a high position at her age. Her Castilian accent betrayed her origins, although he could already tell that she was Iberian from the hue of her olive skin and strong-boned features. Fadrique also thought it unusual that such a prominent Abbess went on progress without a chaperone or another nun to act as her maid. Still, he imagined that this was how senior nuns must travel, so he gave it no more thought.

His unruly and ungodly crew became skittish at a woman on board. The older hands viewed it as bad luck, while some of the younger ones leered at the female body under the dark habit, even though she was a daughter of God.

Fadrique apologised for the behaviour of his crew, but the Abbess waved it away. On this trip, he had two other passengers, a cloth merchant from Bruges and a Tapestry seller from Arras. Both were loud and friendly and had quickly bonded, whereas the Abbess said little and kept herself to herself even in the hours before they sailed. She requested meals be served to her in her accommodation rather than with the other passengers. Fadrique assumed it had something to do with her religious vows, quickly dismissing the thought again.

The incoming tide was at its height as St Mary's and St Dunstan's bells pealed for Nones. The Senyora dels Mars, packed with its cargo of English wool, left its berth at Baudries Wharf and glided with the tide down the Thames towards the Narrow Sea bound for Boulogne.

In her accommodation, the Abbess of San Andreas de Anroyo sensed the gentle pitch and roll of the ship's movement and inwardly gave thanks, but not to God. Jasliena van Leuven, in her, alter ego as Benuic, had failed in her attempt to kill Queen Eleanor. Still, there would be other occasions in the future. That had been made clear to

Guy de Montfort when he first engaged the services of Benuic; the agreement lasted until the task was fulfilled. De Montfort had never met Benuic, but it would be Benuic who decided on the how, the where and most importantly, the when.

Alone in her small sleeping area, Jasliena thought momentarily about Adam. He had been a pleasant youth, without guile and naive. He had done all she had asked of him, all she expected of him. She hadn't witnessed him seized by the soldiers outside St Albans Abbey. However, she had heard the shouts and screams identifying him as the assassin and the cries that he held the weapon still. Jasliena had fully expected a commotion and had used that moment to affect her escape, just as she had planned. Jasliena van Leuven had to disappear, just in case Adam identified her, so she assumed the disguise of the Abbess Constanza of San Andreas de Anroyo. The real Abbess was many hundreds of miles away in her convent and was never likely to discover the impersonation. Poor Adam, he was likely dead now, swinging at the end of a rope, killed by some gruesome method, no doubt.

And, as quickly as that, she put the young man out of her mind. Adam of Brazbourn had served his purpose. The Senyora dels Mars was picking up speed as the river breezes began to fill her sails. To the sound of timbers creaking, canvas flapping, and ropes slapping, Jasliena van Leuven left England, but she would return; Benuic would return.

CHAPTER 67

The Scriptorium, St Albans Abbey, July 1276

It had been the first Abbot, the Benedictine, Paul of Caen, who had established the scriptorium above the monk's Chapter House at St Albans. It had six writing seats on either side of a large west-facing window to maximise the natural daylight. William of Rishanger sat at one such desk, his quill moving in deft strokes across the stretched parchment in front of him. His steady hand-produced neat, perfect Gothic Textura letters with open capital letters left blank for future illumination with red ink.

William was proud to be working in the scriptorium of St Albans Monastery. He knew pride was a sin but was it still sinful when it was for the glory of God? He felt the heavy presence of those who had gone before, especially Roger of Wendover and Matthew Paris. Not yet, in his thirtieth year, Brother William was an accomplished scribe, a cronicator. He was continuing the tradition of Matthew Paris and his *Chronica Majora*, recording the events of the realm. The location of the Abbey on Watling Street meant many important guests passed through the Benedictine complex and were an essential source of information on events that had occurred. He was not yet the official recorder of events, but he hoped that, in time, the Abbot would see the quality of his writing and grant him that title.

But in these past days, the monastery itself had been at the centre of events. Although William had not witnessed it himself, he had taken time to question other Brothers who had been present or who had heard what had happened. Thus, it was that he sat alone in the Scriptorium in the hours between Terce and Sext before the sun was at its height. William contemplated how best to record the momentous events that had occurred here in the past weeks. He felt his start was worthy of Matthew Paris himself:

Eodem anno, anno regni regis Edwardi quarto, filii regis Henrici, in festo sancti Phillipi et beati Jacobi regis gratia, regina venit ad devotionem suam coram beato sancto.

("In that same year, being the fourth year of the reign of King Edward, son of King Henry, on the Feast day of St Philip and St James her grace, the queen did come to pay her devotion before the blessed Saint.")

William dipped his trimmed de-feathered quill into the inkhorn. He had left a small tuft at one end and cut a split in the other to regulate the ink flow. He tapped its tip gently to prevent the ink pooling on the expensive parchment and continued his writing. His desk inclined slightly towards him to allow the ink to flow, but the parchment was, as yet, unilluminated. That he would do that once the page was complete.

Cuius gratia regina, in magna pietate, antea cum Augustinianis apud Sanctam Mariam in Stanmere devoverat, et apud sanctas sorores sanctae Mariae apud Sopuellam manserat. Et factum est ut in festivitate beate Sancti, gratia eius comitata filia sua domina Leonora, pervenerit ad fores ecclesie abbatie ad devotionem suam.

(Her Grace, the Queen, in great piety, had previously paid her devotion with the Augustinians at St Mary's in Stanmere and had stayed with the holy sisters of St Mary, at Sopwell. And it happened that on the Feast day of the Blessed Holy Saint, Her Grace, accompanied by her young daughter, the Lady Leonora, did arrive at the doors of the Abbey Church to pay her devotion.)

William had thought very carefully about what he would write next. At the time, most of the brothers had been unaware of anything occurring. Later, some had told him that they had heard a commotion. A crowd had assembled to see Her Grace the Queen, with some hoping to receive alms or a holy laying on of hands. Some of the monks had sworn that they had witnessed the divine intervention of St. Amphibalus, who had appeared above the Abbey doors to save Queen Eleanor. When Father Abbot, Roger de Norton, spoke in Chapter, he had been quite cautious but was sure that God had intervened to protect Her Grace, the Queen.

William spent nearly an hour scribing the details of the Queen's devotion before the Blessed Saint. In the next part, her exit from the Abbey Church and the attempt upon her life, he had to ensure he found the most suitable expression to record for history. William was dubious about the saint's intervention, but, at the same time, he was sure that God had, in some way, protected and saved the queen from death.

William became aware of a shadow cast across the parchment lain out in front of him. He twisted in his seat, looked up, and before him stood a tall near-bald man with a hooked nose, not a monk, but from his clothing, a man of rank. Penetrating eyes took in the page and William both.

"G...G...Good sir, I do not think... you have permission to be here," William's voice was stuttering, scratchy and a little worried.

The tall man ignored William's question, and he pointed at the unfinished parchment.

"*Is this your account of what occurred with Her Grace the Queen and her daughter?*"

A tremble of unease rippled through William. How did this man gain access to the Scriptorium? Was he one of the men involved in the attempt on Her Grace's life? Was his own life now in danger?

"A... A... Aye... it is the beginning of the account, s... s... sir."

William's unease turned to fear as the man's hand went to his belt and withdrew a jewel-handled dagger. Beads of sweat appeared on the monk's brow, and he put down his quill as his hand began to shake.

"I beg of you, do not hurt me. I am a man of God. I hold you no malice."

"Be not afeared, Brother William. You shall not be hurt this day by my hand."

That the man knew his name only served to increase William's agitation.

"Tell me, William of Rishanger, where do you hail from?" Despite the dagger still being held in his hand, the question was conciliatory, and William stammered a response.

"F... F... From the village of Rishangles, i... i... it lays about four miles distant from Eye, in... in... Suffolk."

"*Indeed! Indeed! Such a lovely place Suffolk. Pray, tell me now, what you intend to scribe about the events of these weeks past?*"

With anxiety still in his voice, William narrated the stories he had heard from his fellow monks and what others present had told him.

"*And some say that it was Saint Amphibalus himself, who miraculously appeared in front of the doors to the Abbey church, to intervene to save Her Grace the Queen. Others, including Father Abbot, say that it was the hand of God that saved her from the deadly crossbow bolt.*"

And the Lord led the saviours to rescue the Lady Leonora from the clutches of the coven of Lucifer's daughters..."

Still looming over the seated William, the man inclined his head with an expression of puzzlement.

"You possess such a fertile mind, Brother. *All that you say now is but imagination."* William was aware of the dagger at his eye level; his face tensed.

The man tapped the dagger on the parchment and continued speaking. *"Her Grace, the Queen, did spend the night with the Holy Sisters at Sopwell and came in the morn, along with her young daughter, to pay her devotion to the blessed St Alban. After which she left to progress her pilgrimage with the Brothers of St Peter's in Dunstable...."*

Now it was Brother William's turn to be puzzled.

"Nay, sir," he said indignantly. "You have that wrong, and what I said is true. I do not know who has told you your version, but they know not of what happened."

The man gently laid the dagger's blade on William's shoulder, leaned in towards the monk, and whispered, *"My version..."* – he spoke his words very slowly – *"my version comes from His Grace, King Edward of England."*

"K... K... K... King Edward of... of... England?"

"Aye, Brother. *The King."*

"But... But.... what about the attempt to slay the Queen? The assassin? The abduction of the young lady?"

"Brother William." The tone of menace had returned. *"The Chronicle of St Albans Abbey, your Chronica Majora* is a most highly regarded history of events. When it is written, when you write it, there will be no attempt to slay the Queen. There was no assassin. The abduction of the Lady Eleanora. All those events..." – he paused – "they never occurred."

William of Rishanger looked wide-eyed at this madman.

"But the witnesses?"

"Nay. These witnesses obviously have thought they saw something but were in error."

With that, the man reached down and sunk the tip of his dagger into the parchment, making three long cuts to destroy William's work. He picked up the ruined document and slipped it into a scrip slung over his back.

"Now, good Brother William. His Grace, the King is most interested to hear your account. Perhaps when it is written, you will send word to John of Berwick at the royal court so that I might read it to him?"

William nervously nodded his assent.

"And you do understand what His Grace, the King expects of you, Brother?"

"Aye." William was still trembling. It was a sin to lie, he knew that, but perhaps, an even greater evil to defy his King. And a man dead could commit no sin.

"It will be as you have said. These days showed Her Grace, the Queen's great piety and devotion. That is all. They were but days of little incident, as my words in the chronicle will record."

It was some time before William of Rishanger returned to record events. He trimmed his quill, and having dipped it in the inkhorn, he began his deft Gothic Textura strokes, the Latin words coming quickly to him.

Eodem anno, cum anno quarto regni regis Edwardi filii regis Henrici, in festo sancte Marie Magdalene, regina et filia eius, domina Eleonora, venit ad devotionem suam ante beatam. Sancte. Cum eleemosynis egenis et manibus impositis infirmis, gratia eius in magna pietate ad septentrionem iter faciebat ad iter faciendum cum Fratribus Sancti Petri in Dunstaplia.

(In that same year, being the fourth year of the reign of King Edward, son of King Henry, on the Feast day St Mary Magdalene, her grace, the queen and her daughter, the lady Eleanora, did come to pay her devotion before the blessed Saint. Having given alms to the poor and laid hands upon the sick, her grace journeyed north in great piety to progress her pilgrimage with the Brothers of St Peter's in Dunstable.)

CHAPTER 68

The Wheatsheaf Inn, St Albans, August 1276

It was two days after the feast of St. Bartholomew when Simon Lowys next rode into St Albans. The late August sun was welcome and warm, and he found the streets familiar. His work in transferring Langlei was all but complete, and the manor was entirely in possession of Her Grace, the Queen. His palfrey crossed the triangular marketplace and entered the wide Magno Vico. Halfway along, outside the gleaming whitewashed walls of the Wheatsheaf Inn, he tethered his mount to an iron ring fixed to the outside wall.

He could have sent word ahead to Isabelle to expect him. Still, he chose not to, telling himself he would surprise her but actually because he feared she might not wish to see him. The tall willowy man who had acted as doorkeeper on his previous visit was not there. In his stead was a hard-faced guard with weather-worn skin. He surveyed the King's Man, eyeing him cautiously but saying nothing.

"I have business to conduct with Mistress de Brun." If the doorkeeper took this in, it did not reflect in his expression. With a nod of his head, he indicated to Simon to enter. Inside young serving lads moved between the few occupied tables, cursorily wiping them down, bringing and removing ale jugs. At the rear, beyond the kitchen, Simon walked towards the stairs up to the first floor as he had done on his previous visit. A man wearing a green cote and linen hose moved to intercept him, hand on the dagger in his belt.

"This is a private area, Meister." His words held an underlying menace.

"I am Simon Lowys, Nuncio and King's Man, and I am here on royal business. I wish to see Mistress de Brun once more."

Simon received a quizzical look and an even more challenging stare before the man indicated to follow him up to the first floor. The familiar long anteroom still had sweet fresh rushes strewn across the floor, and its walls retained the fresh smell of lime wash, but the scent of sandalwood was gone.

The familiarity from his previous visit brought pleasant thoughts to Simon's mind. He looked to the far end of the room and saw Isabelle seated facing the fire, her wimple crisp and white, setting off the bright crimson of her robes. His heart raced; he took in the all-too-familiar smells of crushed rosemary and beeswax. The doorkeeper indicated for Simon to wait and went forward to Isabelle to announce him. If he was truthful to himself, he longed to see Isabelle's beauty once more and secretly hoped she wished to see him too.

The doorkeeper leaned in towards her and whispered in her ear before retiring. The woman's composed herself stood and turned to greet the King's Man. Simon tried to hide his regret. It was not Isabelle. The woman wore fine fashionable robes, which indicated wealth. She had the same slight build as Isabelle but was older, having seen at least fifty summers in her life. Her distinguished face was pale but comely, with signs of emerging wrinkles around her eyes.

Trying not to show his genuine disappointment, Simon made a bow. "God give you good day. Forgive my intrusion. We have not met Mistress; I am Simon Lowys, nuncio and King's Man. I have royal business with Mistress de Brun. Can you bring me to her?"

"Why, I give you good day, Master Lowys." The woman leaned her head in courtly acknowledgement and smiled at the Royal Nuncio.

"I am Mistress Isabelle de Brun. This is my tavern. How may I be of service to a King's Man?"

Historical Note

Shadows on the Queen is a work of fiction; however, most of the central characters in the story are real. Simon Lowys served as a royal nuncio in the household of Queen Eleanor of Castile, the wife of King Edward I. The murder of Roger le Stedeman and Henry Pelliors appears in the Calendar of the Coroners Rolls of the city of London. Margery de Pyritton, Agnes de Bilda, Dulcia, Maud Blount, Notekina de Hoggenhore and Isabella la Rus were real people and present in the house in Fulelane in the city when the murders took place. Along with the owner of the property, Alice le Blunde, they disappeared following the killings. This incident inspired me to create the Daughters of the Shadows. Queen Eleanor of Castile did buy out the debt of Stephen de Chenduit to various Jewish moneylenders in 1276. In so doing, she acquired the manor of Langlei and had a royal place built on top of the hill. One lender owed money by Stephen de Chenduit was Abraham of Berkhamsted.

John of Berwick held the position of Steward to the Queen's Household. However, his role as a royal intelligencer is a product of my imagination. The assassination of Henry of Almain, cousin to the future Edward I, by Guy de Montfort and his older brother Simon, in March 1271 happened in the city of Viterbo, as I have described. One of de Montfort's English mercenary captains present in the church was Walter de Baskerville. So heinous was the crime that years later, Dante placed Guy de Montfort in the seventh circle of his *Inferno*, immersed in a river of boiling blood.

St Albans Abbey was one of the greatest monasteries in medieval England. Its location along the old Roman road north, and a day's journey from London, meant it frequently housed important guests who brought with the news from the royal court. The Abbey drew many thousands of pilgrims each year to the shrine of St Alban. St Albans Abbey had an international reputation for its Chronicles between the 12th and 15th centuries. Roger of Wendover, Matthew Paris, William of Rishanger and Thomas of Walsingham are celebrated as renowned Chroniclers of events in medieval England. St Albans had many inns to accommodate the pilgrim trade. The Wheatsheaf is fictional but based upon similar medieval alehouses in the town. The Abbot of St Albans had significant influence over the townspeople during the medieval period in his capacity as their feudal overlord. This led to a fractious relationship between Abbey and Town, which continued over centuries. The town of St Albans was much smaller than today and defined by a boundary ditch. Its population was perhaps 2,000, though this figure swelled from its pilgrim trade. The street names I have used existed in the late thirteenth century and can be traced in the layout of modern-day St Albans. The mid-summer fair in St Albans was a highlight of the year and brought traders, buyers, and pilgrims from across England and the continent.

The gruesome punishment of hanging, drawing and quartering was not codified until the early 14th century, although there were examples of such executions in the reign of Henry III. Hanging, followed by the severing of the head, was a punishment for treason used often in the reign of Edward I.

Simon Lowys, Isabella la Rus, Alia Parys and Mistress Heacham will return in the second St Albans medieval mystery, '*The Guilt of the Penitent.*'

Michael Long   Apsley, Hertfordshire   July 2022

The Guilt of the Penitent

PROLOGUE

The Church of St. Mary Magdalene, Windridge, Hertfordshire May 1277

A chill night breeze found the cracks in the walls of the Church of St. Mary Magdalene, causing the few lit tallow candles to flicker uncontrollably. Shadows danced up the walls animating the painted frescos in a hallowed glow. Yet, the tops of the round arches were shrouded in darkness. The scratching and scurry of mice interrupted the stillness of the night. The church was empty at this late hour save for a single sinner kneeling before the holy altar. He was oblivious to the acrid stink of the solitary candle burning beside him.

His lips moved quickly, mouthing the 'De Profundis,' the 129th Psalm.

"Out of the depths I have cried to Thee O Lord! Lord, hear my voice. Let Thine ears be attentive to the voice of my supplication." With each line, a whip cracked, biting deep into the boney, hairy back of the parish priest of St Mary's but drawing no cries of pain.

"Bless, O my God, the repose I am about to take, that, renewing my strength, I may be better enabled to serve Thee. Lord, hear my prayer."

Dark red wheals on his back broke into rivulets of blood which flowed down onto Sire Roger's unwashed habit, pulled down to his waist, exposing his hairy back.

"Oh, My Lord. Mea Culpa. Mea Culpa. I have sinned before you." The whip cracked again, its knotted ends biting deep into his flesh. Tears of anguish welled in Sire Roger Wake's eyes. He had failed his flock; he was guilty of more than one mortal sin and had broken the Fifth Commandment. It was a thousand years in Purgatory where his soul would be painfully stripped of its wrongdoing, purged by fire and ice. The light from his single candle flickered and caught the golden crucifix on the altar before him, where the eyes of the crucified Jesus stared reproachfully down at him.

"Oh, dear Lord, help me." He wailed a penitent cry to his maker, dropping the whip and falling prone to the cold stone floor, sobbing uncontrollably.

"O God, who willest not the death of a sinner, protect me this night and keep evil far from me." Sire Roger whimpered his intercession, unaware that death had slipped into his cold, dank Church through a chapel side door as he uttered his lament.

The priest closed his eyes and recalled his transgressions against God; how easily he succumbed to temptation. The flesh was weak; he was weak. The flesh; Oh! The flesh. He knew it was wrong. He knew it could damn his soul for all eternity, yet he had surrendered to desire. Even amid his supplication before God, the thought of the young bodies aroused him.

He had sought repentance and confessed his sins to a fellow priest. He had embarked on the three stages of the penitent; repentance, disclosure, and he intended to make reparation. He would admit all to the Town authorities. He would have to leave St. Mary Magdalene, his home, for more than twelve summers, but it was now necessary for him to go far away where no one knew him.

Sire Roger rose to his knees and clenched his hands in prayer. "Merciful Lord, grant me repentance. Satan has lured me from the path of righteousness, and I am a sinner." His sobbing intonation echoed around the church. He was sure that when the time came for him to meet his maker, a merciful God would have forgiven him.

That time came all too quickly for Sire Roger as death stalked St. Mary's. The praying priest didn't hear the muffled sound of leather on the stone floor of the nave, nor the gentle creak of a longbow drawn. He had just enough time to register the rush of an arrow before he slumped forward on the altar steps, a shaft embedded deep in his bloodied, hairy back. Life ebbed slowly from his bleeding body, with his soul keeping an appointment in the fires of Hell.

9 781399 923712